# InvestiGATORS
## Ants in Our P.A.N.T.S.

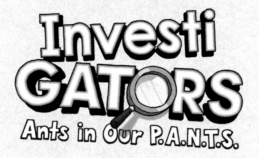

# Investi GATORS
## Ants in Our P.A.N.T.S.

written and illustrated by

## John Patrick Green

with color by **Wes Dzioba**

**:01**

First Second
New York

# For anyone who's stuck in the mud

**First Second**

© 2021 by John Patrick Green

Drawn on Strathmore Smooth Bristol paper with Staedtler Mars Lumograph H pencils, inked with Sakura Pigma Micron and Staedtler Pigment Liner pens, and digitally colored in Photoshop.

Published by First Second
First Second is an imprint of Roaring Brook Press,
a division of Holtzbrinck Publishing Holdings Limited Partnership
120 Broadway, New York, NY 10271
firstsecondbooks.com
mackids.com
All rights reserved

Don't miss your next favorite book from First Second! For the latest updates go to firstsecondnewsletter.com and sign up for our enewsletter.

Library of Congress Cataloging-in-Publication Data is available

ISBN: 978-1-250-22005-9 (Hardcover)
ISBN: 978-1-250-82590-2 (Special Edition)

Our books may be purchased in bulk for promotional, educational, or business use. Please contact your local bookseller or the Macmillan Corporate and Premium Sales Department at (800) 221-7945 ext. 5442 or by email at MacmillanSpecialSales@macmillan.com.

FIRST EDITION

First edition, 2021
Edited by Calista Brill and Dave Roman
Cover design by John Patrick Green and Kirk Benshoff
Interior book design by John Patrick Green
Color by Wes Dzioba
Printed in China by Toppan Leefung Printing Ltd., Dongguan City, Guangdong Province

10 9 8 7 6 5 4 3

# Chapter 1

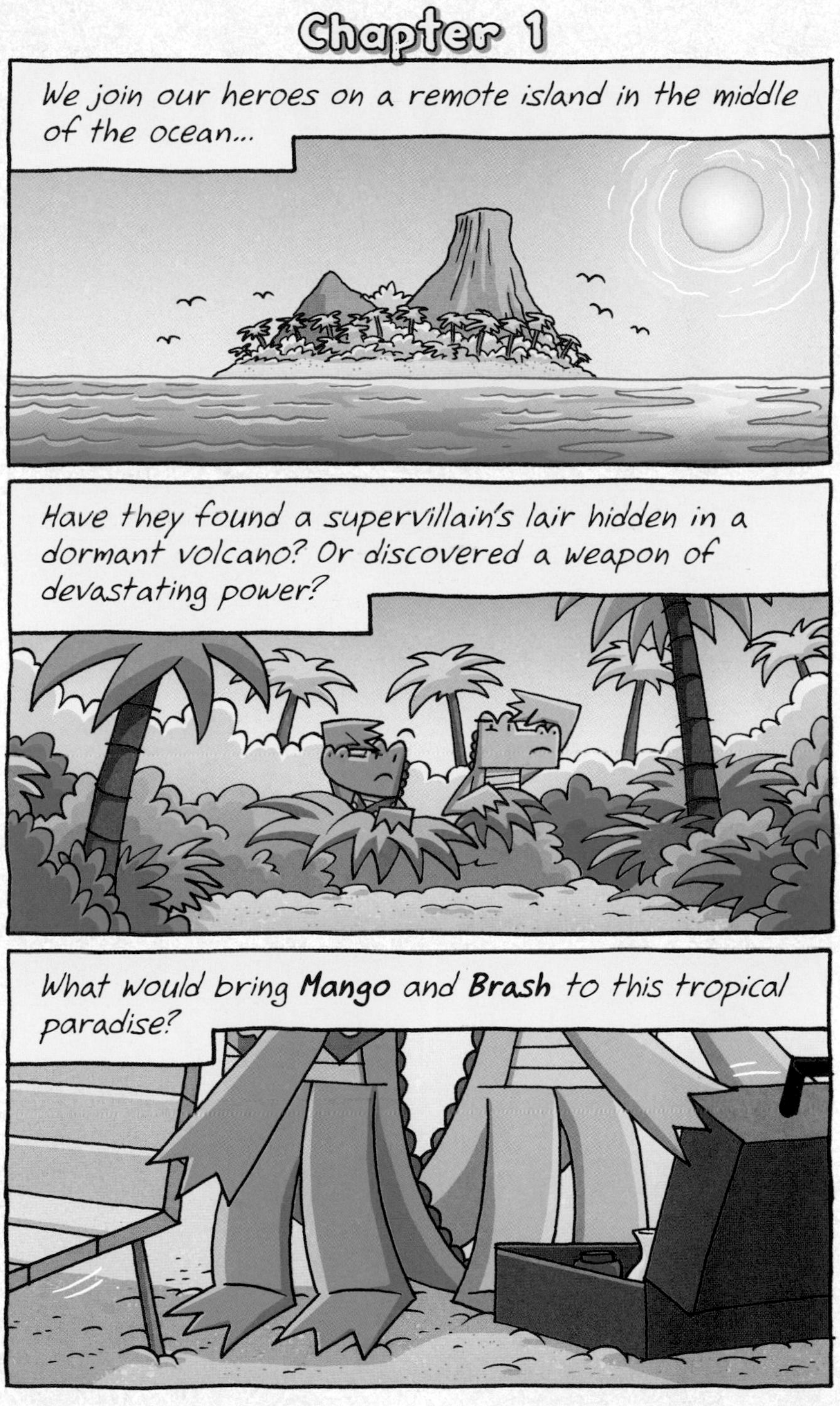

We join our heroes on a remote island in the middle of the ocean...
Have they found a supervillain's lair hidden in a dormant volcano? Or discovered a weapon of devastating power?
What would bring **Mango** and **Brash** to this tropical paradise?

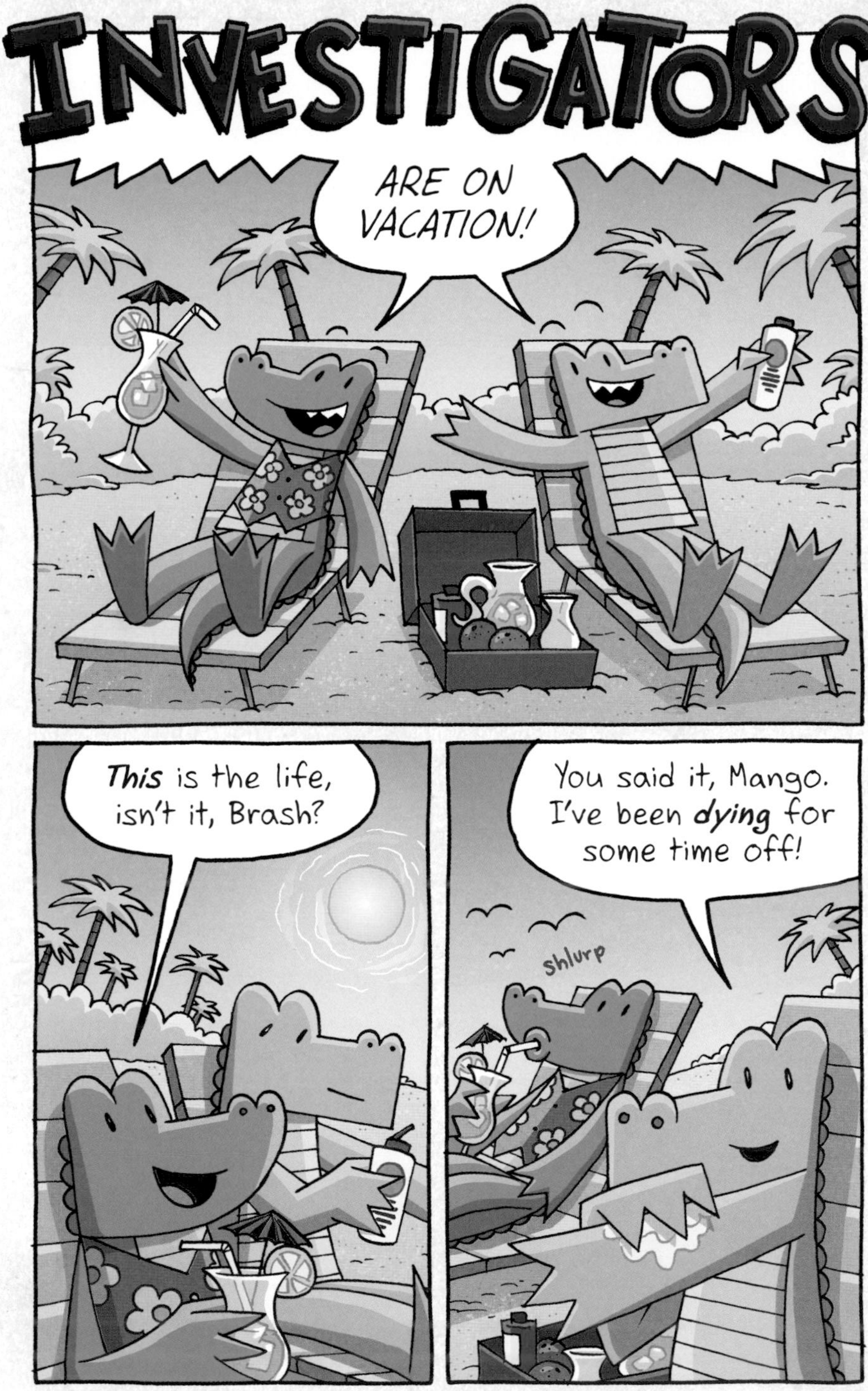
INVESTIGATORS
ARE ON VACATION!
*This* is the life, isn't it, Brash?
shlurp
You said it, Mango. I've been ***dying*** for some time off!

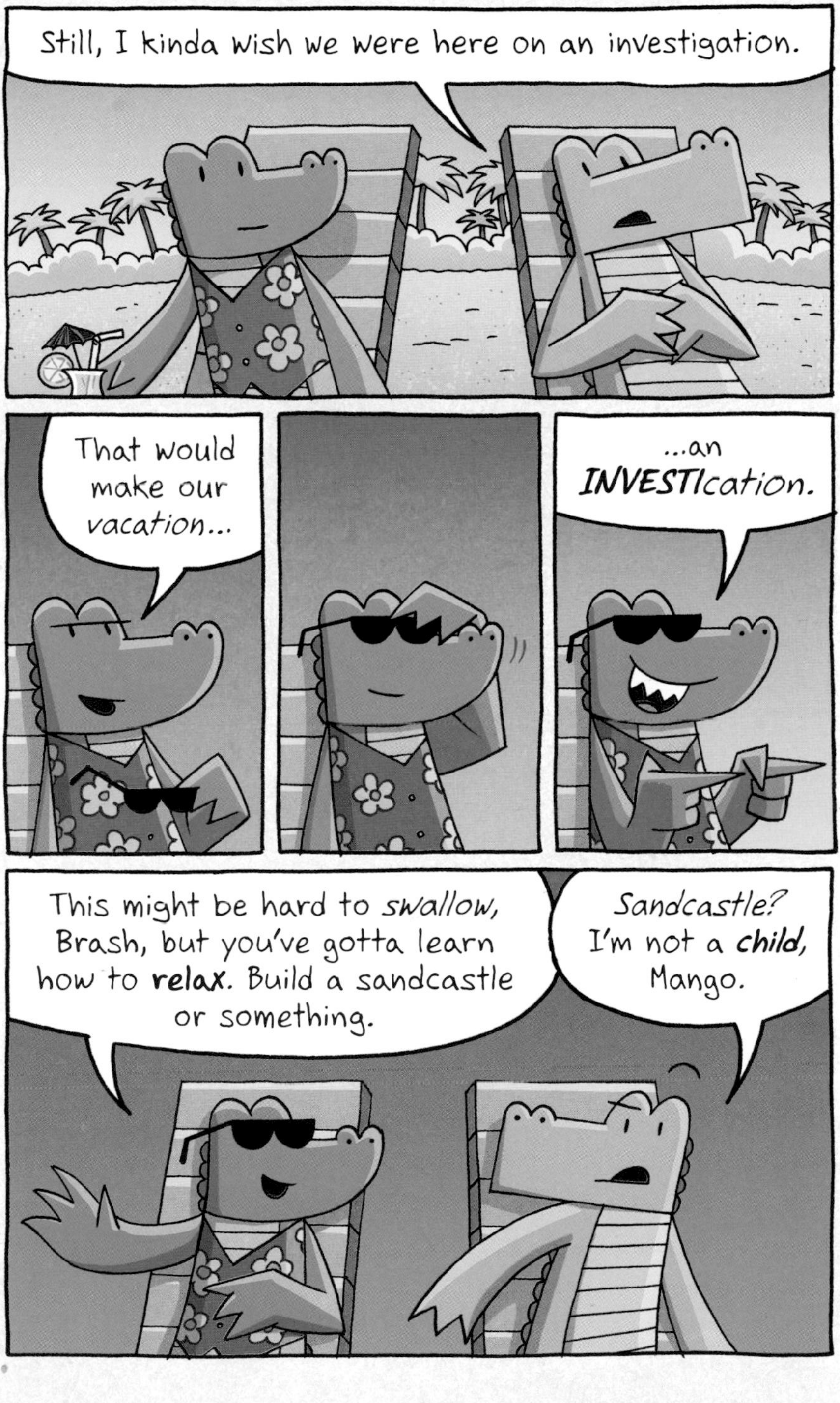
Still, I kinda wish we were here on an investigation.
That would make our vacation...
...an *INVESTI*cation.
This might be hard to *swallow*, Brash, but you've gotta learn how to **relax**. Build a sandcastle or something.
*Sandcastle?* I'm not a ***child***, Mango.

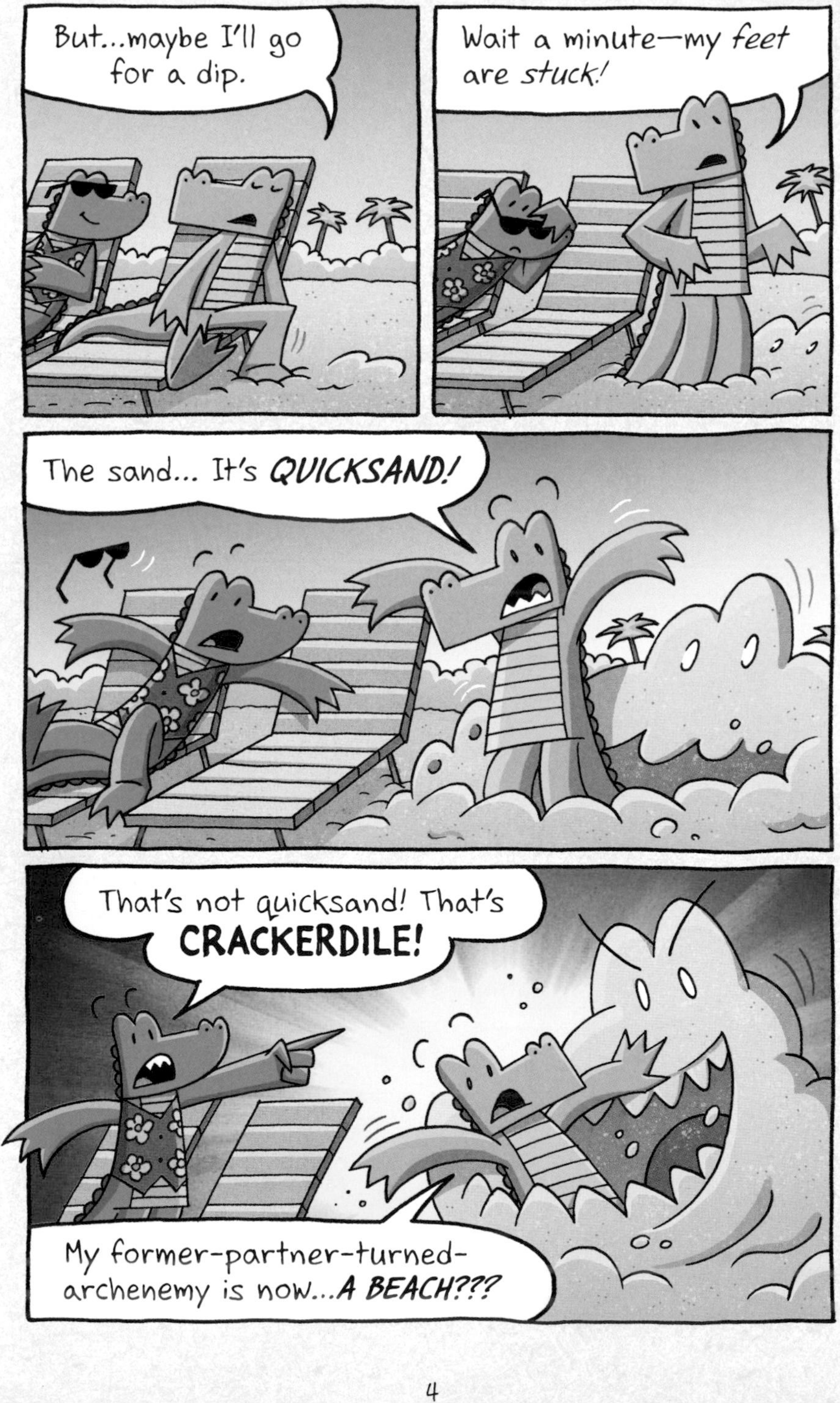

But...maybe I'll go for a dip.
Wait a minute—my *feet* are *stuck!*
The sand... It's ***QUICKSAND!***
That's not quicksand! That's **CRACKERDILE!**
My former-partner-turned-archenemy is now...***A BEACH???***

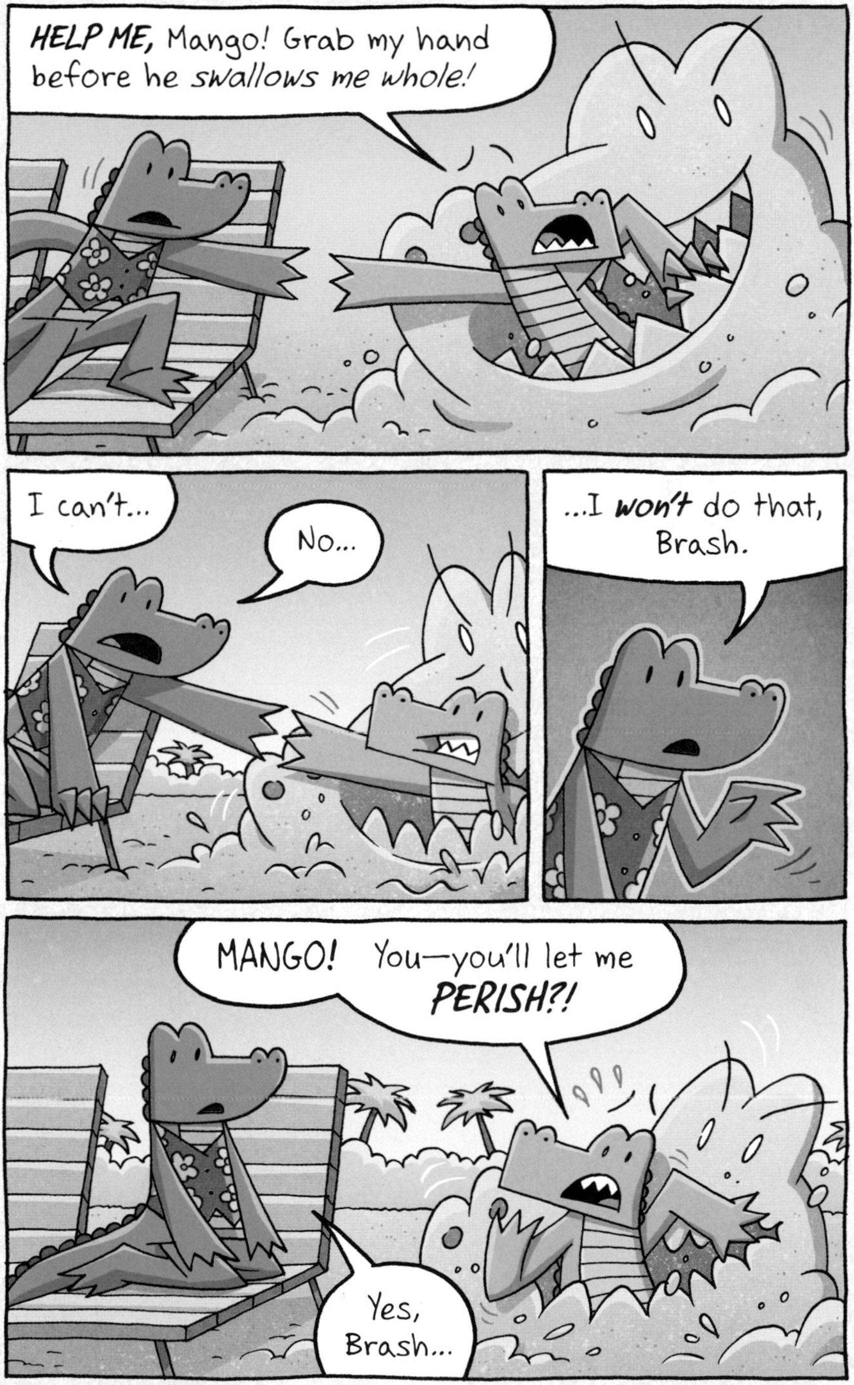

HELP ME, Mango! Grab my hand before he swallows me whole!
I can't...
No...
...I won't do that, Brash.
MANGO! You—you'll let me PERISH?!
Yes, Brash...

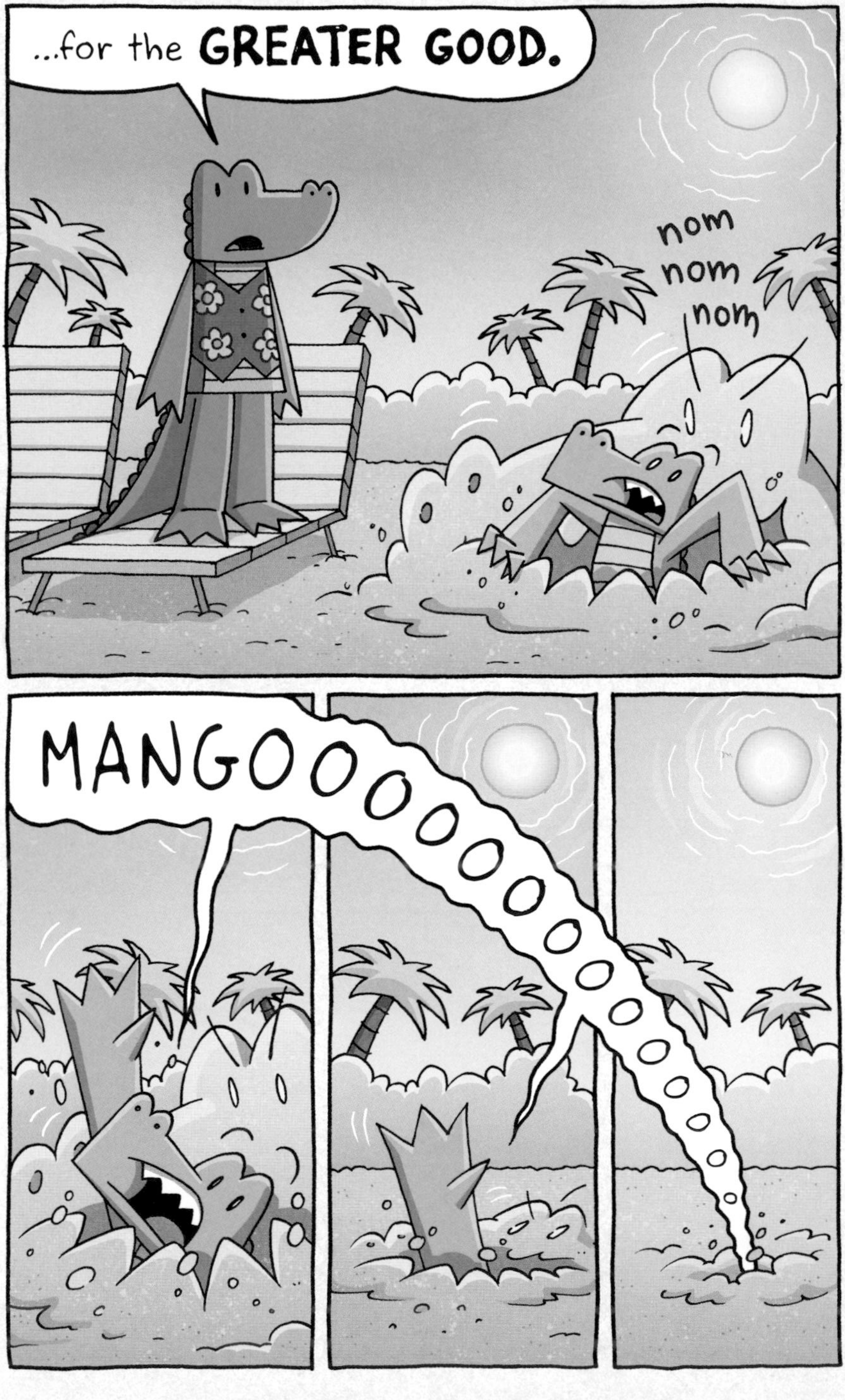
...for the **GREATER GOOD.**
nom
nom
nom
MANGOOOOOOOOOOOOOOOOO

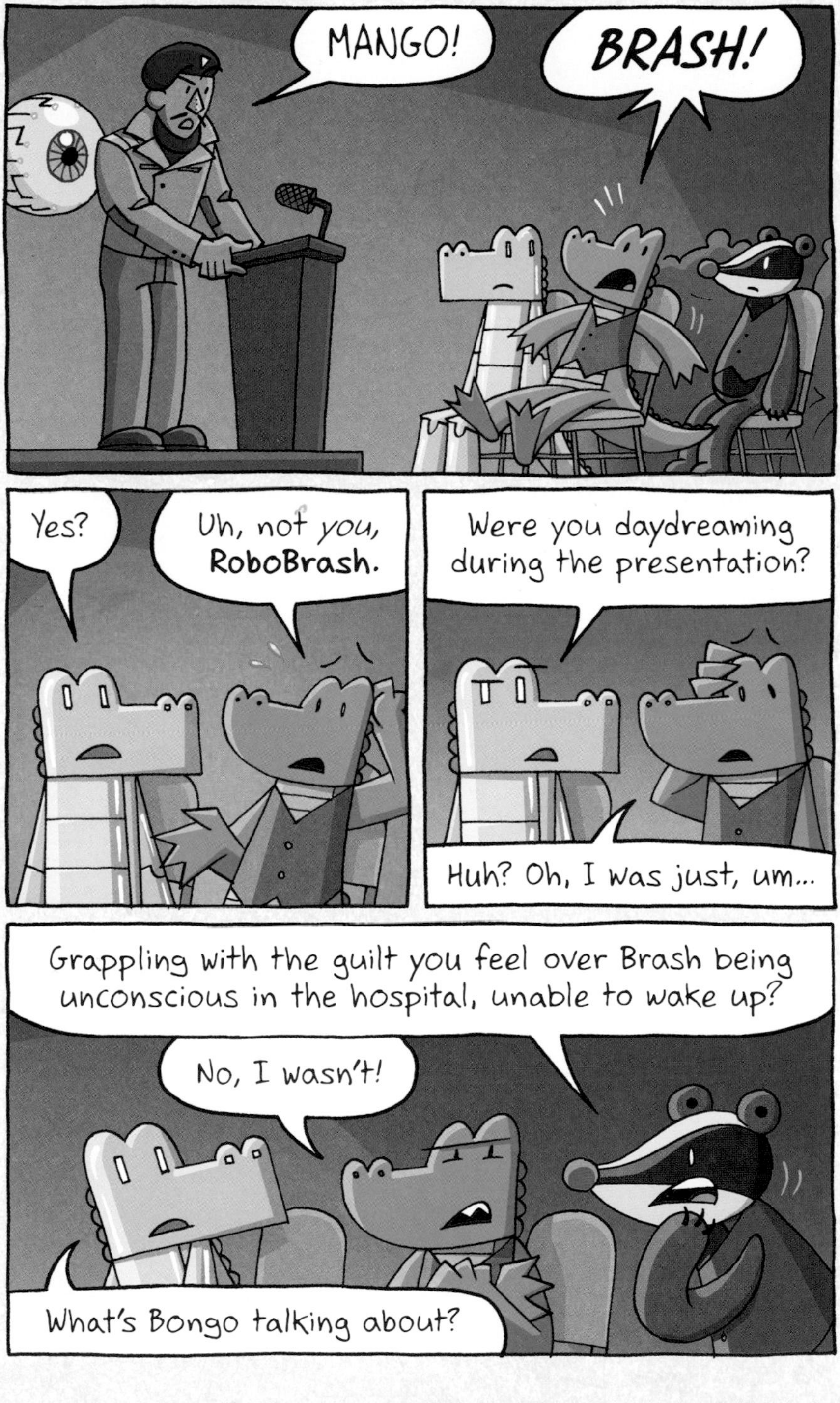
MANGO!
BRASH!
Yes?
Uh, not *you*, **RoboBrash.**
Were you daydreaming during the presentation?
Huh? Oh, I was just, um...
Grappling with the guilt you feel over Brash being unconscious in the hospital, unable to wake up?
No, I wasn't!
What's Bongo talking about?

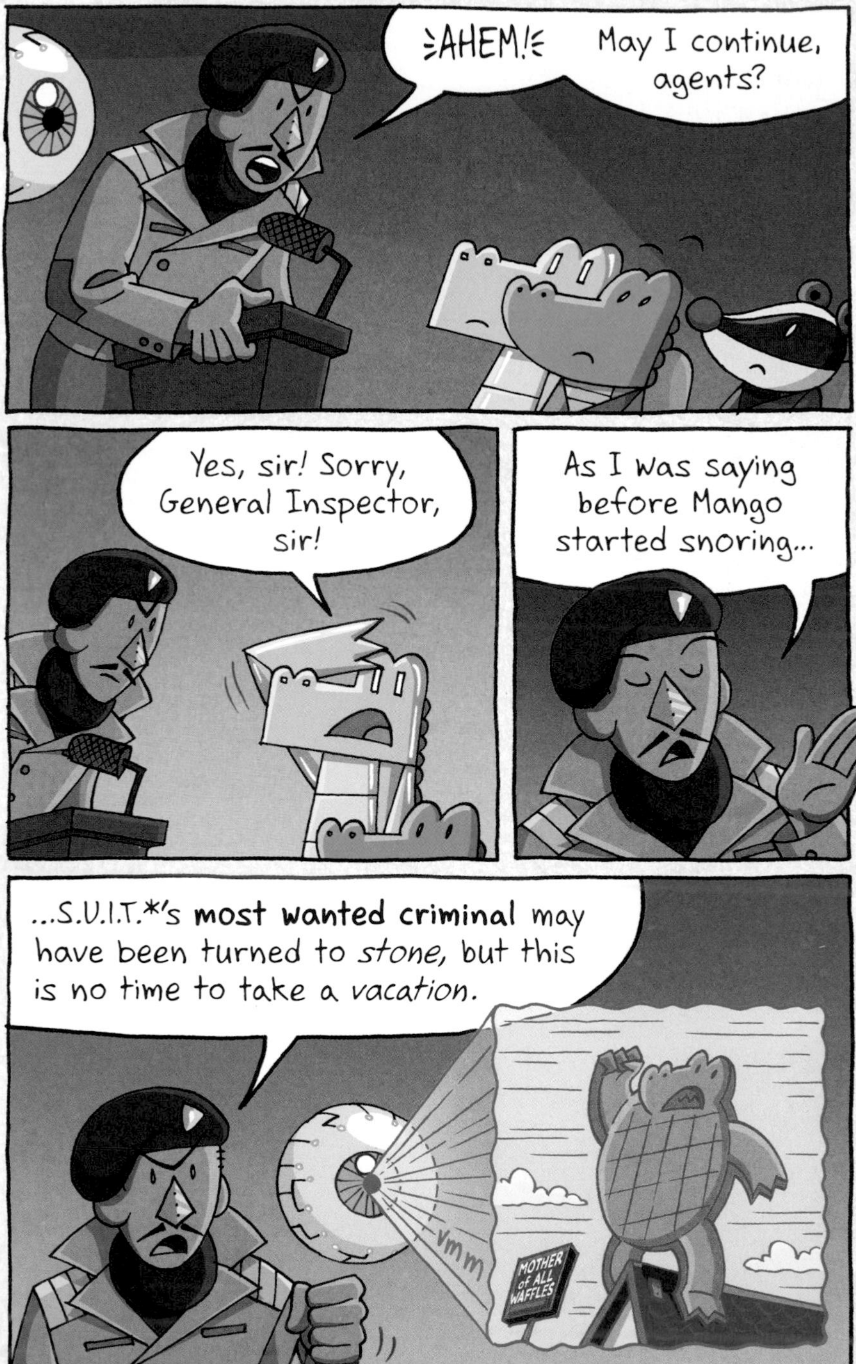

AHEM! May I continue, agents?
Yes, sir! Sorry, General Inspector, sir!
As I was saying before Mango started snoring...
...S.U.I.T.*'s **most wanted criminal** may have been turned to *stone*, but this is no time to take a *vacation*.
VMM
MOTHER of ALL WAFFLES


*Special Undercover Investigation Teams

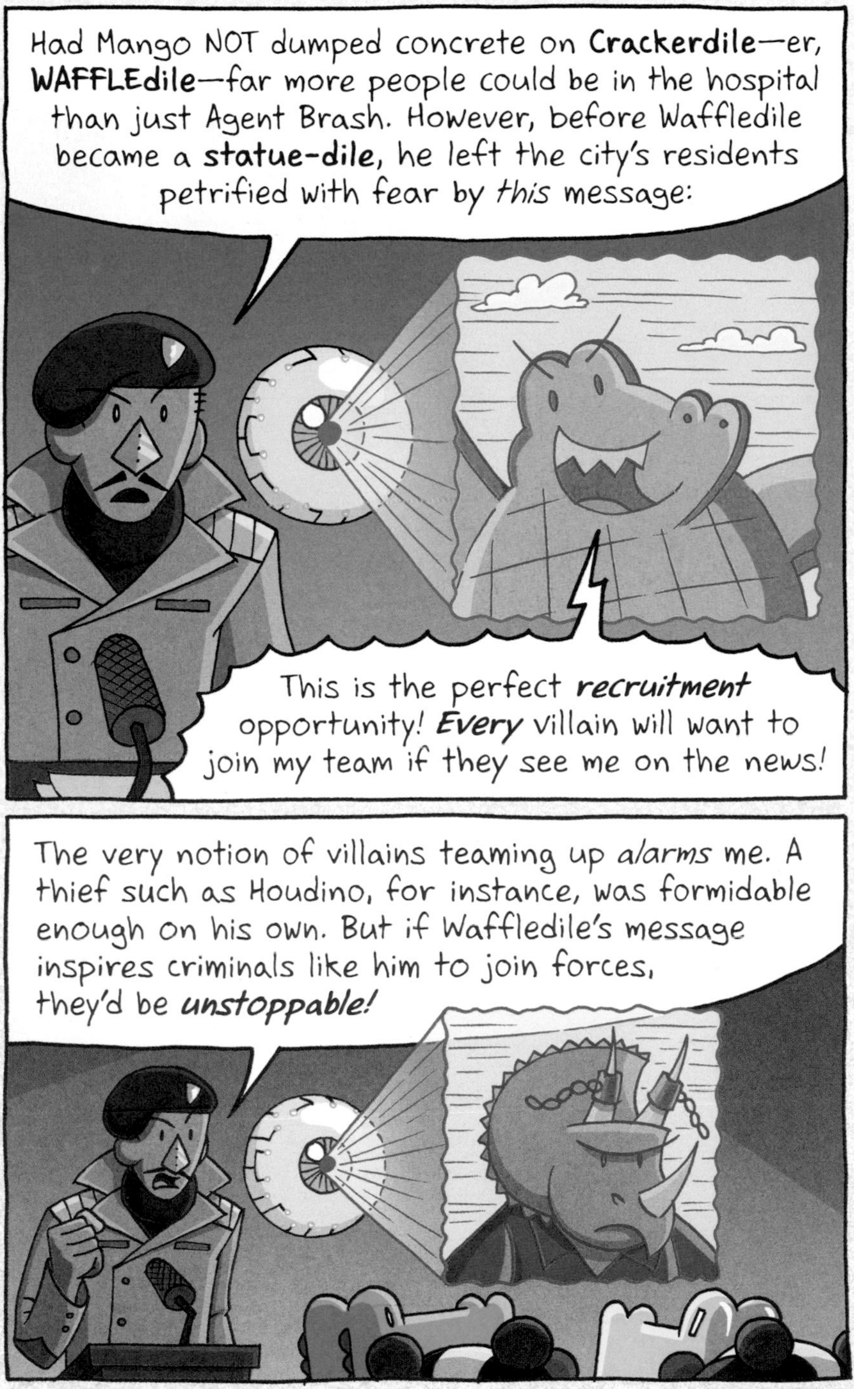
Had Mango NOT dumped concrete on **Crackerdile**—er, **WAFFLEdile**—far more people could be in the hospital than just Agent Brash. However, before Waffledile became a **statue-dile**, he left the city's residents petrified with fear by *this* message:
This is the perfect ***recruitment*** opportunity! ***Every*** villain will want to join my team if they see me on the news!
The very notion of villains teaming up *alarms* me. A thief such as Houdino, for instance, was formidable enough on his own. But if Waffledile's message inspires criminals like him to join forces, they'd be ***unstoppable!***

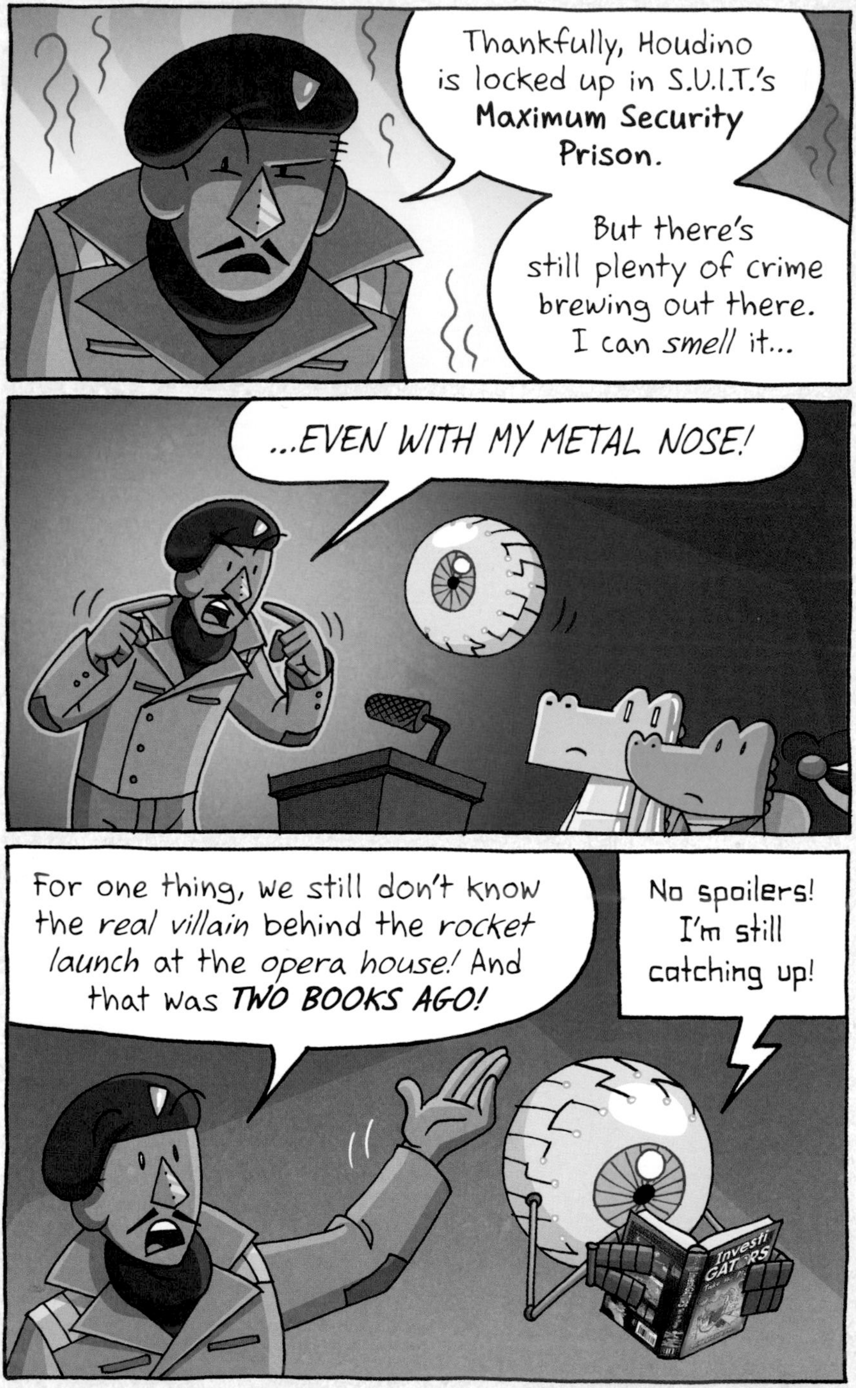
Thankfully, Houdino is locked up in S.U.I.T.'s **Maximum Security Prison.**
But there's still plenty of crime brewing out there. I can *smell* it...
...EVEN WITH MY METAL NOSE!
For one thing, we still don't know the *real villain* behind the *rocket launch* at the *opera house!* And that was **TWO BOOKS AGO!**
No spoilers! I'm still catching up!

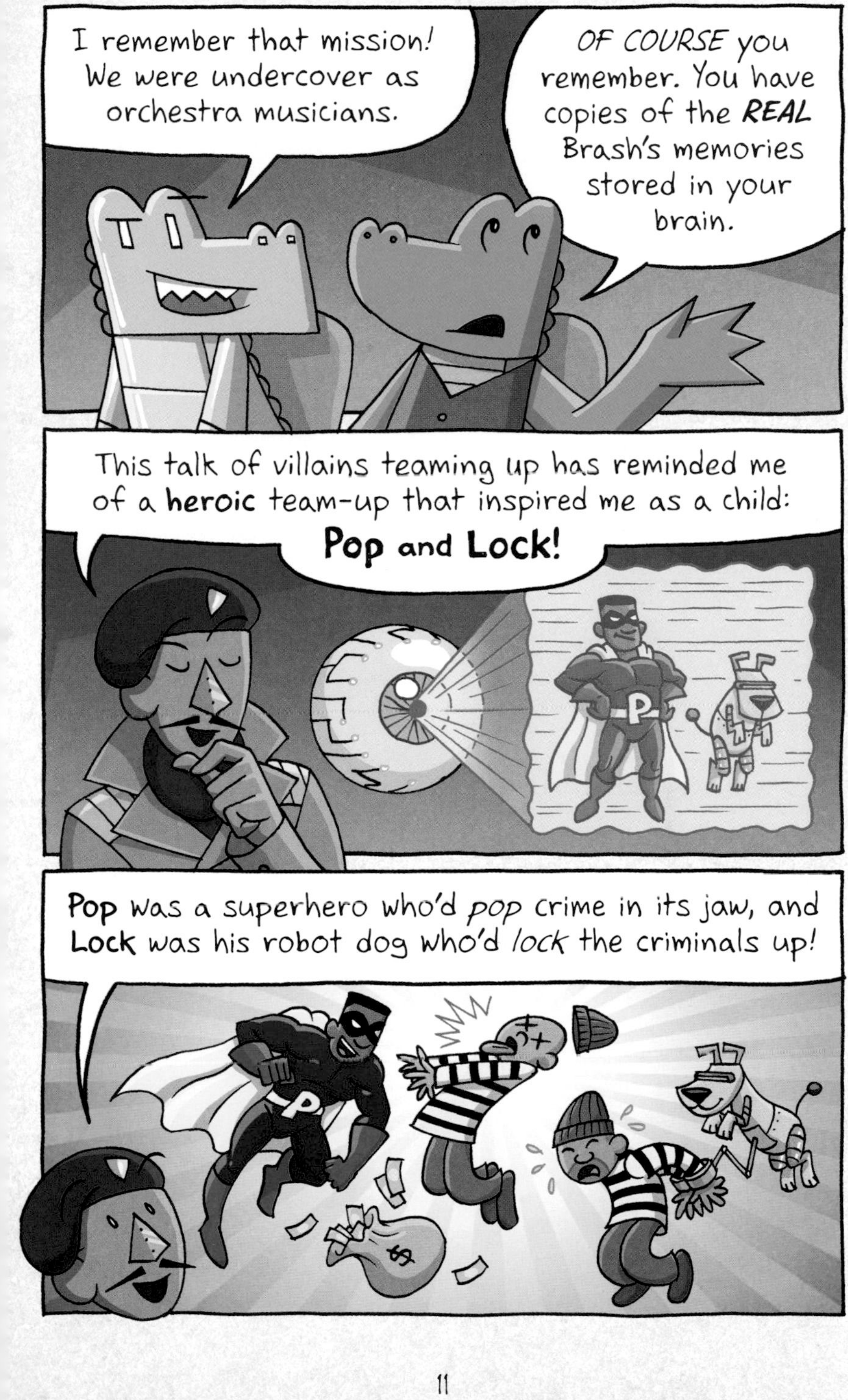
I remember that mission! We were undercover as orchestra musicians.
OF COURSE you remember. You have copies of the REAL Brash's memories stored in your brain.
This talk of villains teaming up has reminded me of a heroic team-up that inspired me as a child: Pop and Lock!
Pop was a superhero who'd pop crime in its jaw, and Lock was his robot dog who'd lock the criminals up!

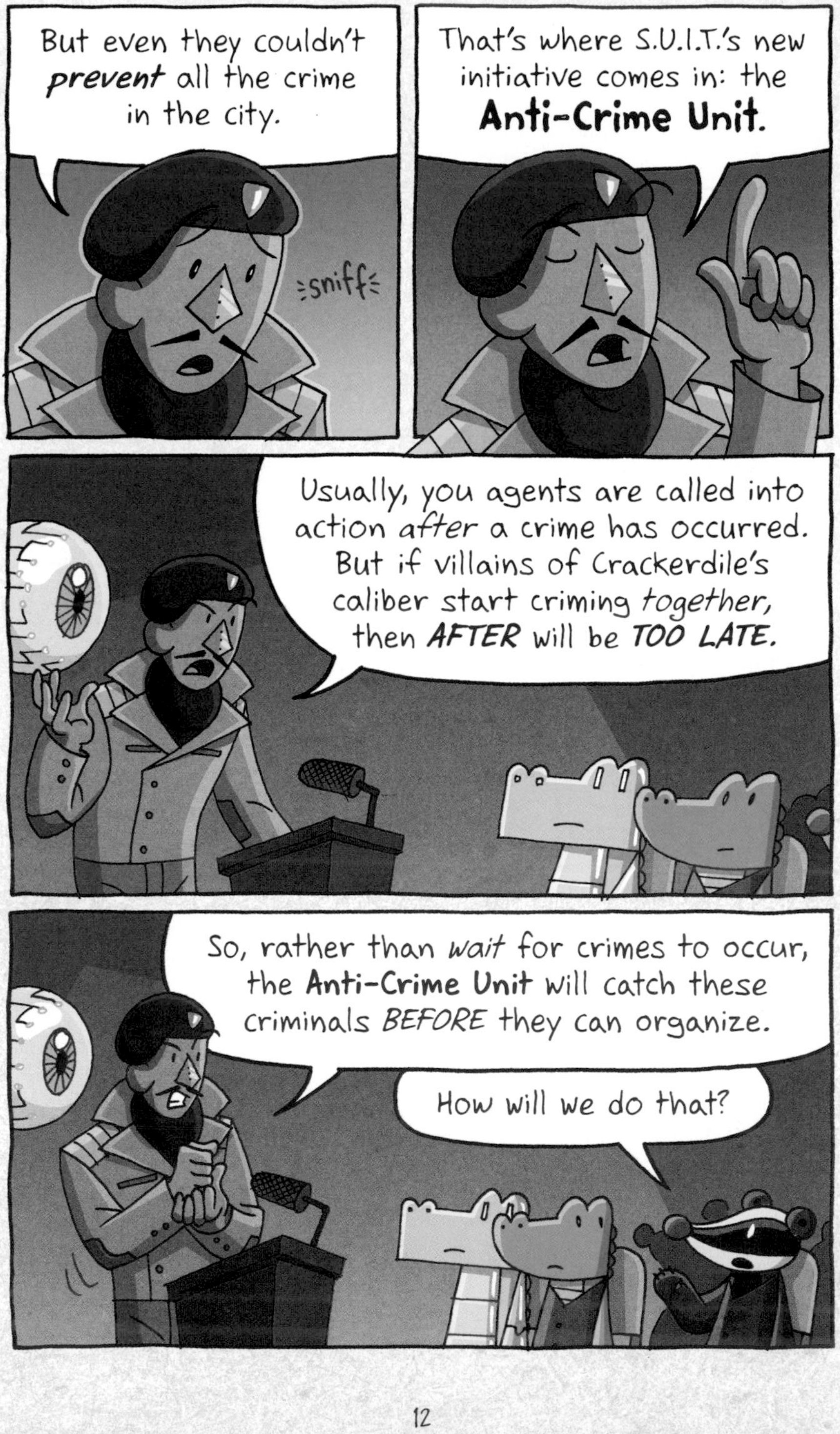
But even they couldn't *prevent* all the crime in the city.
sniff
That's where S.U.I.T.'s new initiative comes in: the **Anti-Crime Unit.**
Usually, you agents are called into action *after* a crime has occurred. But if villains of Crackerdile's caliber start criming *together*, then ***AFTER*** will be ***TOO LATE.***
So, rather than *wait* for crimes to occur, the **Anti-Crime Unit** will catch these criminals *BEFORE* they can organize.
How will we do that?

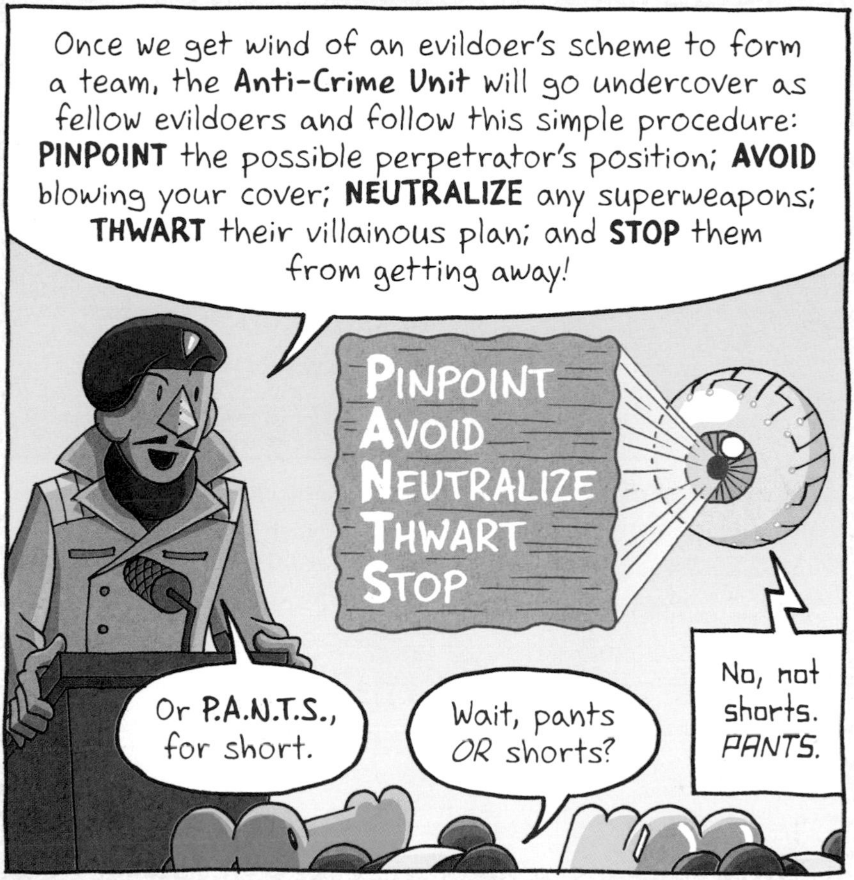
Once we get wind of an evildoer's scheme to form a team, the Anti-Crime Unit will go undercover as fellow evildoers and follow this simple procedure: PINPOINT the possible perpetrator's position; AVOID blowing your cover; NEUTRALIZE any superweapons; THWART their villainous plan; and STOP them from getting away!
PINPOINT
AVOID
NEUTRALIZE
THWART
STOP
Or P.A.N.T.S., for short.
Wait, pants OR shorts?
No, not shorts. PANTS.

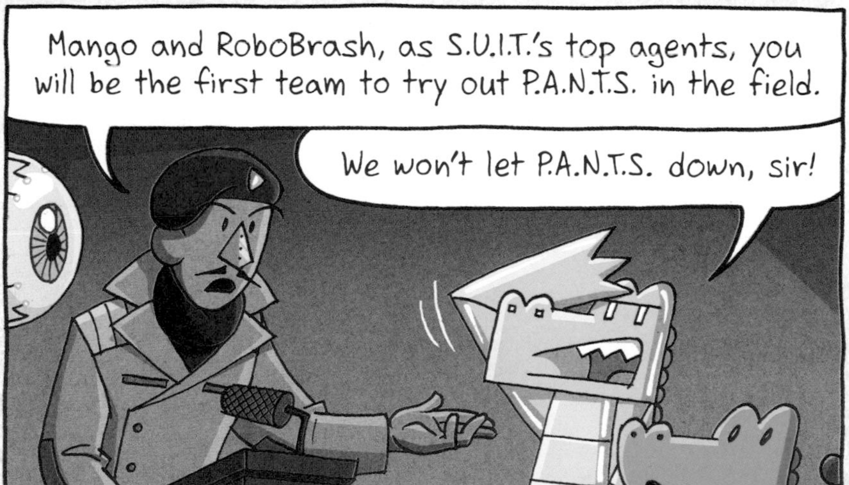
Mango and RoboBrash, as S.U.I.T.'s top agents, you will be the first team to try out P.A.N.T.S. in the field.
We won't let P.A.N.T.S. down, sir!

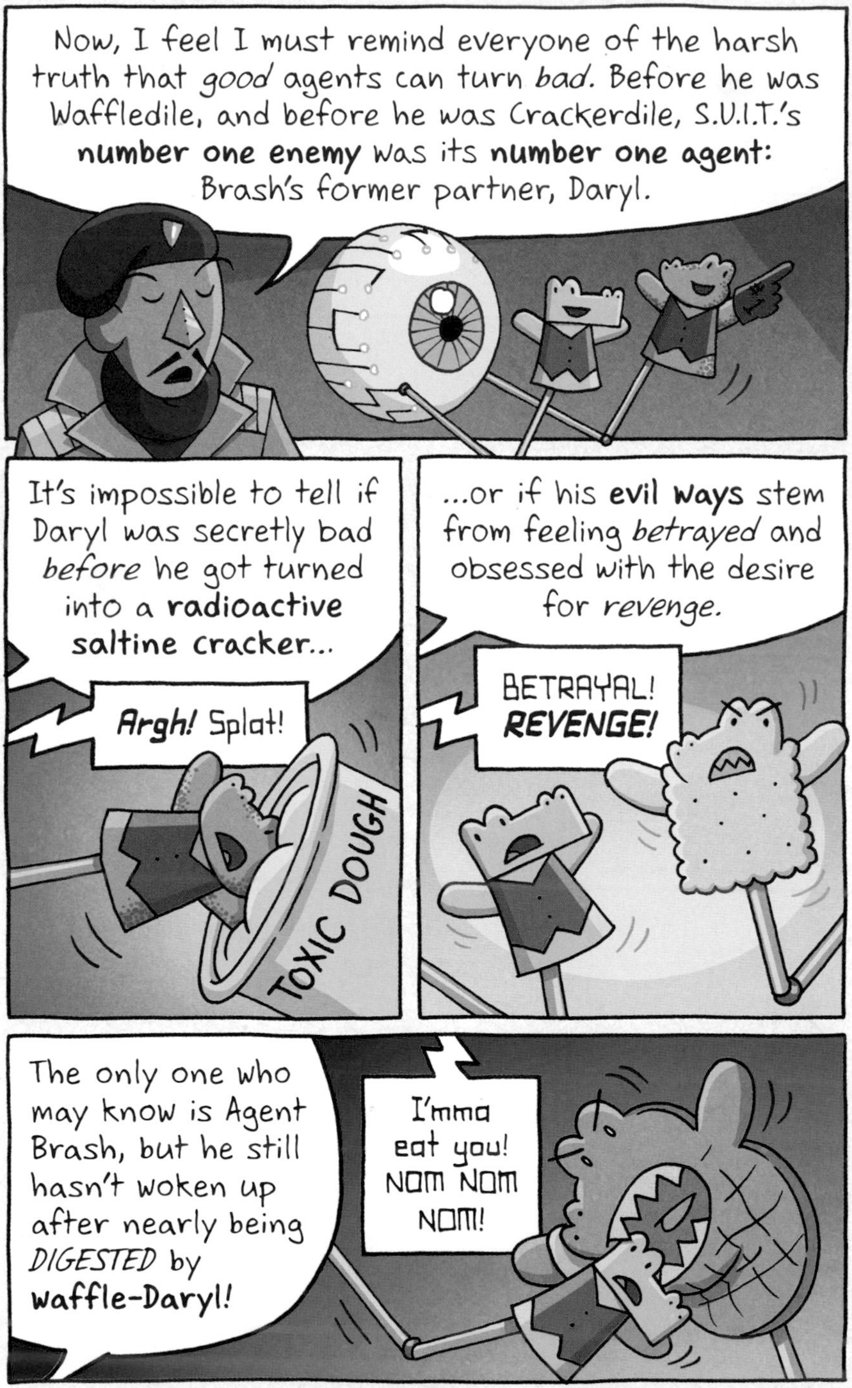
Now, I feel I must remind everyone of the harsh truth that *good* agents can turn *bad*. Before he was Waffledile, and before he was Crackerdile, S.U.I.T.'s **number one enemy** was its **number one agent:** Brash's former partner, Daryl.
It's impossible to tell if Daryl was secretly bad *before* he got turned into a **radioactive saltine cracker...**
**Argh!** Splat!
TOXIC DOUGH
...or if his **evil ways** stem from feeling *betrayed* and obsessed with the desire for *revenge.*
BETRAYAL! **REVENGE!**
The only one who may know is Agent Brash, but he still hasn't woken up after nearly being *DIGESTED* by **waffle-Daryl!**
I'mma eat you! NOM NOM NOM!

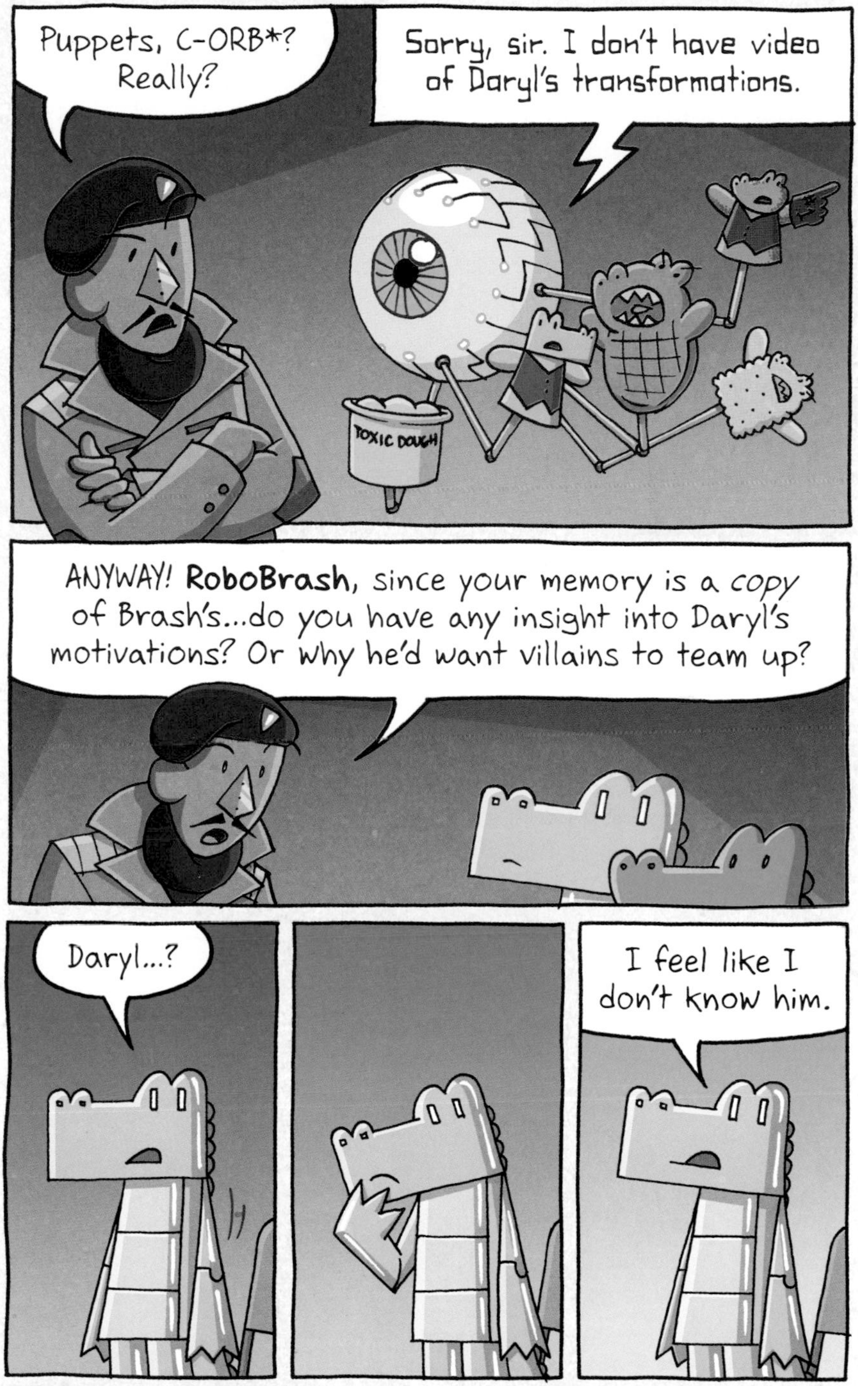
Puppets, C-ORB*? Really?
Sorry, sir. I don't have video of Daryl's transformations.
TOXIC DOUGH
ANYWAY! **RoboBrash**, since your memory is a *copy* of Brash's...do you have any insight into Daryl's motivations? Or why he'd want villains to team up?
Daryl...?
I feel like I don't know him.

*Computerized Ocular Remote Butler

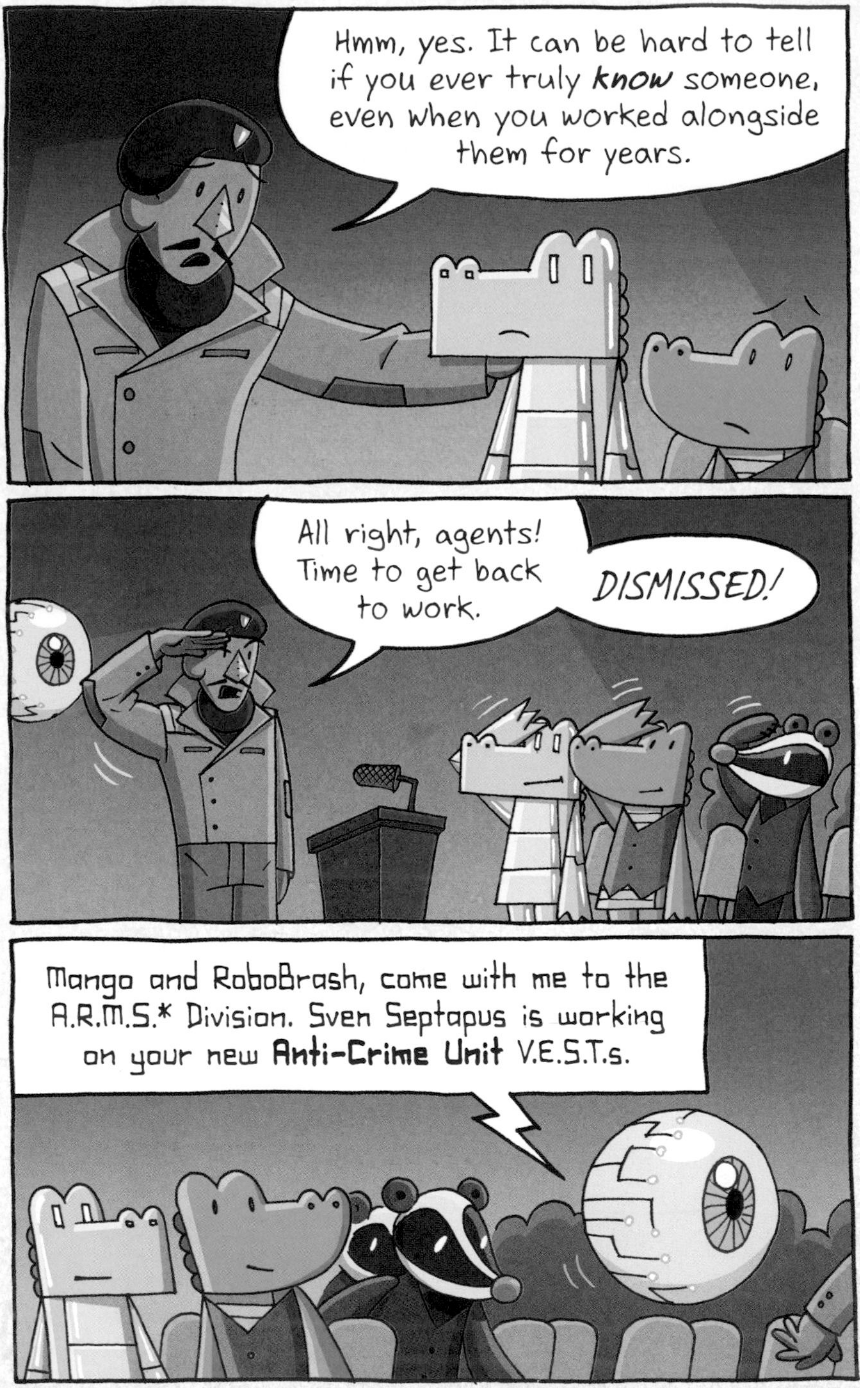
Hmm, yes. It can be hard to tell if you ever truly **know** someone, even when you worked alongside them for years.
All right, agents! Time to get back to work.
DISMISSED!
Mango and RoboBrash, come with me to the A.R.M.S.* Division. Sven Septapus is working on your new **Anti-Crime Unit** V.E.S.T.s.

*Apparel Research and Manufacturing...by Sven!

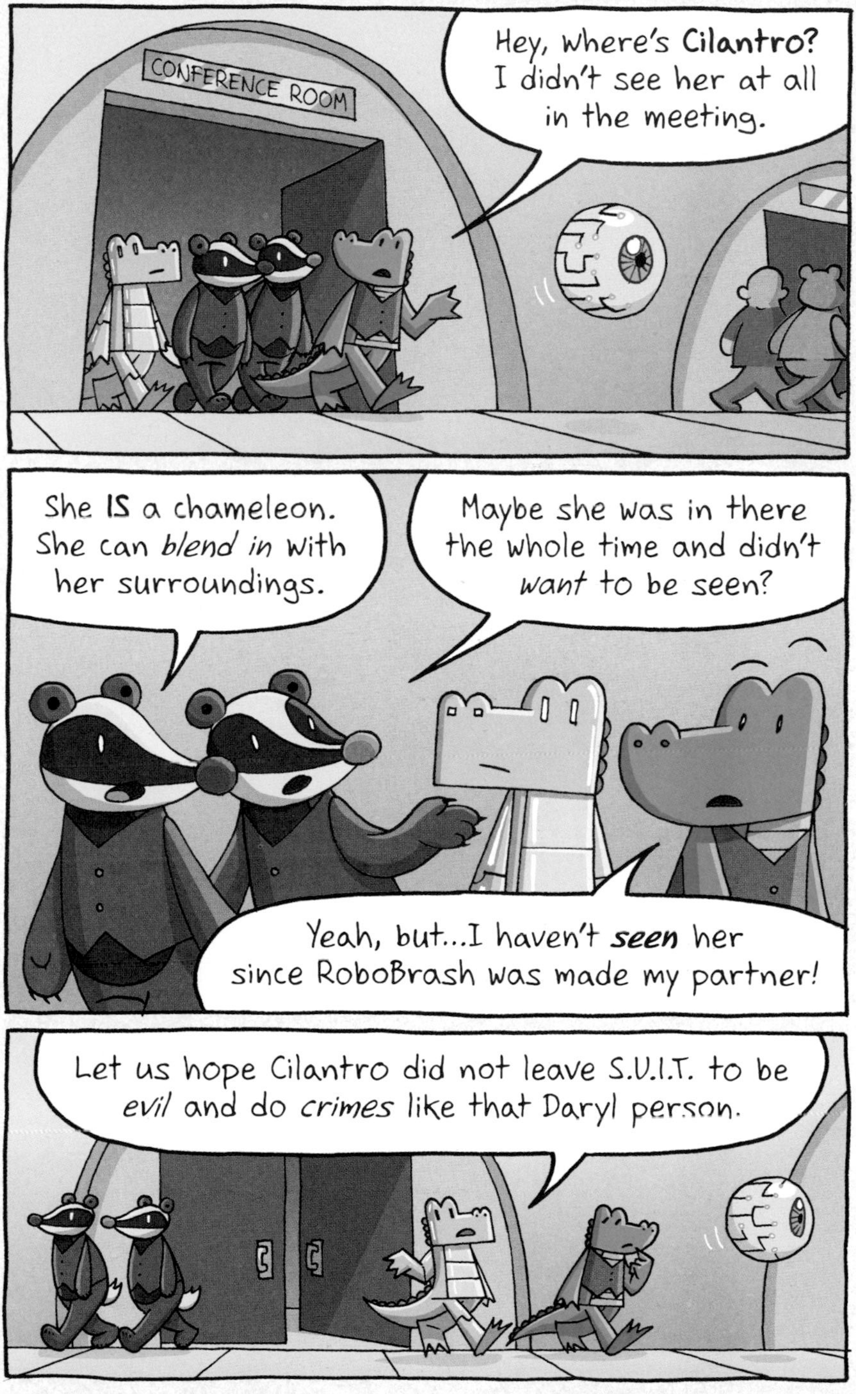
CONFERENCE ROOM
Hey, where's Cilantro? I didn't see her at all in the meeting.
She IS a chameleon. She can blend in with her surroundings.
Maybe she was in there the whole time and didn't want to be seen?
Yeah, but...I haven't seen her since RoboBrash was made my partner!
Let us hope Cilantro did not leave S.U.I.T. to be evil and do crimes like that Daryl person.

# Chapter 2

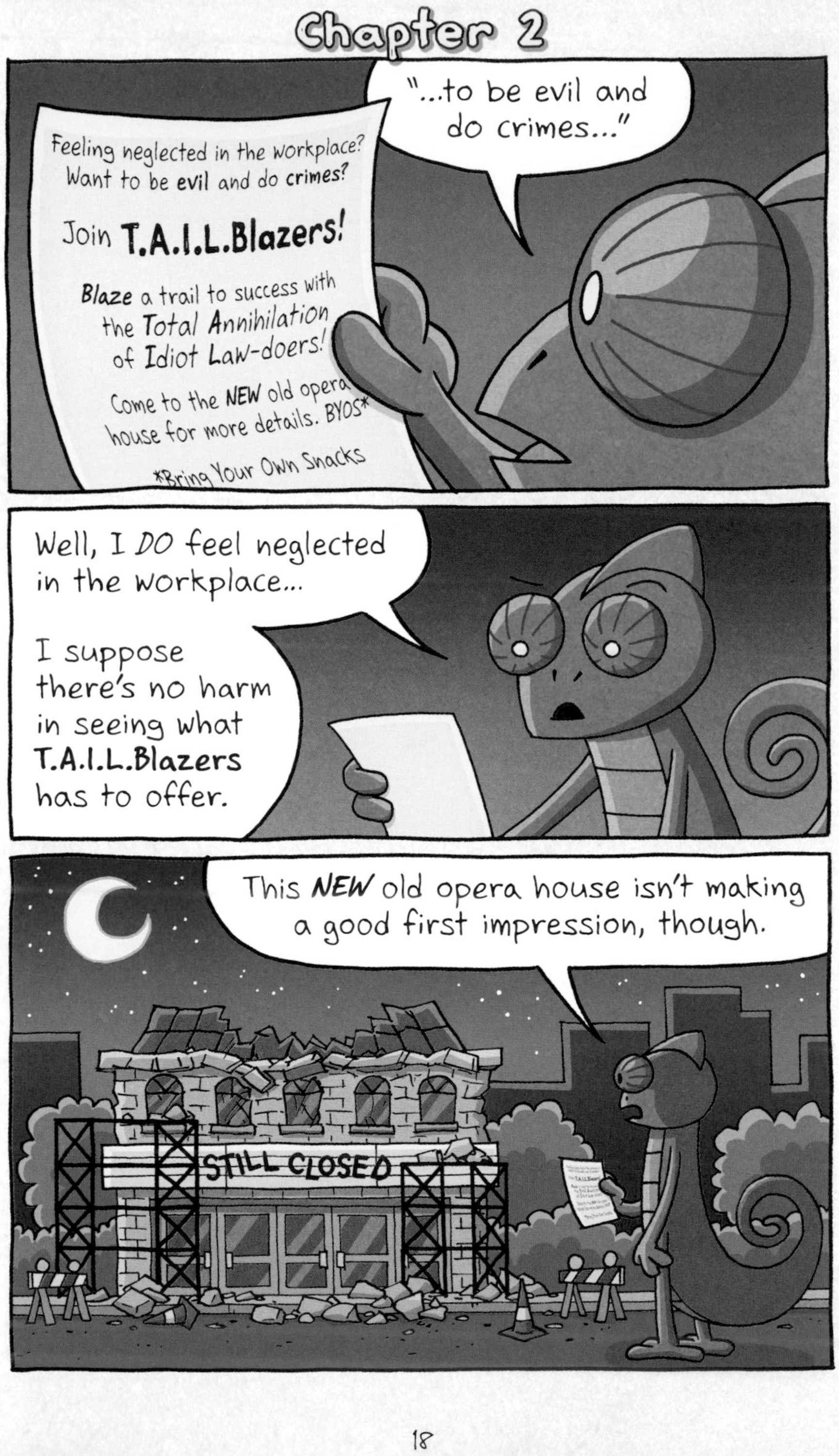
Feeling neglected in the workplace? Want to be evil and do crimes?
Join T.A.I.L.Blazers!
Blaze a trail to success with the Total Annihilation of Idiot Law-doers!
Come to the NEW old opera house for more details. BYOS*
*Bring Your Own Snacks
"...to be evil and do crimes..."
Well, I DO feel neglected in the workplace...
I suppose there's no harm in seeing what T.A.I.L.Blazers has to offer.
This NEW old opera house isn't making a good first impression, though.
STILL CLOSED

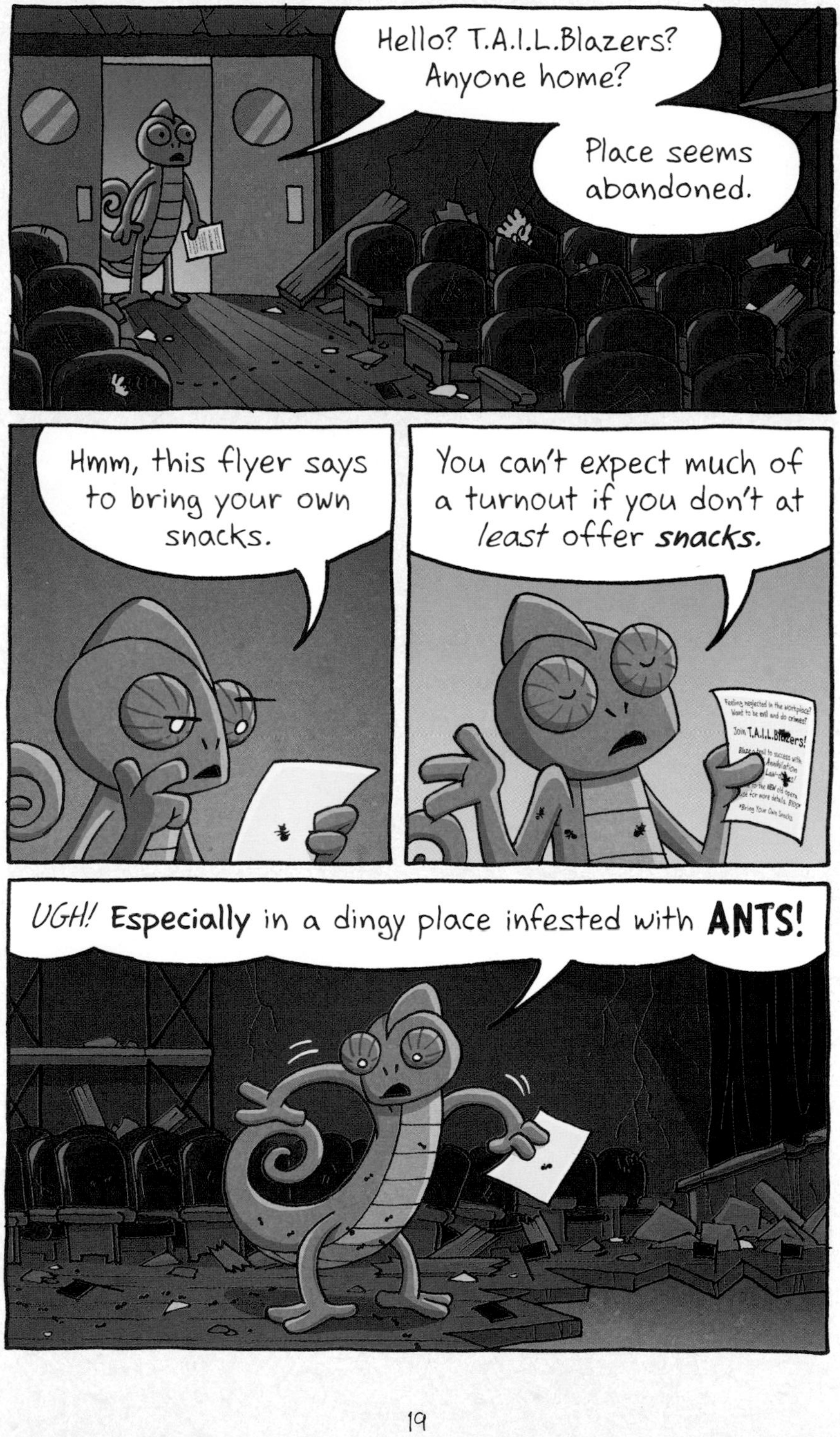
Hello? T.A.I.L.Blazers? Anyone home?
Place seems abandoned.
Hmm, this flyer says to bring your own snacks.
You can't expect much of a turnout if you don't at *least* offer **snacks.**
*UGH!* **Especially** in a dingy place infested with **ANTS!**

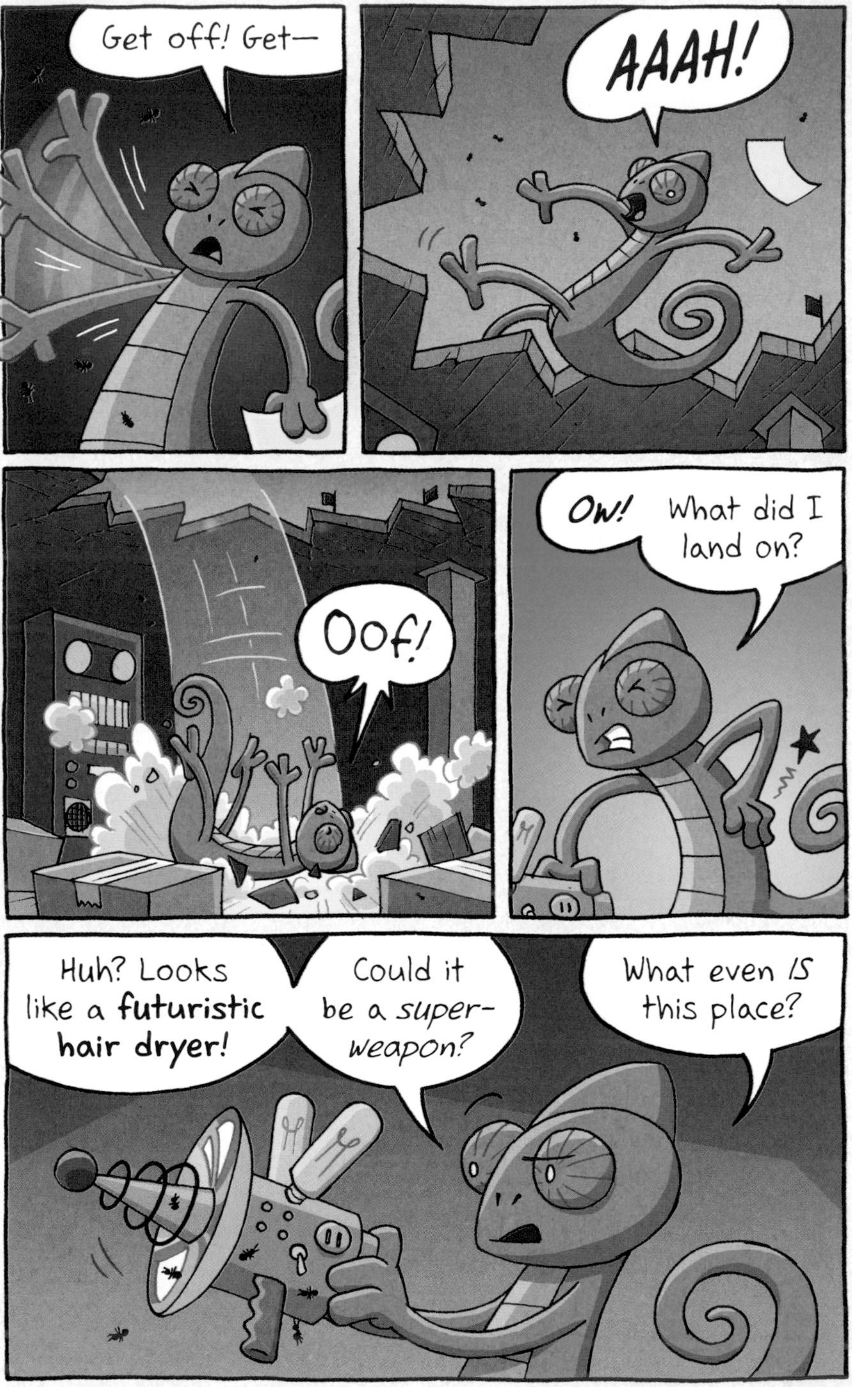
Get off! Get—
AAAH!
Oof!
OW! What did I land on?
Huh? Looks like a **futuristic hair dryer**!
Could it be a *super-weapon*?
What even *IS* this place?

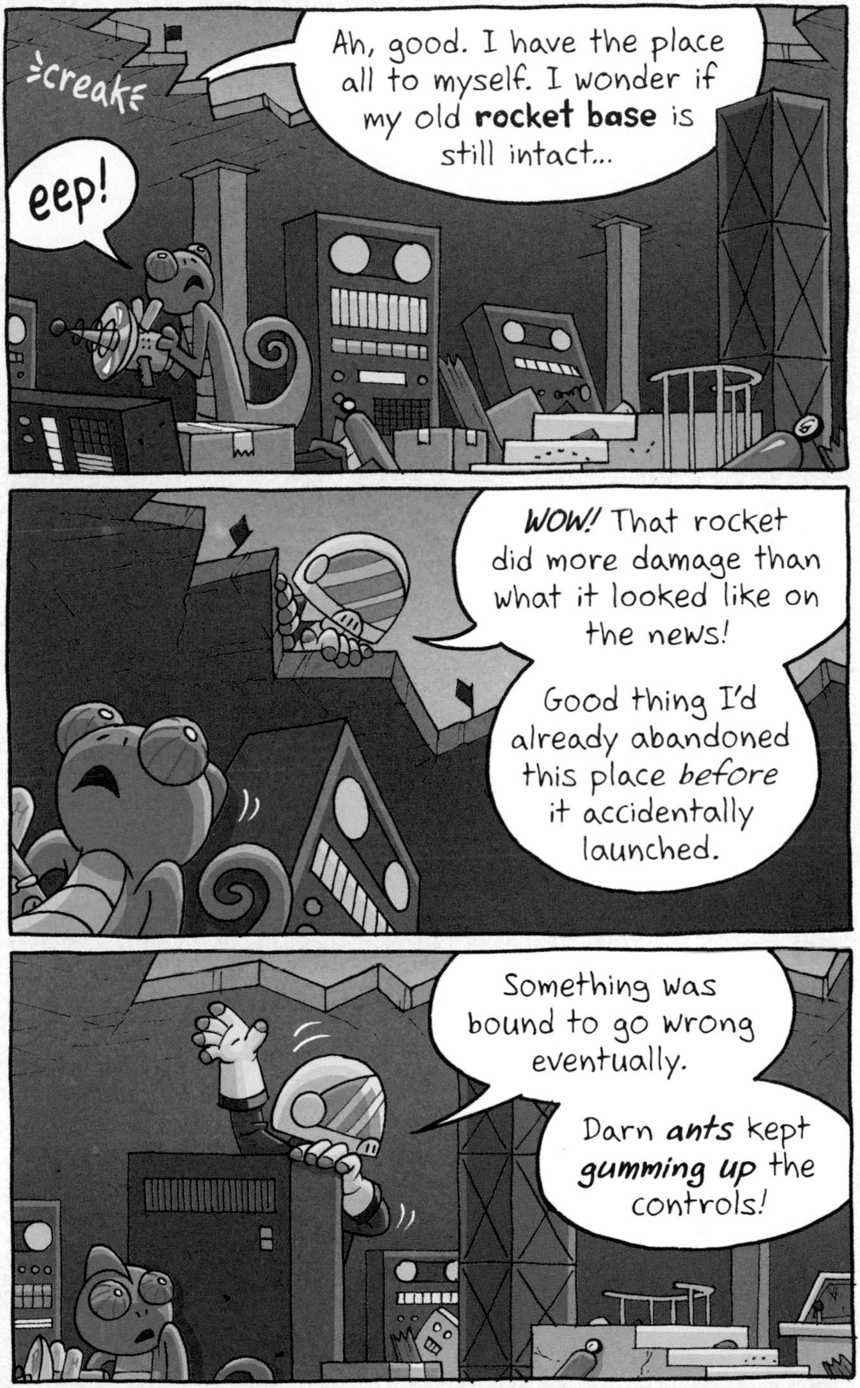
creak
Ah, good. I have the place all to myself. I wonder if my old **rocket base** is still intact...
eep!
***WOW!*** That rocket did more damage than what it looked like on the news!
Good thing I'd already abandoned this place *before* it accidentally launched.
Something was bound to go wrong eventually.
Darn ***ants*** kept ***gumming up*** the controls!

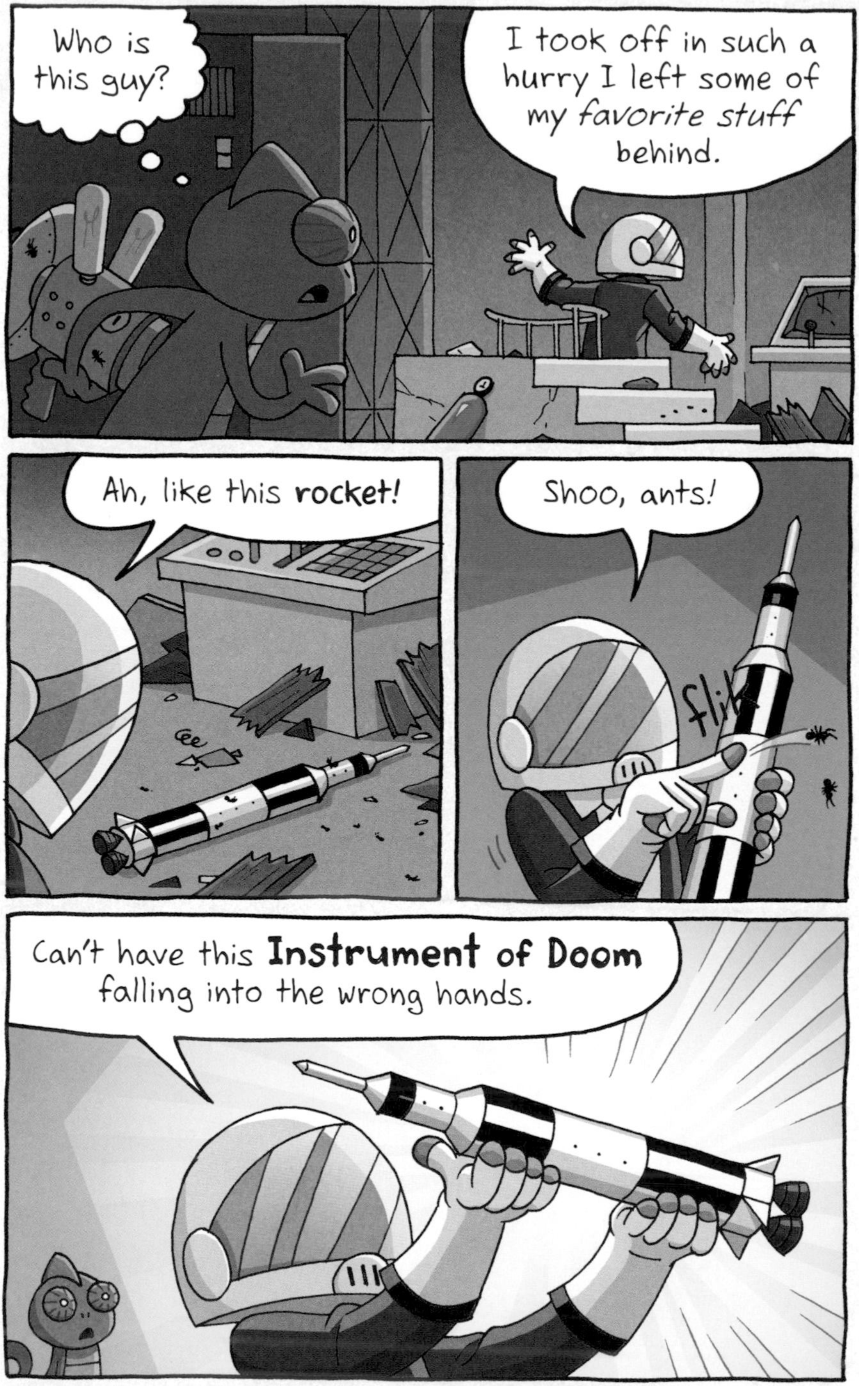
Who is this guy?
I took off in such a hurry I left some of my *favorite stuff* behind.
Ah, like this **rocket!**
Shoo, ants!
flik
Can't have this **Instrument of Doom** falling into the wrong hands.

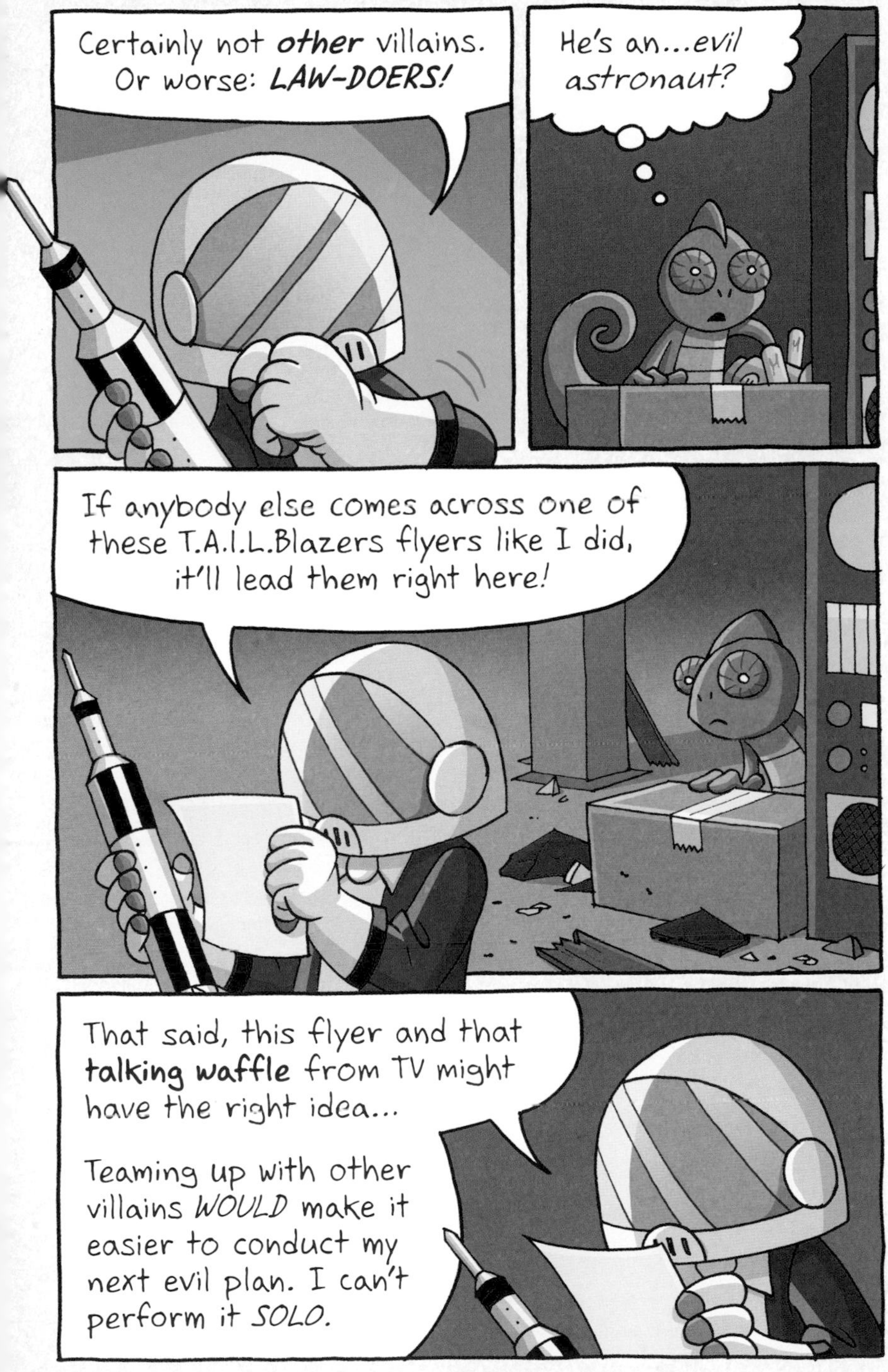
Certainly not **other** villains. Or worse: ***LAW-DOERS!***
He's an...*evil* astronaut?
If anybody else comes across one of these T.A.I.L.Blazers flyers like I did, it'll lead them right here!
That said, this flyer and that **talking waffle** from TV might have the right idea...
Teaming up with other villains *WOULD* make it easier to conduct my next evil plan. I can't perform it *SOLO*.

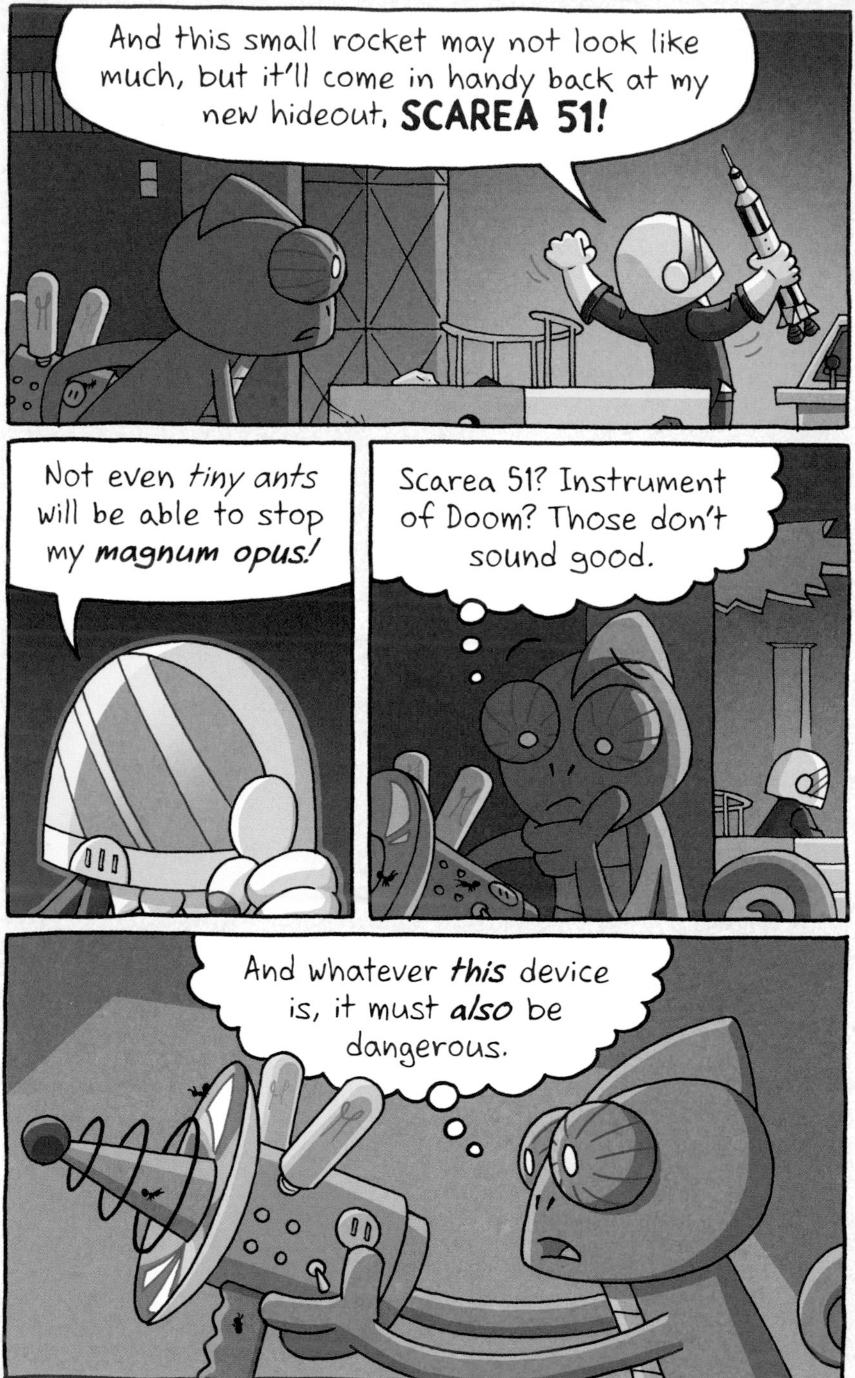
And this small rocket may not look like much, but it'll come in handy back at my new hideout, SCAREA 51!
Not even tiny ants will be able to stop my magnum opus!
Scarea 51? Instrument of Doom? Those don't sound good.
And whatever this device is, it must also be dangerous.

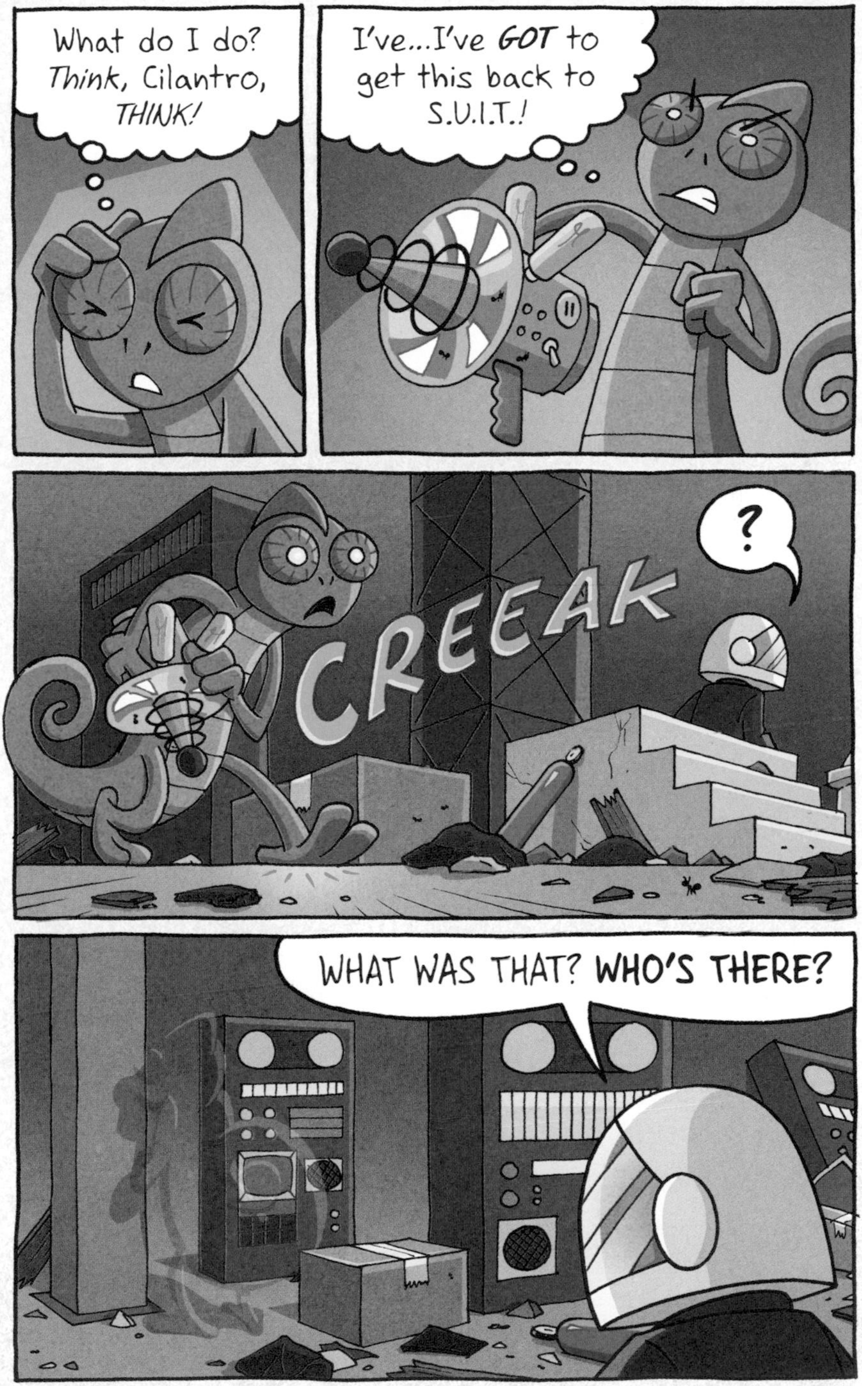
What do I do? Think, Cilantro, THINK!
I've...I've GOT to get this back to S.U.I.T.!
?
CREEAK
WHAT WAS THAT? WHO'S THERE?

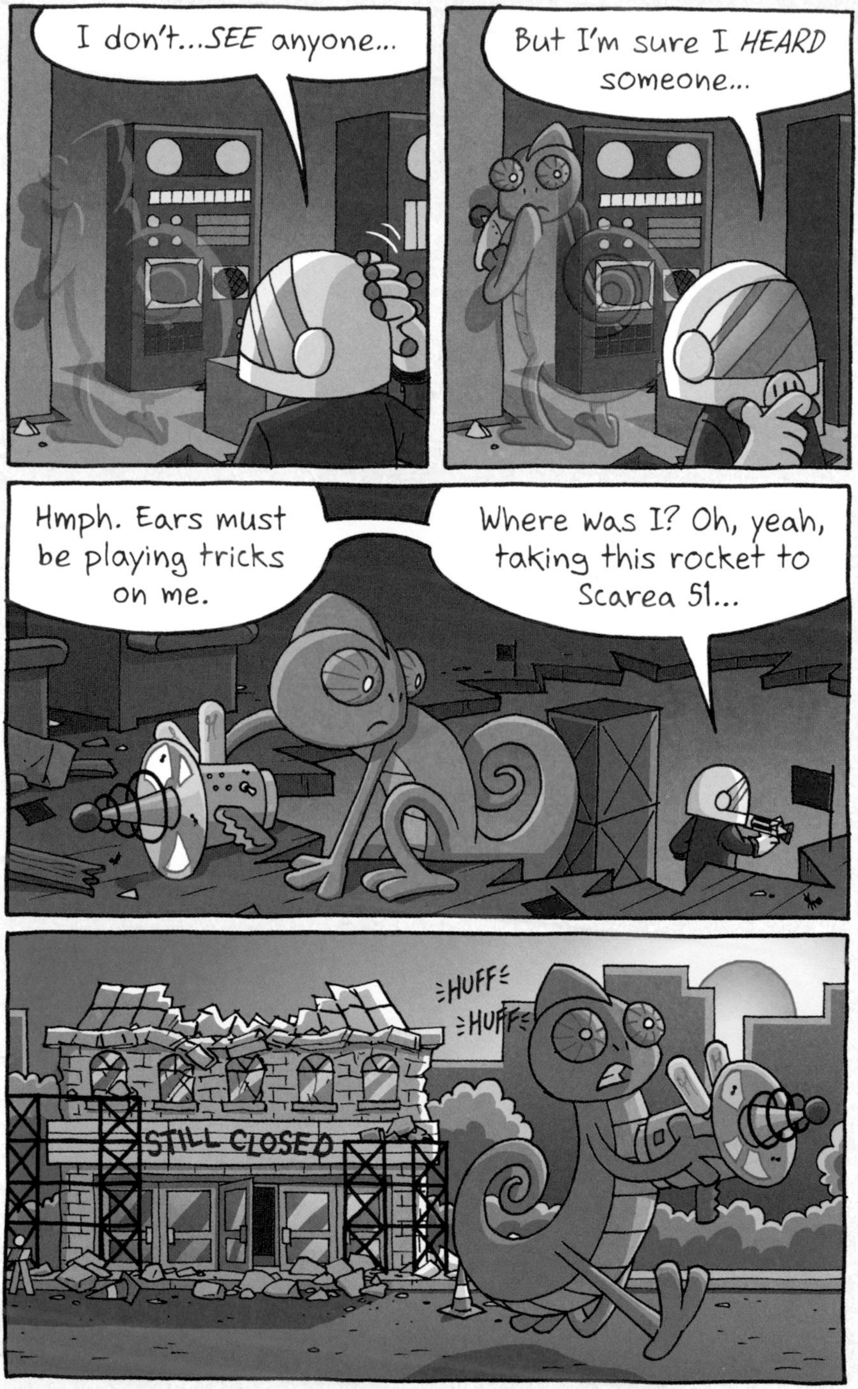
I don't...SEE anyone...
But I'm sure I HEARD someone...
Hmph. Ears must be playing tricks on me.
Where was I? Oh, yeah, taking this rocket to Scarea 51...
HUFF
HUFF
STILL CLOSED

# Chapter 3

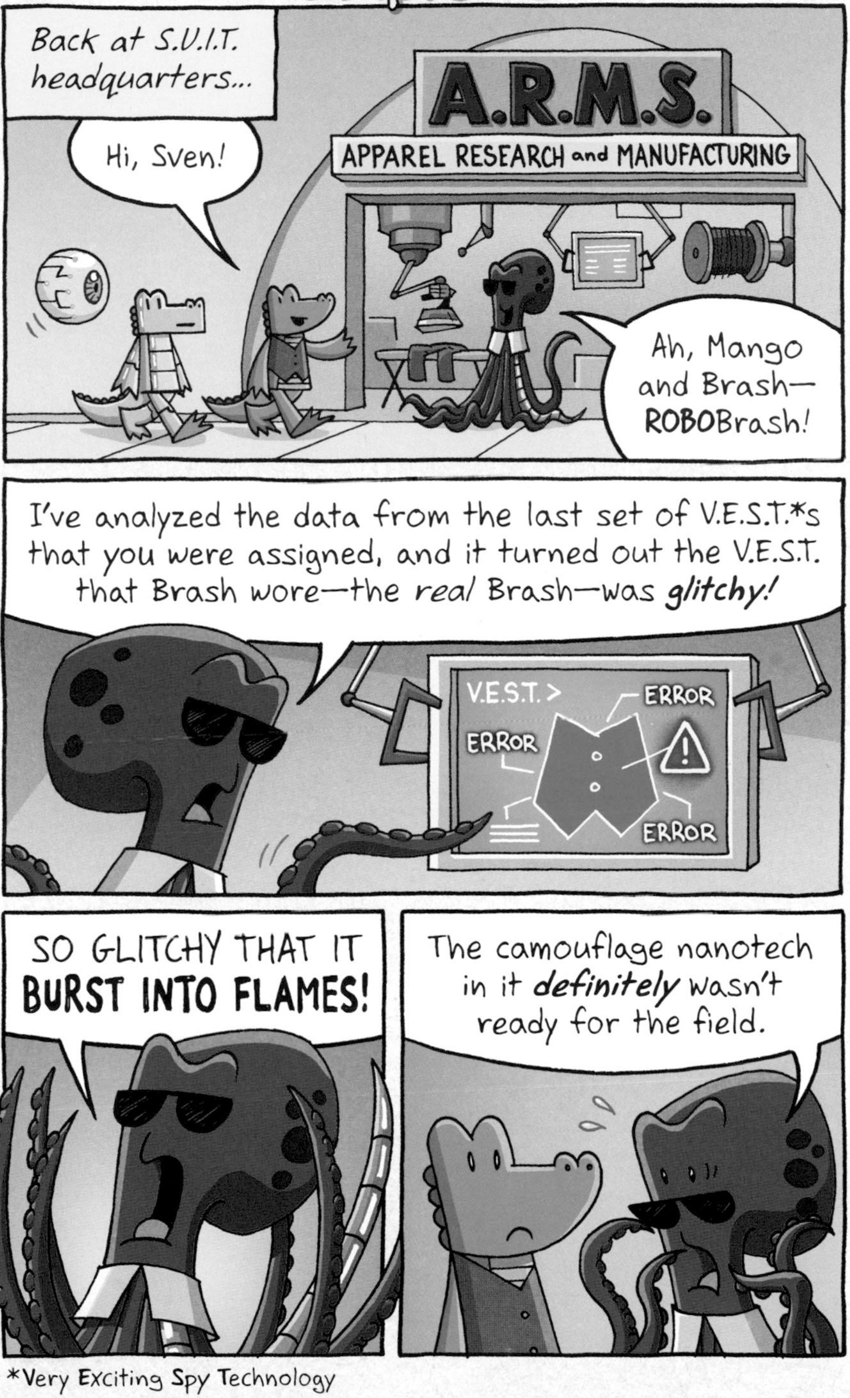

Back at S.U.I.T. headquarters...
Hi, Sven!
A.R.M.S.
APPAREL RESEARCH and MANUFACTURING
Ah, Mango and Brash—ROBOBrash!
I've analyzed the data from the last set of V.E.S.T.*s that you were assigned, and it turned out the V.E.S.T. that Brash wore—the *real* Brash—was *glitchy!*
V.E.S.T. >
ERROR
ERROR
ERROR
SO GLITCHY THAT IT **BURST INTO FLAMES!**
The camouflage nanotech in it *definitely* wasn't ready for the field.


*Very Exciting Spy Technology

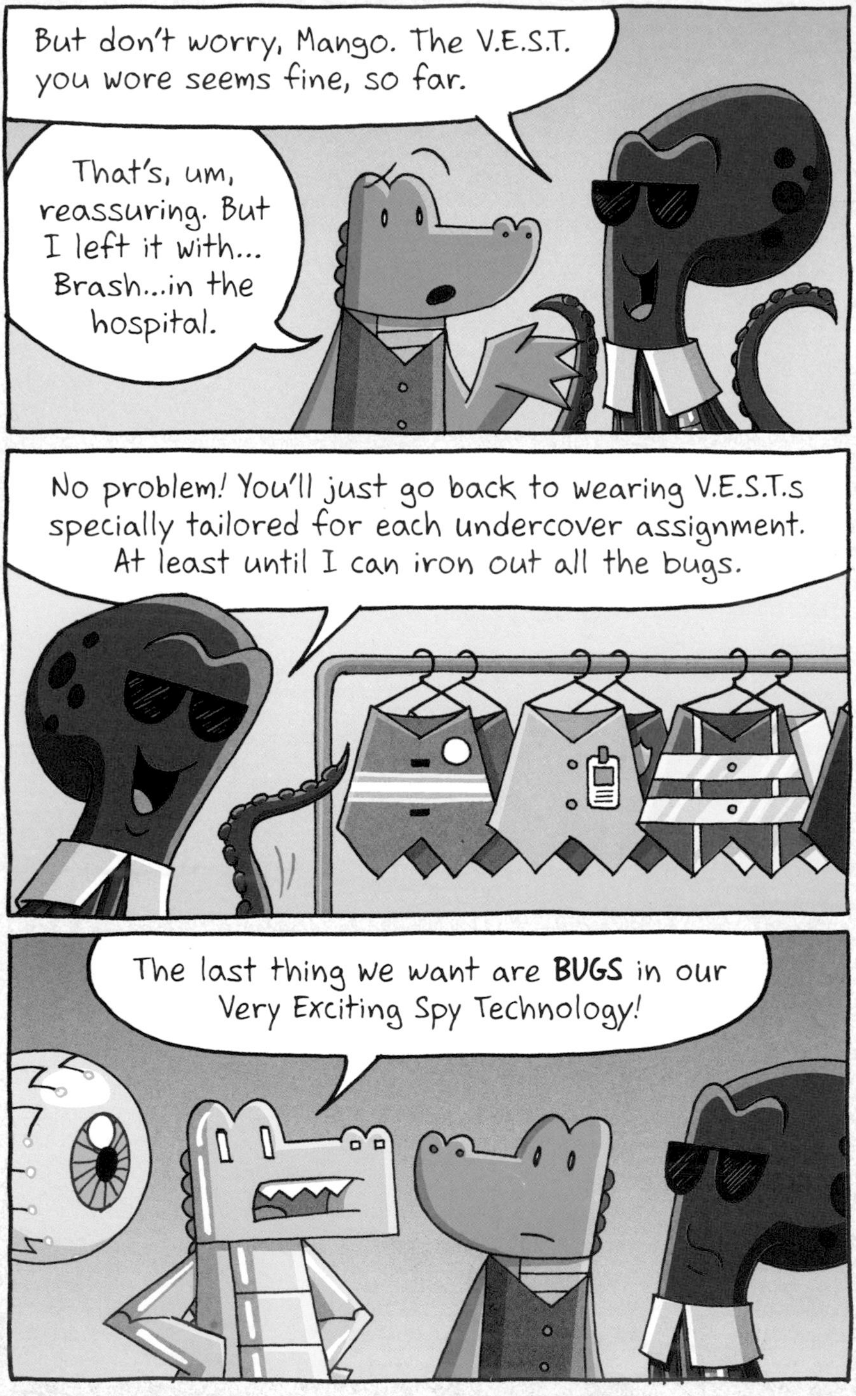

But don't worry, Mango. The V.E.S.T. you wore seems fine, so far.
That's, um, reassuring. But I left it with... Brash...in the hospital.
No problem! You'll just go back to wearing V.E.S.T.s specially tailored for each undercover assignment. At least until I can iron out all the bugs.
The last thing we want are **BUGS** in our Very Exciting Spy Technology!

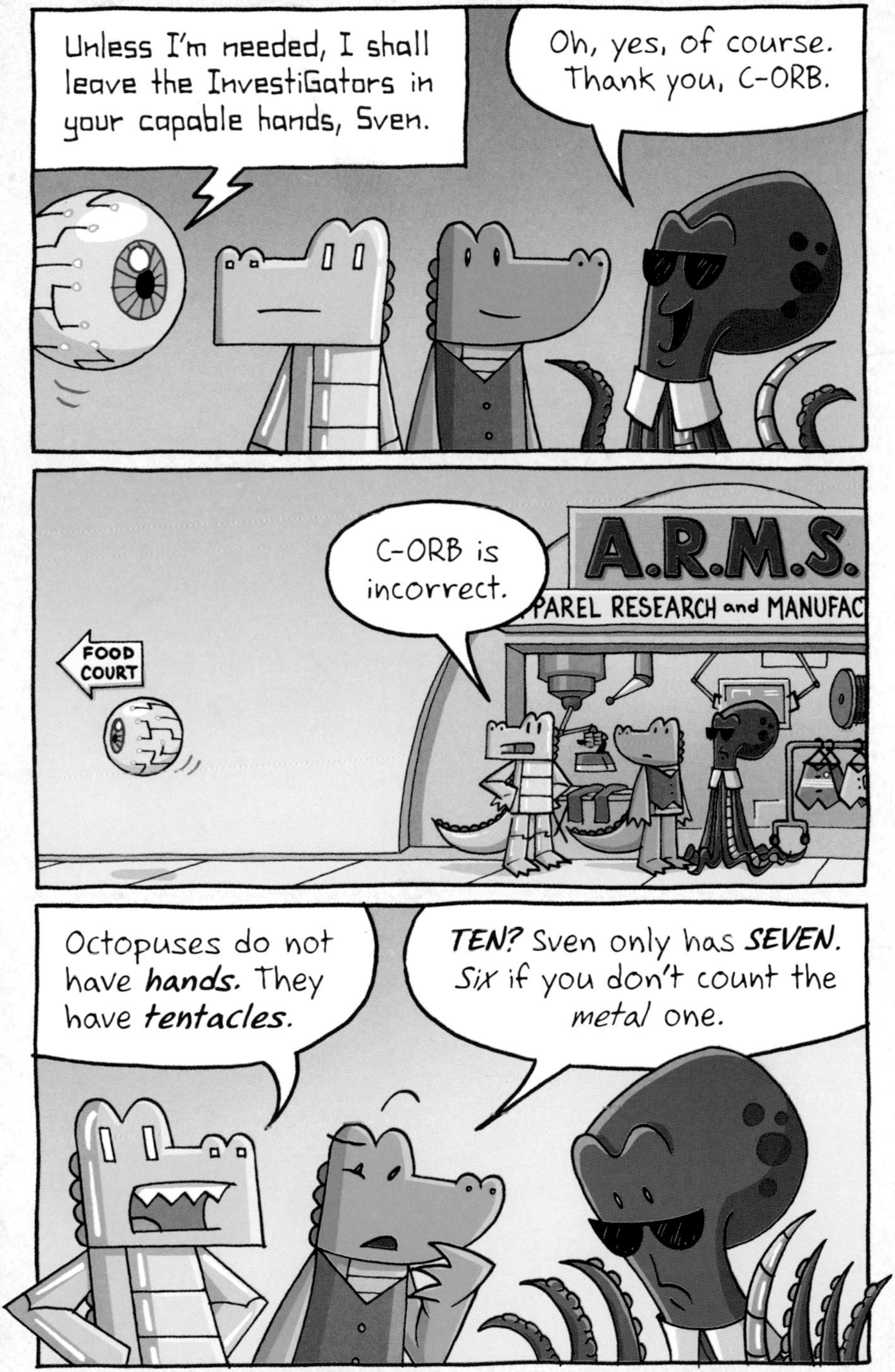
Unless I'm needed, I shall leave the InvestiGators in your capable hands, Sven.
Oh, yes, of course. Thank you, C-ORB.
FOOD COURT
A.R.M.S.
PPAREL RESEARCH and MANUFAC
C-ORB is incorrect.
Octopuses do not have **hands**. They have ***tentacles***.
***TEN?*** Sven only has ***SEVEN***. *Six* if you don't count the *metal* one.

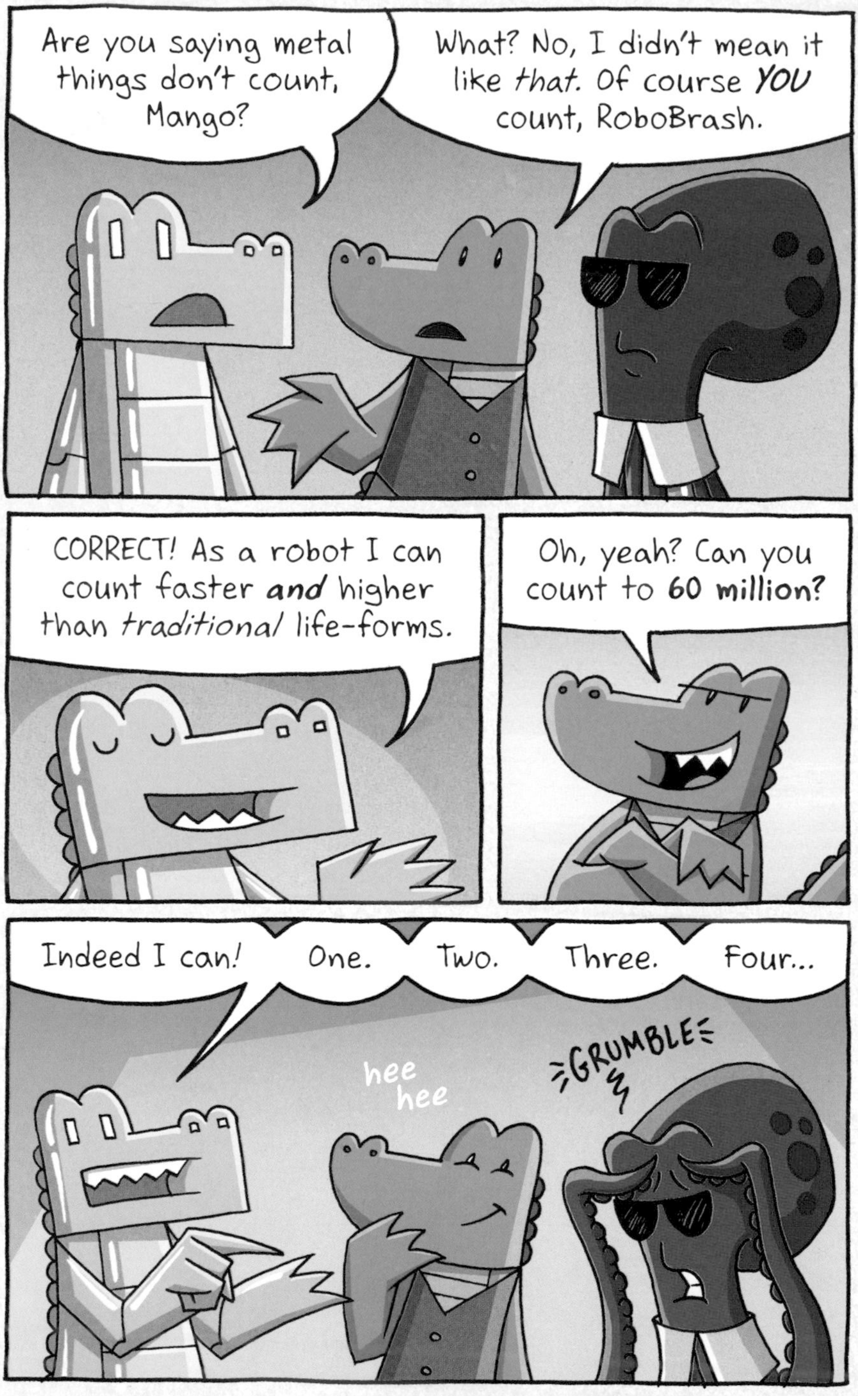
Are you saying metal things don't count, Mango?
What? No, I didn't mean it like *that*. Of course **YOU** count, RoboBrash.
CORRECT! As a robot I can count faster **and** higher than *traditional* life-forms.
Oh, yeah? Can you count to **60 million?**
Indeed I can! One. Two. Three. Four...
hee hee
GRUMBLE

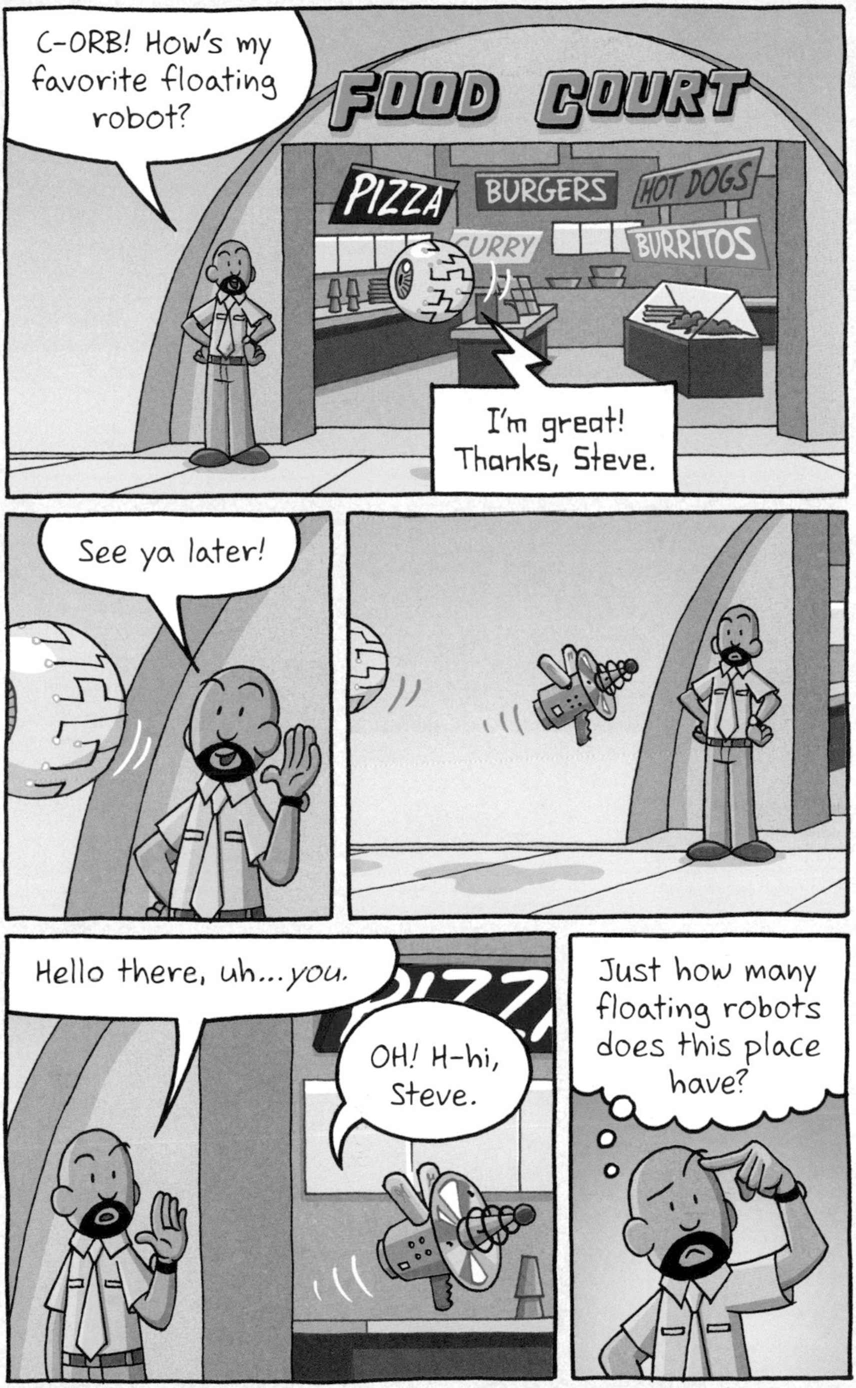
C-ORB! HOW'S my favorite floating robot?
FOOD COURT
PIZZA
BURGERS
HOT DOGS
CURRY
BURRITOS
I'm great! Thanks, Steve.
See ya later!
Hello there, uh... *you.*
OH! H-hi, Steve.
Just how many floating robots does this place have?

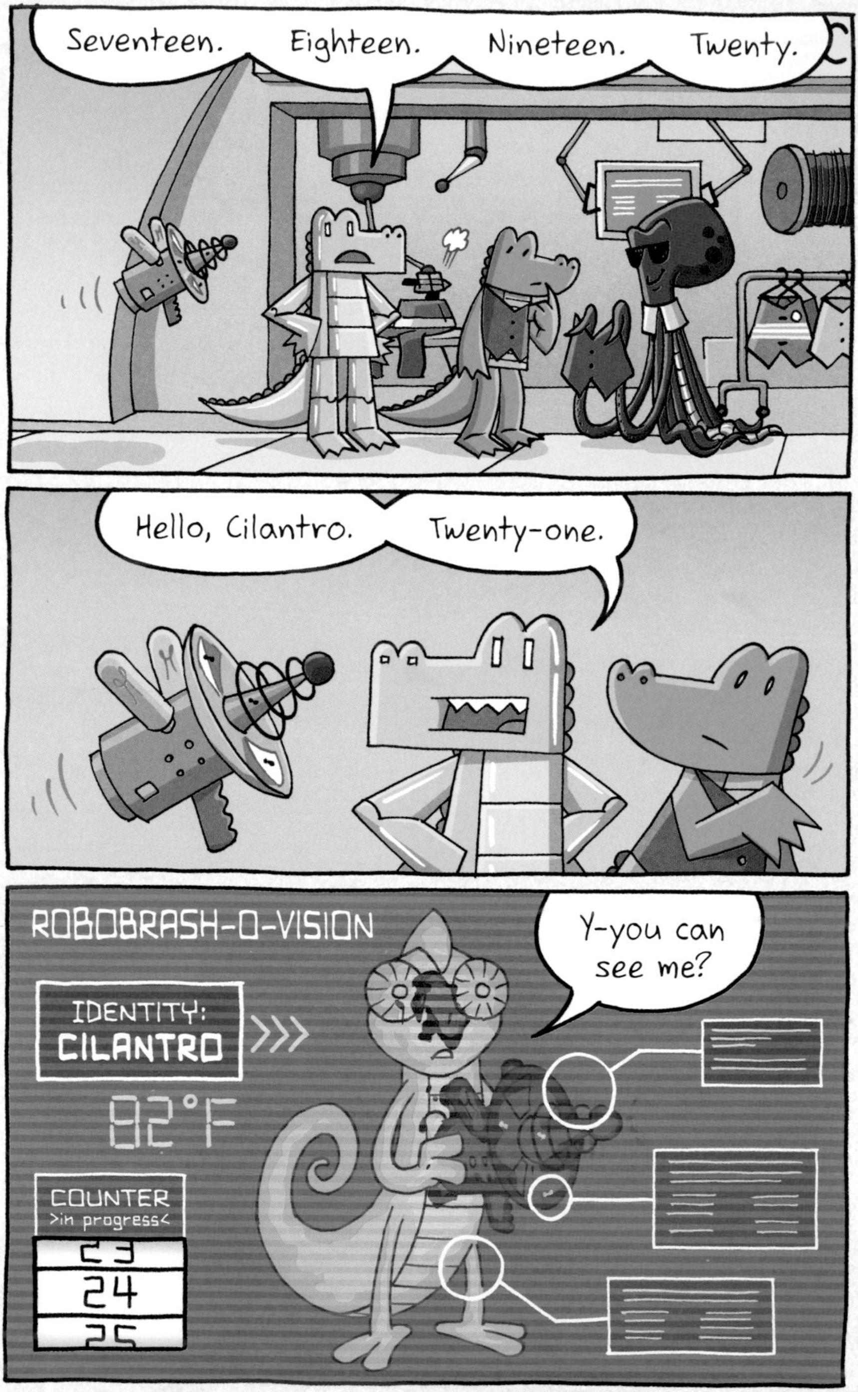
Seventeen. Eighteen. Nineteen. Twenty.
Hello, Cilantro. Twenty-one.
ROBOBRASH-O-VISION
Y-you can see me?
IDENTITY:
CILANTRO
82°F
COUNTER
>in progress<
23
24
25

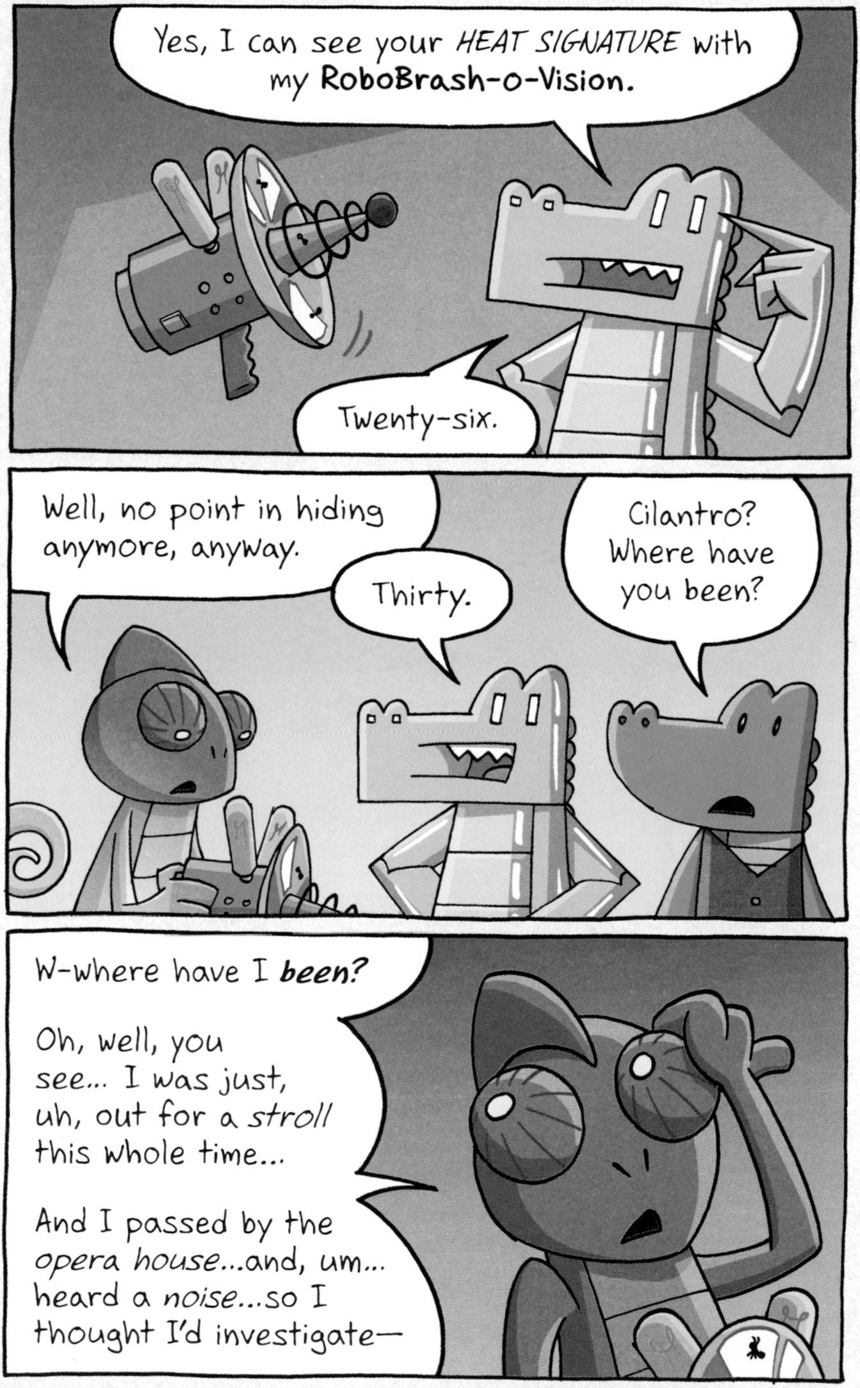
Yes, I can see your *HEAT SIGNATURE* with my **RoboBrash-o-Vision.**
Twenty-six.
Well, no point in hiding anymore, anyway.
Thirty.
Cilantro? Where have you been?
W-where have I ***been?***
Oh, well, you see... I was just, uh, out for a *stroll* this whole time...
And I passed by the *opera house*...and, um... heard a *noise*...so I thought I'd investigate—

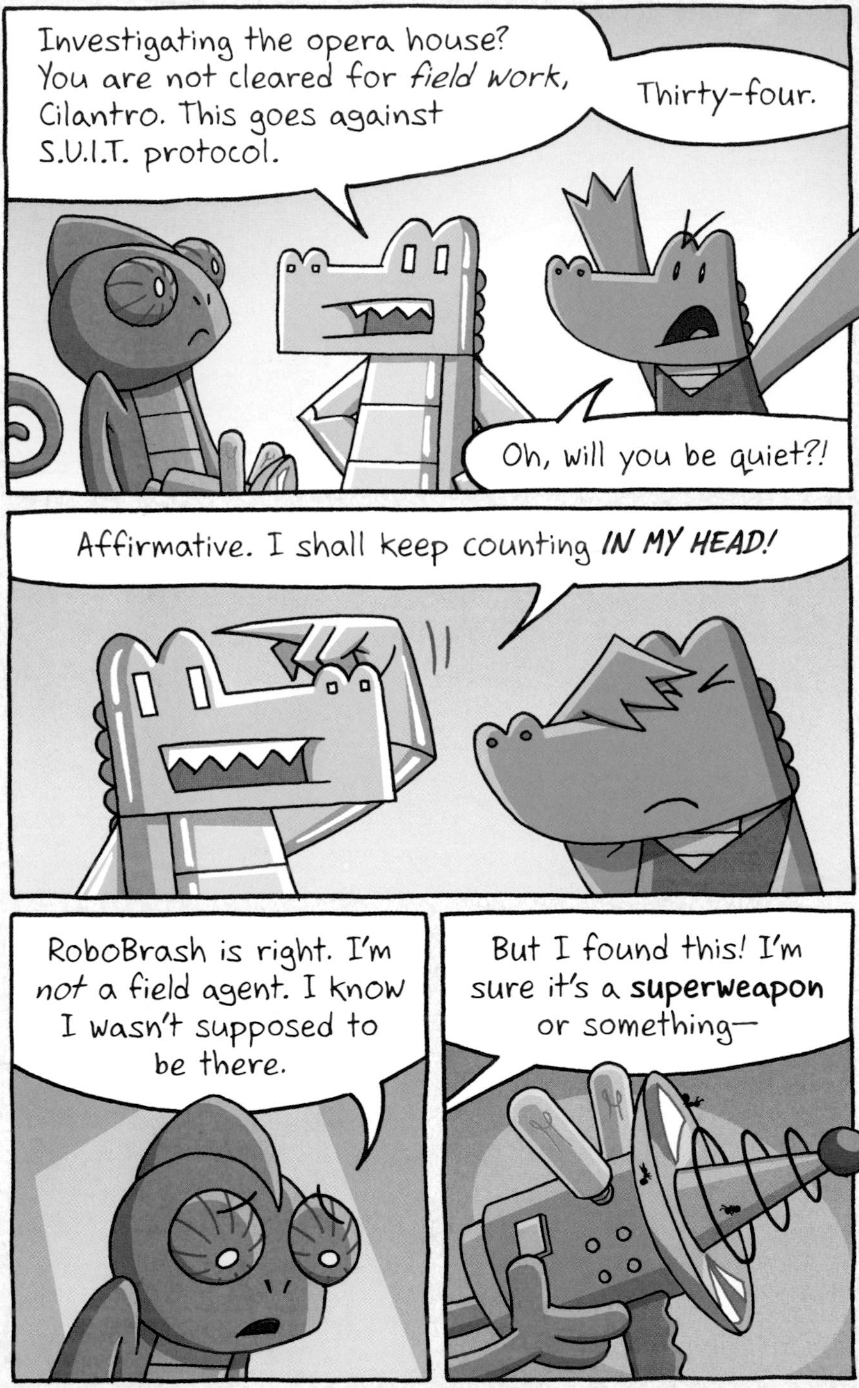
Investigating the opera house? You are not cleared for *field work*, Cilantro. This goes against S.U.I.T. protocol.
Thirty-four.
Oh, will you be quiet?!
Affirmative. I shall keep counting ***IN MY HEAD!***
RoboBrash is right. I'm *not* a field agent. I know I wasn't supposed to be there.
But I found this! I'm sure it's a **superweapon** or something—

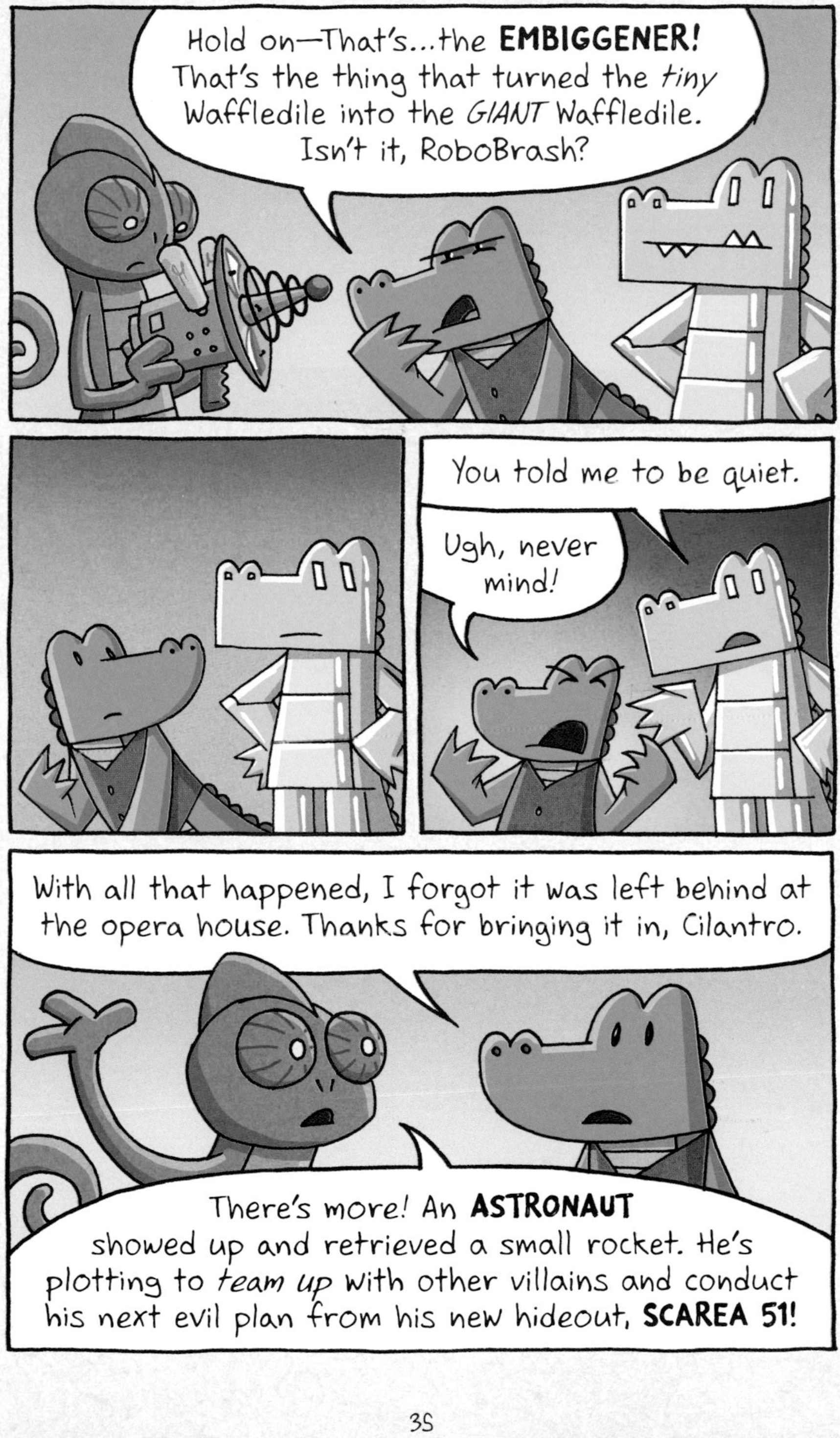

Hold on—That's...the **EMBIGGENER!** That's the thing that turned the *tiny* Waffledile into the *GIANT* Waffledile. Isn't it, RoboBrash?
You told me to be quiet.
Ugh, never mind!
With all that happened, I forgot it was left behind at the opera house. Thanks for bringing it in, Cilantro.
There's more! An **ASTRONAUT** showed up and retrieved a small rocket. He's plotting to *team up* with other villains and conduct his next evil plan from his new hideout, **SCAREA 51!**

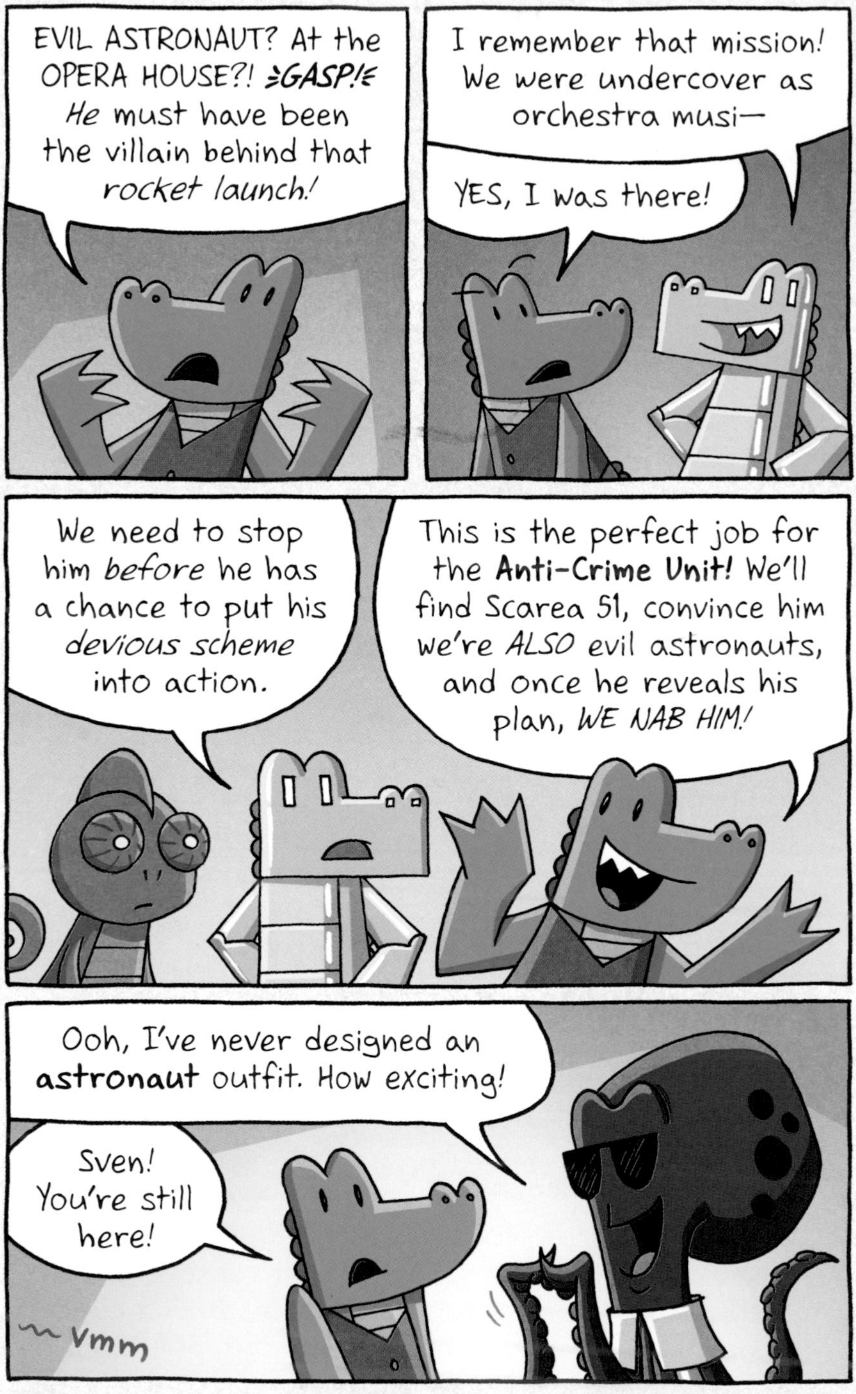
EVIL ASTRONAUT? At the OPERA HOUSE?! GASP! He must have been the villain behind that rocket launch!
I remember that mission! We were undercover as orchestra musi—
YES, I was there!
We need to stop him before he has a chance to put his devious scheme into action.
This is the perfect job for the Anti-Crime Unit! We'll find Scarea 51, convince him we're ALSO evil astronauts, and once he reveals his plan, WE NAB HIM!
Ooh, I've never designed an astronaut outfit. How exciting!
Sven! You're still here!
vmm

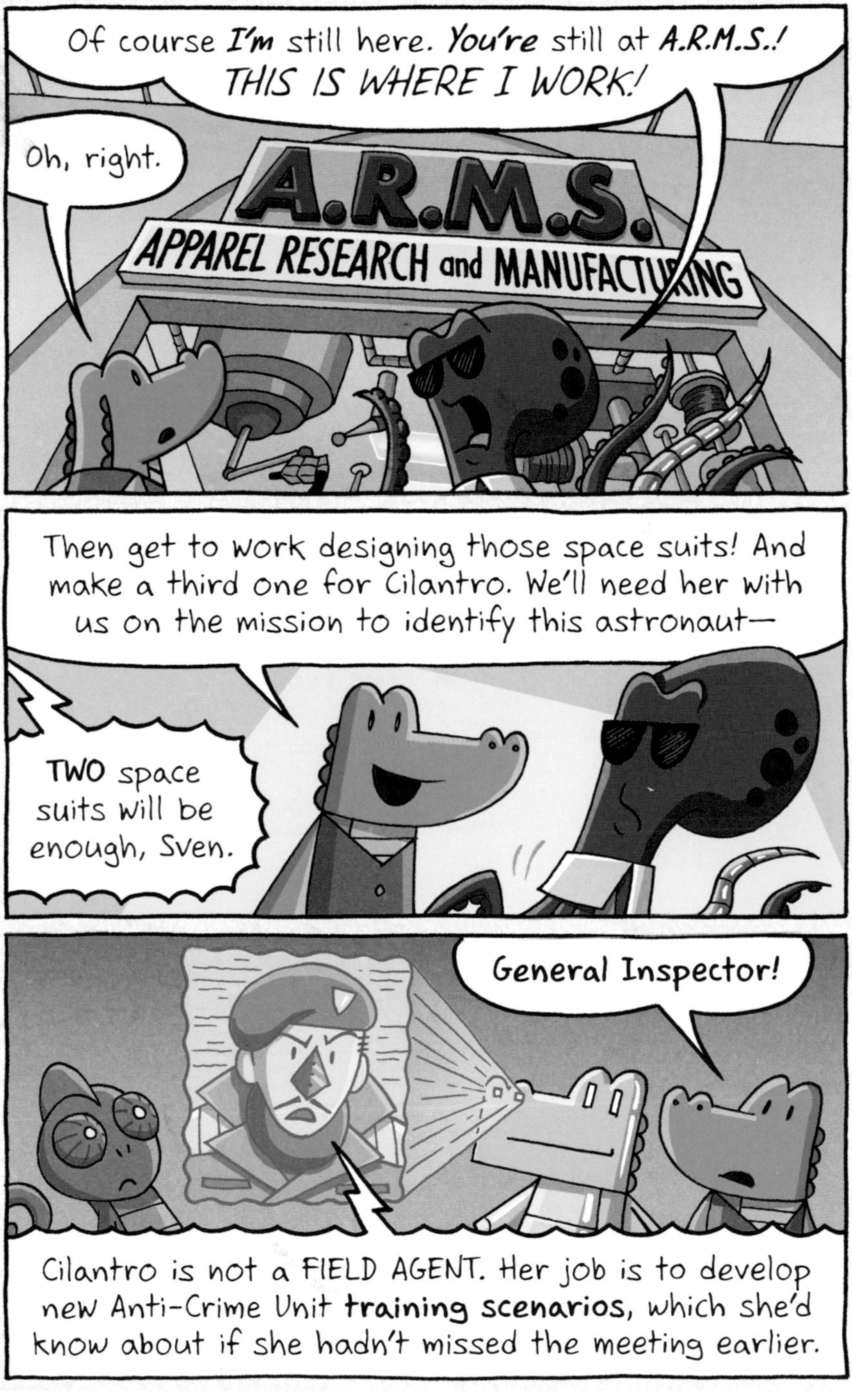

Of course I'm still here. You're still at A.R.M.S.! THIS IS WHERE I WORK!
Oh, right.
A.R.M.S.
APPAREL RESEARCH and MANUFACTURING
Then get to work designing those space suits! And make a third one for Cilantro. We'll need her with us on the mission to identify this astronaut—
TWO space suits will be enough, Sven.
General Inspector!
Cilantro is not a FIELD AGENT. Her job is to develop new Anti-Crime Unit training scenarios, which she'd know about if she hadn't missed the meeting earlier.

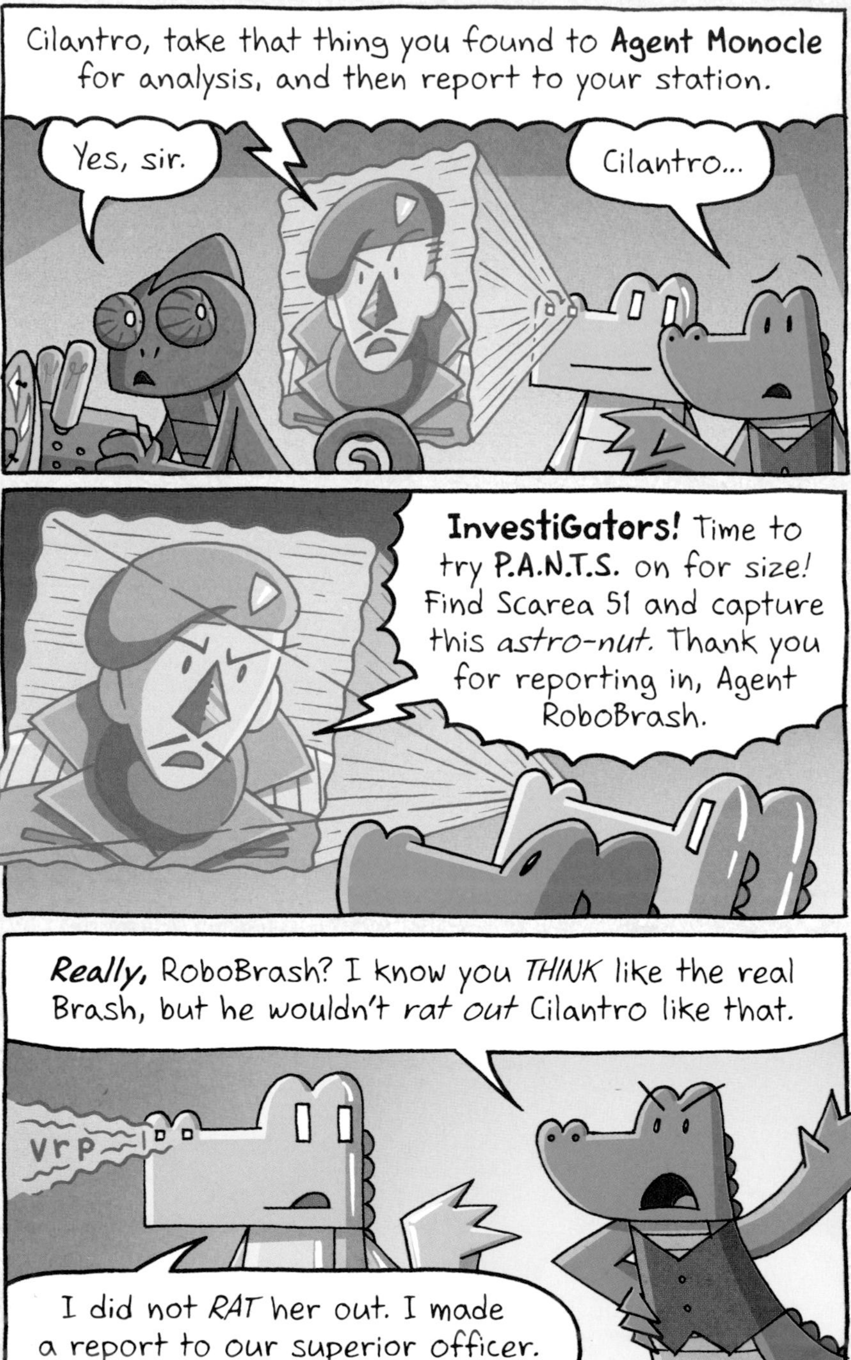
Cilantro, take that thing you found to **Agent Monocle** for analysis, and then report to your station.
Yes, sir.
Cilantro...
**InvestiGators!** Time to try **P.A.N.T.S.** on for size! Find Scarea 51 and capture this *astro-nut*. Thank you for reporting in, Agent RoboBrash.
***Really,*** RoboBrash? I know you *THINK* like the real Brash, but he wouldn't *rat out* Cilantro like that.
VRP
I did not *RAT* her out. I made a report to our superior officer.

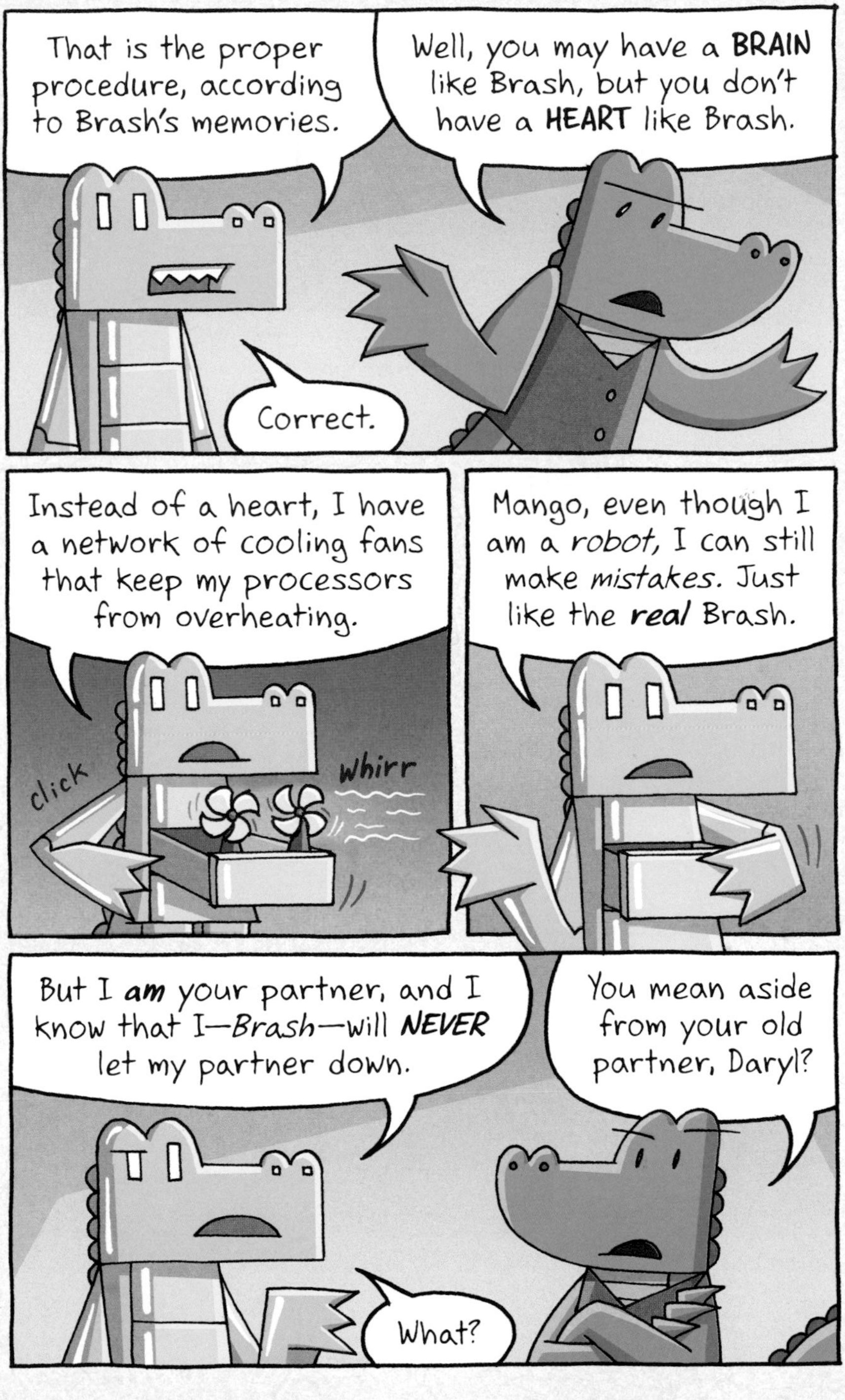
That is the proper procedure, according to Brash's memories.
Well, you may have a BRAIN like Brash, but you don't have a HEART like Brash.
Correct.
Instead of a heart, I have a network of cooling fans that keep my processors from overheating.
click
whirr
Mango, even though I am a robot, I can still make mistakes. Just like the real Brash.
But I am your partner, and I know that I—Brash—will NEVER let my partner down.
You mean aside from your old partner, Daryl?
What?

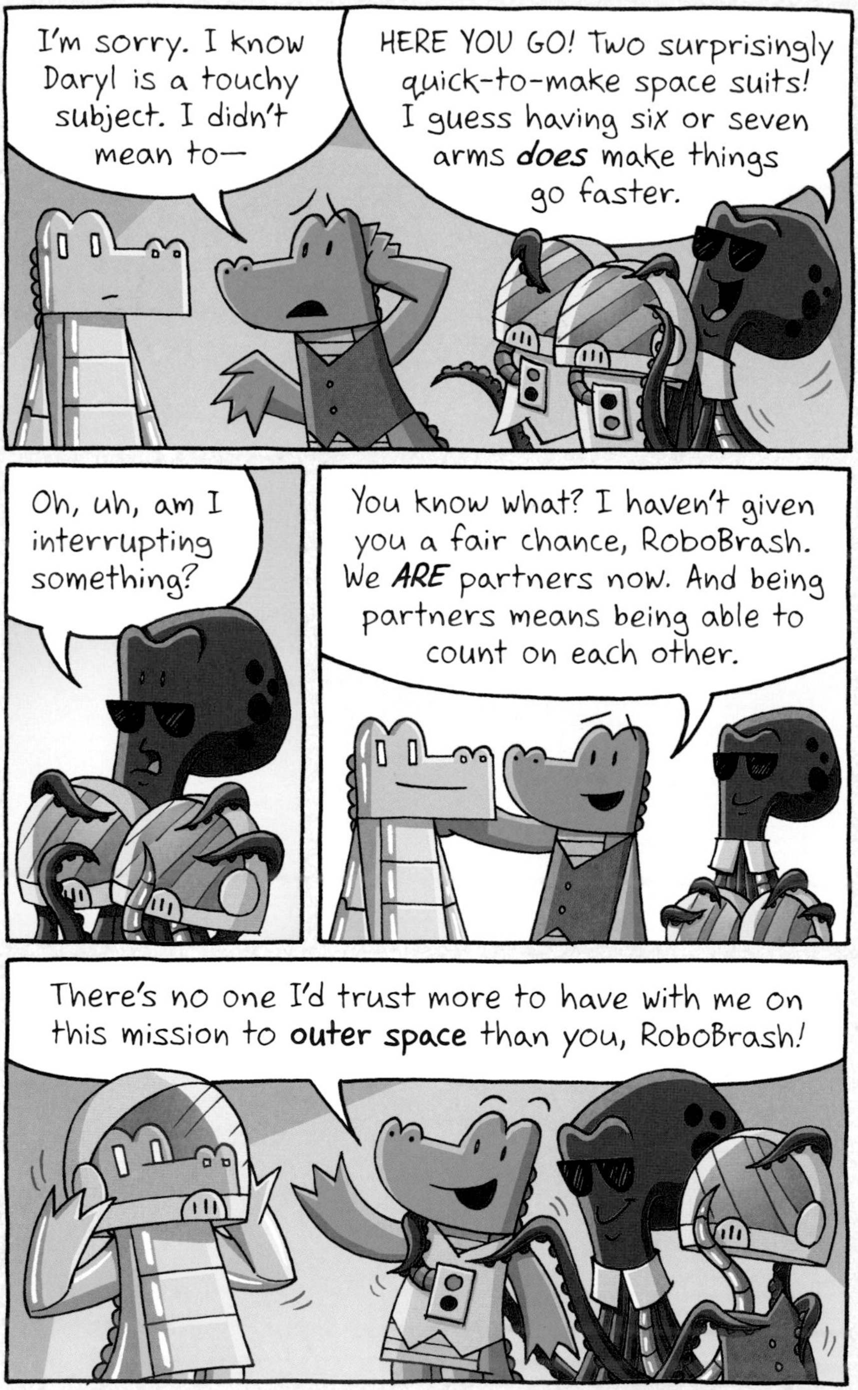

I'm sorry. I know Daryl is a touchy subject. I didn't mean to—
HERE YOU GO! Two surprisingly quick-to-make space suits! I guess having six or seven arms *does* make things go faster.
Oh, uh, am I interrupting something?
You know what? I haven't given you a fair chance, RoboBrash. We *ARE* partners now. And being partners means being able to count on each other.
There's no one I'd trust more to have with me on this mission to **outer space** than you, RoboBrash!

# Chapter 4

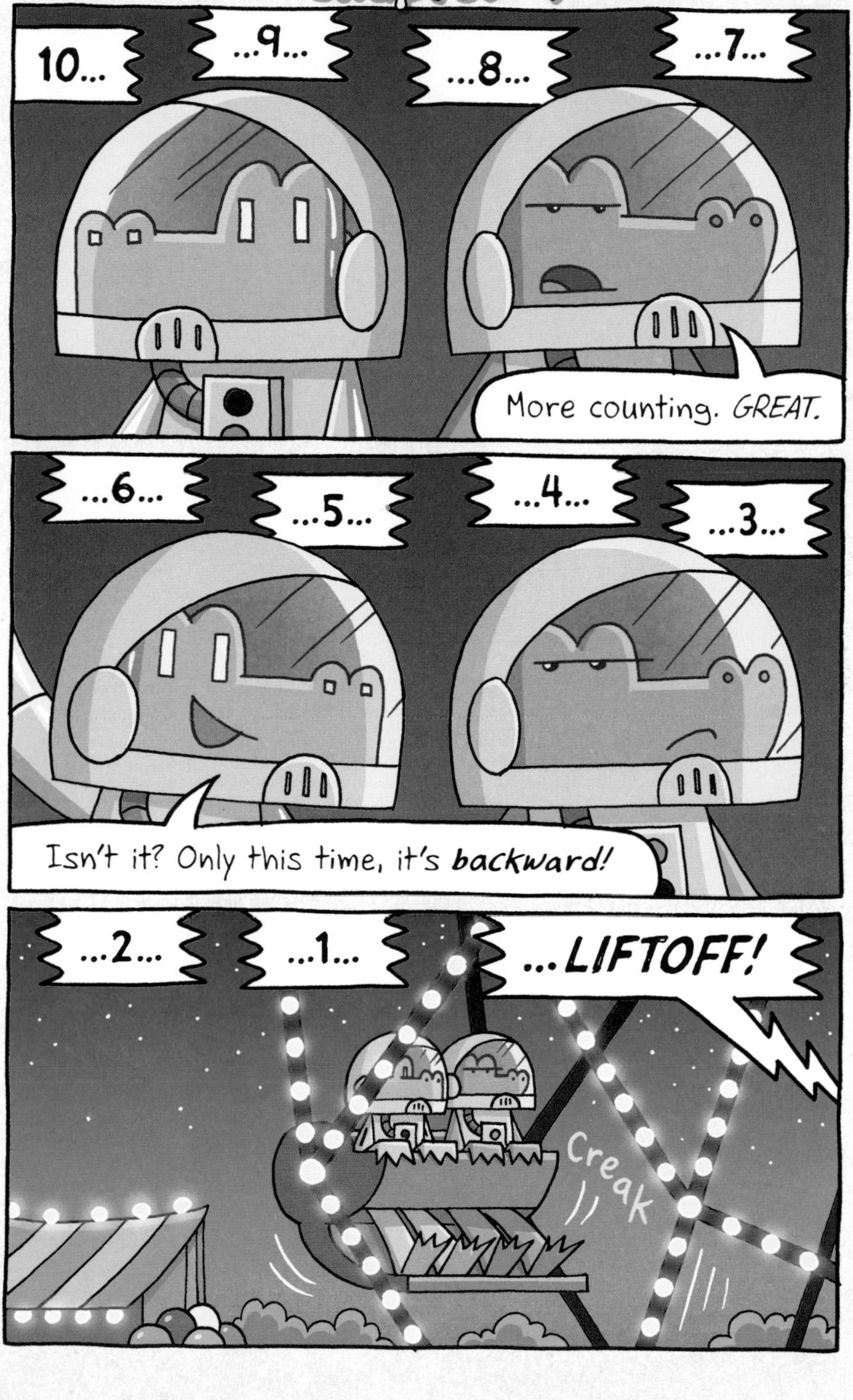
10...
...9...
...8...
...7...
More counting. *GREAT.*
...6...
...5...
...4...
...3...
Isn't it? Only this time, it's **backward!**
...2...
...1...
...*LIFTOFF!*
Creak

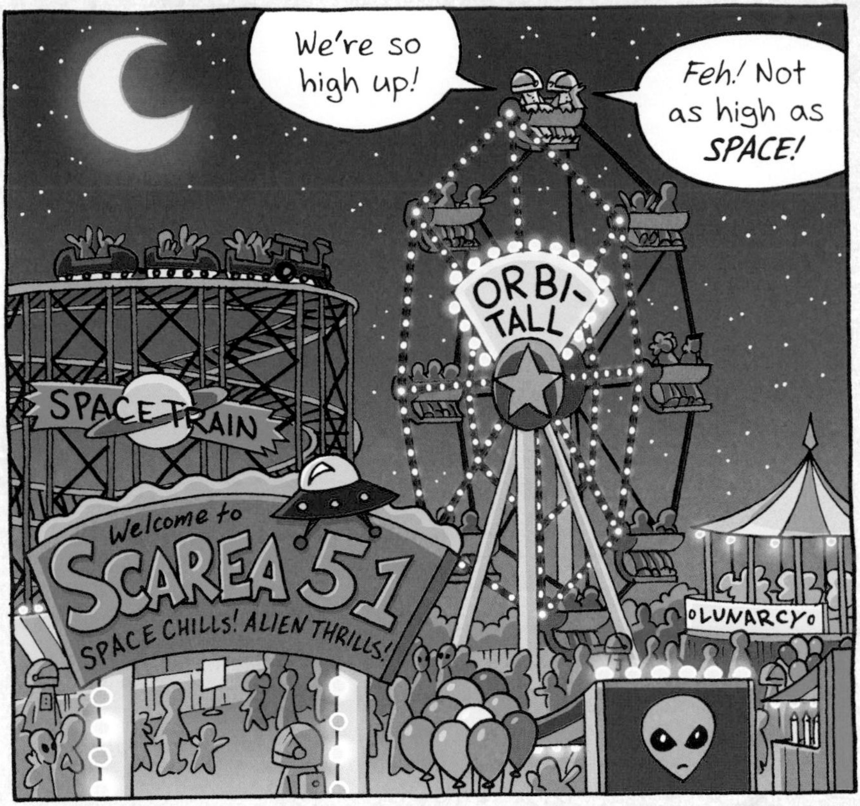
We're so high up!
Feh! Not as high as SPACE!
SPACE TRAIN
ORBI-TALL
Welcome to SCAREA 51
SPACE CHILLS! ALIEN THRILLS!
LUNARCY

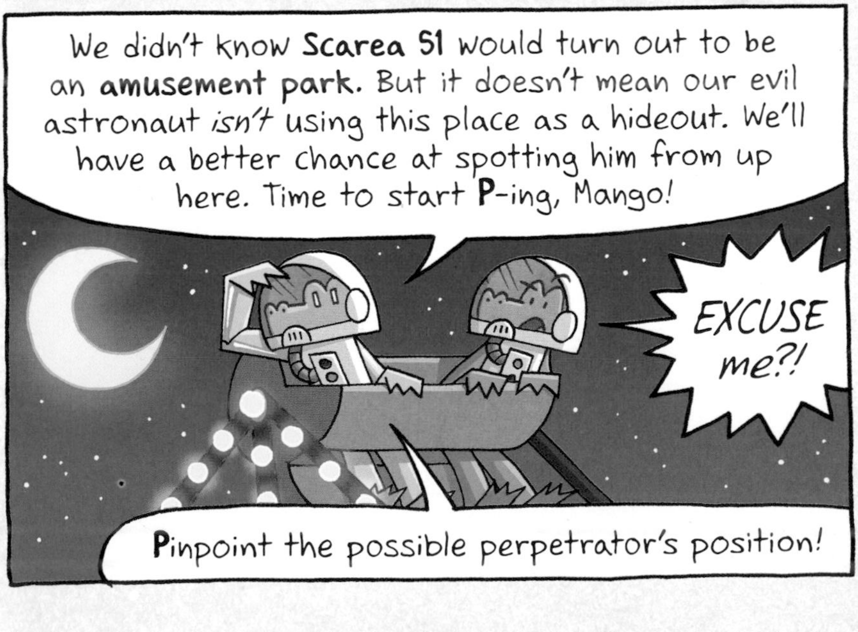
We didn't know **Scarea 51** would turn out to be an **amusement park**. But it doesn't mean our evil astronaut *isn't* using this place as a hideout. We'll have a better chance at spotting him from up here. Time to start **P**-ing, Mango!
EXCUSE me?!
**P**inpoint the possible perpetrator's position!

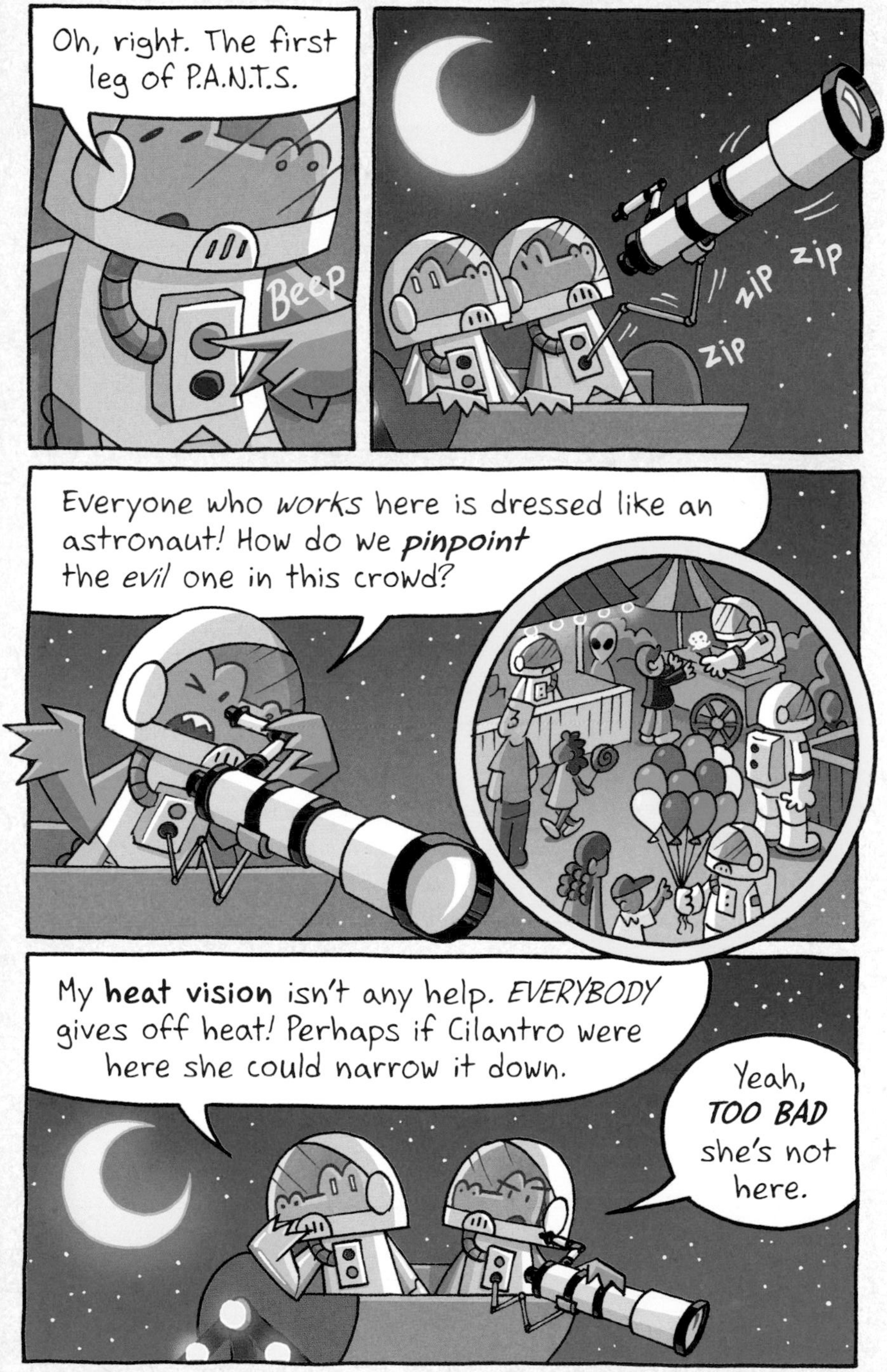

Oh, right. The first leg of P.A.N.T.S.
Beep
zip zip zip zip
Everyone who *works* here is dressed like an astronaut! How do we **pinpoint** the *evil* one in this crowd?
My **heat vision** isn't any help. *EVERYBODY* gives off heat! Perhaps if Cilantro were here she could narrow it down.
Yeah, **TOO BAD** she's not here.

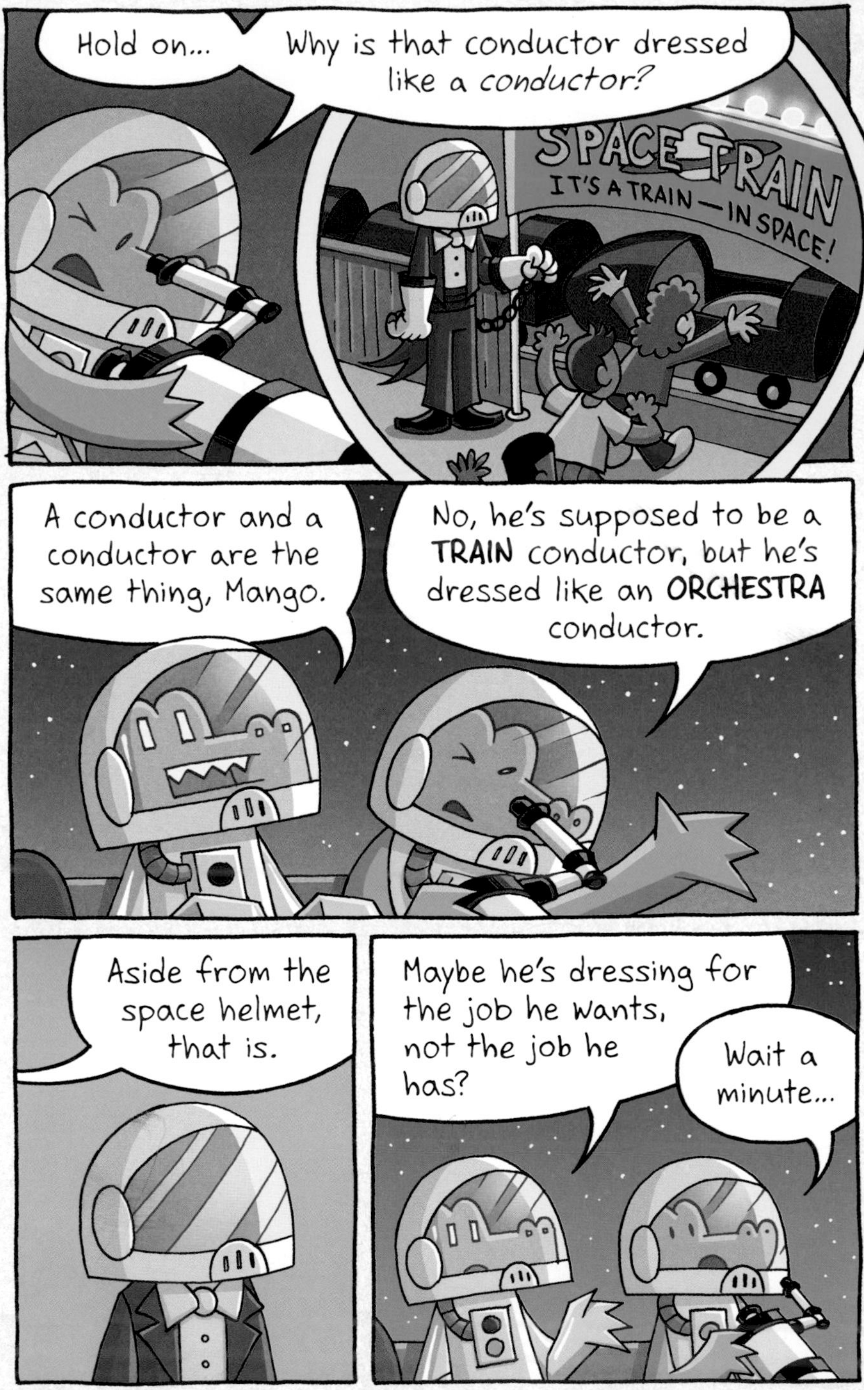
Hold on...
Why is that conductor dressed like a *conductor?*
SPACE TRAIN
IT'S A TRAIN — IN SPACE!
A conductor and a conductor are the same thing, Mango.
No, he's supposed to be a **TRAIN** conductor, but he's dressed like an **ORCHESTRA** conductor.
Aside from the space helmet, that is.
Maybe he's dressing for the job he wants, not the job he has?
Wait a minute...

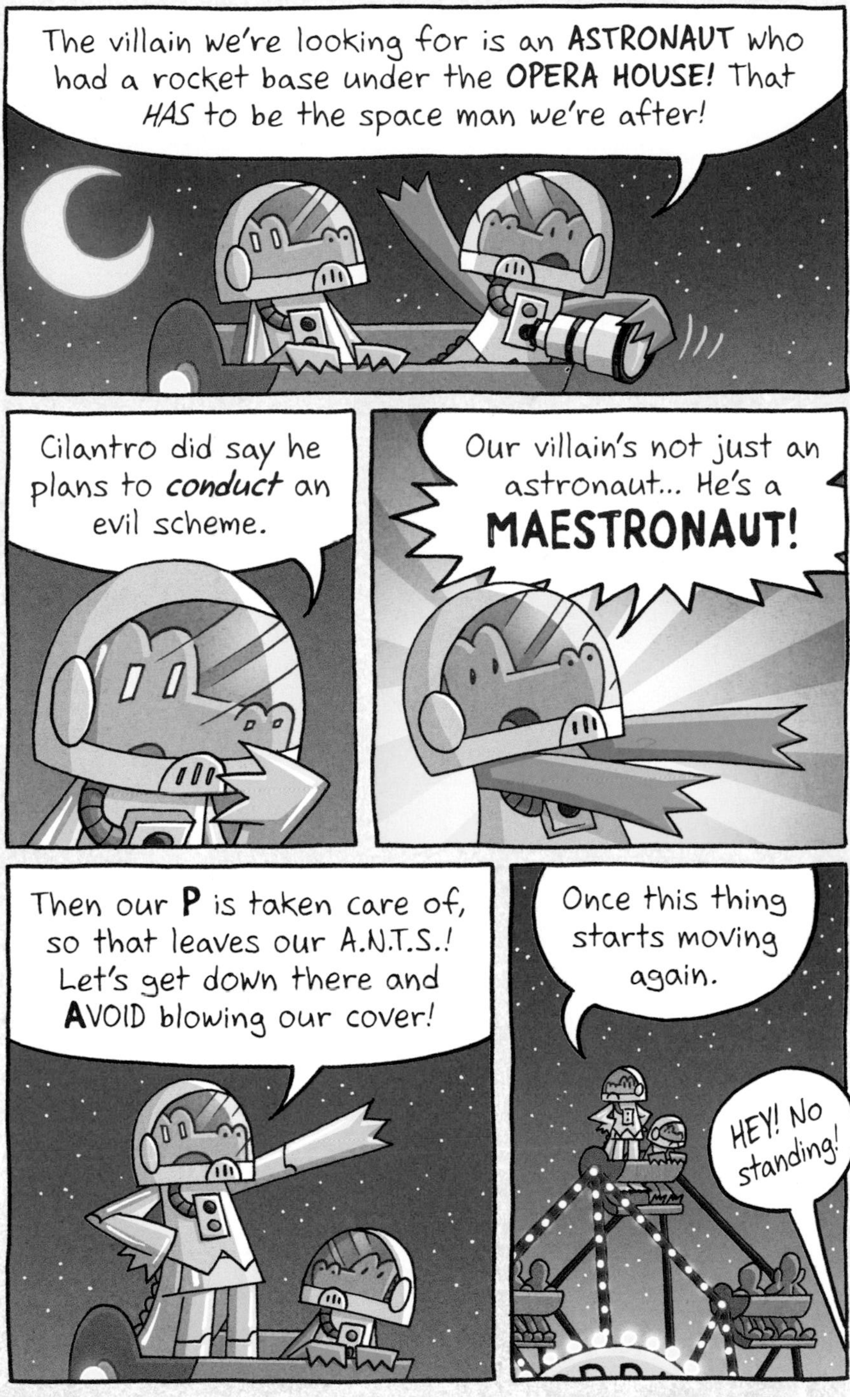
The villain we're looking for is an **ASTRONAUT** who had a rocket base under the **OPERA HOUSE!** That *HAS* to be the space man we're after!
Cilantro did say he plans to ***conduct*** an evil scheme.
Our villain's not just an astronaut... He's a **MAESTRONAUT!**
Then our **P** is taken care of, so that leaves our A.N.T.S.! Let's get down there and **A**VOID blowing our cover!
Once this thing starts moving again.
HEY! No standing!

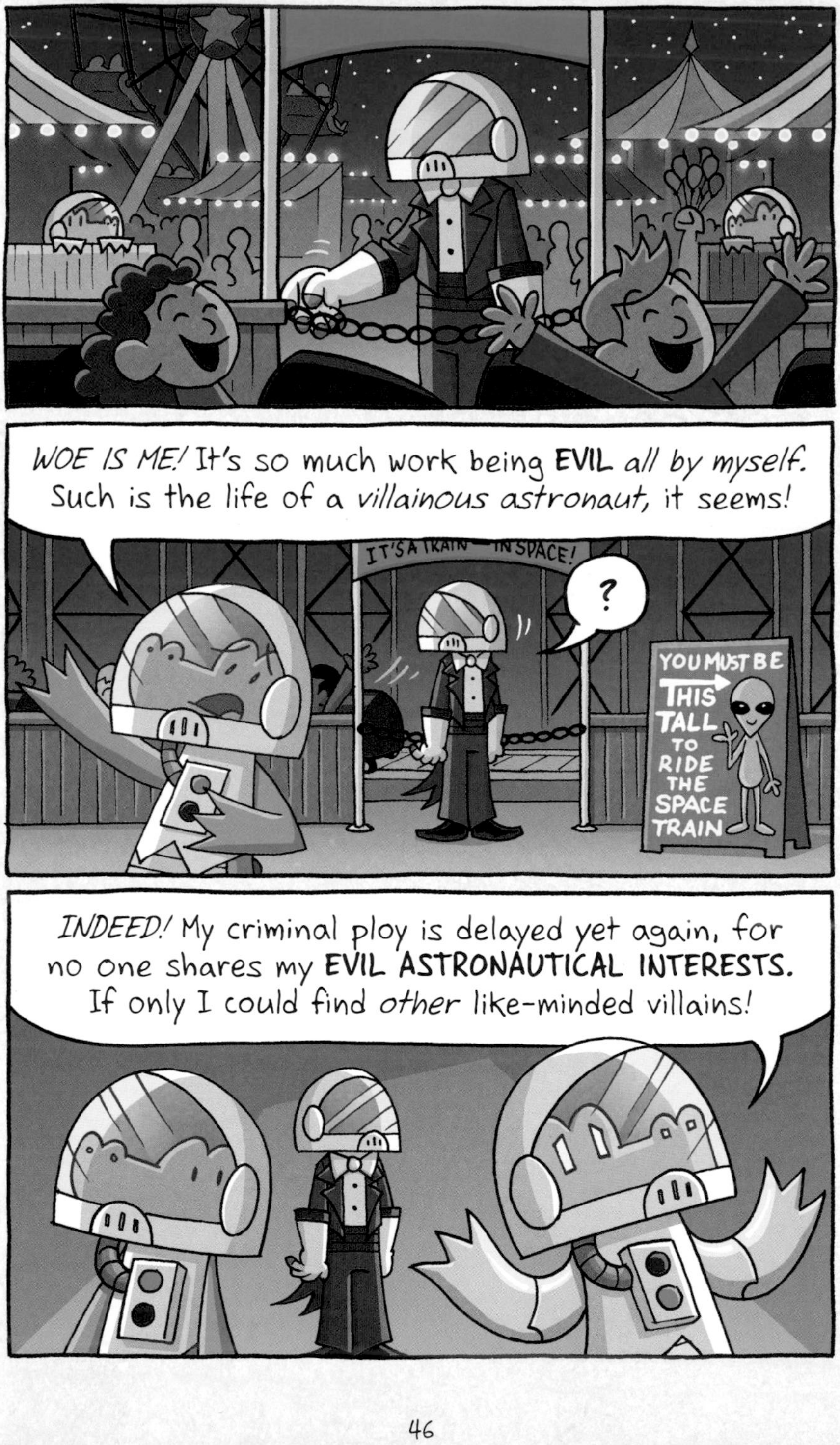
WOE IS ME! It's so much work being EVIL all by myself. Such is the life of a villainous astronaut, it seems!
IT'S A TRAIN IN SPACE!
?
YOU MUST BE THIS TALL TO RIDE THE SPACE TRAIN
INDEED! My criminal ploy is delayed yet again, for no one shares my EVIL ASTRONAUTICAL INTERESTS. If only I could find other like-minded villains!

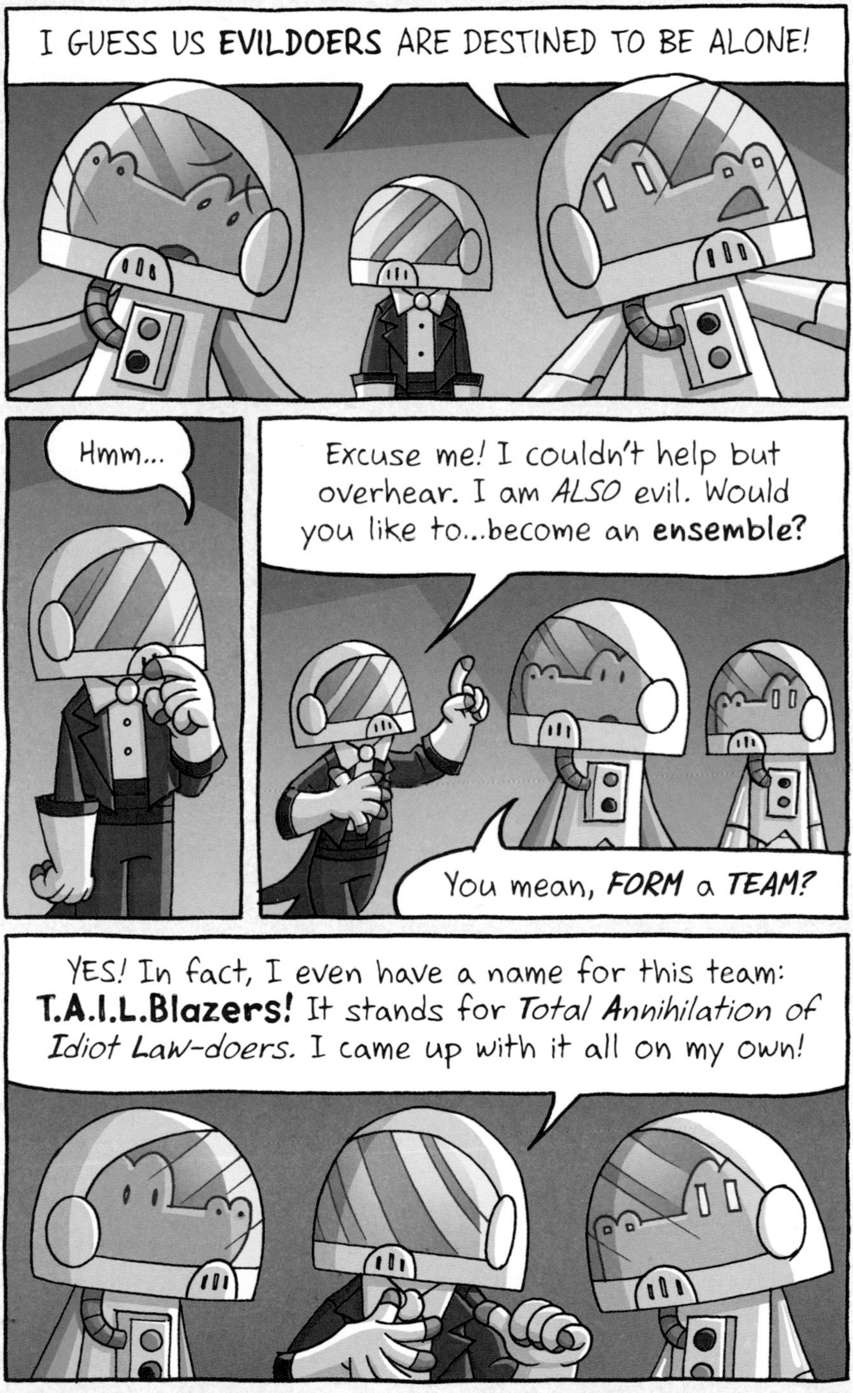
I GUESS US **EVILDOERS** ARE DESTINED TO BE ALONE!
Hmm...
Excuse me! I couldn't help but overhear. I am *ALSO* evil. Would you like to...become an **ensemble**?
You mean, ***FORM*** a ***TEAM?***
YES! In fact, I even have a name for this team: **T.A.I.L.Blazers!** It stands for *Total Annihilation of Idiot Law-doers.* I came up with it all on my own!

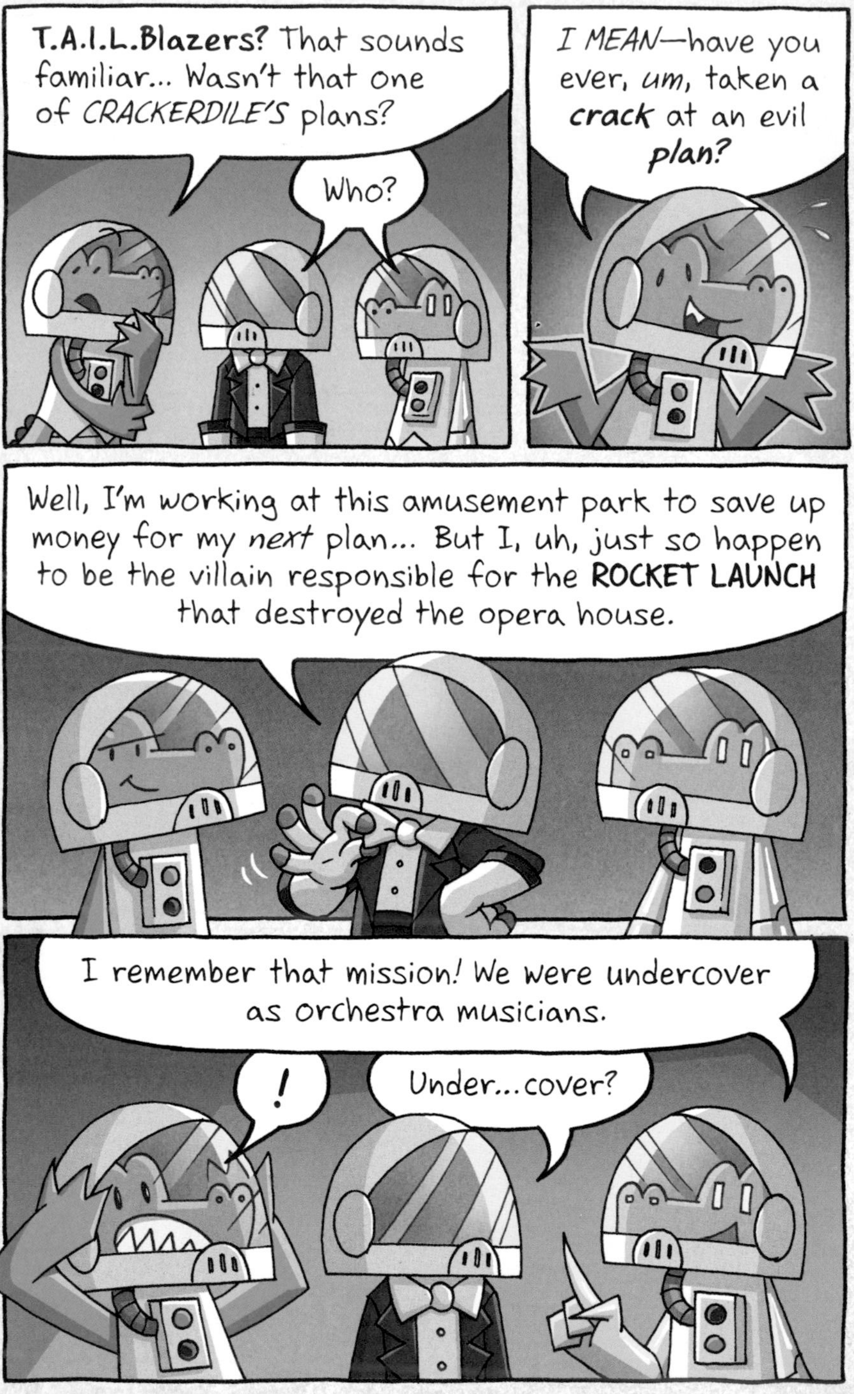
T.A.I.L.Blazers? That sounds familiar... Wasn't that one of CRACKERDILE'S plans?
Who?
I MEAN—have you ever, um, taken a crack at an evil plan?
Well, I'm working at this amusement park to save up money for my next plan... But I, uh, just so happen to be the villain responsible for the ROCKET LAUNCH that destroyed the opera house.
I remember that mission! We were undercover as orchestra musicians.
!
Under...cover?

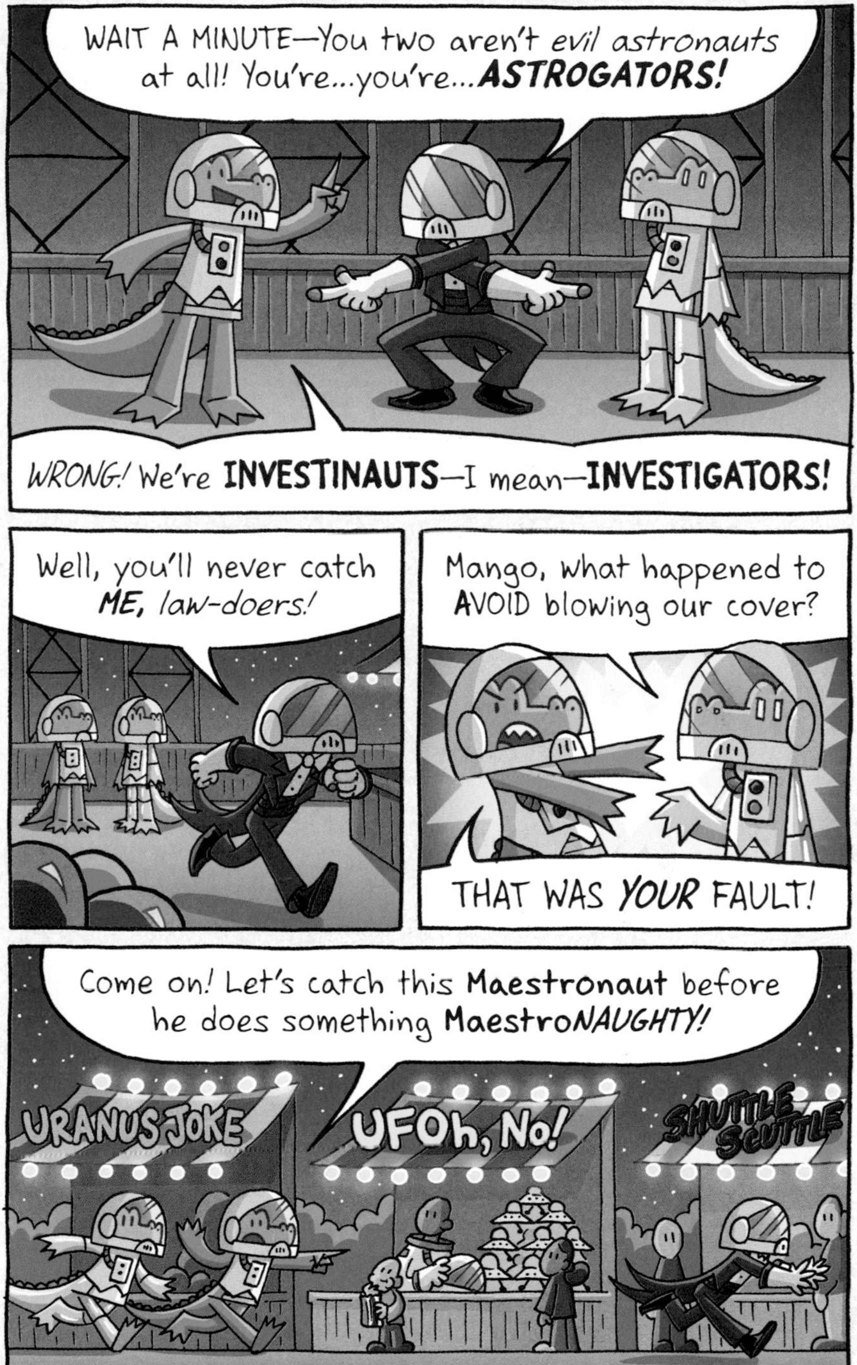
WAIT A MINUTE—You two aren't evil astronauts at all! You're...you're...ASTROGATORS!
WRONG! We're INVESTINAUTS—I mean—INVESTIGATORS!
Well, you'll never catch ME, law-doers!
Mango, what happened to AVOID blowing our cover?
THAT WAS YOUR FAULT!
Come on! Let's catch this Maestronaut before he does something MaestroNAUGHTY!
URANUS JOKE
UFOh, No!
SHUTTLE SCUTTLE

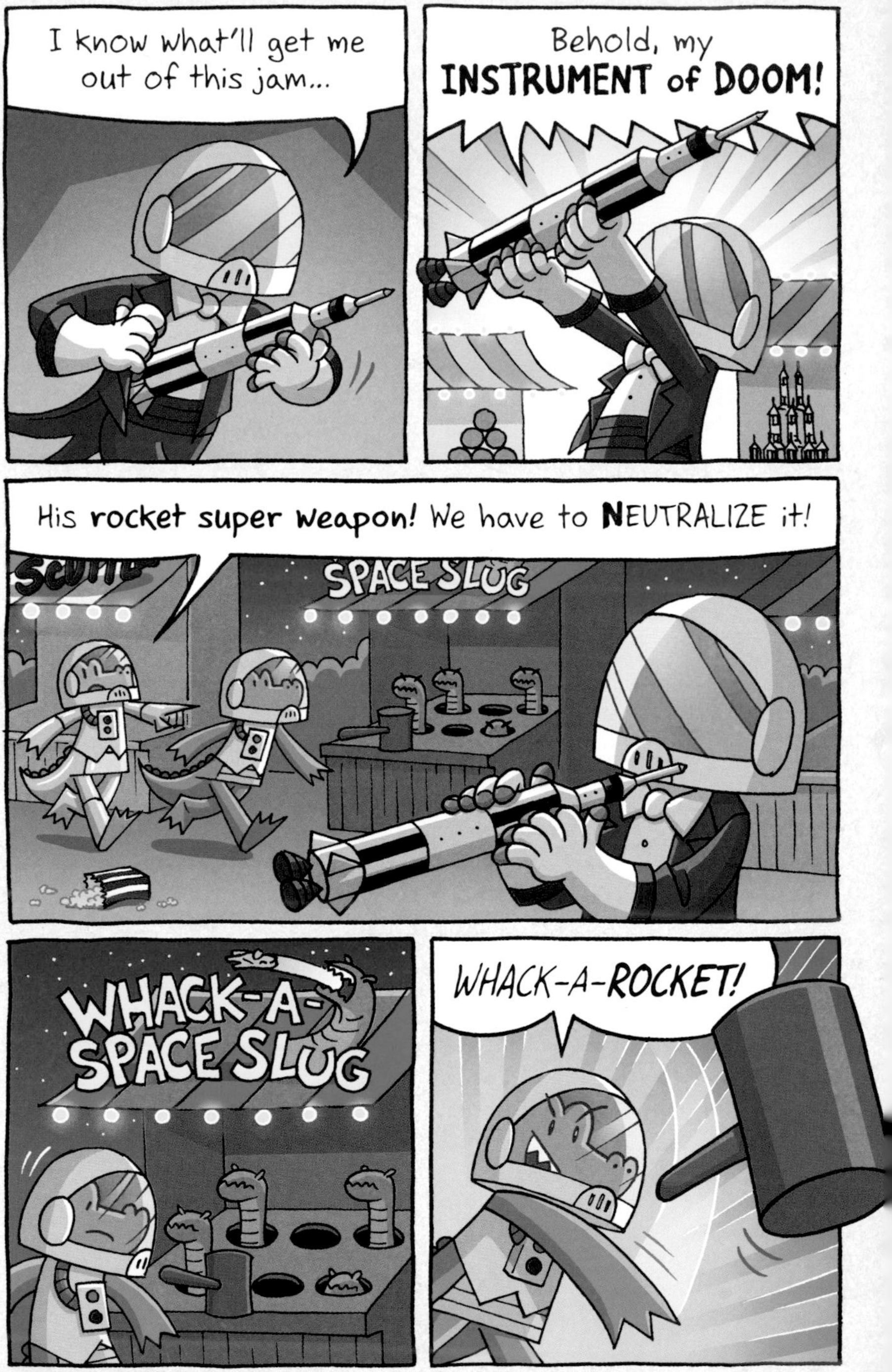
I know what'll get me out of this jam...
Behold, my INSTRUMENT of DOOM!
His rocket super weapon! We have to NEUTRALIZE it!
SPACE SLUG
WHACK-A-SPACE SLUG
WHACK-A-ROCKET!

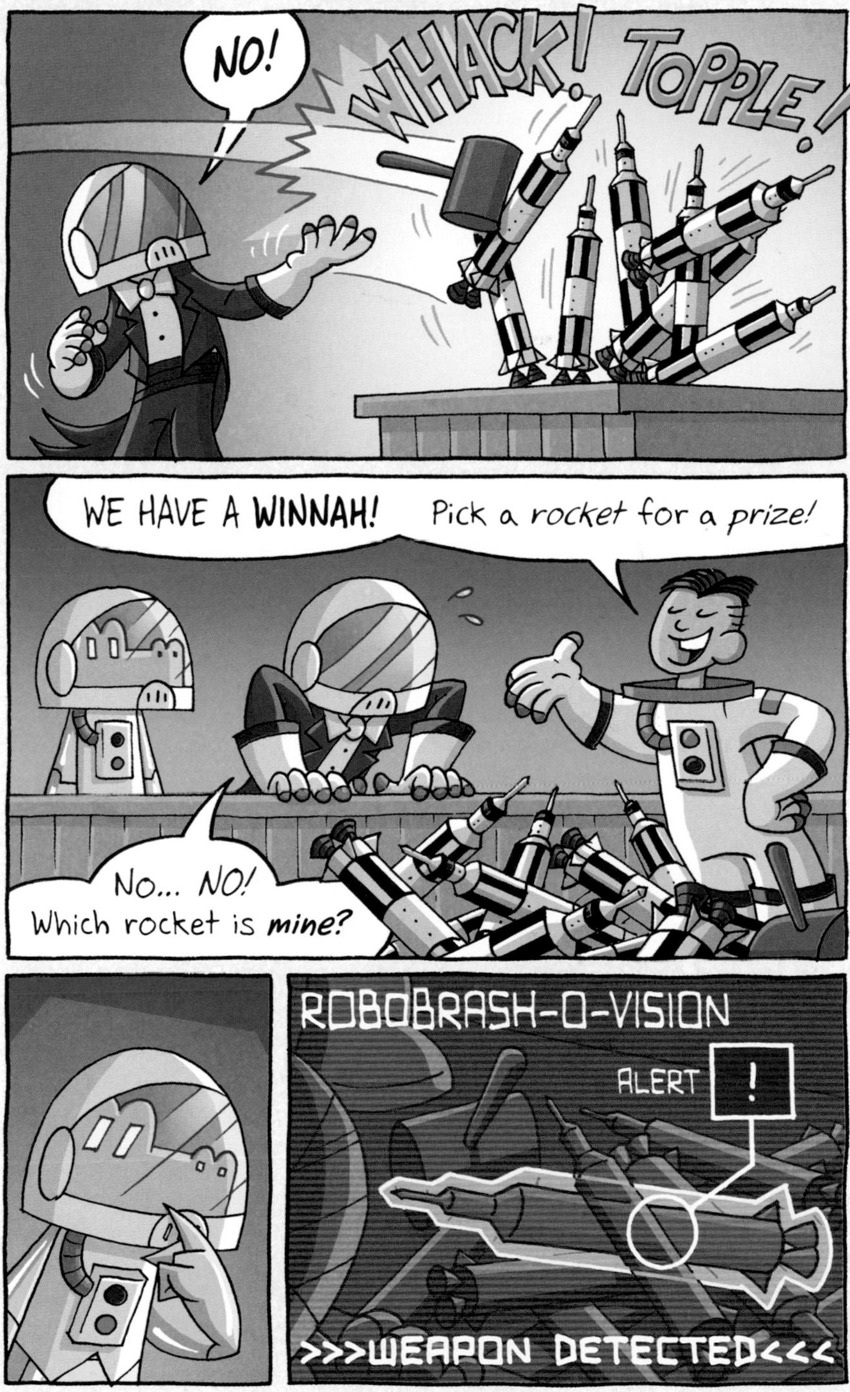
NO!
WHACK! TOPPLE!
WE HAVE A WINNAH! Pick a rocket for a prize!
No... NO! Which rocket is mine?
ROBOBRASH-O-VISION
ALERT
!
>>>WEAPON DETECTED<<<

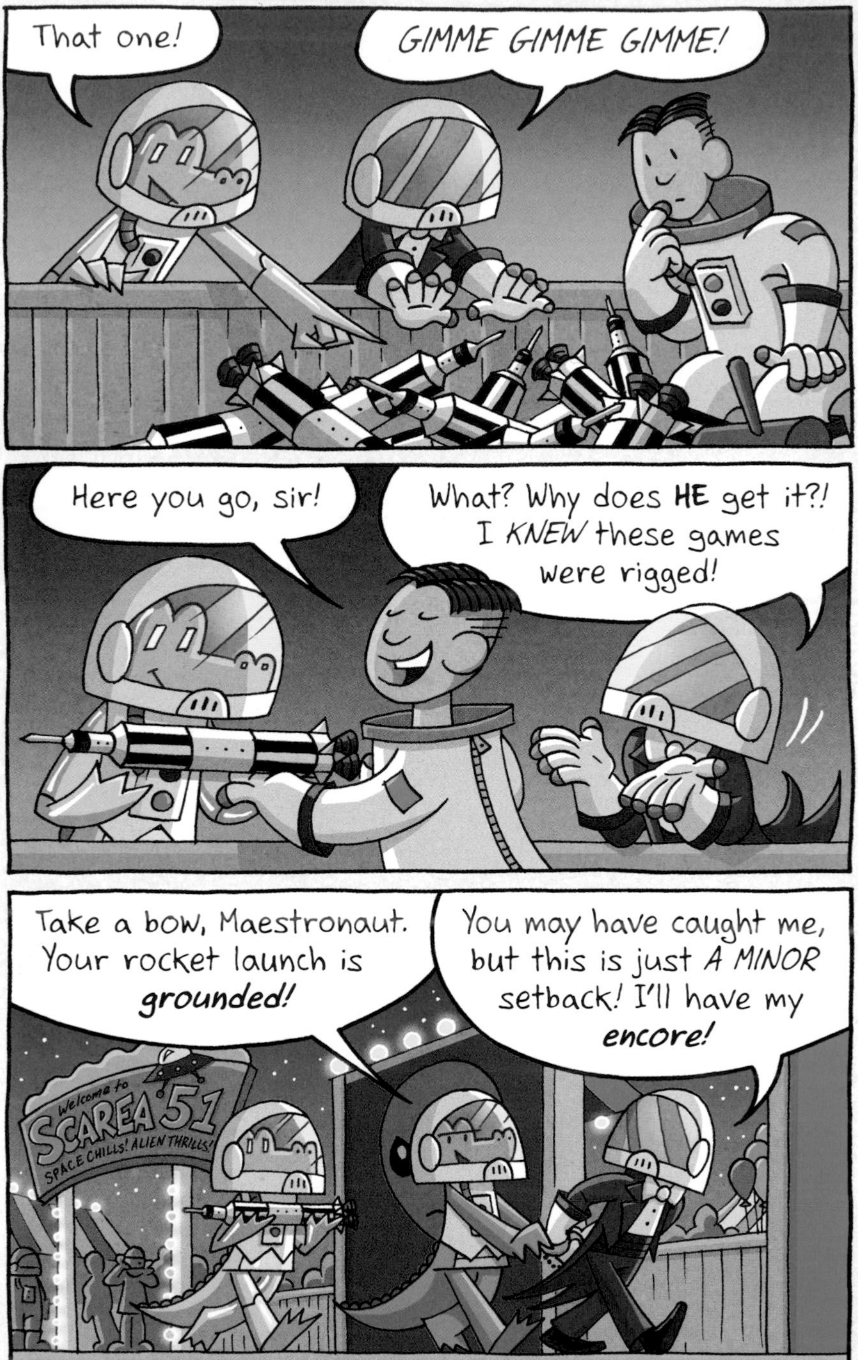

That one!
GIMME GIMME GIMME!
Here you go, sir!
What? Why does HE get it?! I KNEW these games were rigged!
Take a bow, Maestronaut. Your rocket launch is grounded!
You may have caught me, but this is just A MINOR setback! I'll have my encore!
Welcome to SCAREA 51
SPACE CHILLS! ALIEN THRILLS!

# Chapter 5

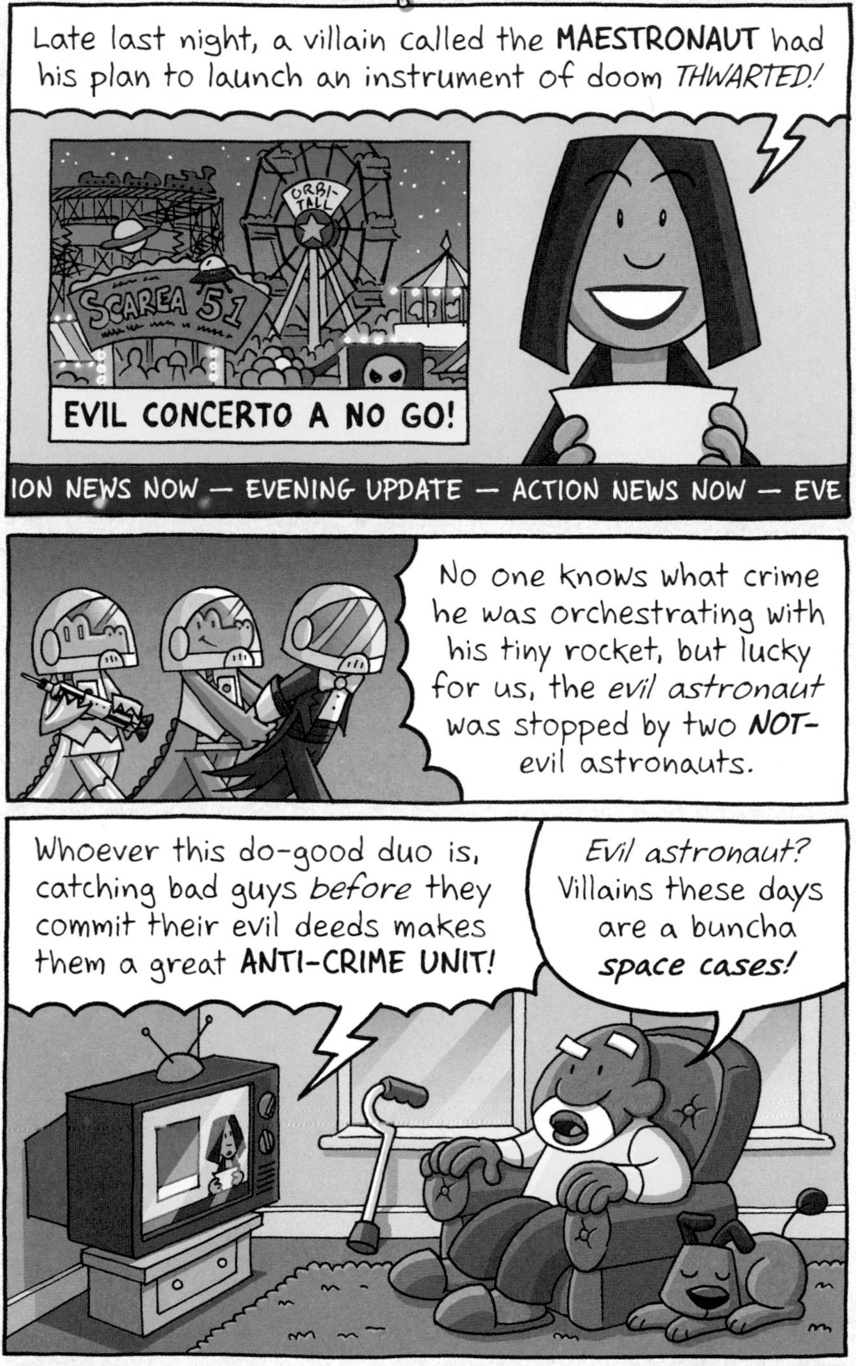
Late last night, a villain called the **MAESTRONAUT** had his plan to launch an instrument of doom *THWARTED!*
ORBI-TALL
SCAREA 51
EVIL CONCERTO A NO GO!
ION NEWS NOW — EVENING UPDATE — ACTION NEWS NOW — EVE
No one knows what crime he was orchestrating with his tiny rocket, but lucky for us, the *evil astronaut* was stopped by two **NOT**-evil astronauts.
Whoever this do-good duo is, catching bad guys *before* they commit their evil deeds makes them a great **ANTI-CRIME UNIT!**
*Evil astronaut?* Villains these days are a buncha ***space cases!***

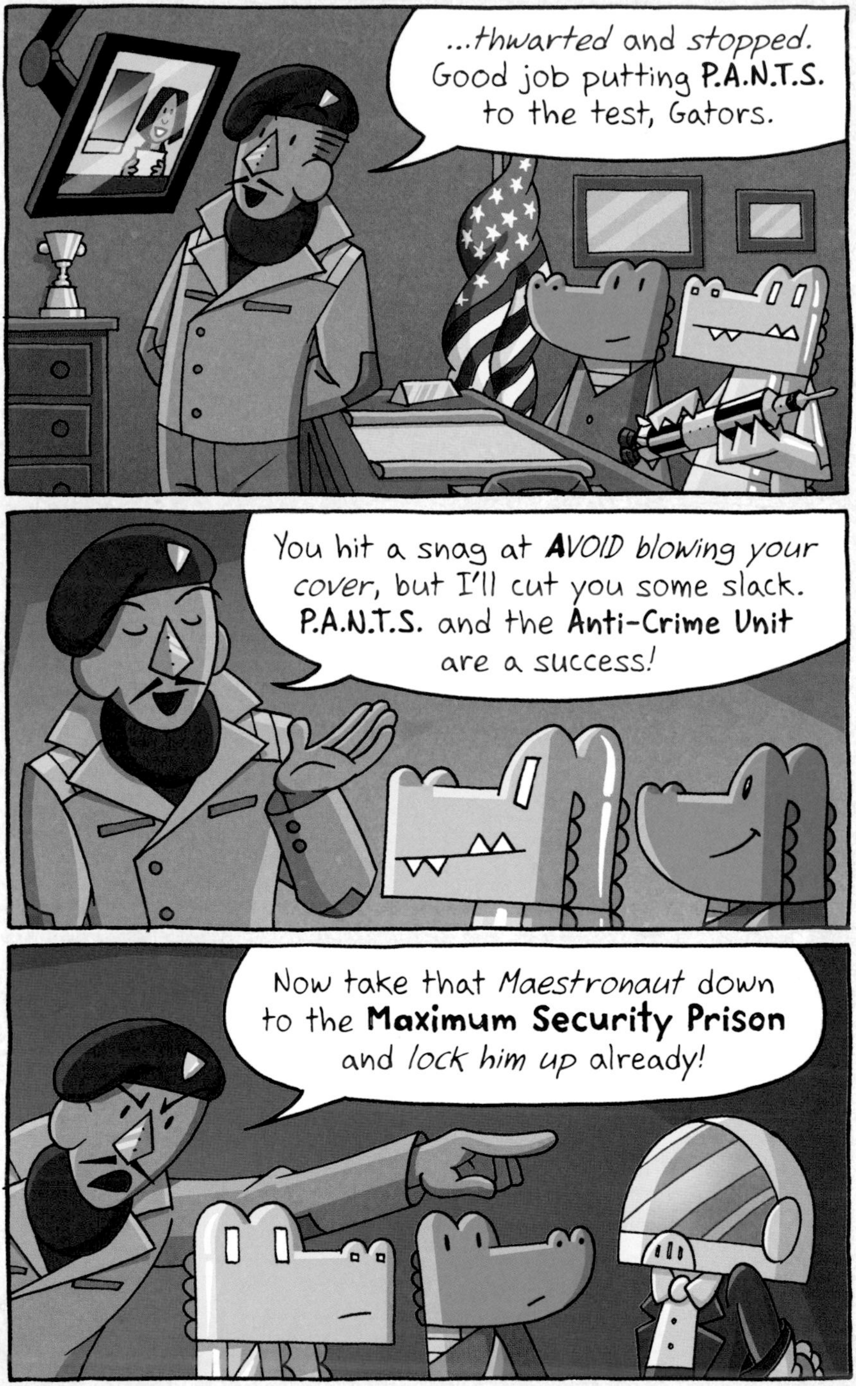
...*thwarted* and *stopped*. Good job putting **P.A.N.T.S.** to the test, Gators.
You hit a snag at ***AVOID** blowing your cover*, but I'll cut you some slack. **P.A.N.T.S.** and the **Anti-Crime Unit** are a success!
Now take that *Maestronaut* down to the **Maximum Security Prison** and *lock him up* already!

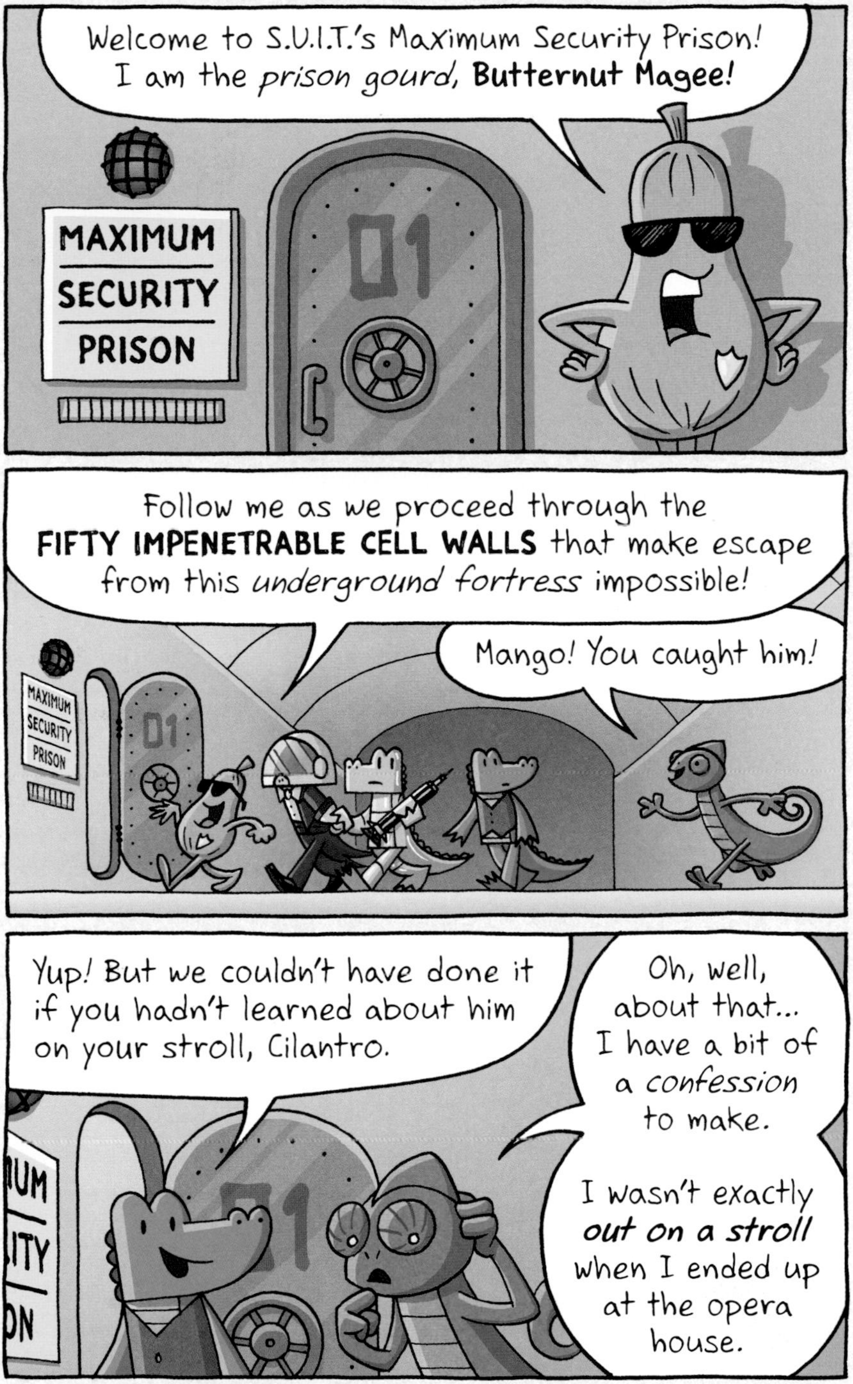
Welcome to S.U.I.T.'s Maximum Security Prison! I am the *prison gourd,* **Butternut Magee!**
MAXIMUM SECURITY PRISON
01
Follow me as we proceed through the **FIFTY IMPENETRABLE CELL WALLS** that make escape from this *underground fortress* impossible!
Mango! You caught him!
Yup! But we couldn't have done it if you hadn't learned about him on your stroll, Cilantro.
Oh, well, about that... I have a bit of a *confession* to make.
I wasn't exactly ***out on a stroll*** when I ended up at the opera house.

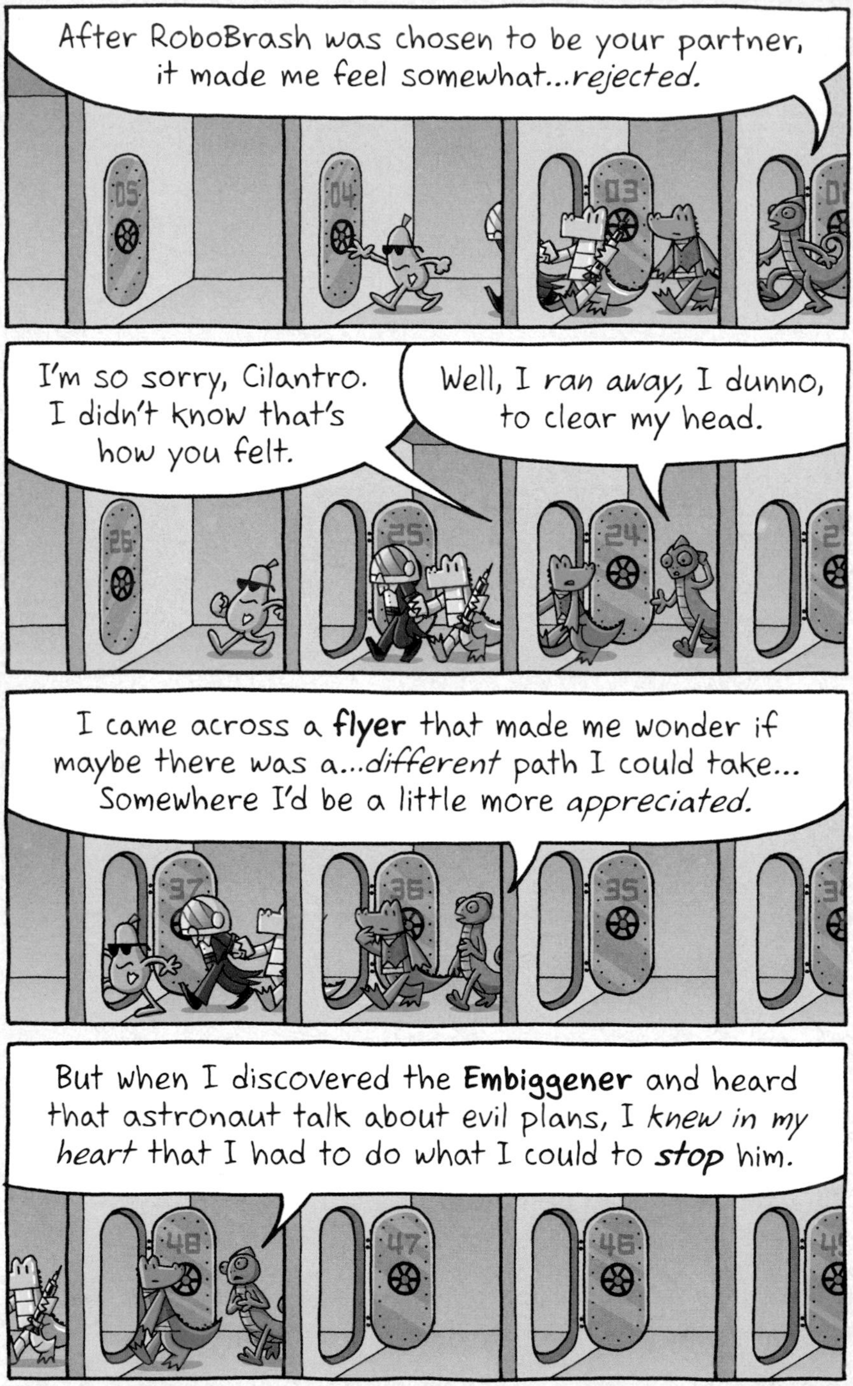
After RoboBrash was chosen to be your partner, it made me feel somewhat...*rejected.*
I'm so sorry, Cilantro. I didn't know that's how you felt.
Well, I *ran away,* I dunno, to clear my head.
I came across a **flyer** that made me wonder if maybe there was a...*different* path I could take... Somewhere I'd be a little more *appreciated.*
But when I discovered the **Embiggener** and heard that astronaut talk about evil plans, I *knew in my heart* that I had to do what I could to ***stop*** him.

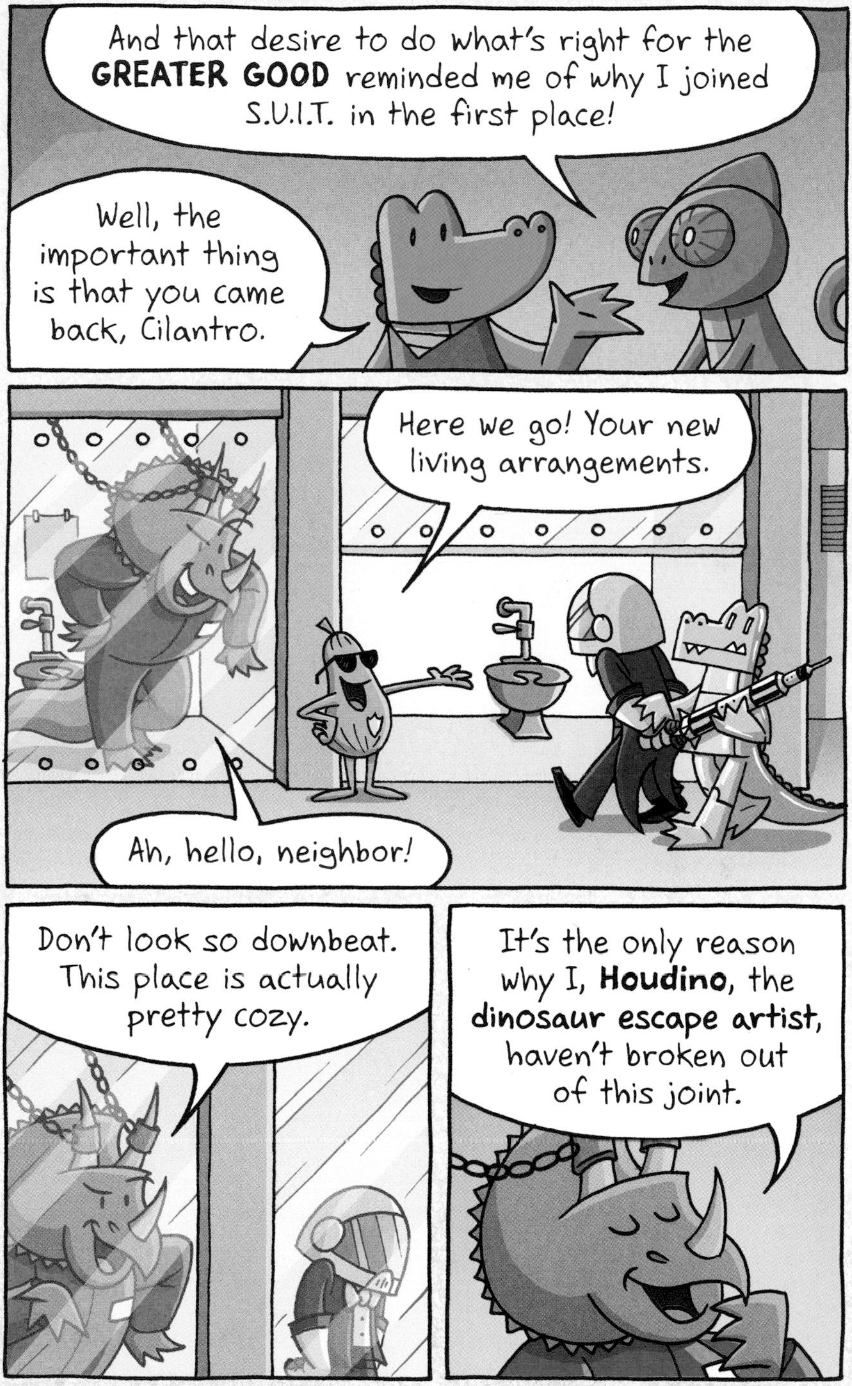
And that desire to do what's right for the **GREATER GOOD** reminded me of why I joined S.U.I.T. in the first place!
Well, the important thing is that you came back, Cilantro.
Here we go! Your new living arrangements.
Ah, hello, neighbor!
Don't look so downbeat. This place is actually pretty cozy.
It's the only reason why I, **Houdino**, the **dinosaur escape artist**, haven't broken out of this joint.

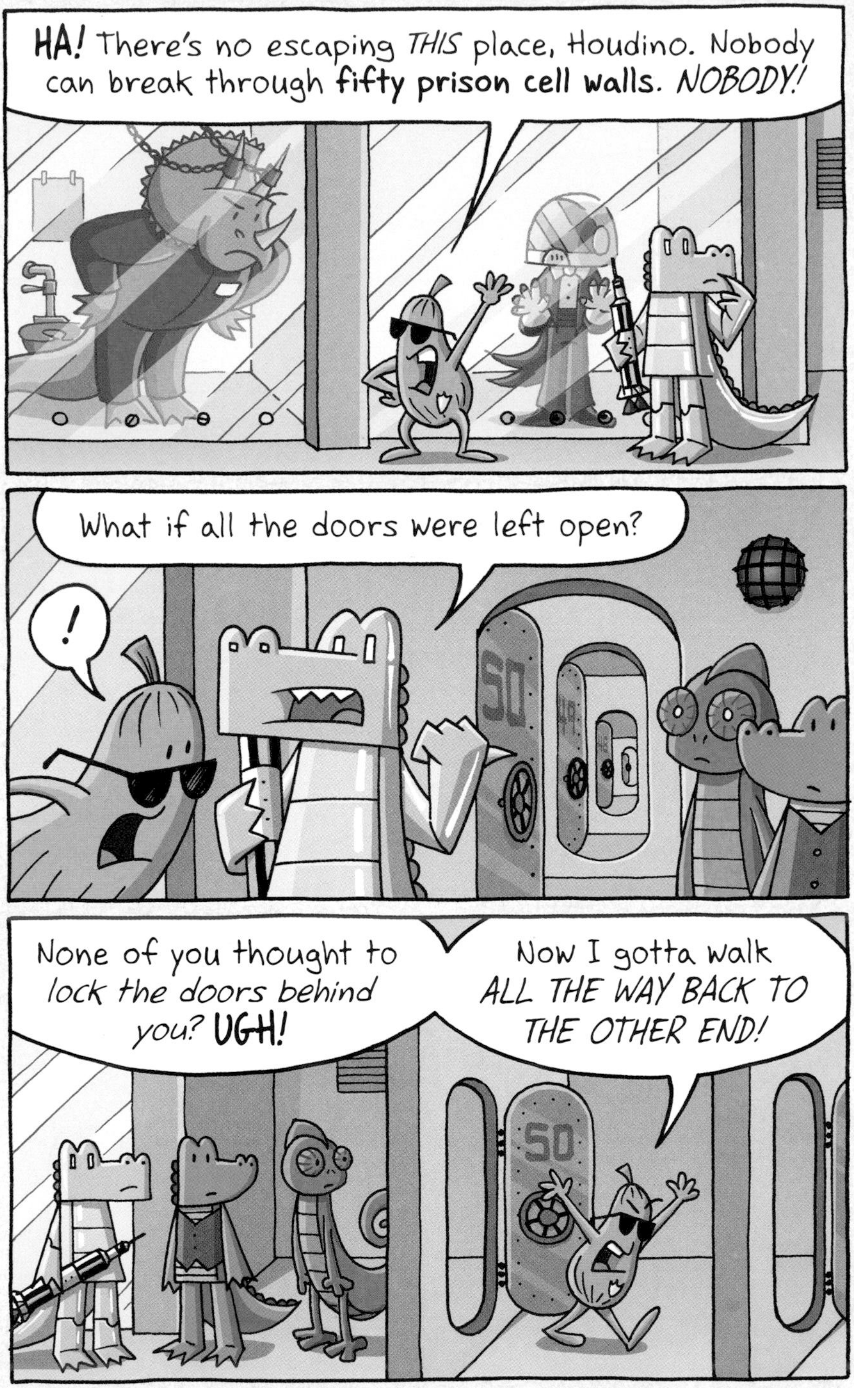

HA! There's no escaping THIS place, Houdino. Nobody can break through fifty prison cell walls. NOBODY!
What if all the doors were left open?
!
50
49
48
None of you thought to lock the doors behind you? UGH!
Now I gotta walk ALL THE WAY BACK TO THE OTHER END!
50

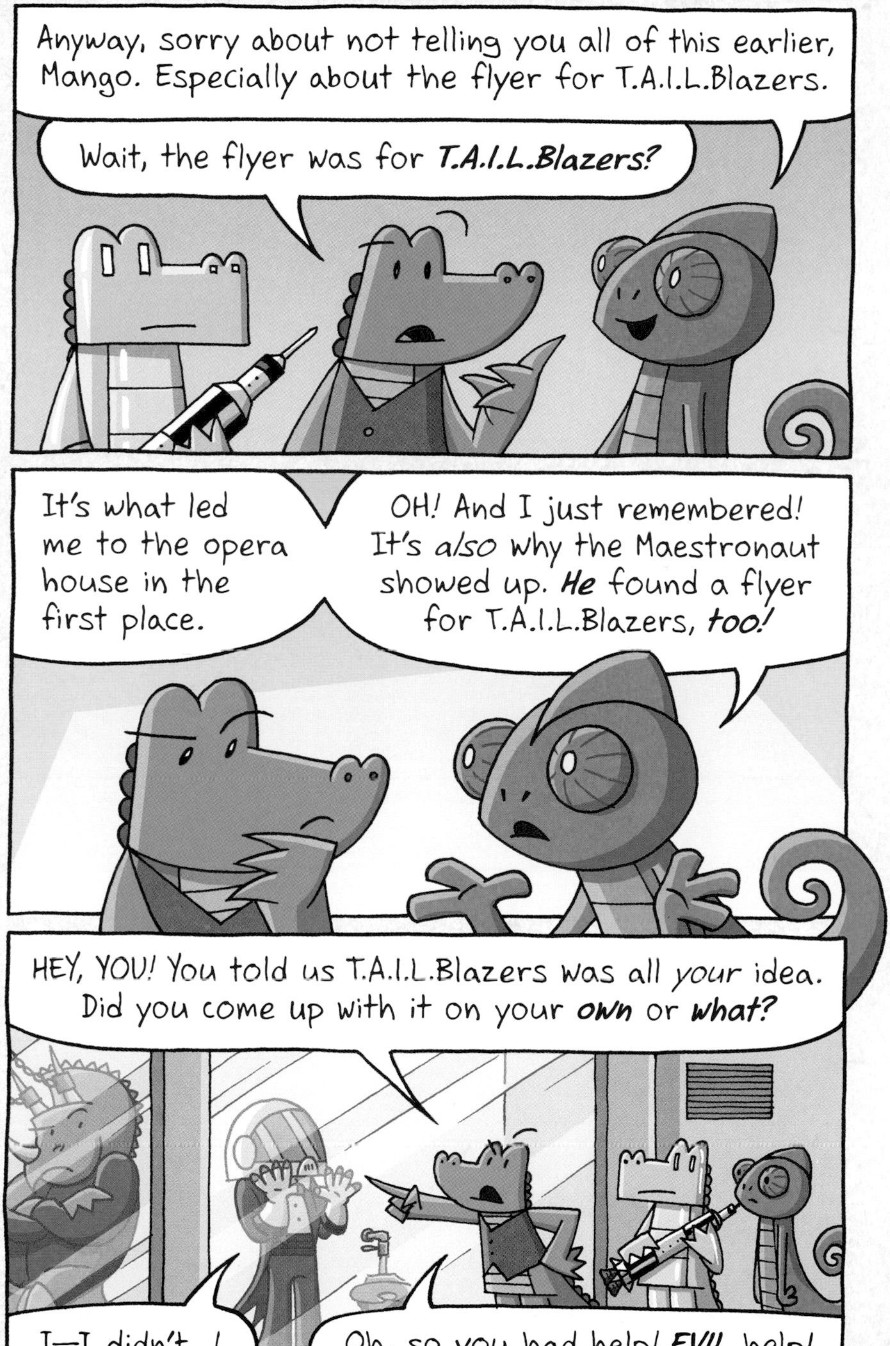
Anyway, sorry about not telling you all of this earlier, Mango. Especially about the flyer for T.A.I.L.Blazers.
Wait, the flyer was for ***T.A.I.L.Blazers?***
It's what led me to the opera house in the first place.
OH! And I just remembered! It's *also* why the Maestronaut showed up. ***He*** found a flyer for T.A.I.L.Blazers, ***too!***
HEY, YOU! You told us T.A.I.L.Blazers was all *your* idea. Did you come up with it on your ***own*** or ***what?***
I—I didn't...!
Oh, so you had help! ***EVIL*** help!

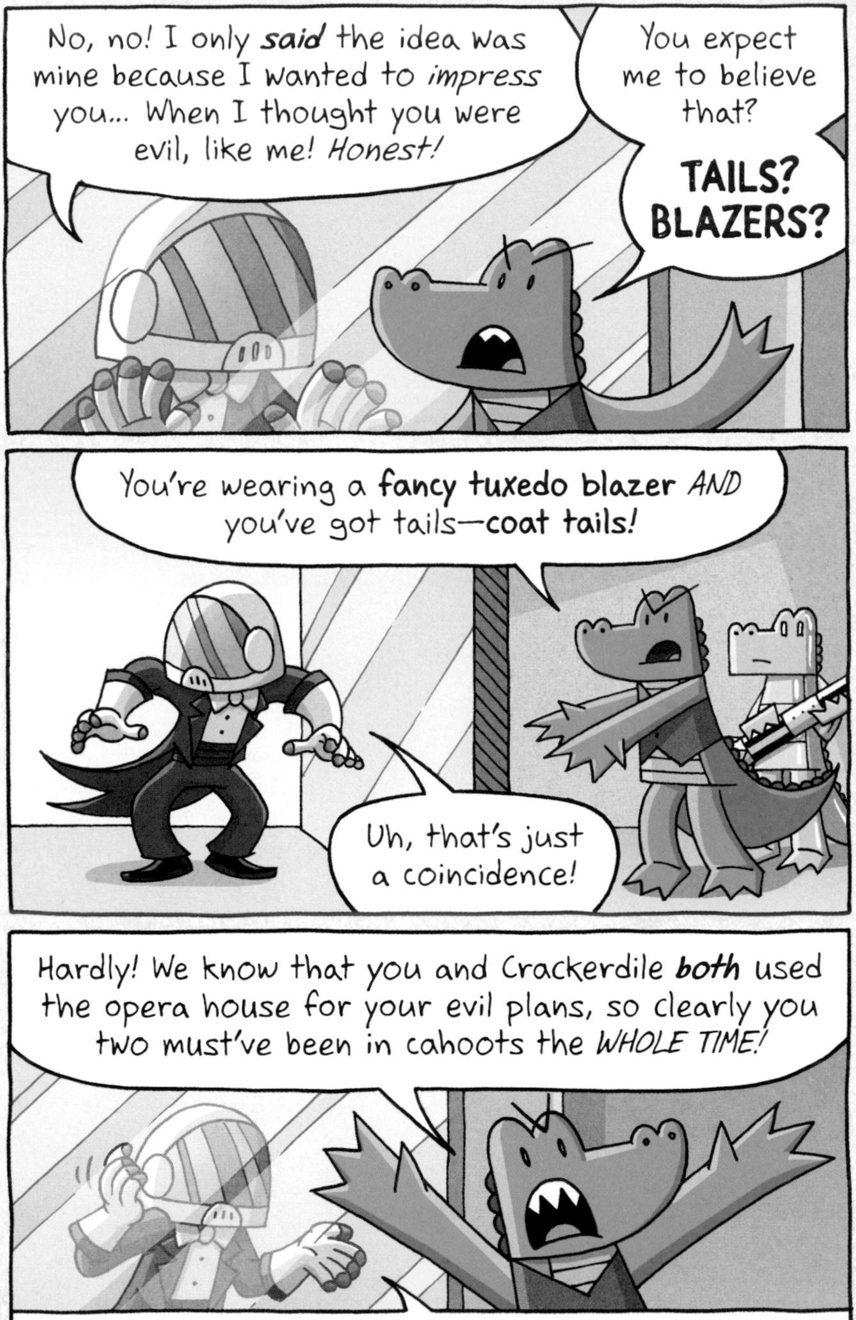
No, no! I only said the idea was mine because I wanted to impress you... When I thought you were evil, like me! Honest!
You expect me to believe that?
TAILS? BLAZERS?
You're wearing a fancy tuxedo blazer AND you've got tails—coat tails!
Uh, that's just a coincidence!
Hardly! We know that you and Crackerdile both used the opera house for your evil plans, so clearly you two must've been in cahoots the WHOLE TIME!
I don't even know what a Crackerdile is! Or cahoots!

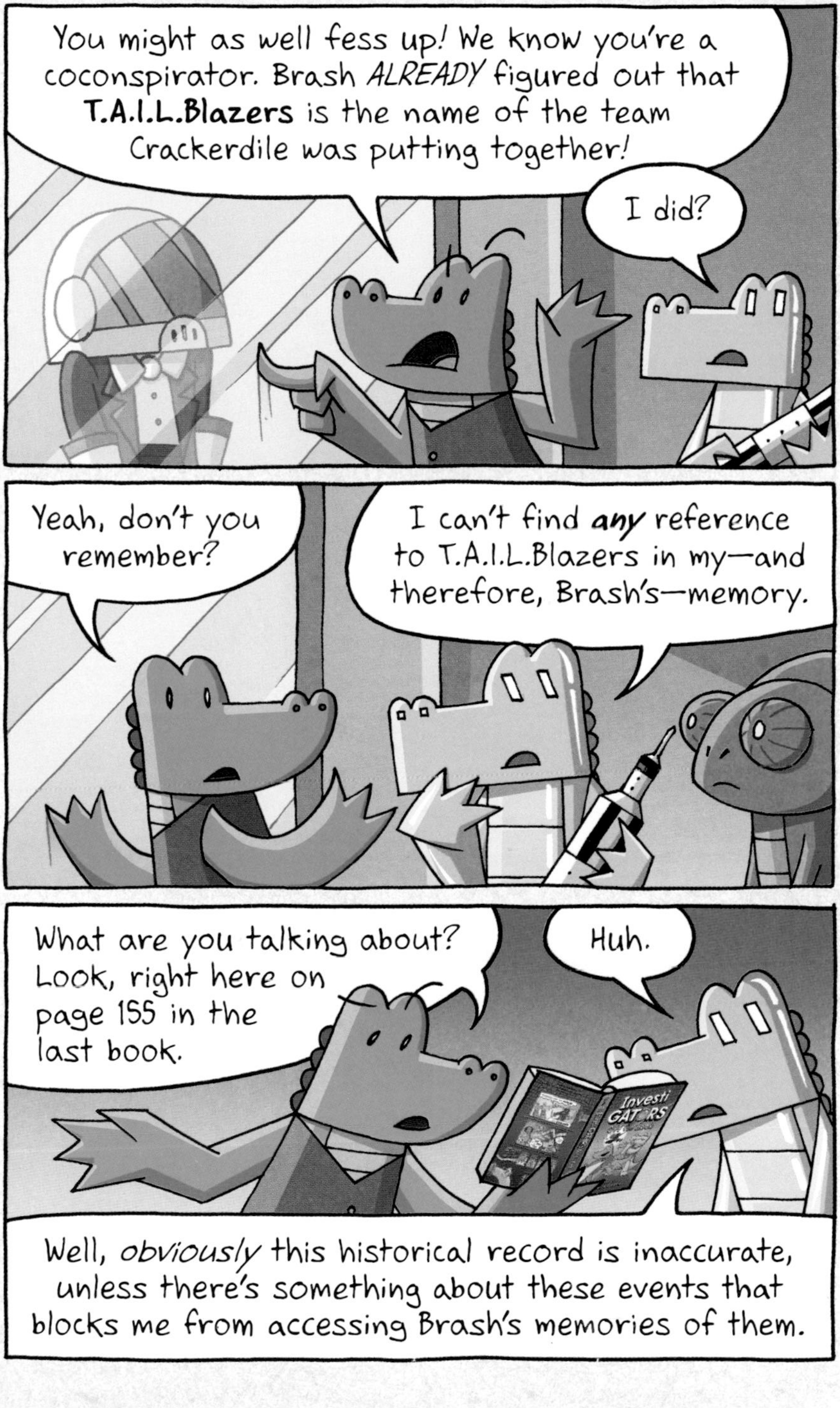
You might as well fess up! We know you're a coconspirator. Brash *ALREADY* figured out that **T.A.I.L.Blazers** is the name of the team Crackerdile was putting together!
I did?
Yeah, don't you remember?
I can't find ***any*** reference to T.A.I.L.Blazers in my—and therefore, Brash's—memory.
What are you talking about? Look, right here on page 155 in the last book.
Huh.
Well, *obviously* this historical record is inaccurate, unless there's something about these events that blocks me from accessing Brash's memories of them.

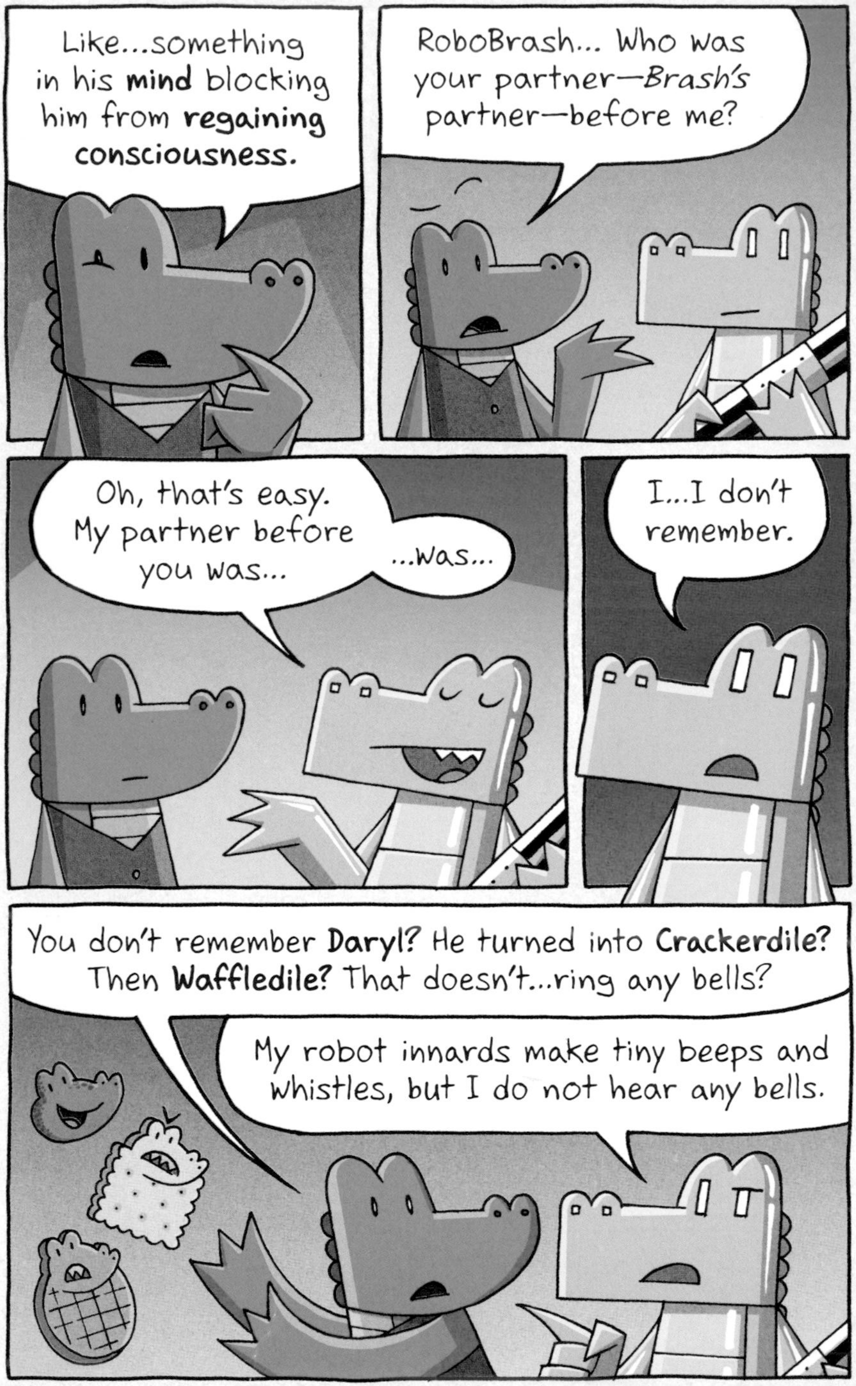
Like...something in his **mind** blocking him from **regaining consciousness.**
RoboBrash... Who was your partner—*Brash's* partner—before me?
Oh, that's easy. My partner before you was...
...was...
I...I don't remember.
You don't remember **Daryl?** He turned into **Crackerdile?** Then **Waffledile?** That doesn't...ring any bells?
My robot innards make tiny beeps and whistles, but I do not hear any bells.

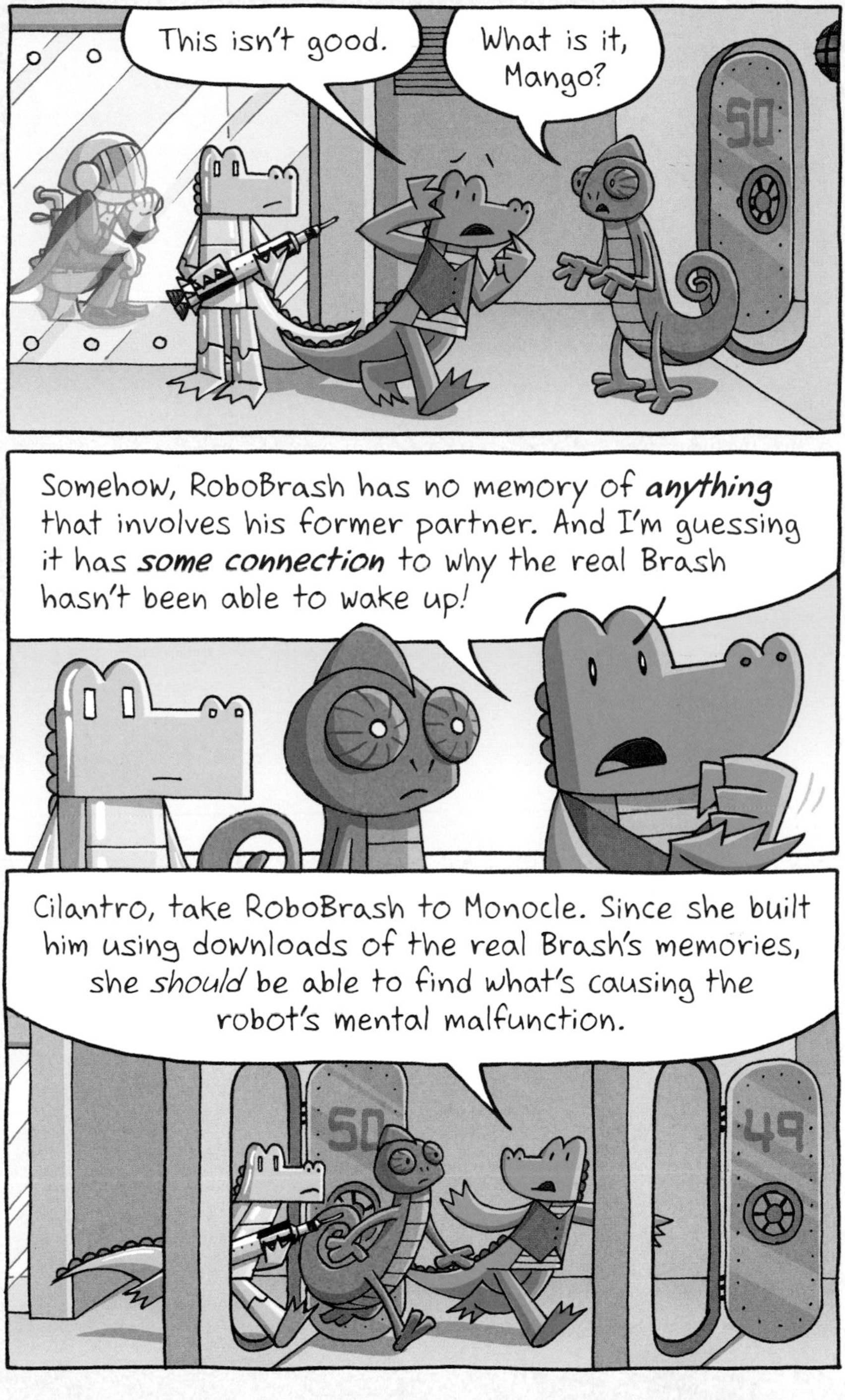
This isn't good.
What is it, Mango?
50
Somehow, RoboBrash has no memory of ***anything*** that involves his former partner. And I'm guessing it has ***some connection*** to why the real Brash hasn't been able to wake up!
Cilantro, take RoboBrash to Monocle. Since she built him using downloads of the real Brash's memories, she *should* be able to find what's causing the robot's mental malfunction.
50
49

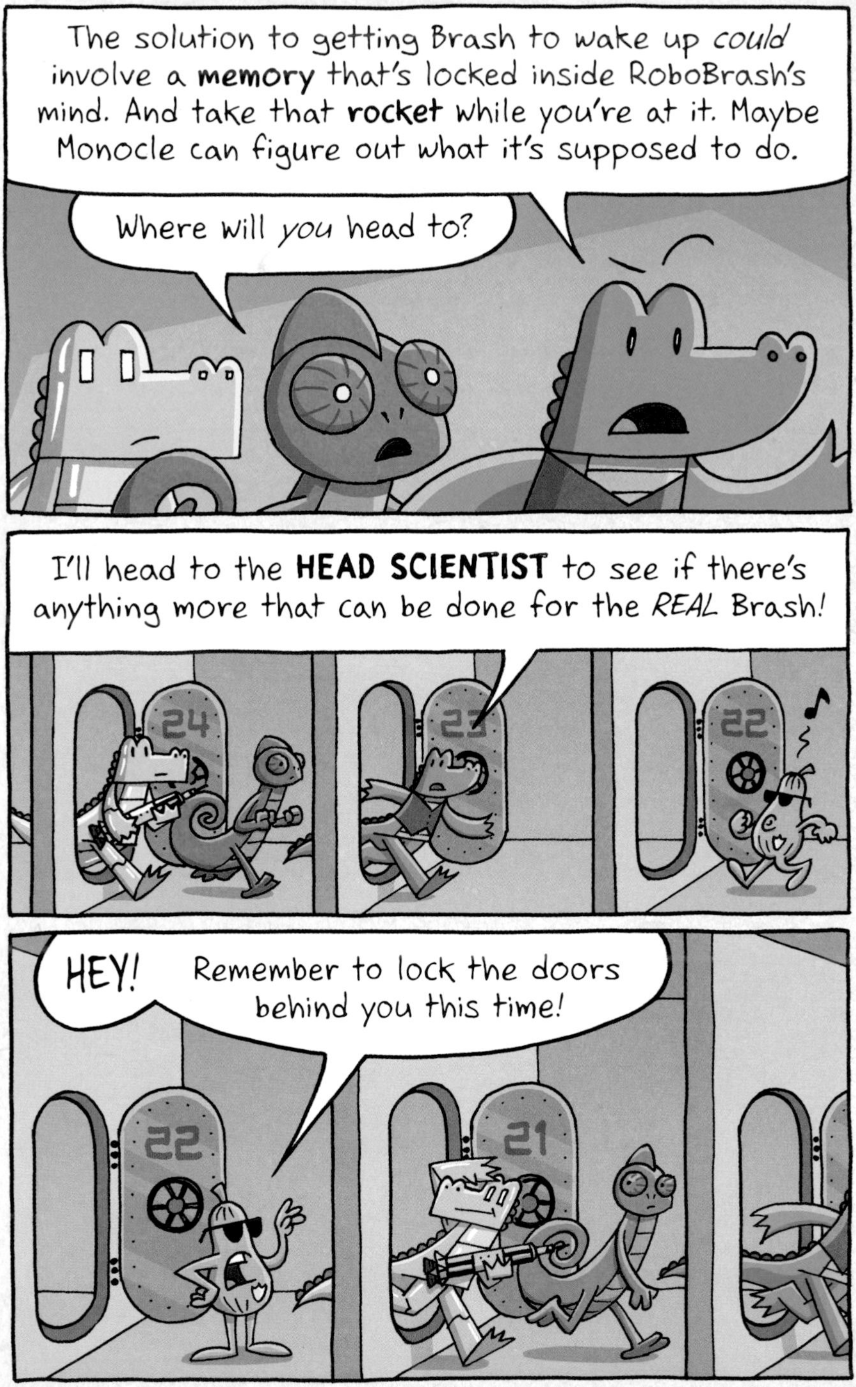
The solution to getting Brash to wake up *could* involve a **memory** that's locked inside RoboBrash's mind. And take that **rocket** while you're at it. Maybe Monocle can figure out what it's supposed to do.
Where will *you* head to?
I'll head to the **HEAD SCIENTIST** to see if there's anything more that can be done for the *REAL* Brash!
24
23
22
HEY! Remember to lock the doors behind you this time!
22
21

# Chapter 6

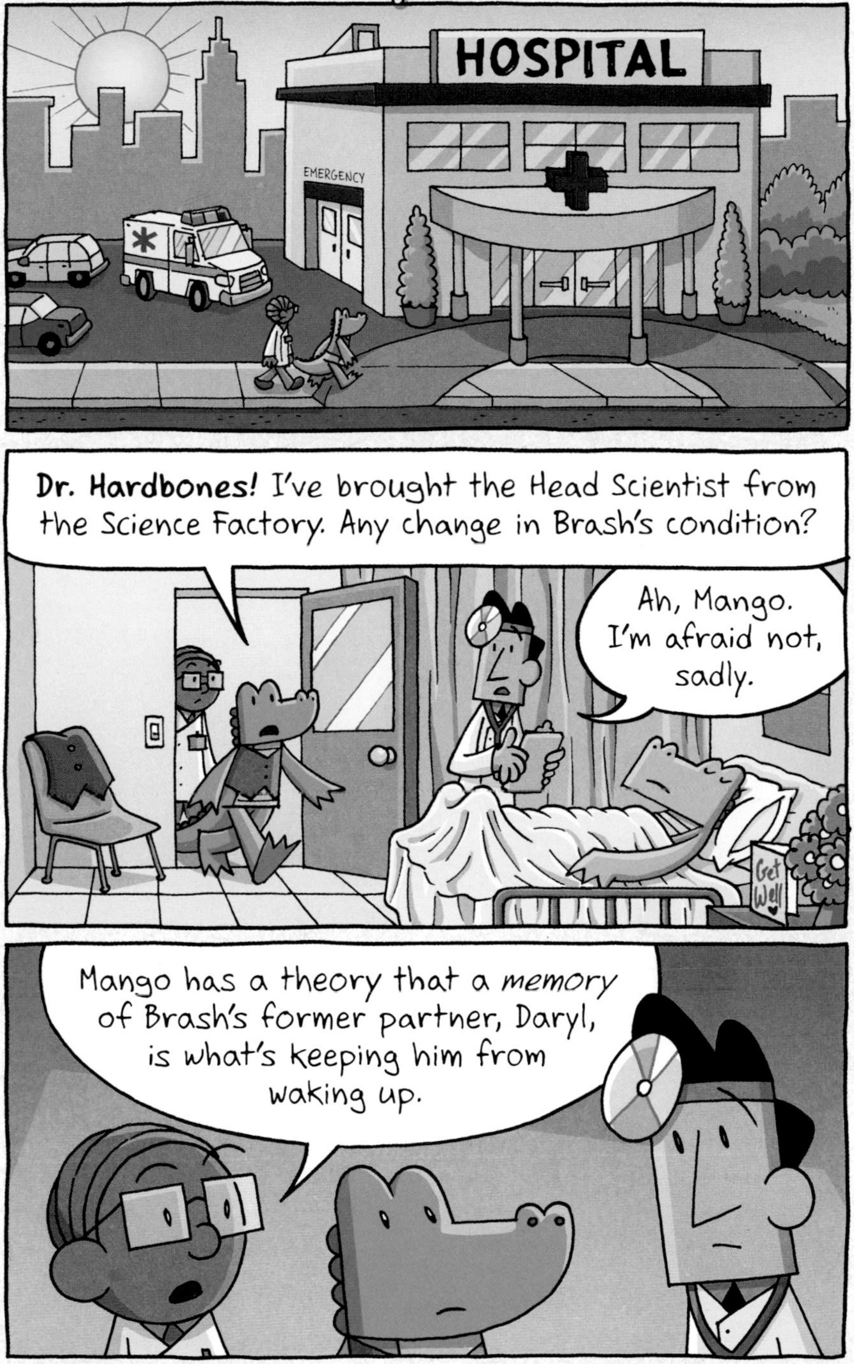
HOSPITAL
EMERGENCY
Dr. Hardbones! I've brought the Head Scientist from the Science Factory. Any change in Brash's condition?
Ah, Mango. I'm afraid not, sadly.
Get Well
Mango has a theory that a *memory* of Brash's former partner, Daryl, is what's keeping him from waking up.

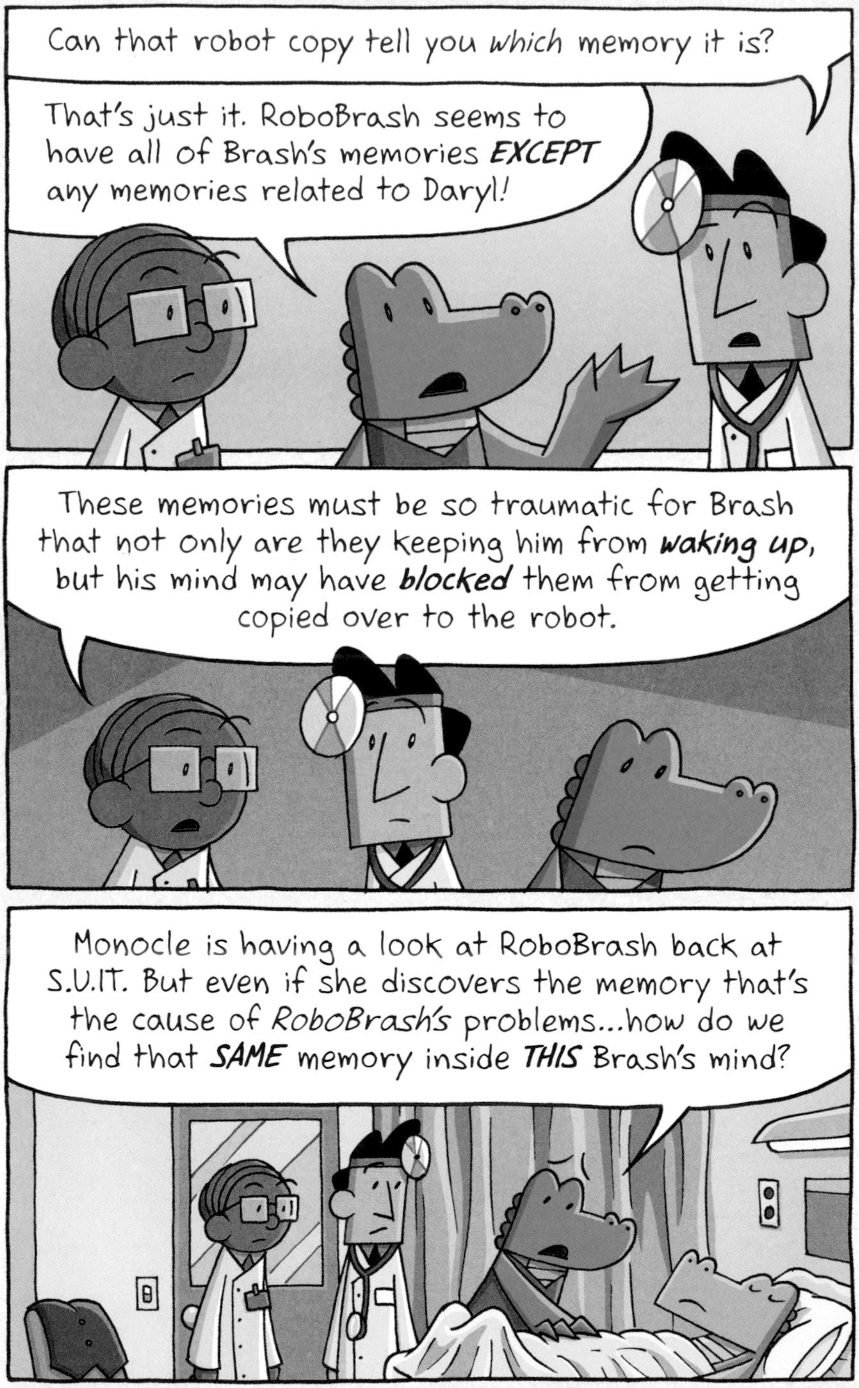
Can that robot copy tell you *which* memory it is?
That's just it. RoboBrash seems to have all of Brash's memories ***EXCEPT*** any memories related to Daryl!
These memories must be so traumatic for Brash that not only are they keeping him from ***waking up***, but his mind may have ***blocked*** them from getting copied over to the robot.
Monocle is having a look at RoboBrash back at S.U.IT. But even if she discovers the memory that's the cause of *RoboBrash's* problems...how do we find that ***SAME*** memory inside ***THIS*** Brash's mind?

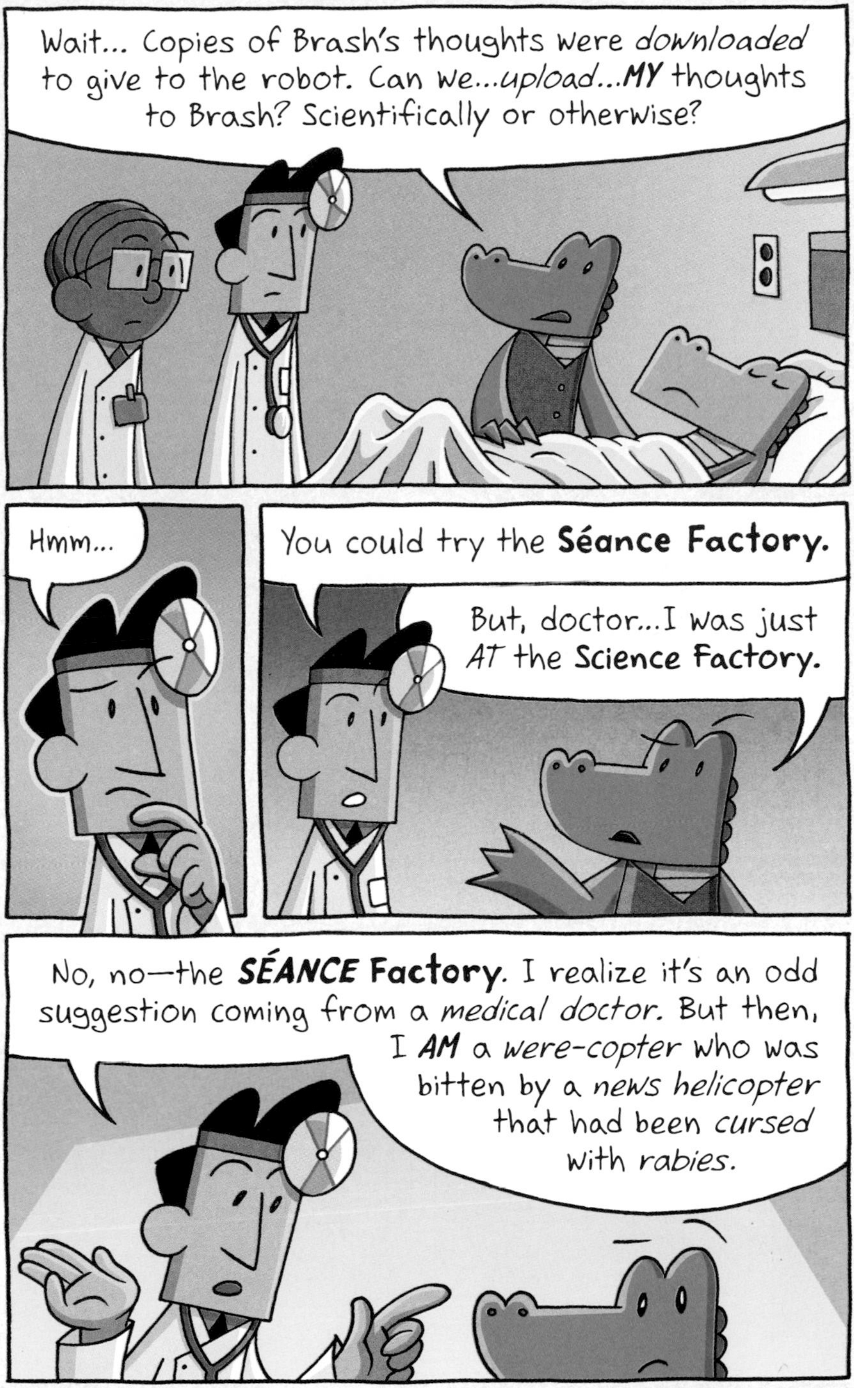
Wait... Copies of Brash's thoughts were *downloaded* to give to the robot. Can we...*upload*...**MY** thoughts to Brash? Scientifically or otherwise?
Hmm...
You could try the **Séance Factory.**
But, doctor...I was just *AT* the **Science Factory.**
No, no—the ***SÉANCE* Factory**. I realize it's an odd suggestion coming from a *medical doctor.* But then, I ***AM*** a *were-copter* who was bitten by a *news helicopter* that had been *cursed* with *rabies.*

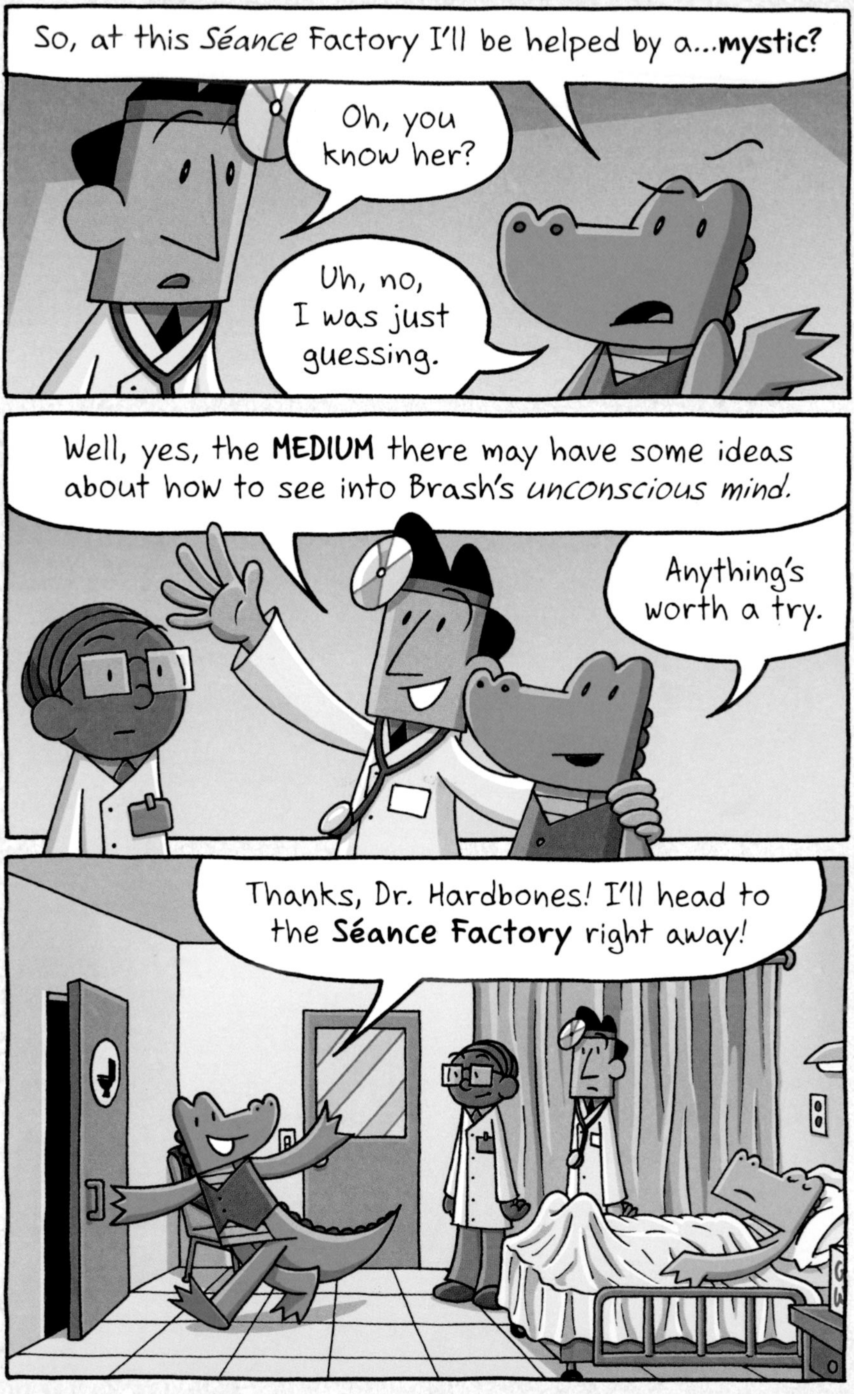
So, at this *Séance* Factory I'll be helped by a...**mystic?**
Oh, you know her?
Uh, no, I was just guessing.
Well, yes, the **MEDIUM** there may have some ideas about how to see into Brash's *unconscious mind.*
Anything's worth a try.
Thanks, Dr. Hardbones! I'll head to the **Séance Factory** right away!

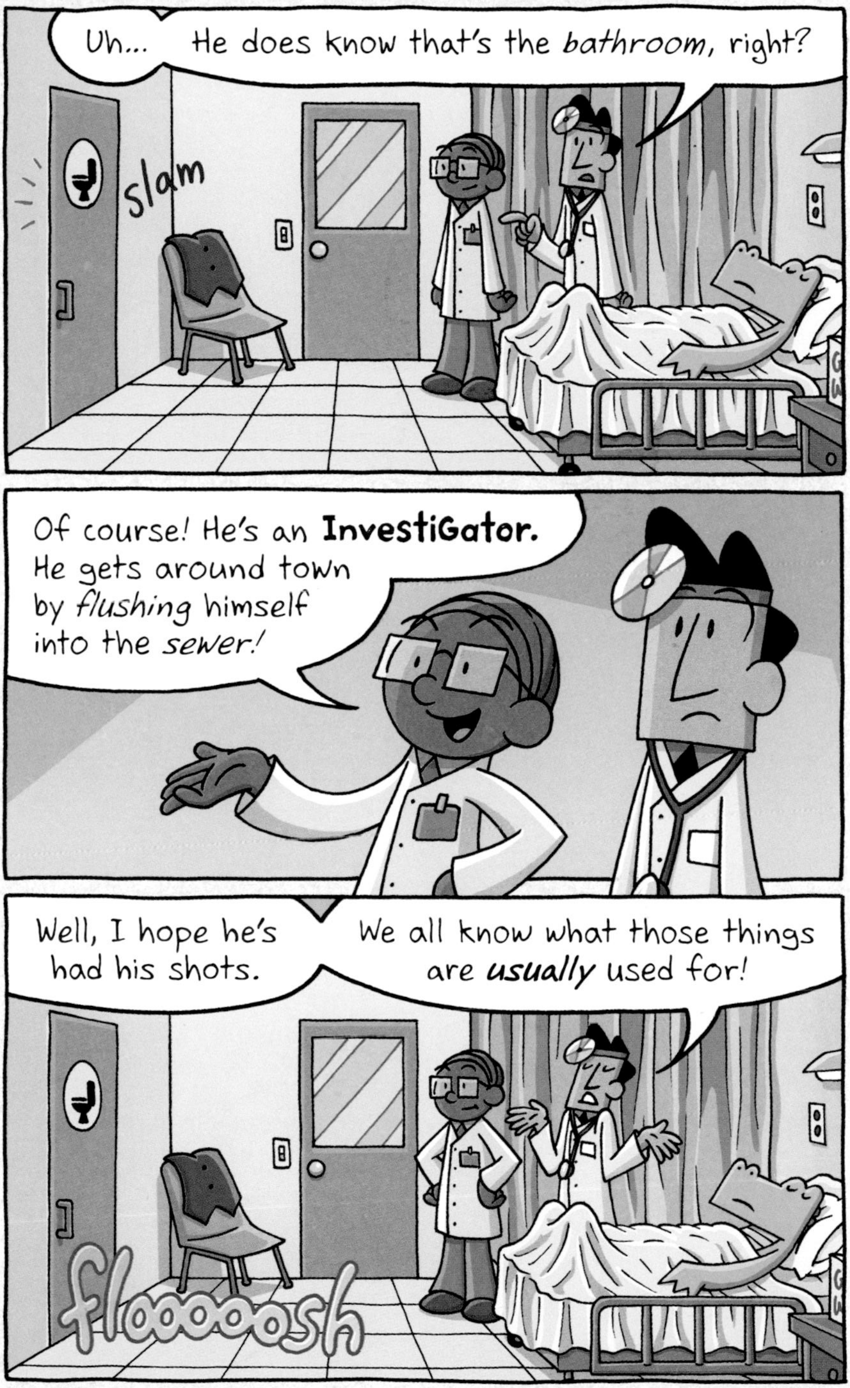
Uh... He does know that's the *bathroom*, right?
slam
Of course! He's an **InvestiGator.** He gets around town by *flushing* himself into the *sewer!*
Well, I hope he's had his shots.
We all know what those things are ***usually*** used for!
flooooosh

# Chapter 7

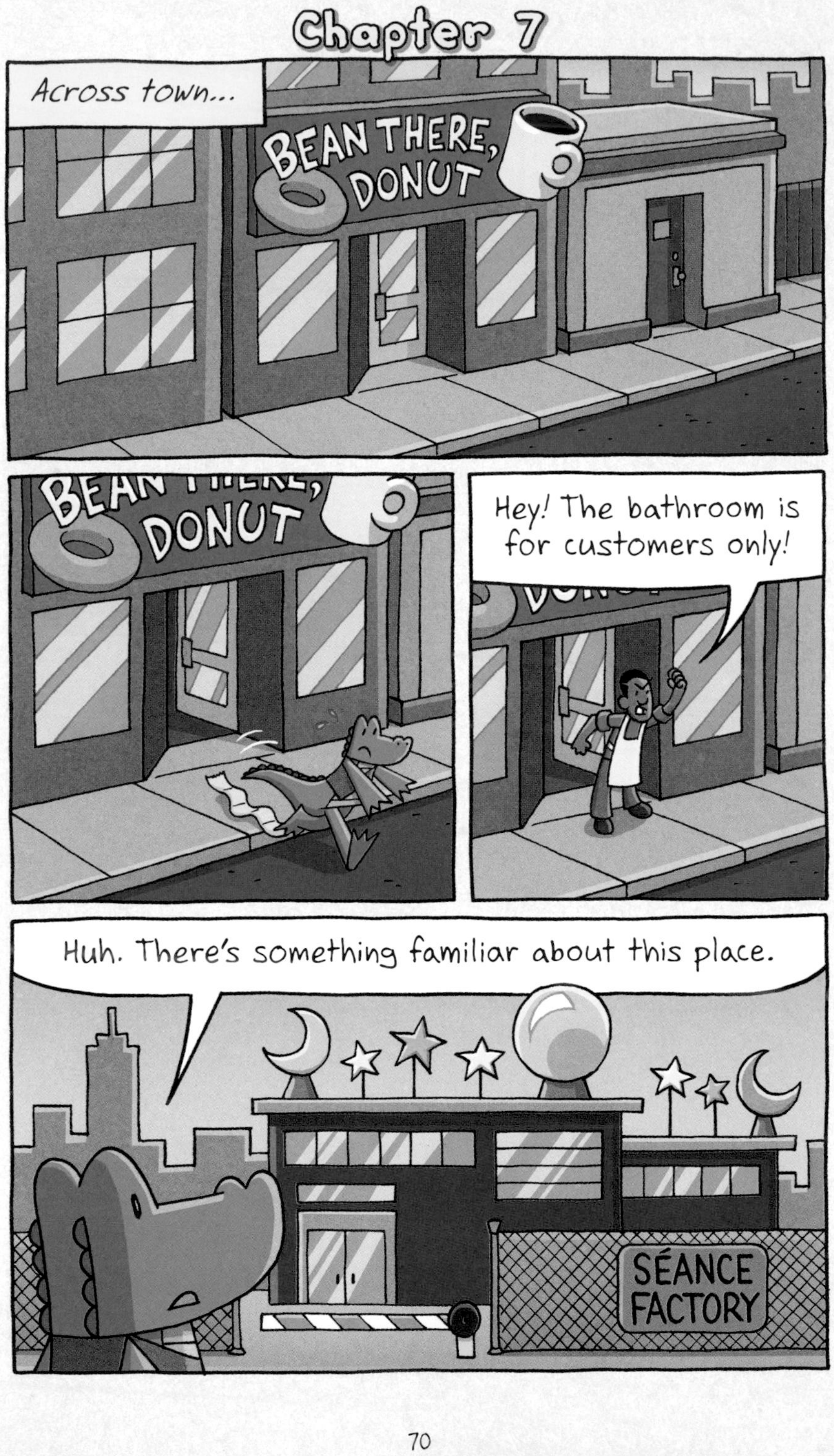

Across town...
BEAN THERE, DONUT
DONUT
Hey! The bathroom is for customers only!
Huh. There's something familiar about this place.
SÉANCE FACTORY

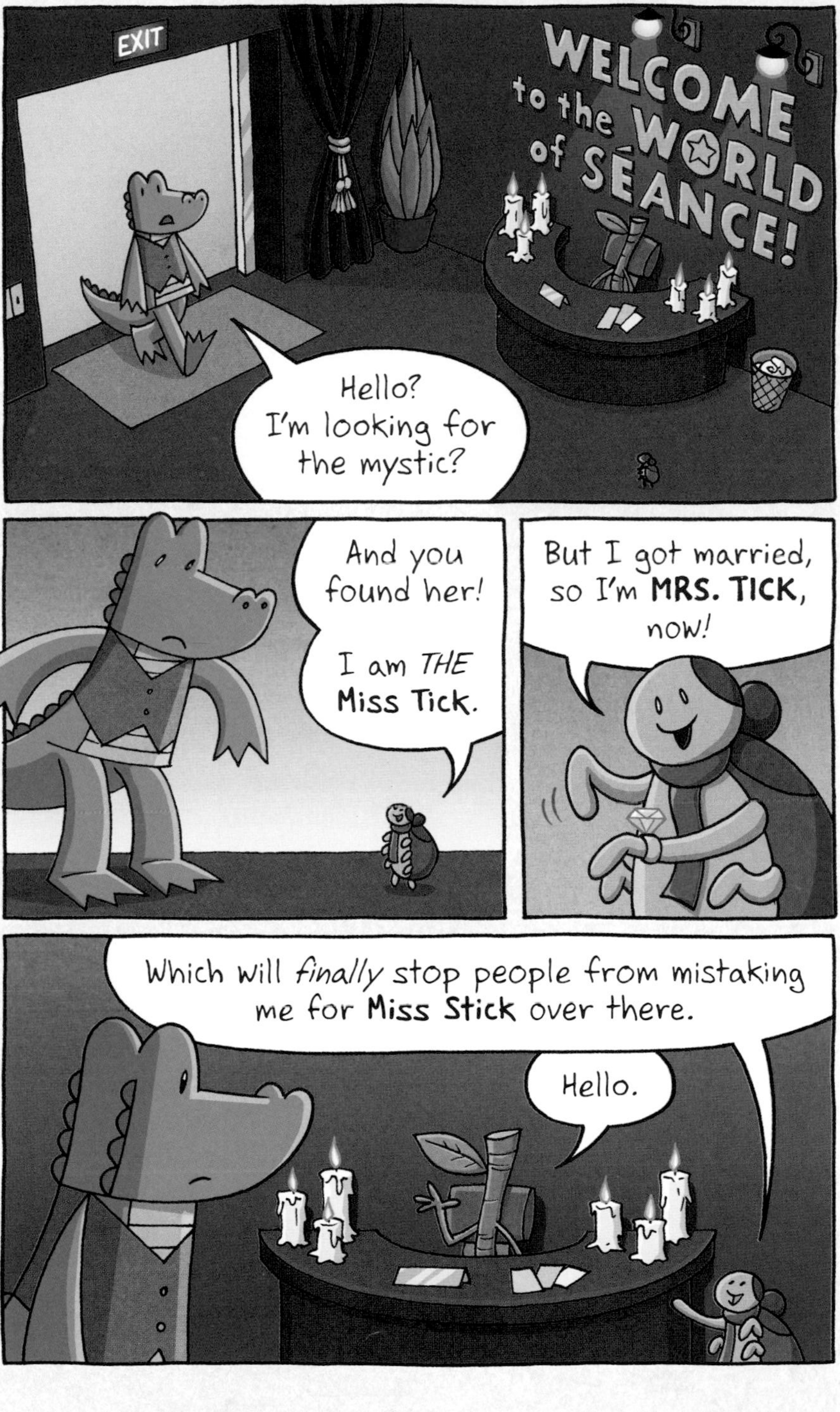
EXIT
WELCOME to the WORLD of SÉANCE!
Hello? I'm looking for the mystic?
And you found her!
I am *THE* **Miss Tick**.
But I got married, so I'm **MRS. TICK**, now!
Which will *finally* stop people from mistaking me for **Miss Stick** over there.
Hello.

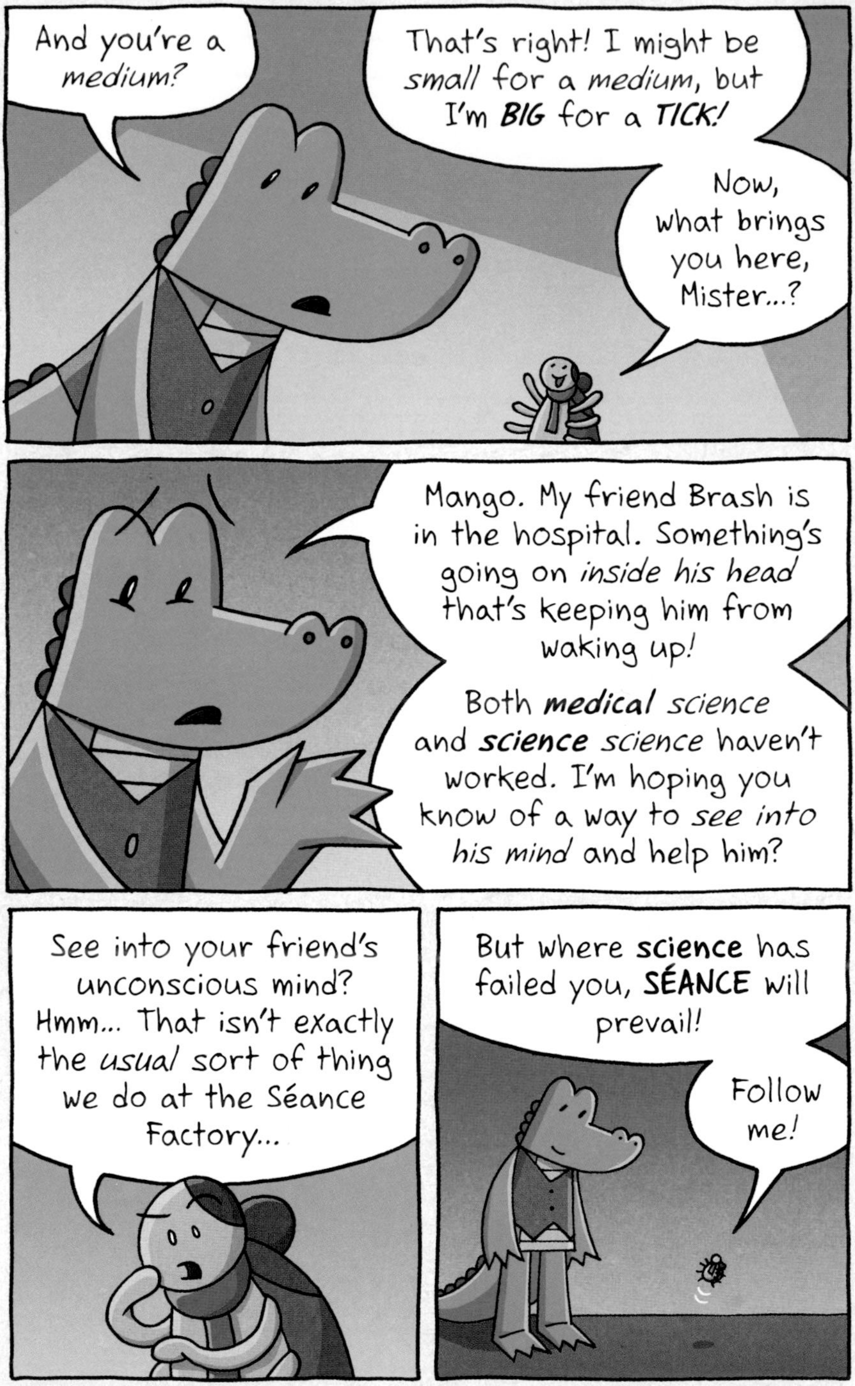
And you're a *medium?*
That's right! I might be *small* for a *medium,* but I'm ***BIG*** for a ***TICK!***
Now, what brings you here, Mister...?
Mango. My friend Brash is in the hospital. Something's going on *inside his head* that's keeping him from waking up!
Both ***medical*** *science* and ***science*** *science* haven't worked. I'm hoping you know of a way to *see into his mind* and help him?
See into your friend's unconscious mind? Hmm... That isn't exactly the *usual* sort of thing we do at the Séance Factory...
But where **science** has failed you, **SÉANCE** will prevail!
Follow me!

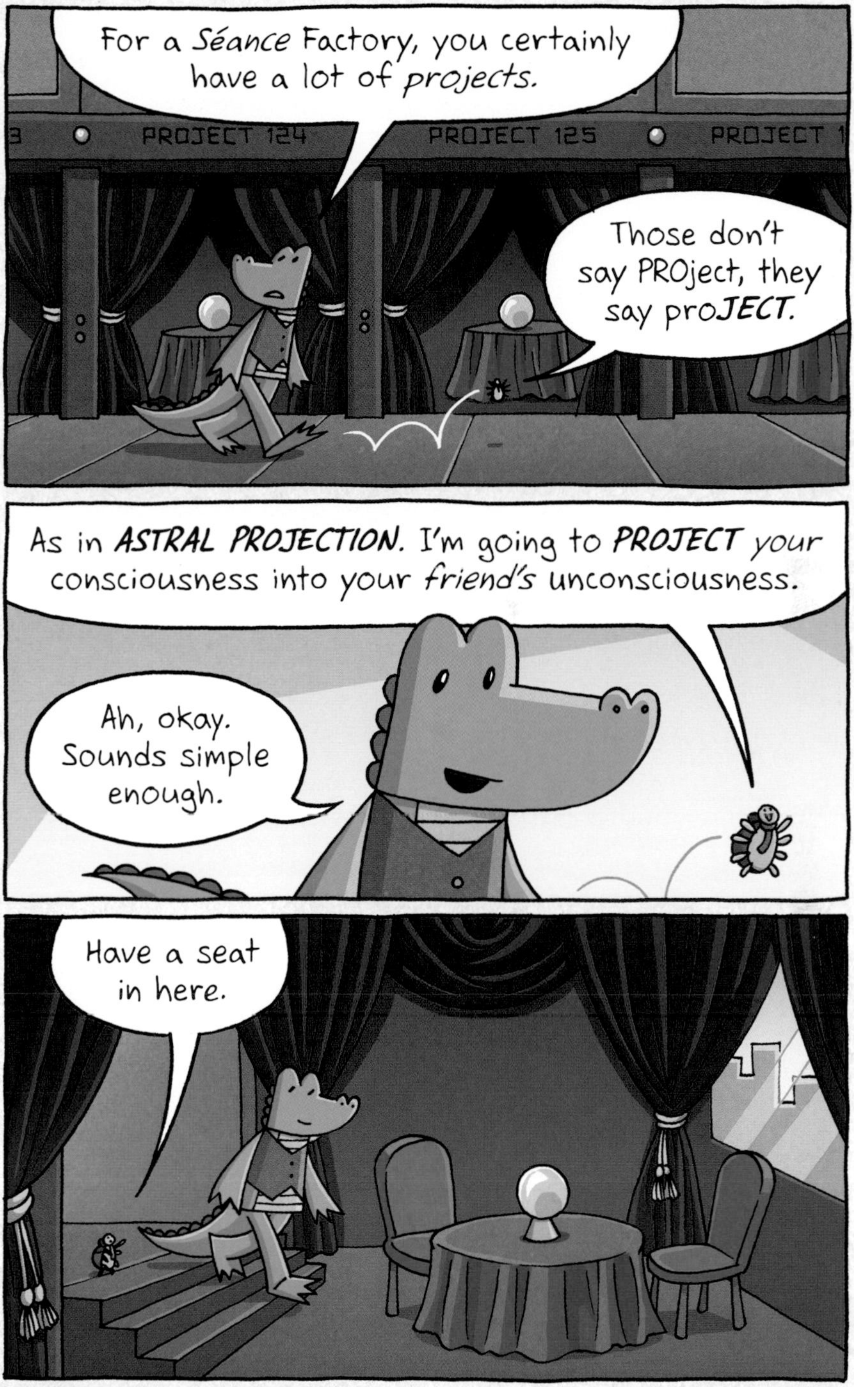
For a *Séance* Factory, you certainly have a lot of *projects.*
PROJECT 124
PROJECT 125
Those don't say PROject, they say pro***JECT.***
As in ***ASTRAL PROJECTION.*** I'm going to ***PROJECT*** *your* consciousness into your *friend's* unconsciousness.
Ah, okay. Sounds simple enough.
Have a seat in here.

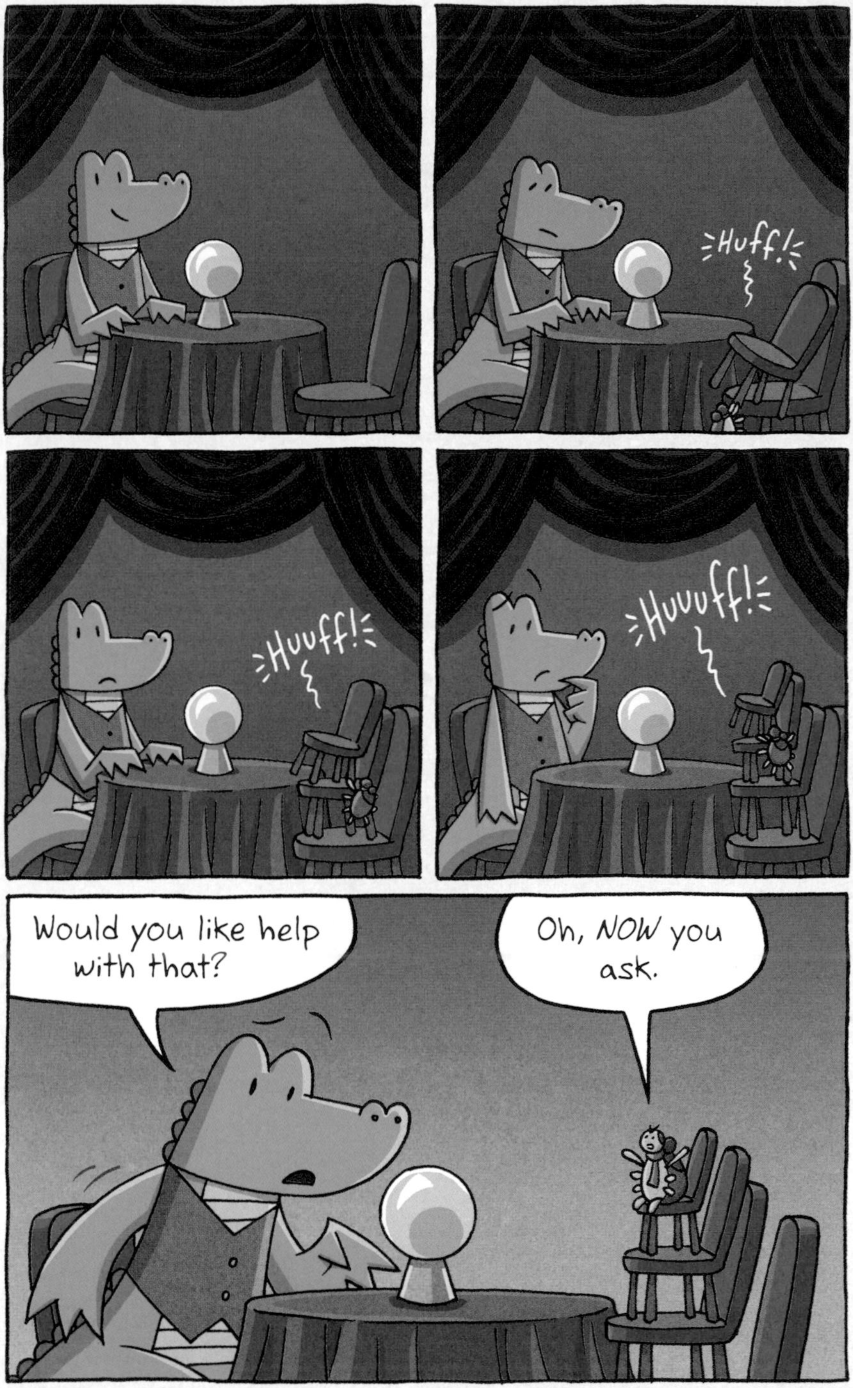
Huff!
Huuff!
Huuuff!
Would you like help with that?
Oh, NOW you ask.

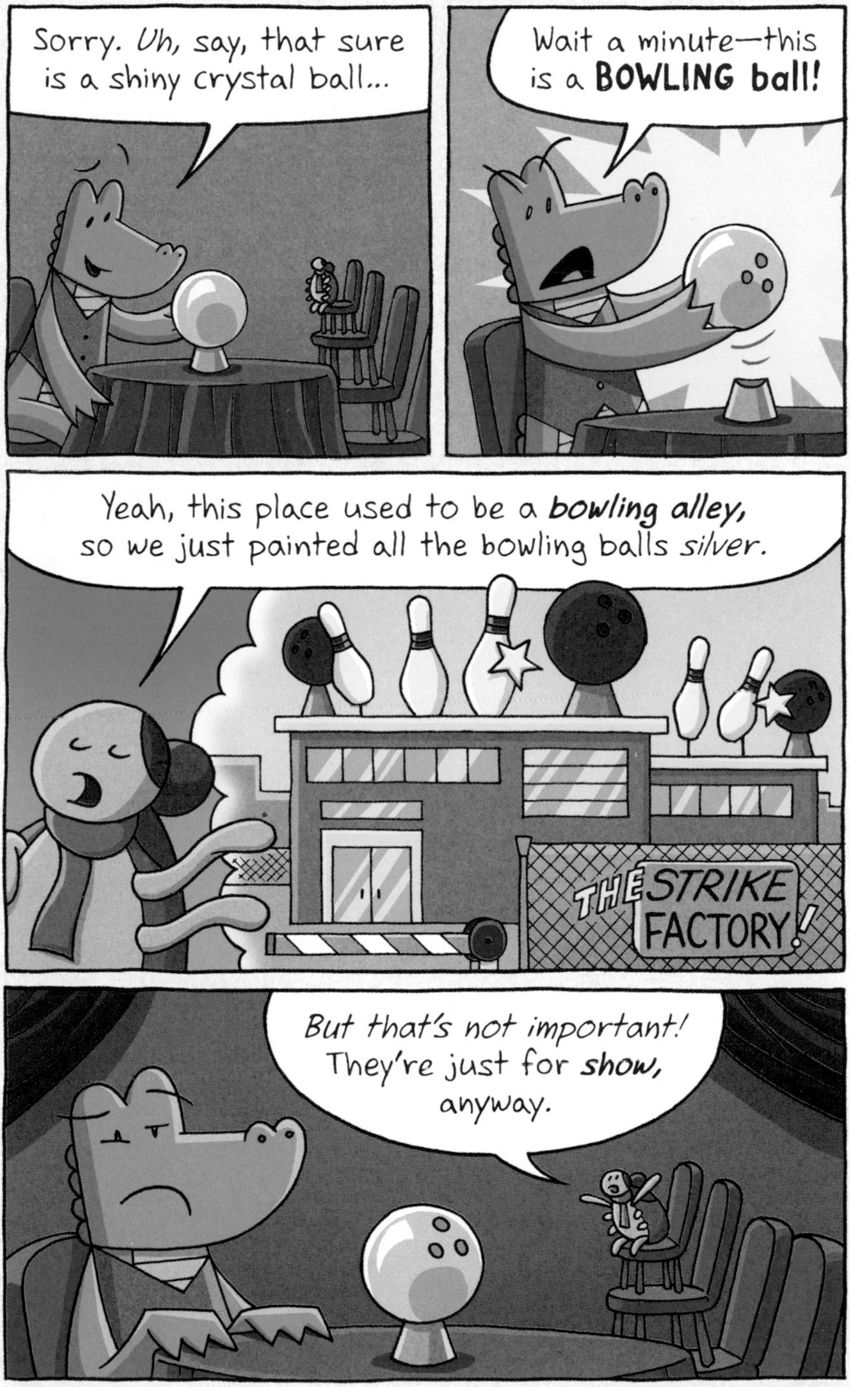
Sorry. *Uh, say,* that sure is a shiny crystal ball...
Wait a minute—this is a **BOWLING ball!**
Yeah, this place used to be a ***bowling alley,*** so we just painted all the bowling balls *silver.*
THE STRIKE FACTORY!
*But that's not important!* They're just for ***show,*** anyway.

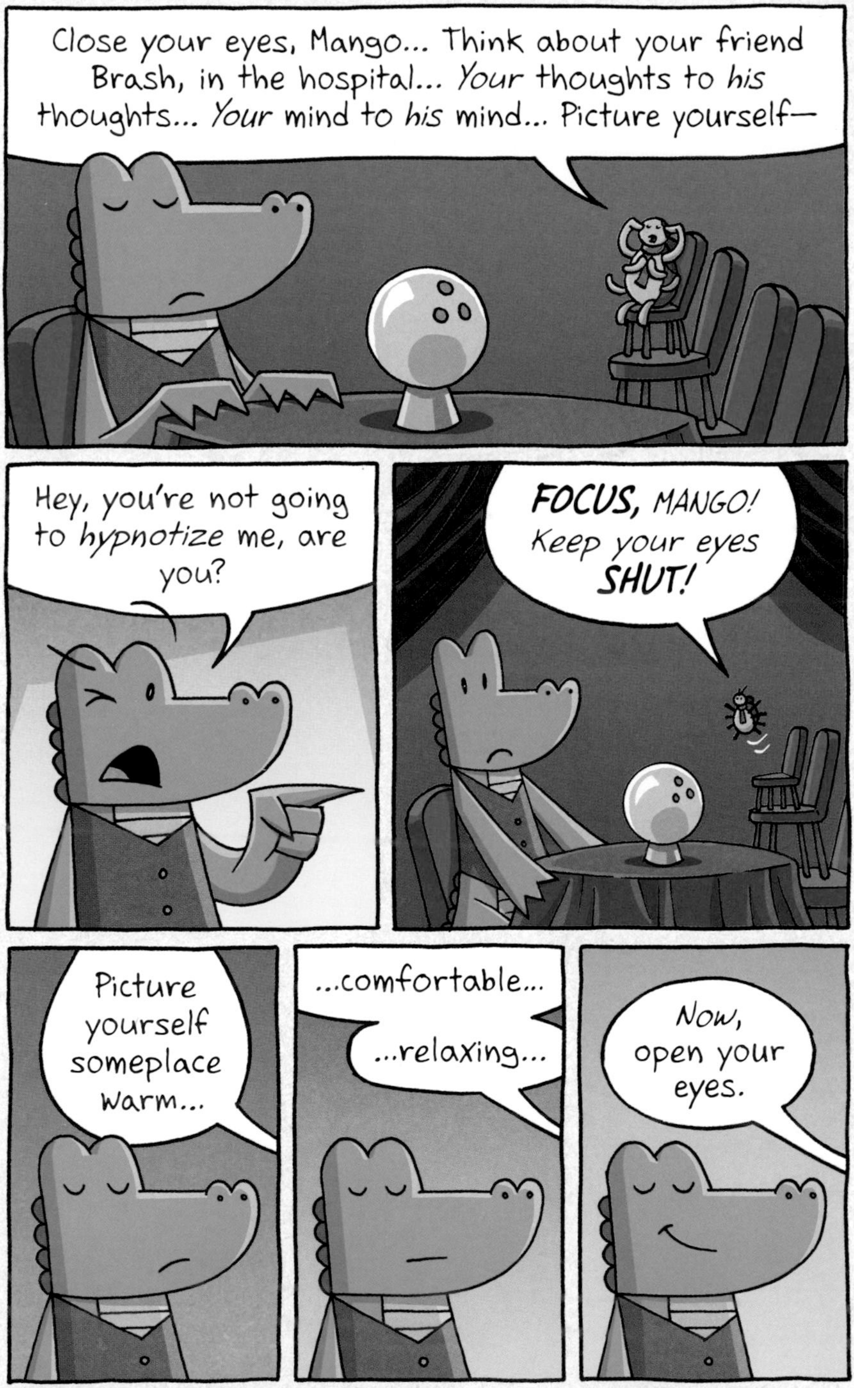
Close your eyes, Mango... Think about your friend Brash, in the hospital... *Your* thoughts to *his* thoughts... *Your* mind to *his* mind... Picture yourself—
Hey, you're not going to *hypnotize* me, are you?
**FOCUS,** MANGO! Keep your eyes **SHUT!**
Picture yourself someplace warm...
...comfortable...
...relaxing...
Now, open your eyes.

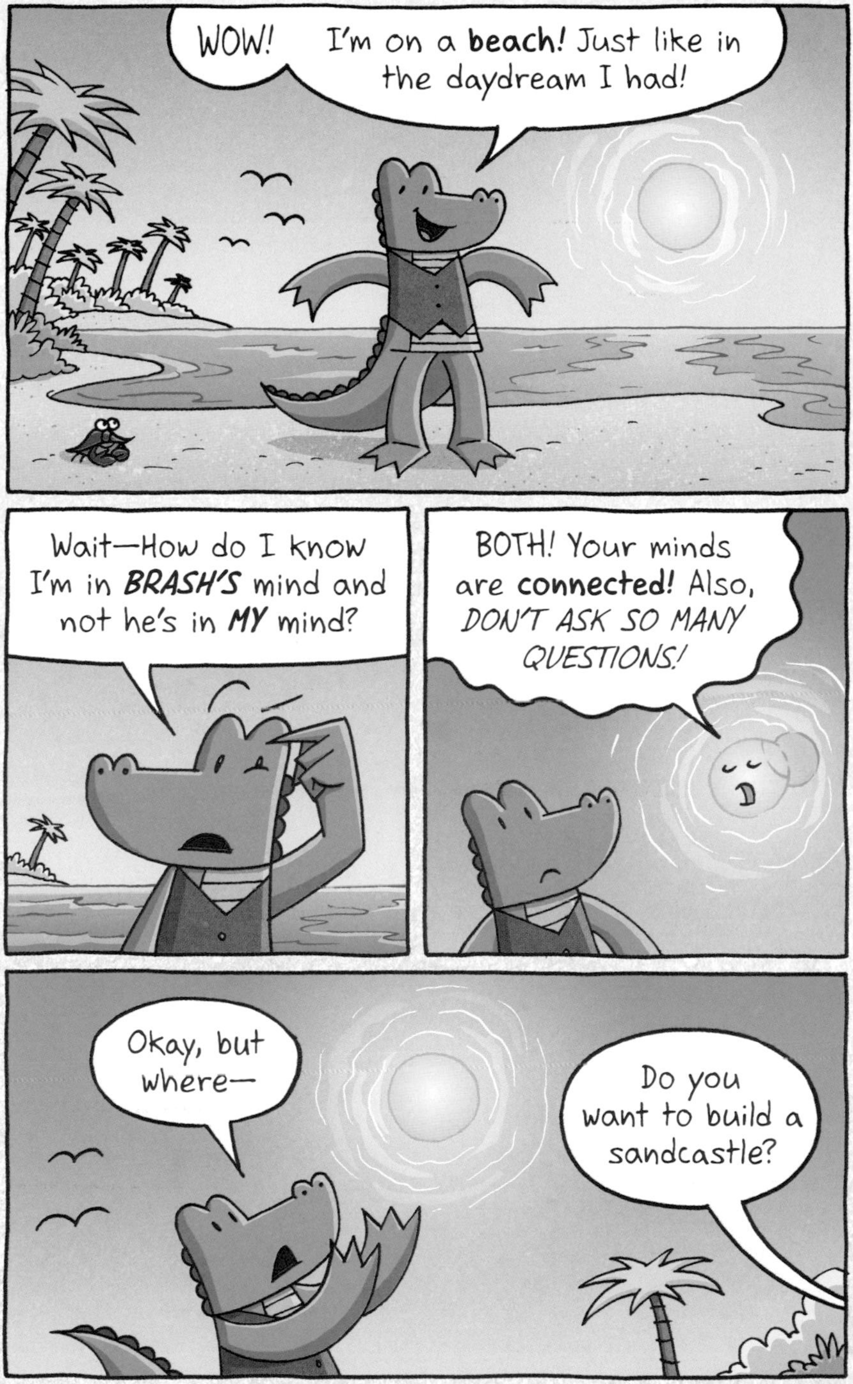
WOW! I'm on a **beach!** Just like in the daydream I had!
Wait—How do I know I'm in ***BRASH'S*** mind and not he's in ***MY*** mind?
BOTH! Your minds are **connected!** Also, *DON'T ASK SO MANY QUESTIONS!*
Okay, but where—
Do you want to build a sandcastle?

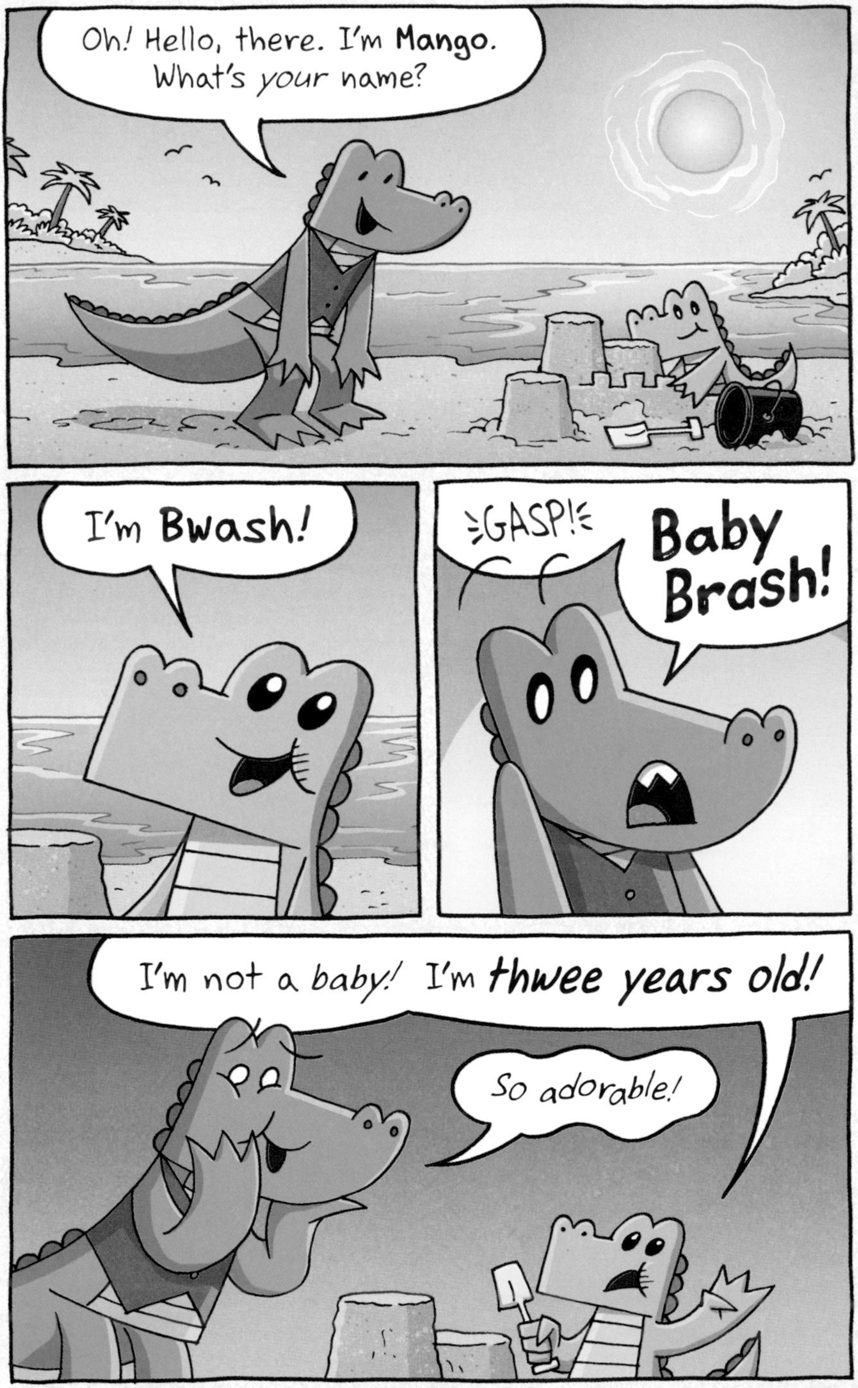
Oh! Hello, there. I'm Mango. What's your name?
I'm Bwash!
GASP!
Baby Brash!
I'm not a baby! I'm thwee years old!
So adorable!

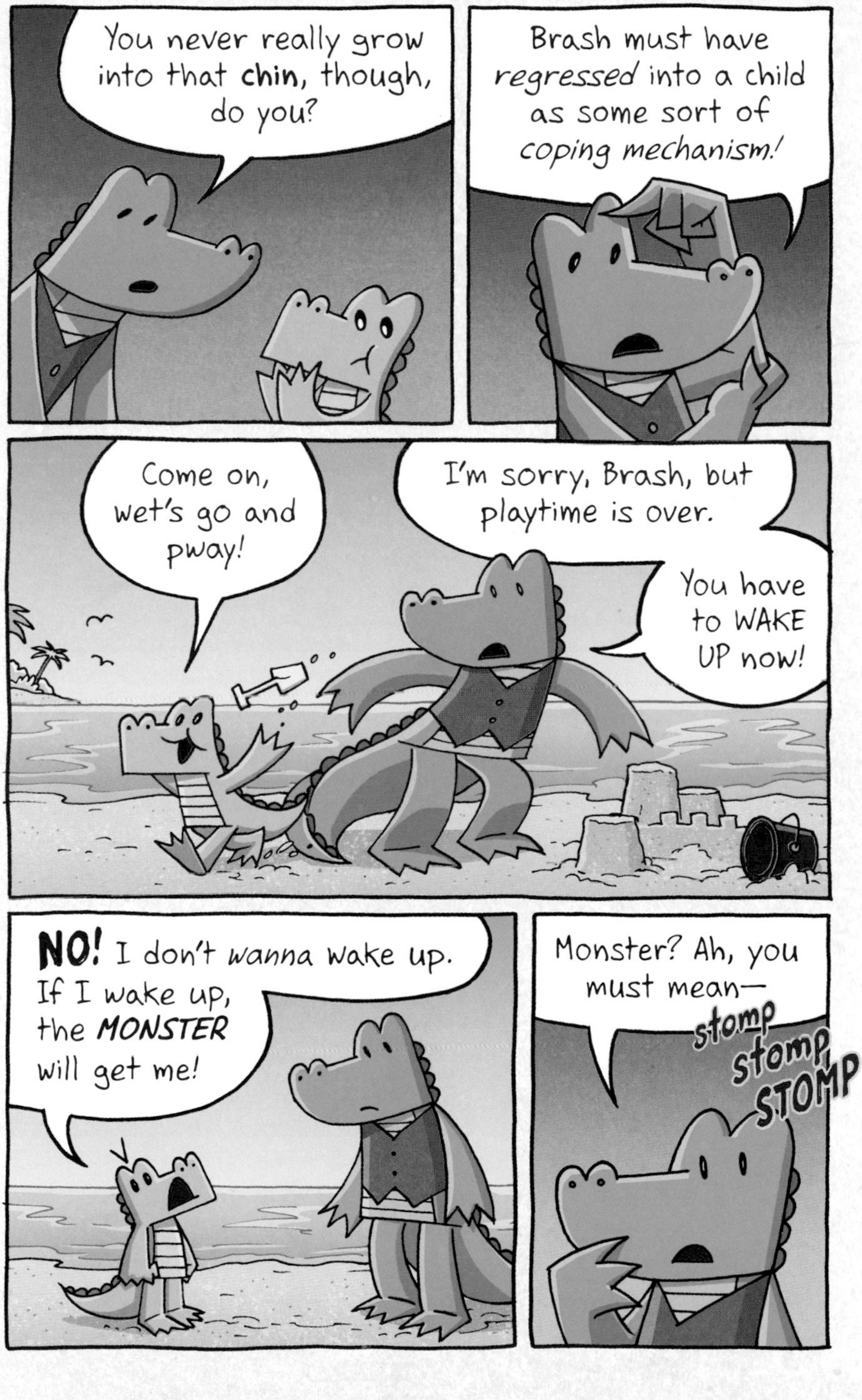
You never really grow into that **chin**, though, do you?
Brash must have *regressed* into a child as some sort of *coping mechanism!*
Come on, wet's go and pway!
I'm sorry, Brash, but playtime is over.
You have to WAKE UP now!
**NO!** I don't *wanna* wake up. If I wake up, the ***MONSTER*** will get me!
Monster? Ah, you must mean—
stomp
stomp
STOMP

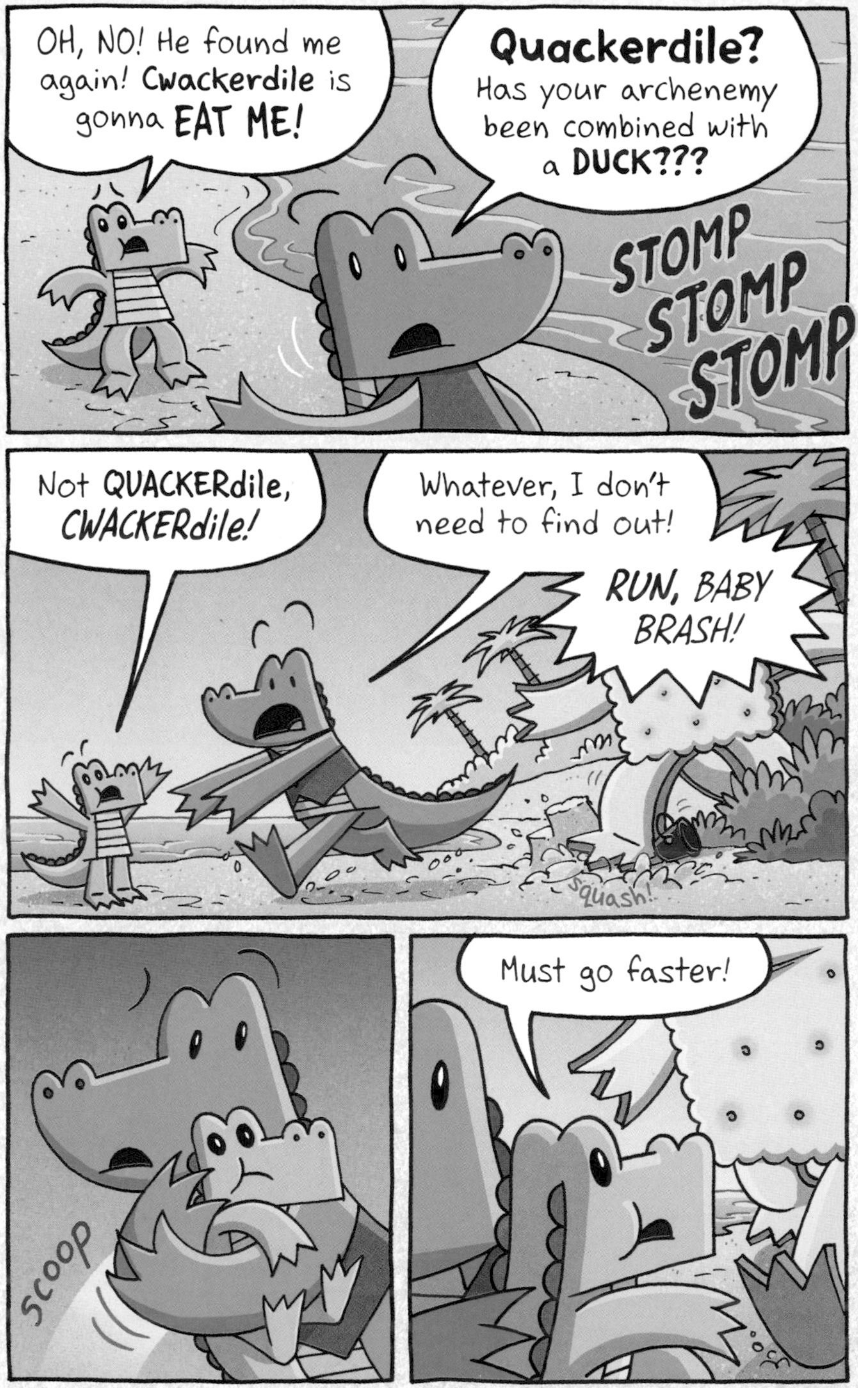
OH, NO! He found me again! Cwackerdile is gonna EAT ME!
Quackerdile? Has your archenemy been combined with a DUCK???
STOMP STOMP STOMP
Not QUACKERdile, CWACKERdile!
Whatever, I don't need to find out!
RUN, BABY BRASH!
squash!
SCOOP
Must go faster!

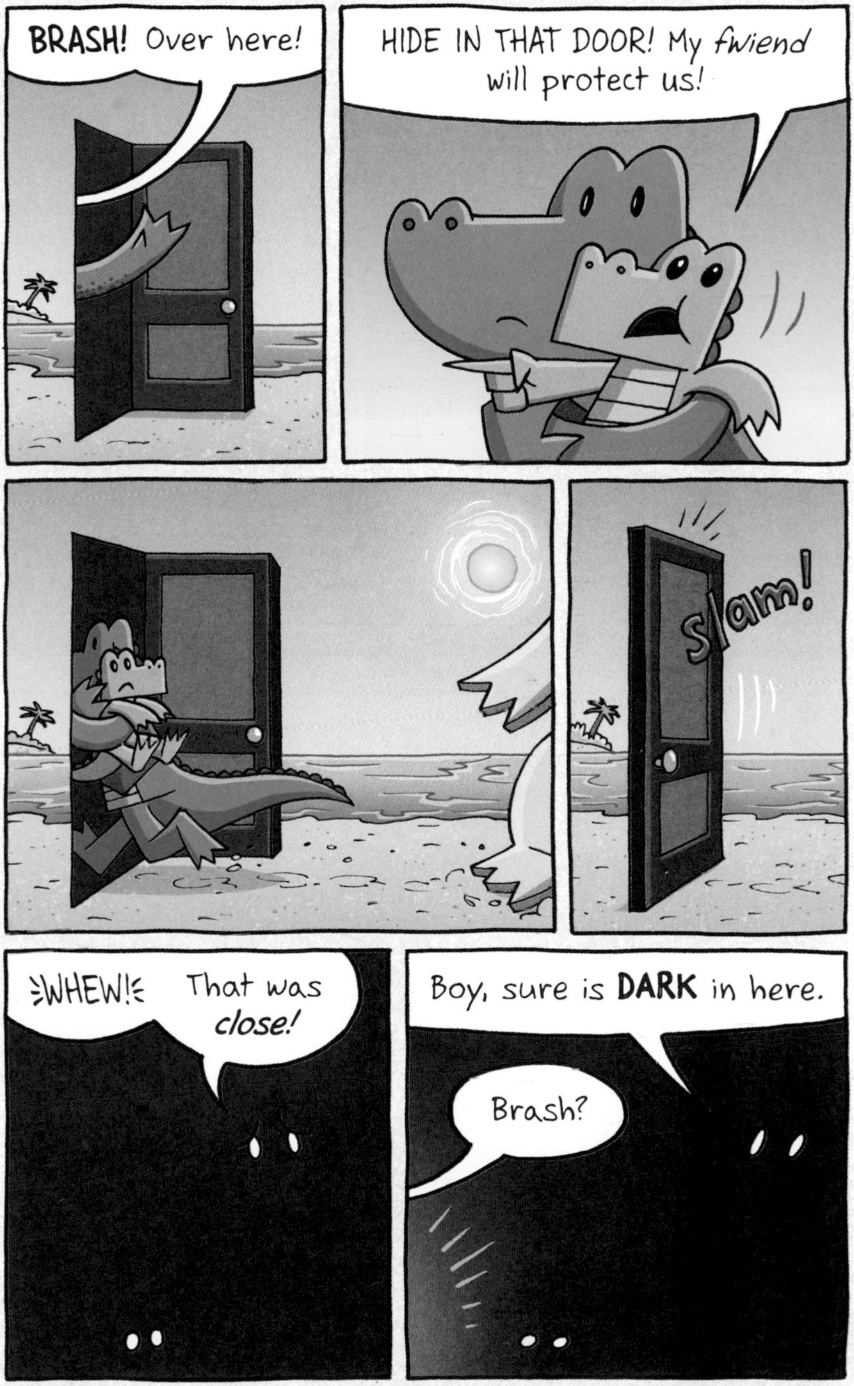
**BRASH!** Over here!
HIDE IN THAT DOOR! My *fwiend* will protect us!
slam!
WHEW! That was *close!*
Boy, sure is **DARK** in here.
Brash?

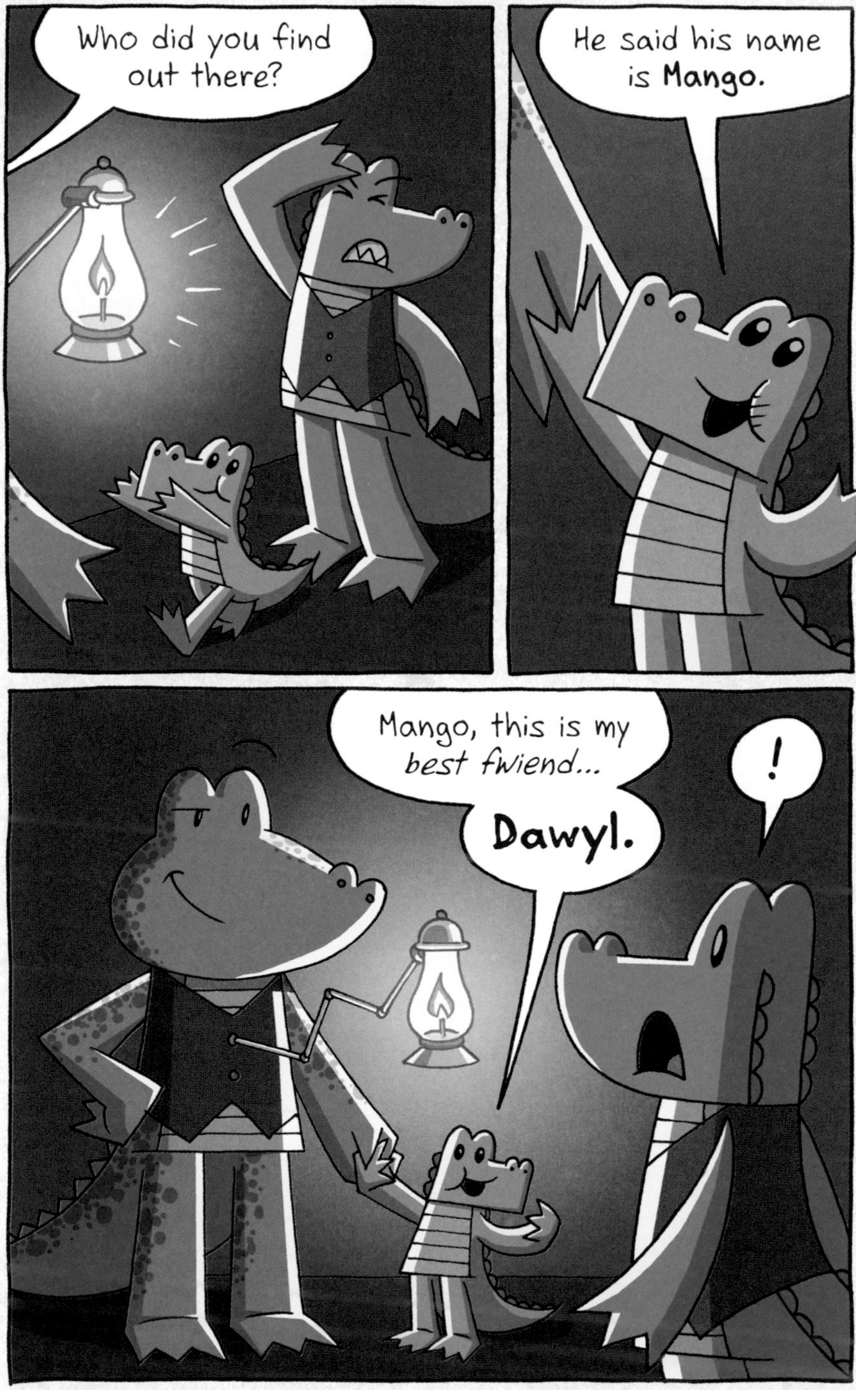
Who did you find out there?
He said his name is **Mango.**
Mango, this is my *best fwiend...*
**Dawyl.**
!

# Chapter 8

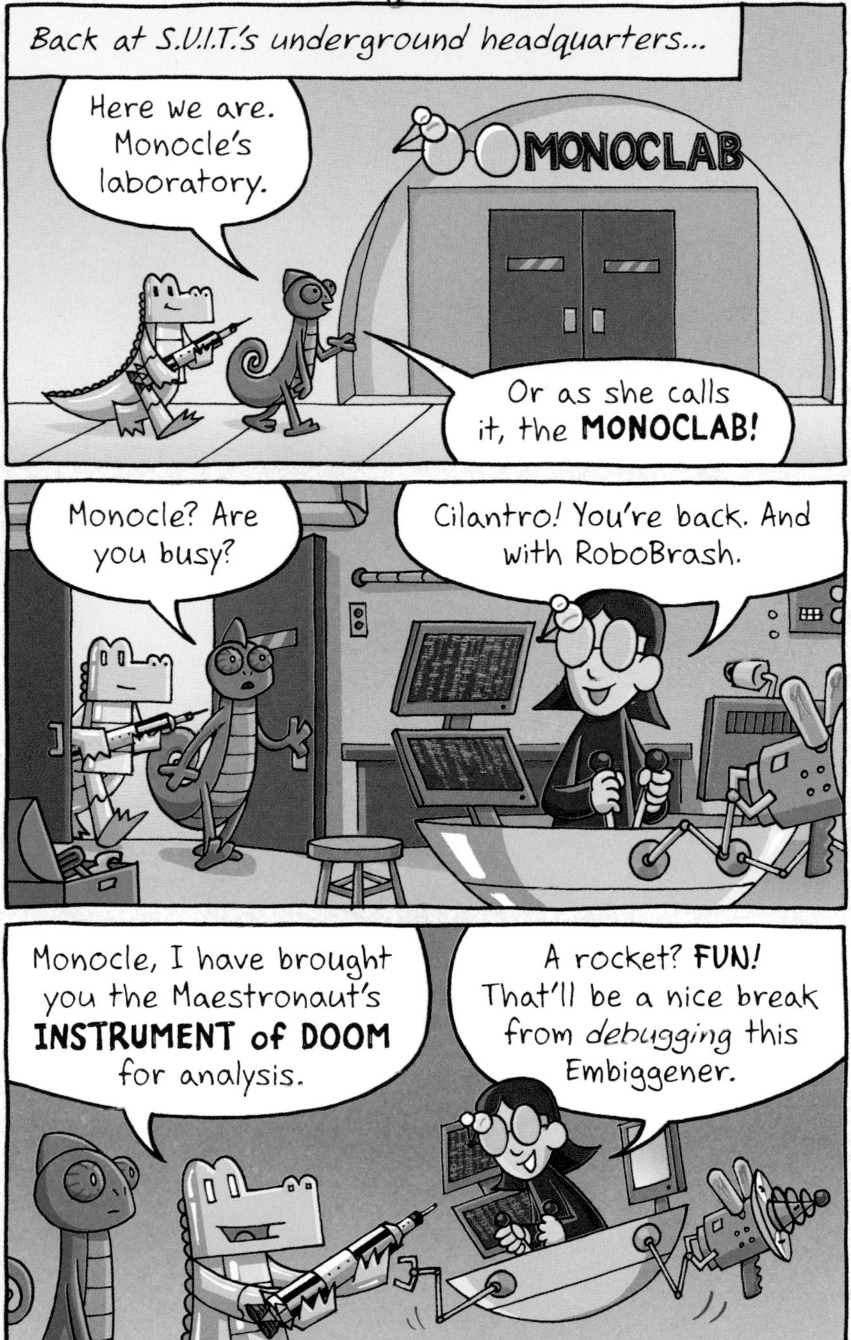
Back at S.U.I.T.'s underground headquarters...
Here we are. Monocle's laboratory.
MONOCLAB
Or as she calls it, the **MONOCLAB!**
Monocle? Are you busy?
Cilantro! You're back. And with RoboBrash.
Monocle, I have brought you the Maestronaut's **INSTRUMENT of DOOM** for analysis.
A rocket? **FUN!** That'll be a nice break from *debugging* this Embiggener.

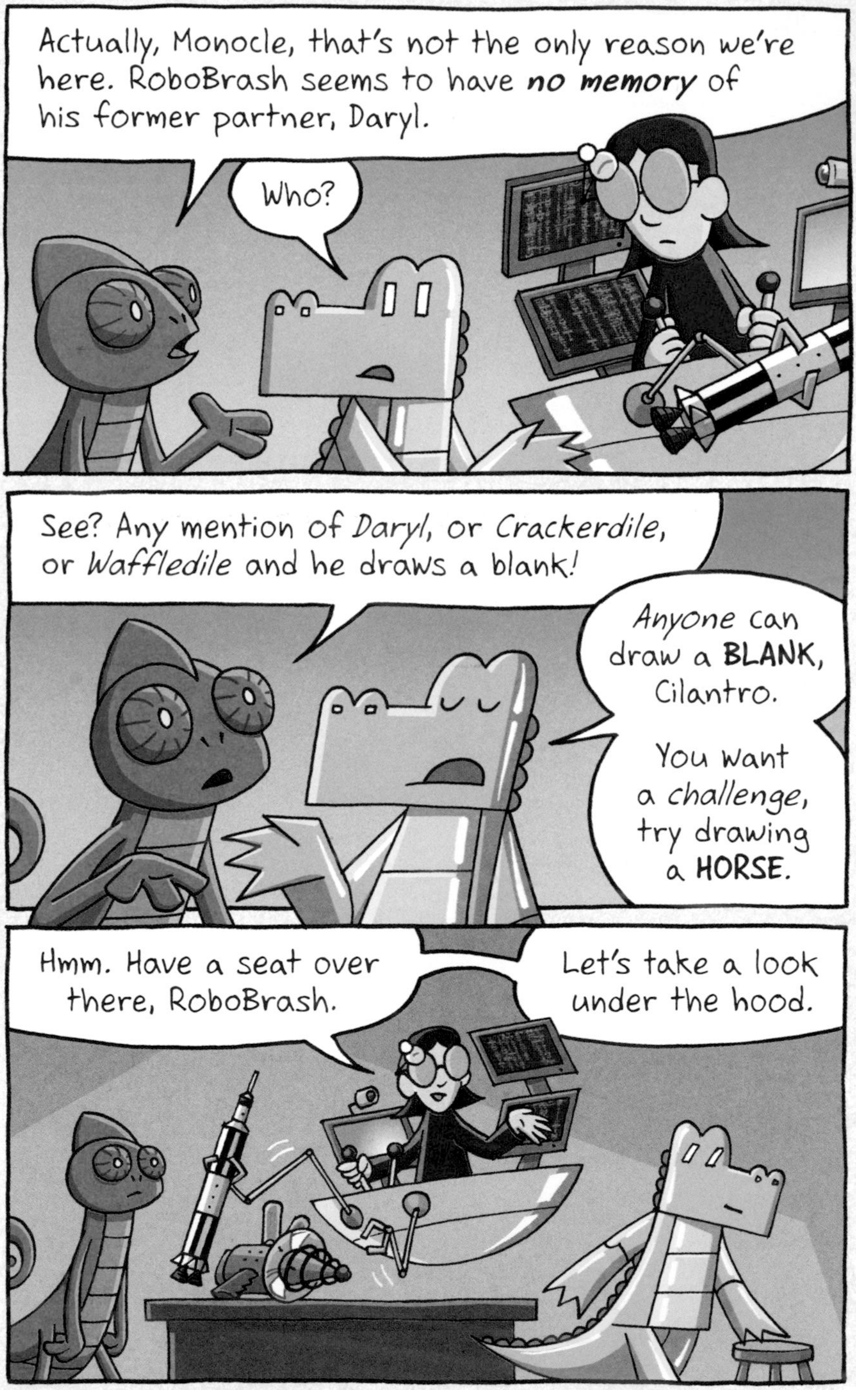
Actually, Monocle, that's not the only reason we're here. RoboBrash seems to have **no memory** of his former partner, Daryl.
Who?
See? Any mention of *Daryl*, or *Crackerdile*, or *Waffledile* and he draws a blank!
*Anyone* can draw a **BLANK**, Cilantro.
You want a *challenge*, try drawing a **HORSE**.
Hmm. Have a seat over there, RoboBrash.
Let's take a look under the hood.

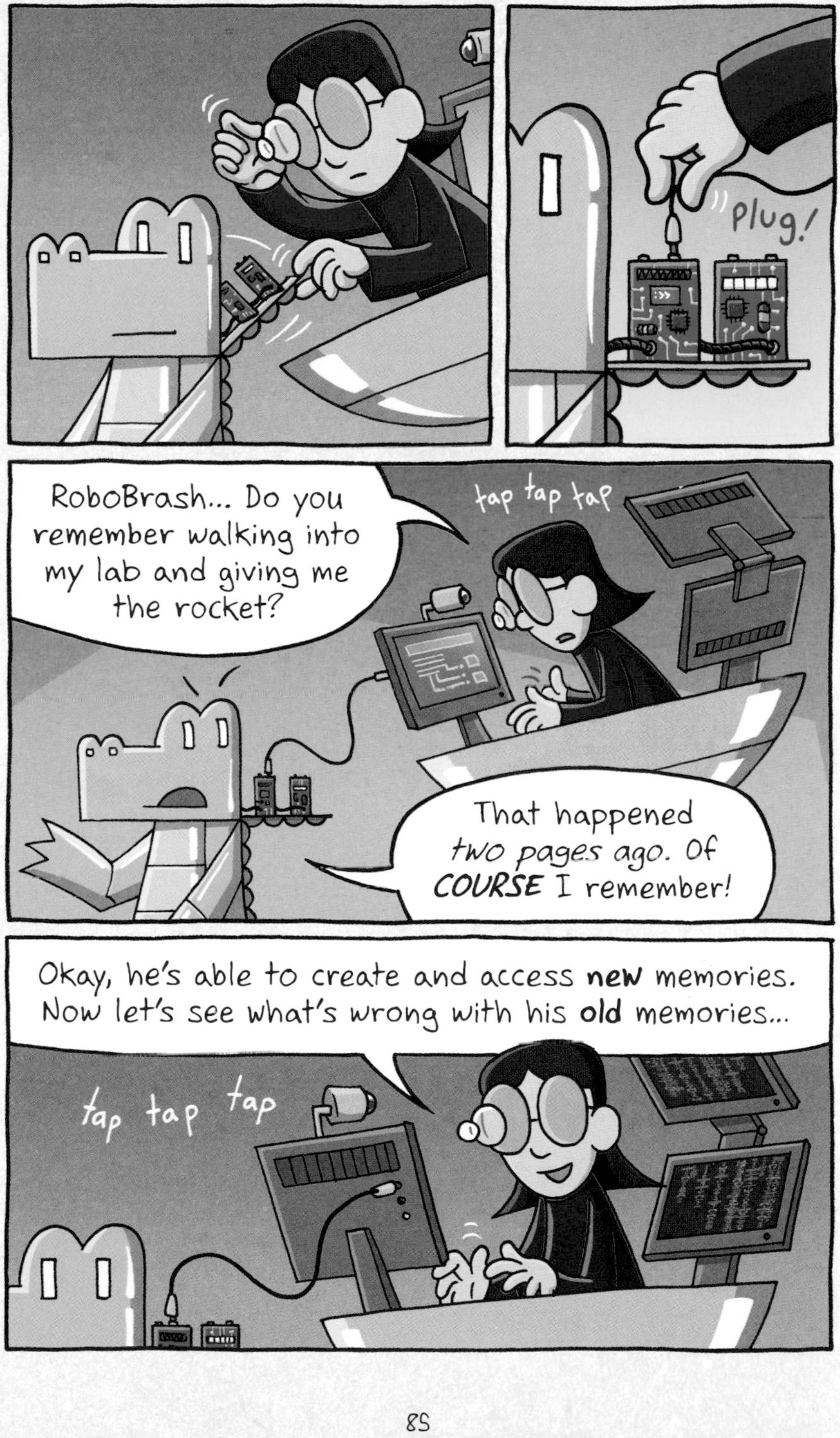
Plug!
RoboBrash... Do you remember walking into my lab and giving me the rocket?
tap tap tap
That happened two pages ago. Of COURSE I remember!
Okay, he's able to create and access new memories. Now let's see what's wrong with his old memories...
tap tap tap

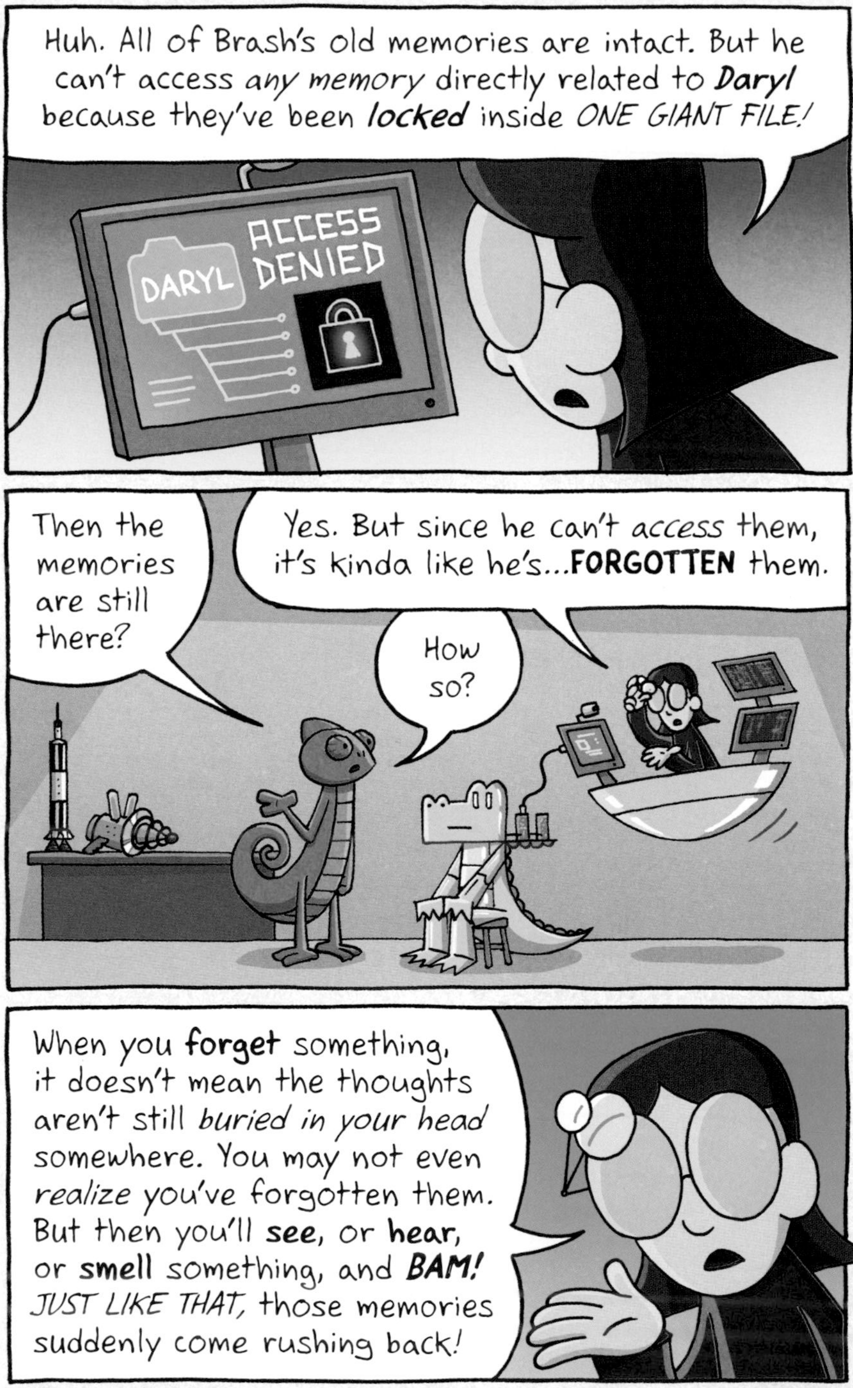
Huh. All of Brash's old memories are intact. But he can't access *any memory* directly related to ***Daryl*** because they've been ***locked*** inside *ONE GIANT FILE!*
DARYL
ACCESS DENIED
Then the memories are still there?
Yes. But since he can't *access* them, it's kinda like he's...**FORGOTTEN** them.
How so?
When you **forget** something, it doesn't mean the thoughts aren't still *buried in your head* somewhere. You may not even *realize* you've forgotten them. But then you'll **see**, or **hear**, or **smell** something, and ***BAM!*** *JUST LIKE THAT,* those memories suddenly come rushing back!

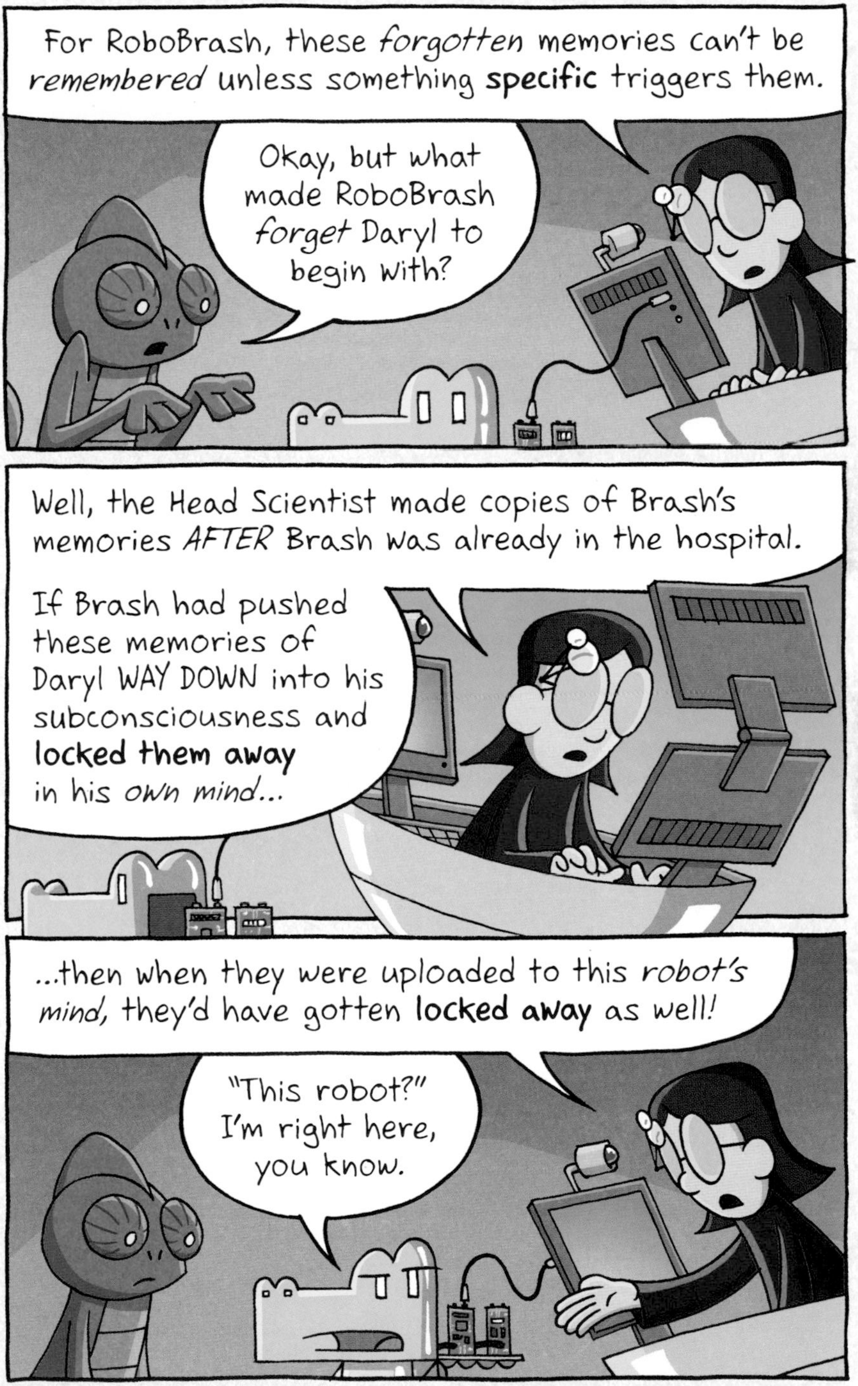

For RoboBrash, these *forgotten* memories can't be *remembered* unless something **specific** triggers them.
Okay, but what made RoboBrash *forget* Daryl to begin with?
Well, the Head Scientist made copies of Brash's memories *AFTER* Brash was already in the hospital.
If Brash had pushed these memories of Daryl WAY DOWN into his subconsciousness and **locked them away** in his *own mind*...
...then when they were uploaded to this *robot's mind*, they'd have gotten **locked away** as well!
"This robot?" I'm right here, you know.

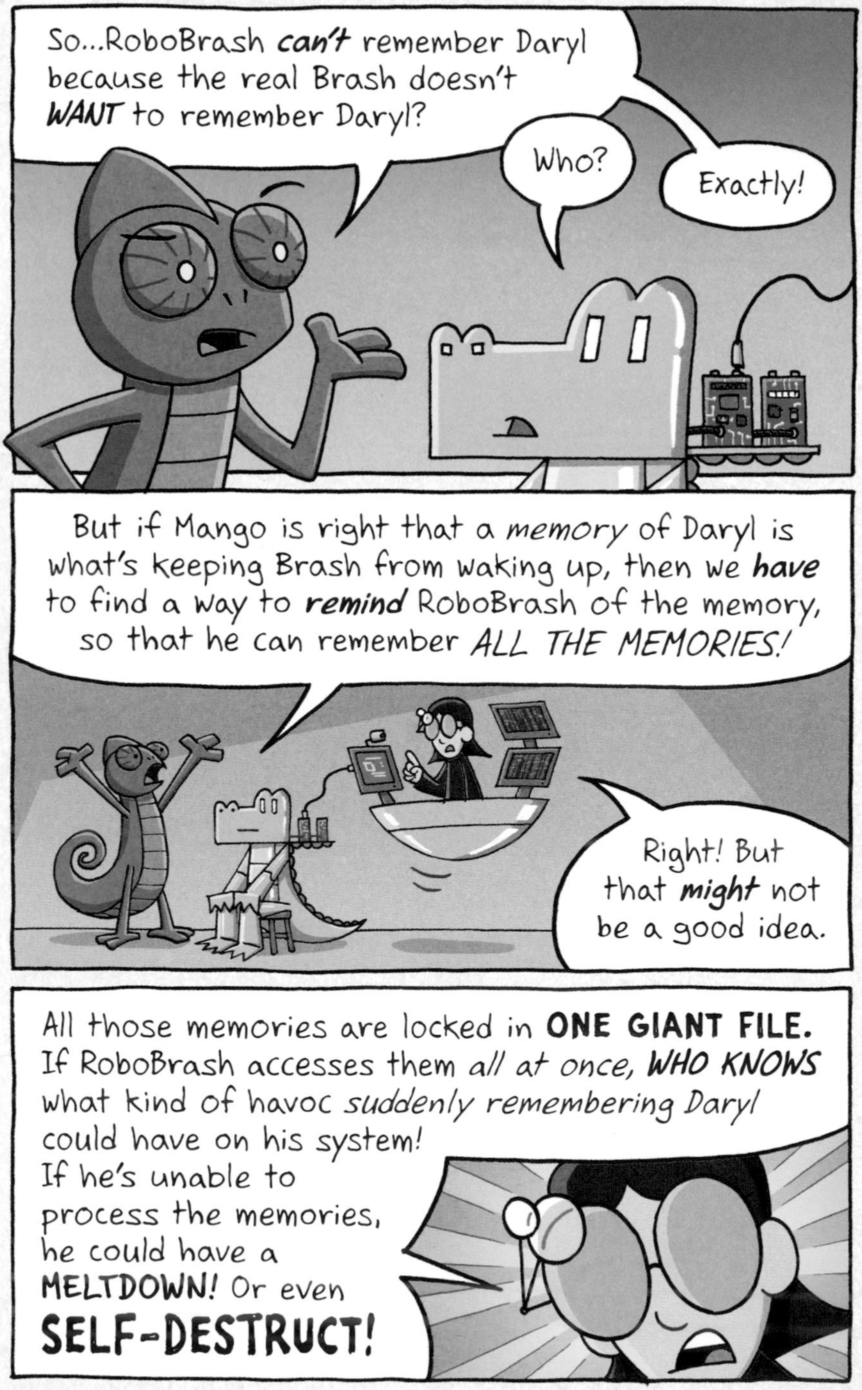
So...RoboBrash *can't* remember Daryl because the real Brash doesn't *WANT* to remember Daryl?
Who?
Exactly!
But if Mango is right that a *memory* of Daryl is what's keeping Brash from waking up, then we *have* to find a way to *remind* RoboBrash of the memory, so that he can remember *ALL THE MEMORIES!*
Right! But that *might* not be a good idea.
All those memories are locked in **ONE GIANT FILE.** If RoboBrash accesses them *all at once*, ***WHO KNOWS*** what kind of havoc *suddenly remembering Daryl* could have on his system!
If he's unable to process the memories, he could have a **MELTDOWN!** Or even **SELF-DESTRUCT!**

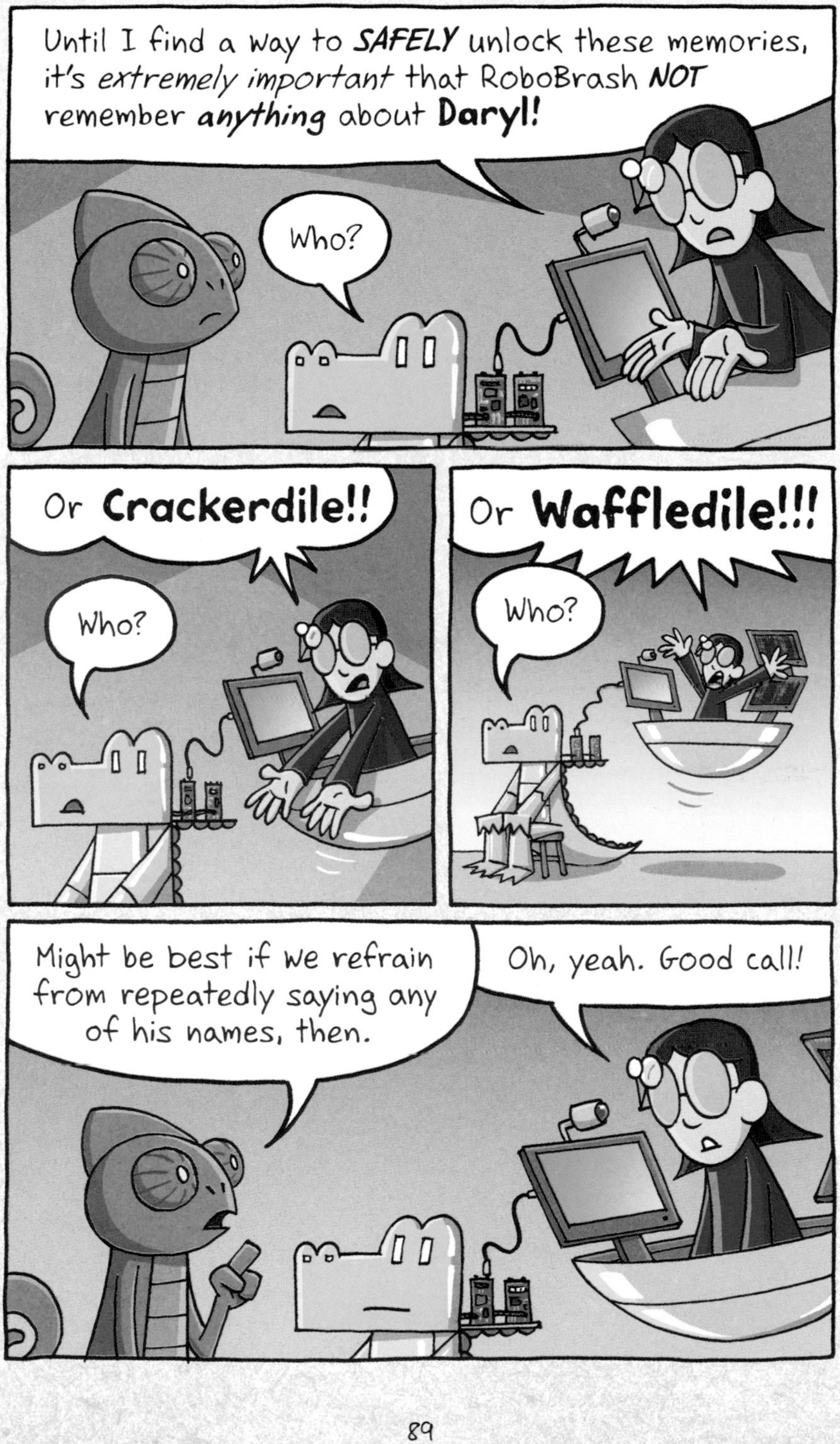
Until I find a way to *SAFELY* unlock these memories, it's *extremely important* that RoboBrash ***NOT*** remember ***anything*** about **Daryl!**
Who?
Or **Crackerdile!!**
Who?
Or **Waffledile!!!**
Who?
Might be best if we refrain from repeatedly saying any of his names, then.
Oh, yeah. Good call!

# Chapter 9

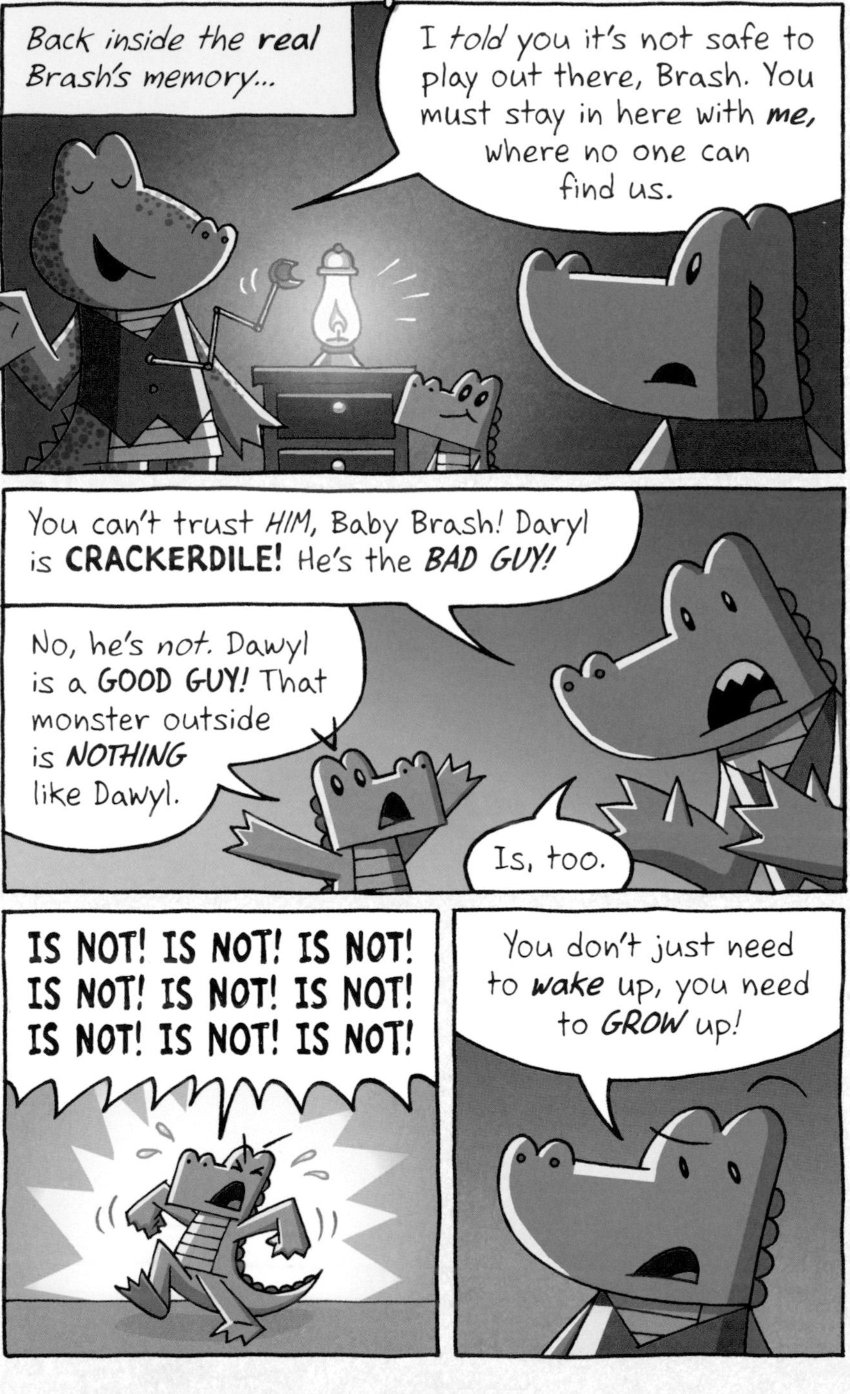

Back inside the *real* Brash's memory...
I *told* you it's not safe to play out there, Brash. You must stay in here with *me,* where no one can find us.
You can't trust *HIM*, Baby Brash! Daryl is **CRACKERDILE!** He's the ***BAD GUY!***
No, he's *not.* Dawyl is a **GOOD GUY!** That monster outside is ***NOTHING*** like Dawyl.
Is, too.
IS NOT! IS NOT! IS NOT! IS NOT! IS NOT! IS NOT! IS NOT! IS NOT! IS NOT!
You don't just need to ***wake*** up, you need to ***GROW*** up!

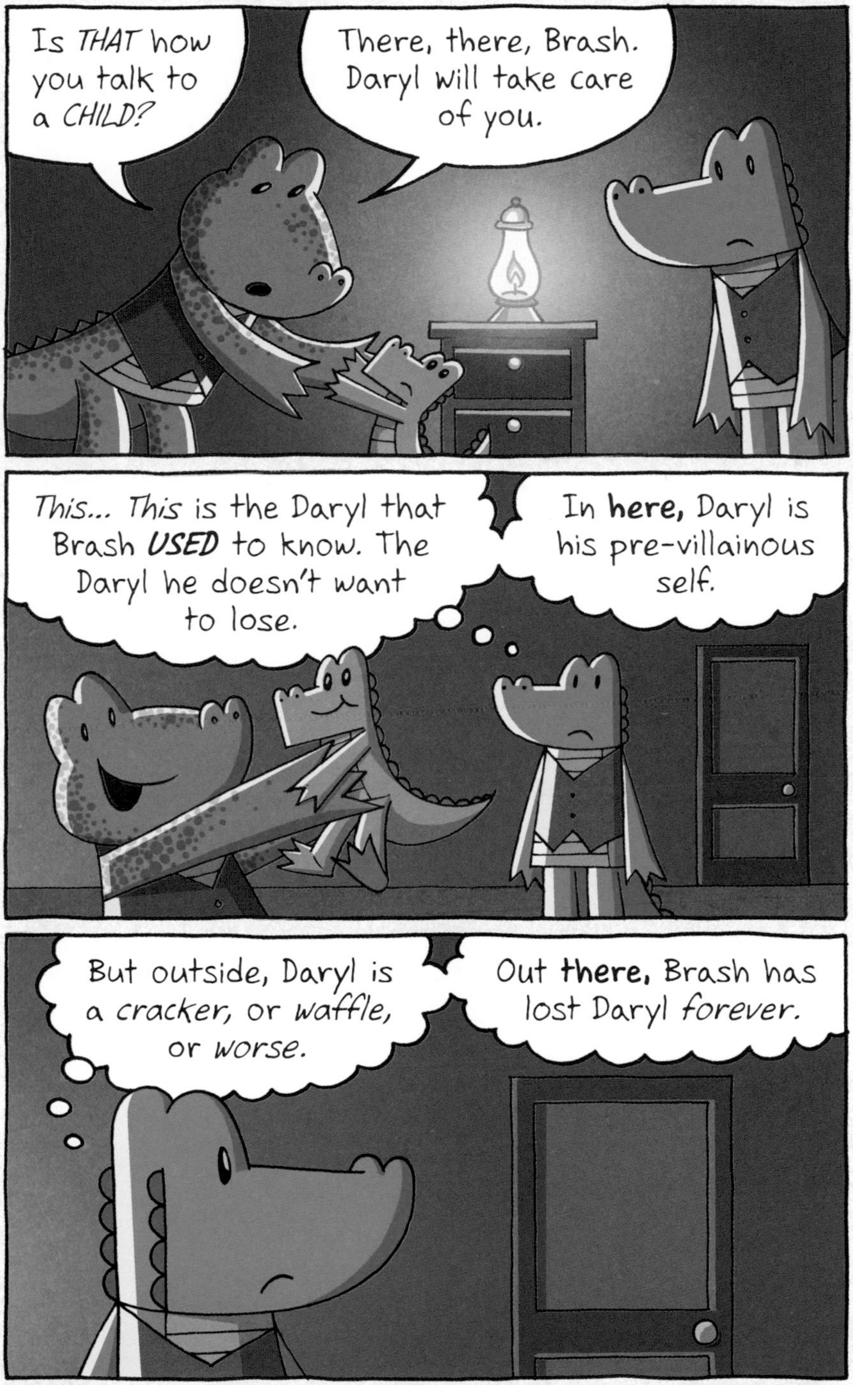
Is *THAT* how you talk to a *CHILD?*
There, there, Brash. Daryl will take care of you.
*This... This* is the Daryl that Brash ***USED*** to know. The Daryl he doesn't want to lose.
In **here,** Daryl is his pre-villainous self.
But outside, Daryl is a *cracker,* or *waffle,* or *worse.*
Out **there,** Brash has lost Daryl *forever.*

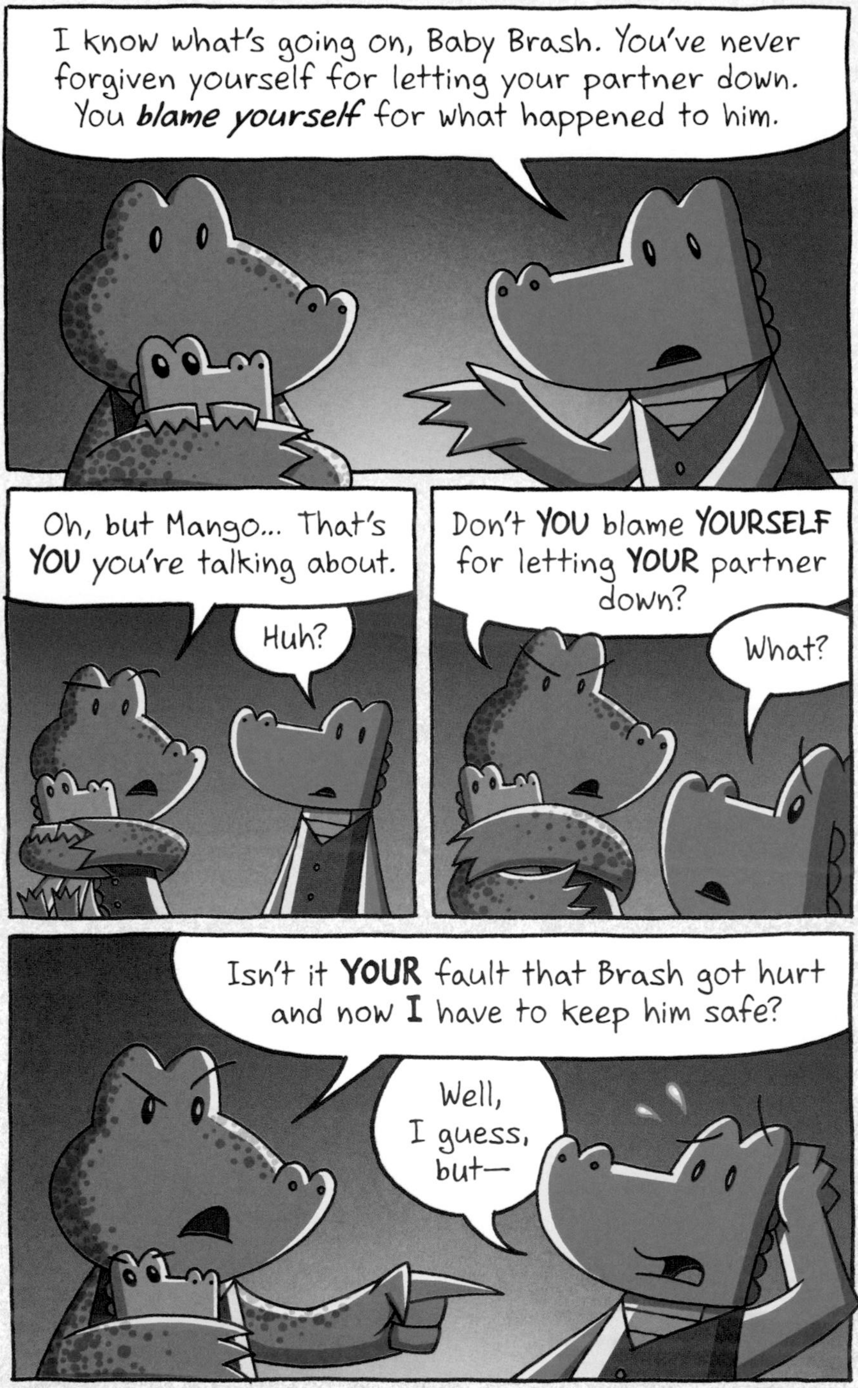
I know what's going on, Baby Brash. You've never forgiven yourself for letting your partner down. You *blame yourself* for what happened to him.
Oh, but Mango... That's **YOU** you're talking about.
Huh?
Don't **YOU** blame **YOURSELF** for letting **YOUR** partner down?
What?
Isn't it **YOUR** fault that Brash got hurt and now **I** have to keep him safe?
Well, I guess, but—

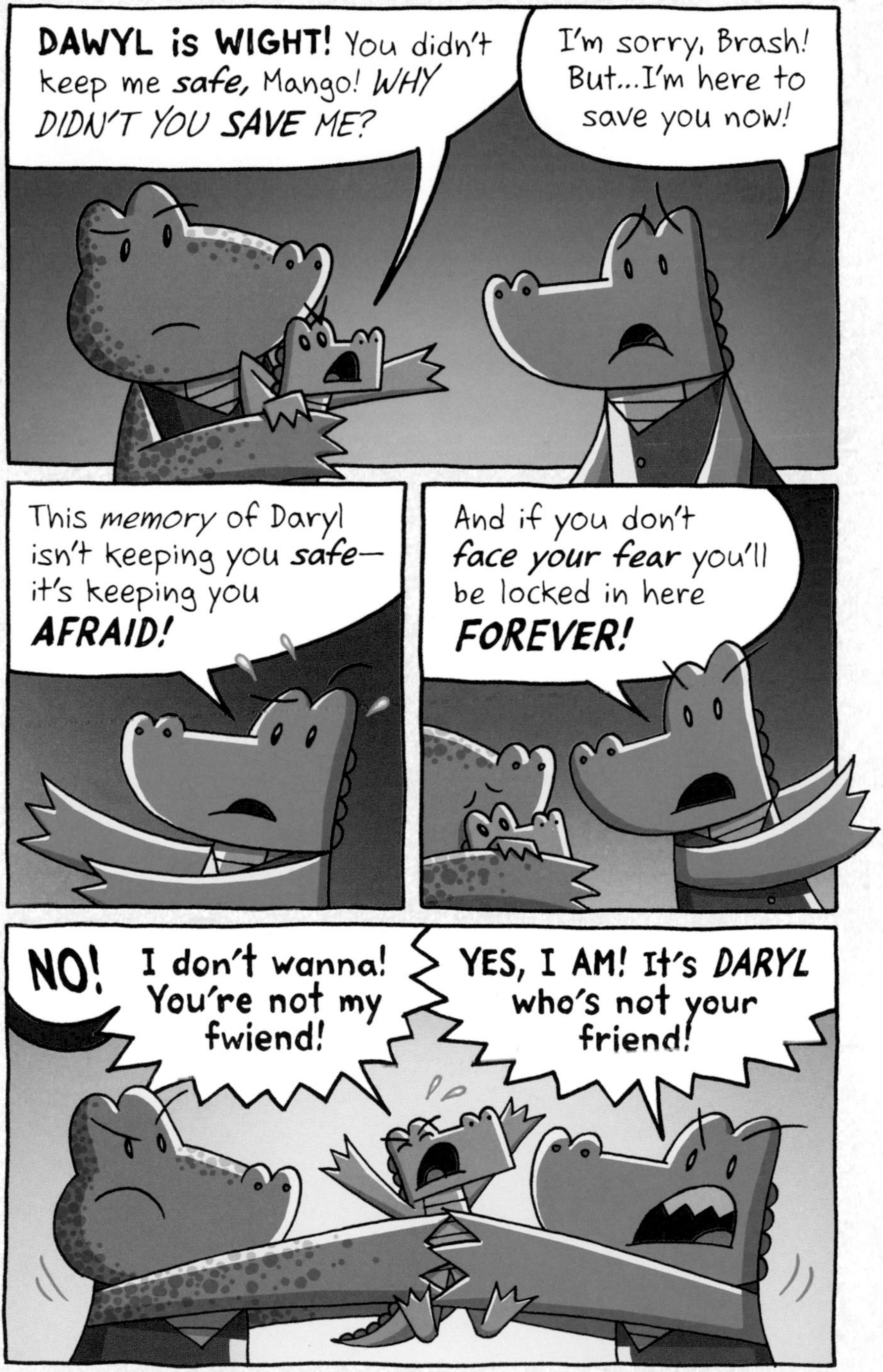
DAWYL is WIGHT! You didn't keep me safe, Mango! WHY DIDN'T YOU SAVE ME?
I'm sorry, Brash! But...I'm here to save you now!
This memory of Daryl isn't keeping you safe—it's keeping you AFRAID!
And if you don't face your fear you'll be locked in here FOREVER!
NO! I don't wanna! You're not my fwiend!
YES, I AM! It's DARYL who's not your friend!

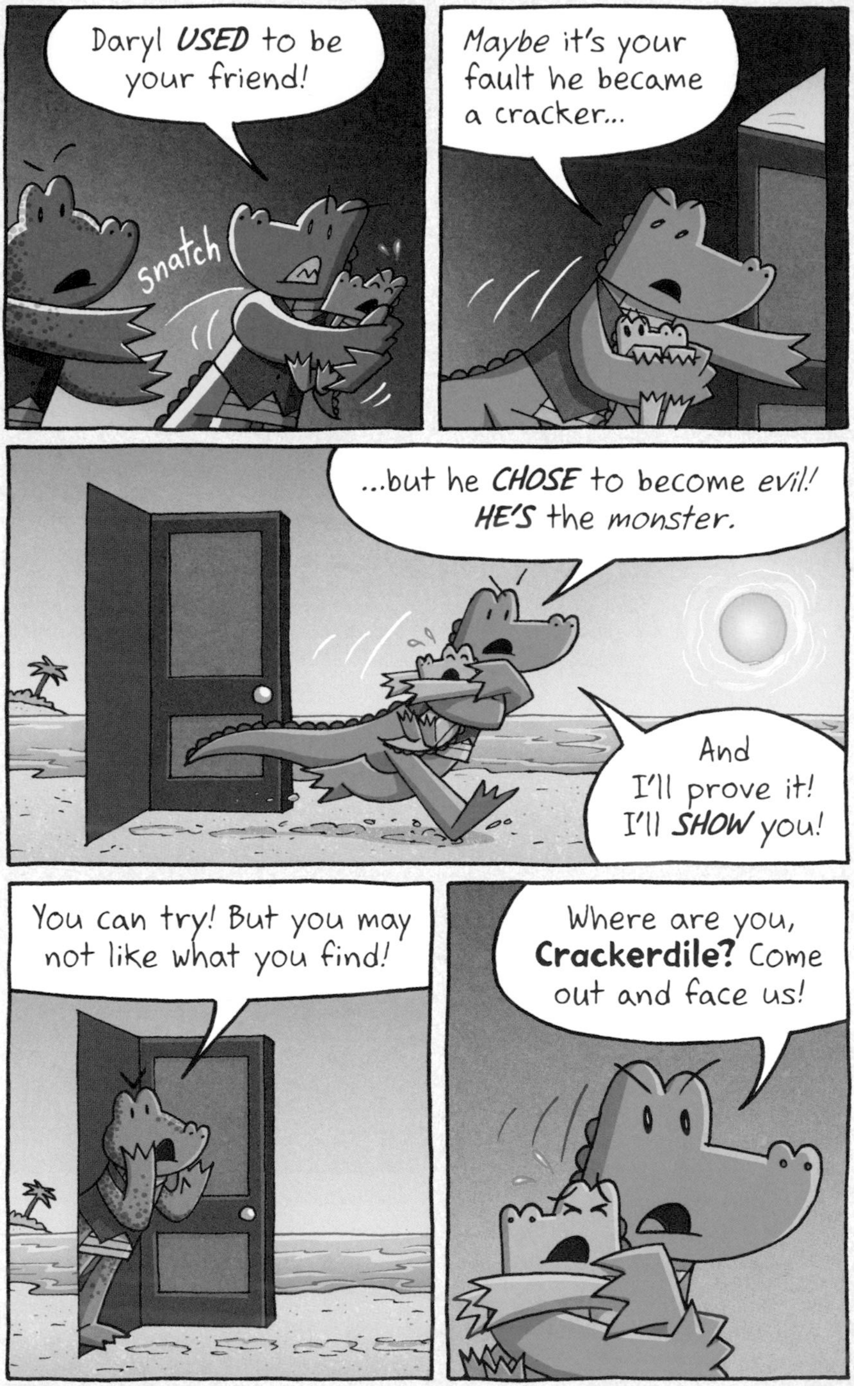
Daryl USED to be your friend!
Snatch
Maybe it's your fault he became a cracker...
...but he CHOSE to become evil! HE'S the monster.
And I'll prove it! I'll SHOW you!
You can try! But you may not like what you find!
Where are you, Crackerdile? Come out and face us!

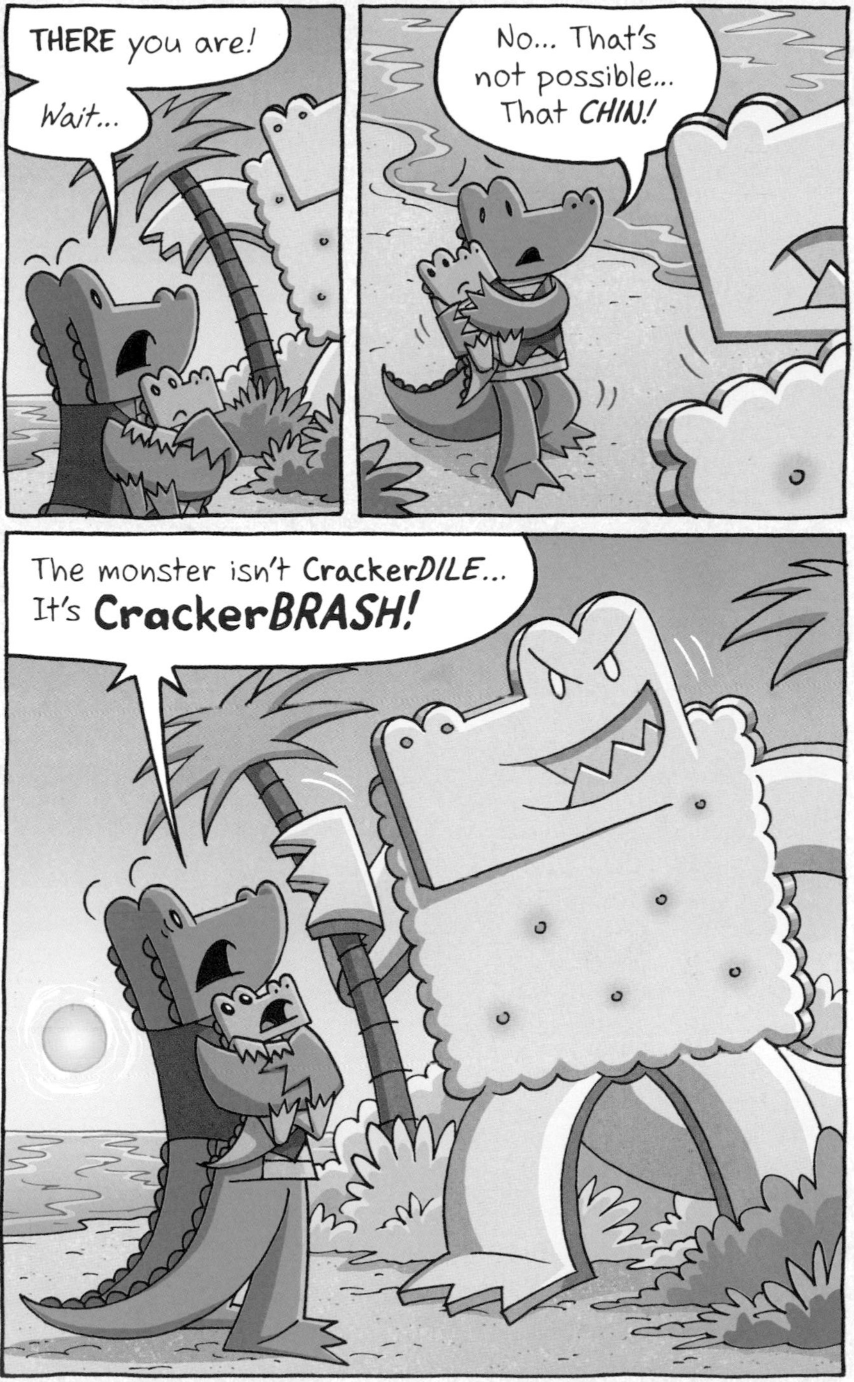
THERE you are!
Wait...
No... That's not possible... That CHIN!
The monster isn't CrackerDILE... It's CrackerBRASH!

# Chapter 10

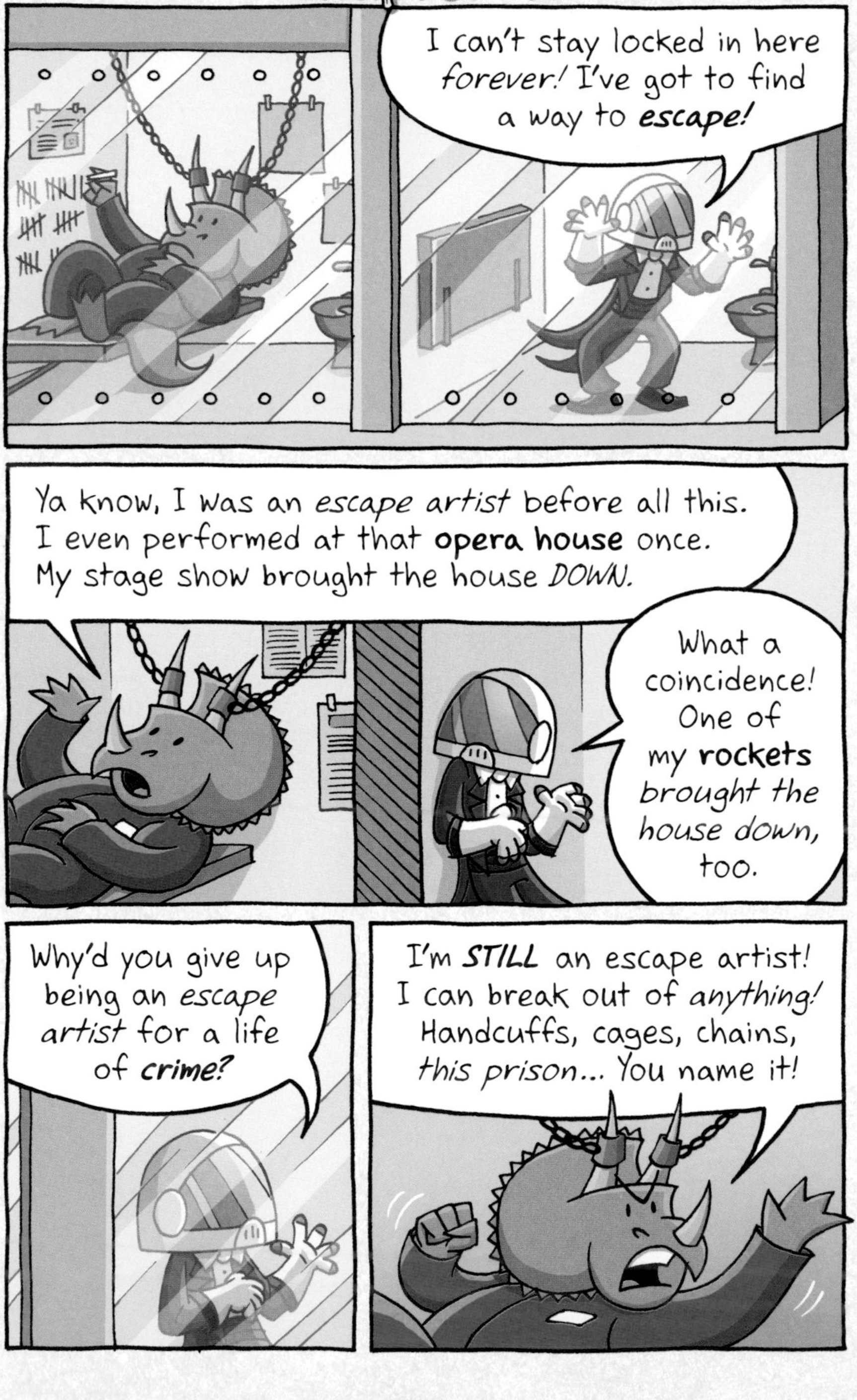

I can't stay locked in here *forever!* I've got to find a way to **escape!**
Ya know, I was an *escape artist* before all this. I even performed at that **opera house** once. My stage show brought the house *DOWN.*
What a coincidence! One of my **rockets** *brought the house down,* too.
Why'd you give up being an *escape artist* for a life of **crime?**
I'm ***STILL*** an escape artist! I can break out of *anything!* Handcuffs, cages, chains, *this prison*... You name it!

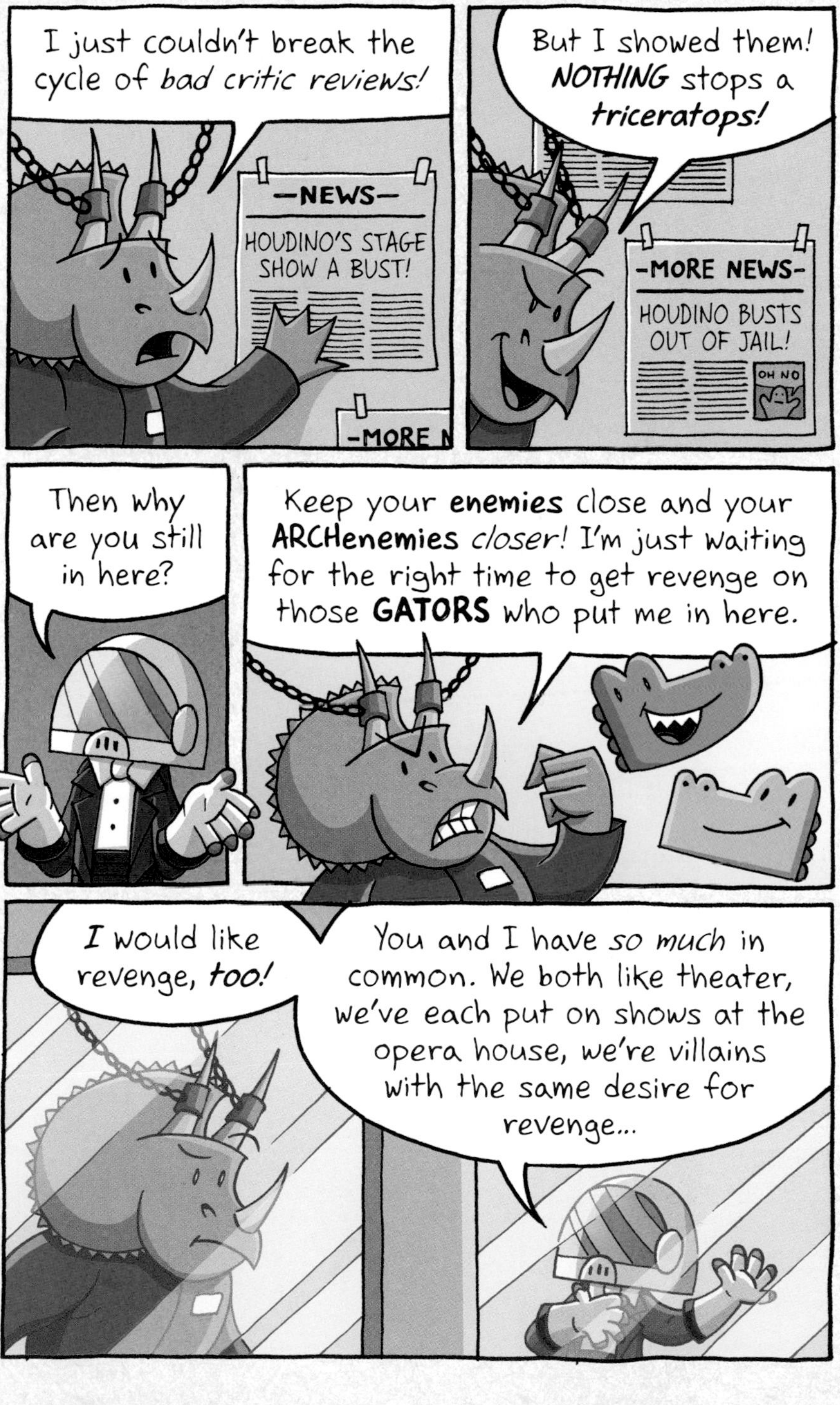
I just couldn't break the cycle of bad critic reviews!
—NEWS—
HOUDINO'S STAGE SHOW A BUST!
-MORE N
But I showed them! NOTHING stops a triceratops!
-MORE NEWS-
HOUDINO BUSTS OUT OF JAIL!
OH NO
Then why are you still in here?
Keep your enemies close and your ARCHenemies closer! I'm just waiting for the right time to get revenge on those GATORS who put me in here.
I would like revenge, too!
You and I have so much in common. We both like theater, we've each put on shows at the opera house, we're villains with the same desire for revenge...

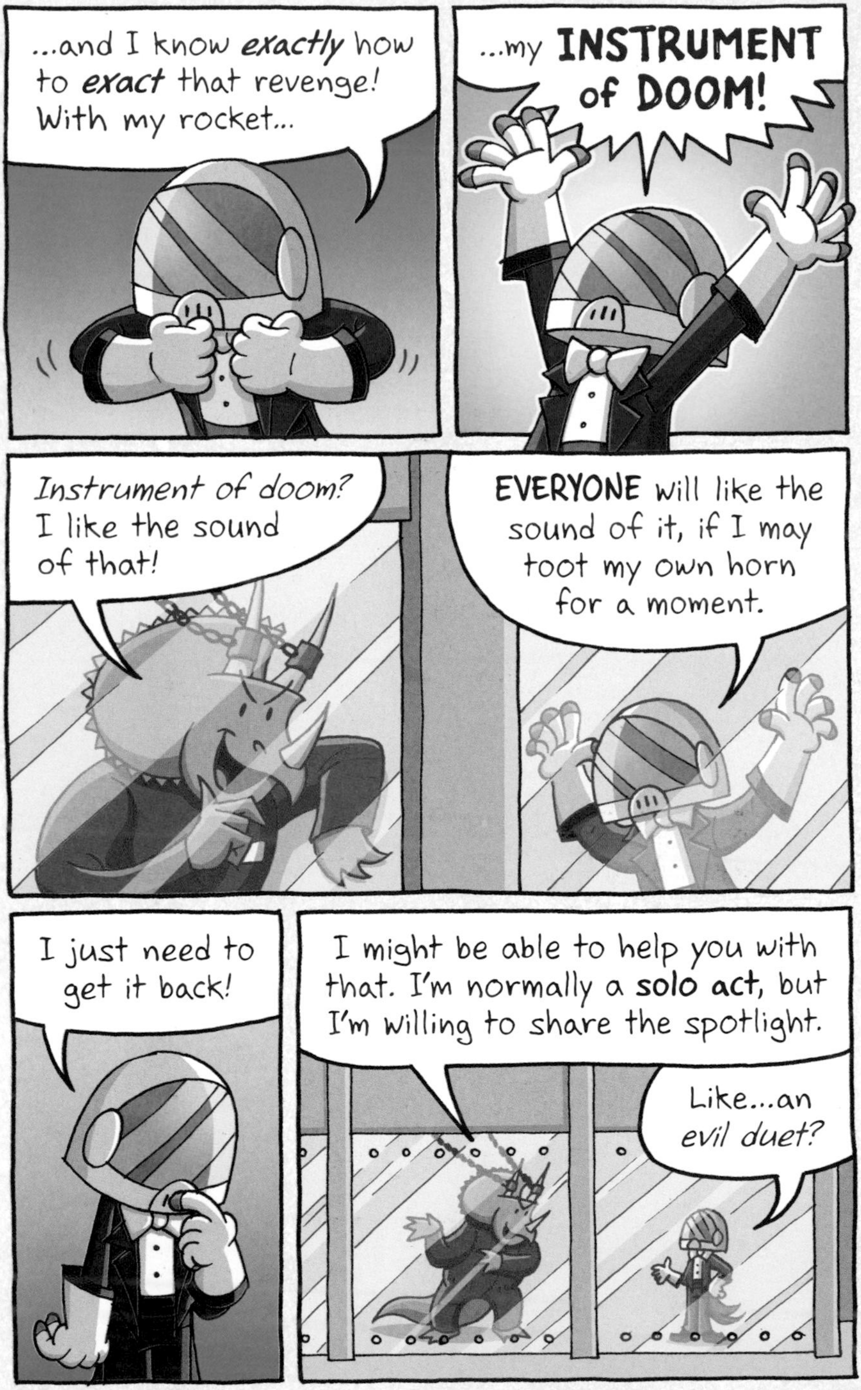
...and I know *exactly* how to *exact* that revenge! With my rocket...
...my **INSTRUMENT of DOOM!**
*Instrument of doom?* I like the sound of that!
**EVERYONE** will like the sound of it, if I may toot my own horn for a moment.
I just need to get it back!
I might be able to help you with that. I'm normally a **solo act**, but I'm willing to share the spotlight.
Like...an *evil duet?*

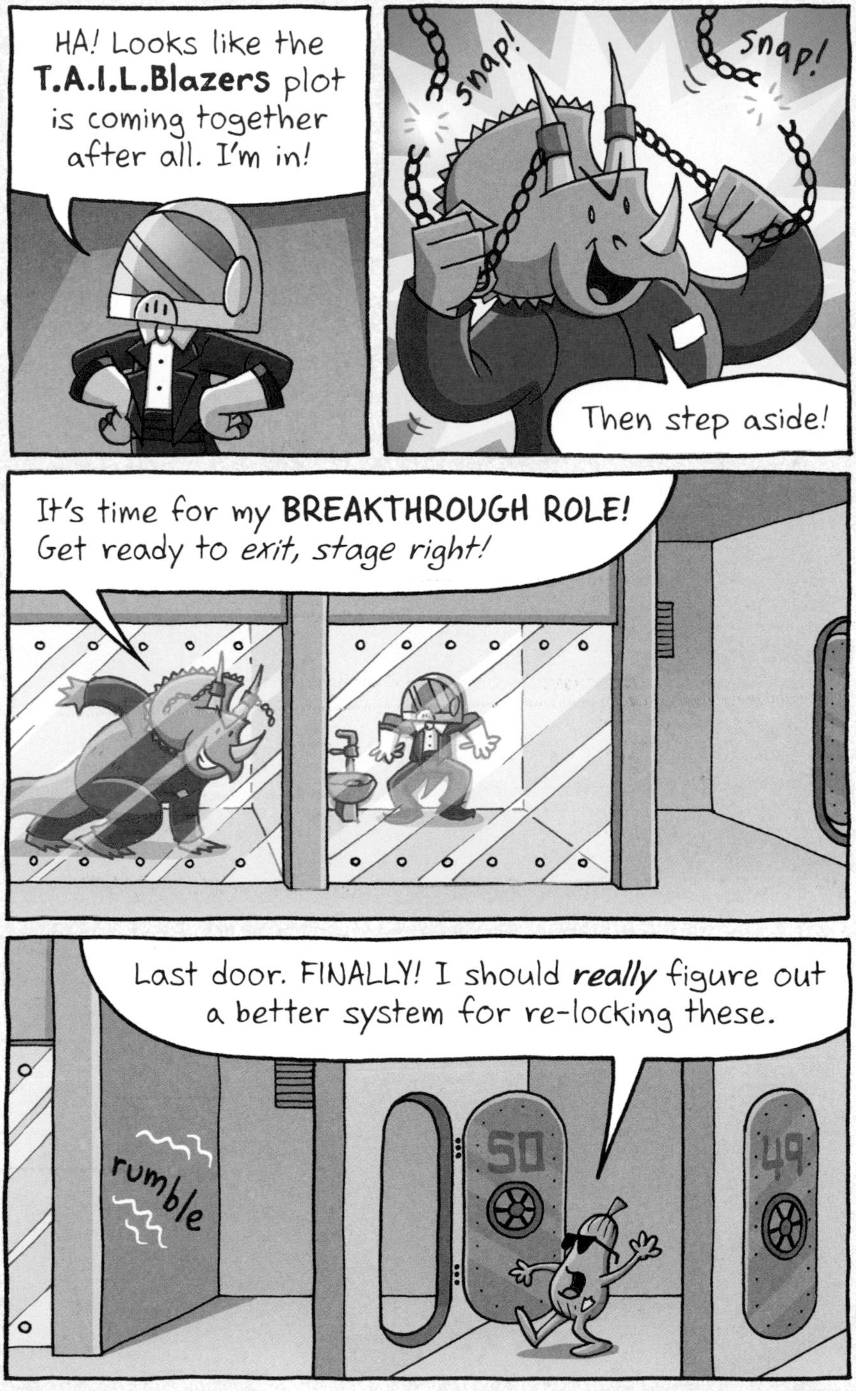
HA! Looks like the **T.A.I.L.Blazers** plot is coming together after all. I'm in!
Snap!
Snap!
Then step aside!
It's time for my **BREAKTHROUGH ROLE!** Get ready to *exit, stage right!*
Last door. FINALLY! I should ***really*** figure out a better system for re-locking these.
rumble
50
49

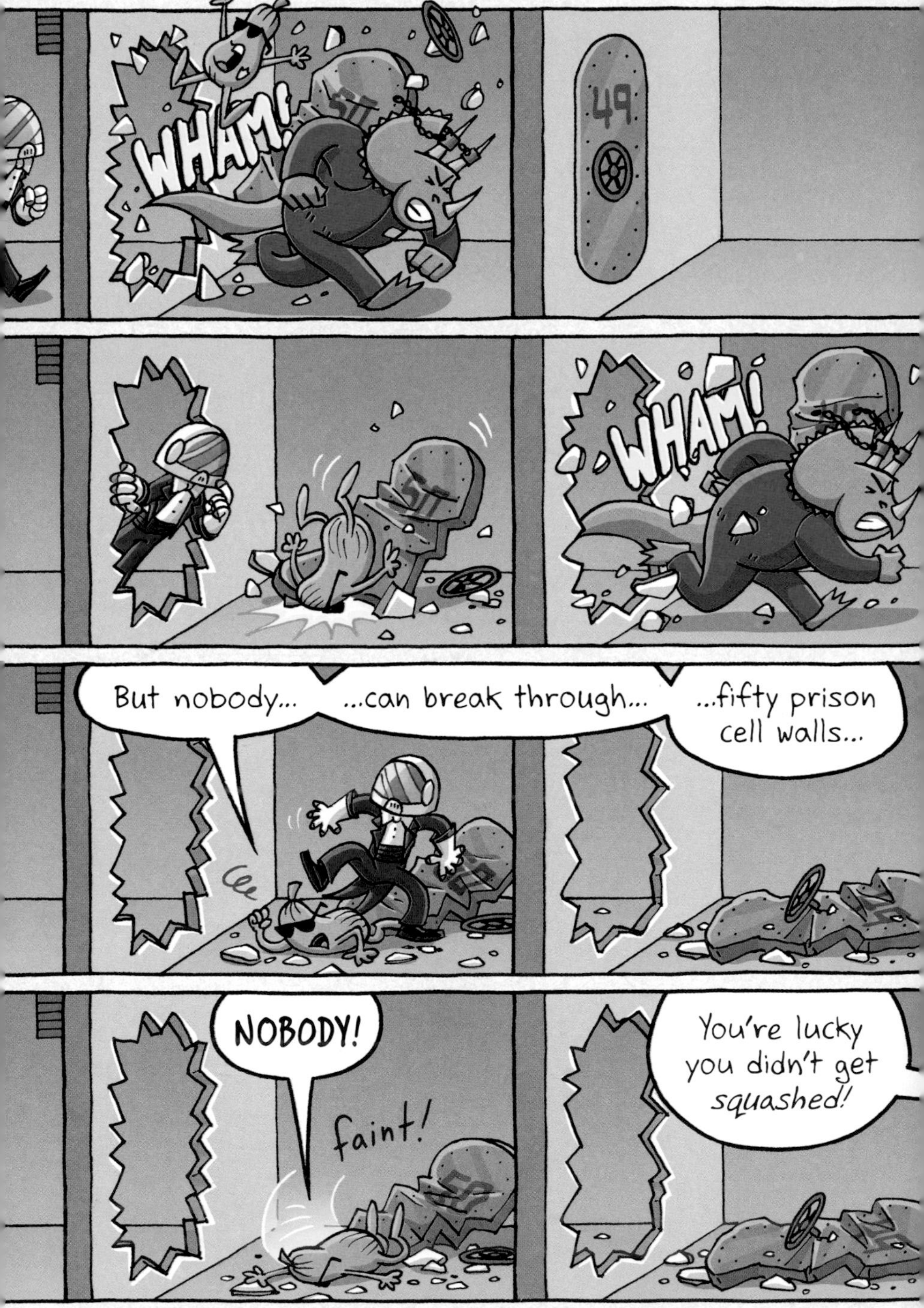
WHAM!
WHAM!
But nobody...
...can break through...
...fifty prison cell walls...
NOBODY!
faint!
You're lucky you didn't get *squashed*!

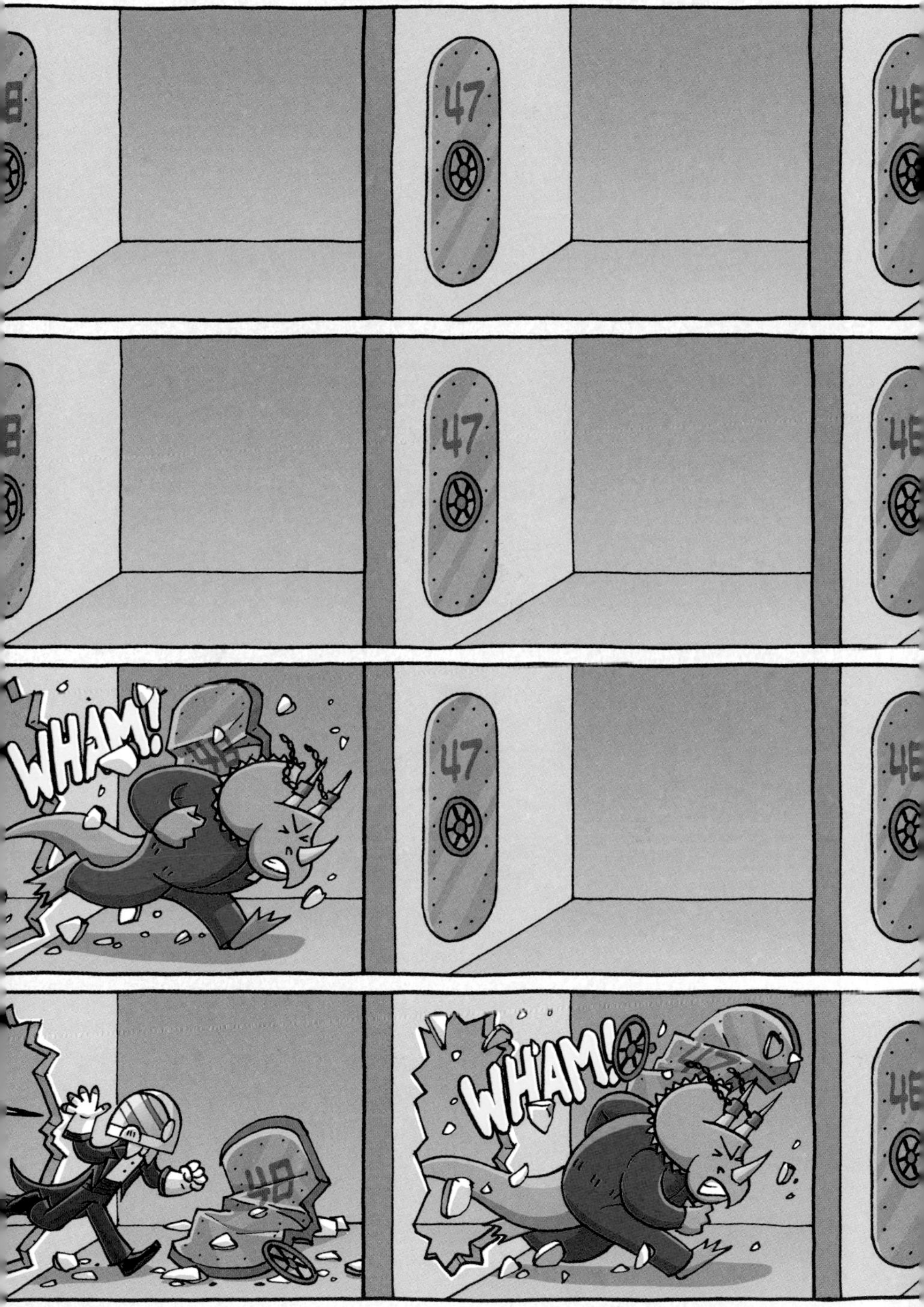

WHAM!
WHAM!

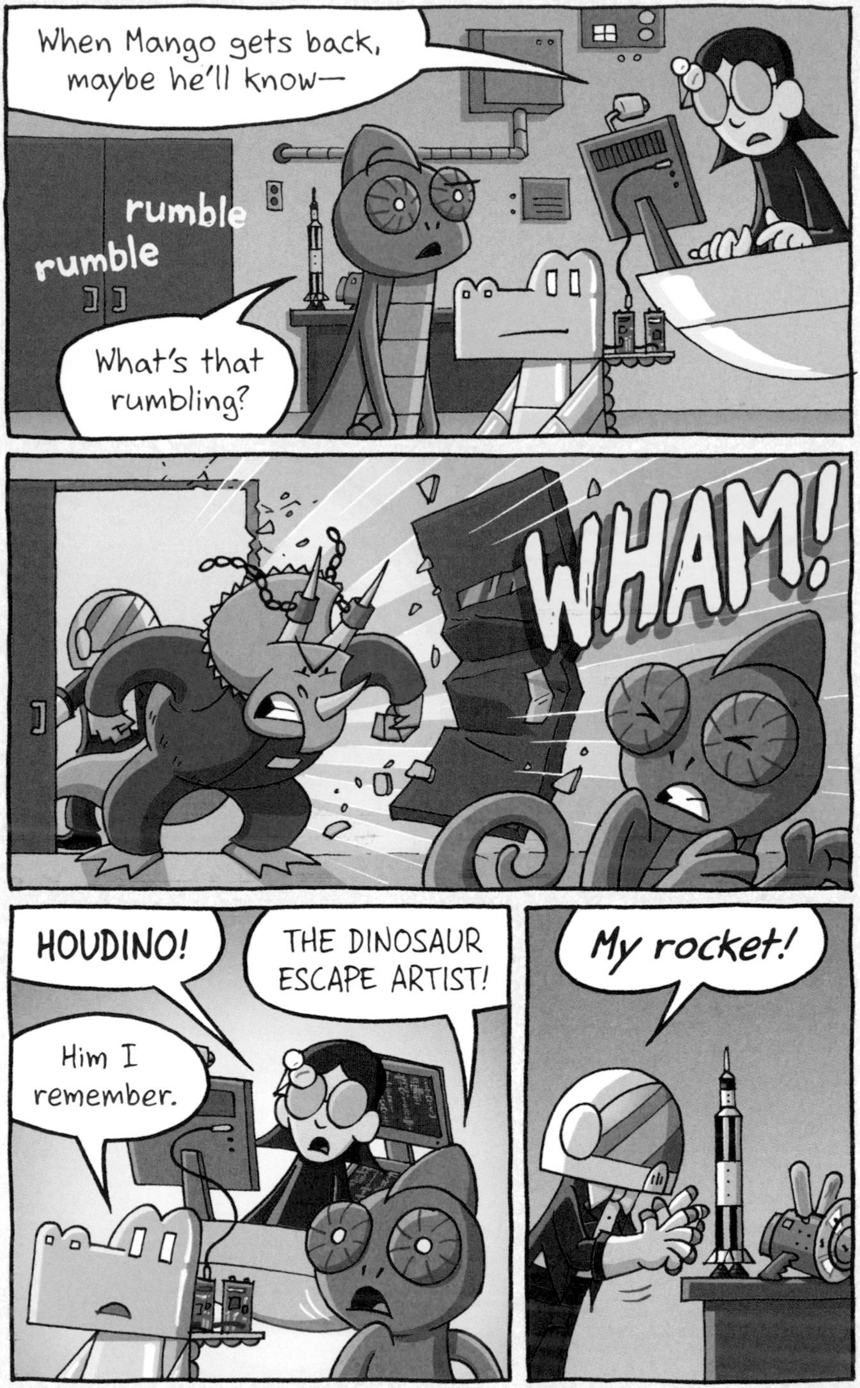
When Mango gets back, maybe he'll know—
rumble
rumble
What's that rumbling?
WHAM!
HOUDINO!
THE DINOSAUR ESCAPE ARTIST!
Him I remember.
My rocket!

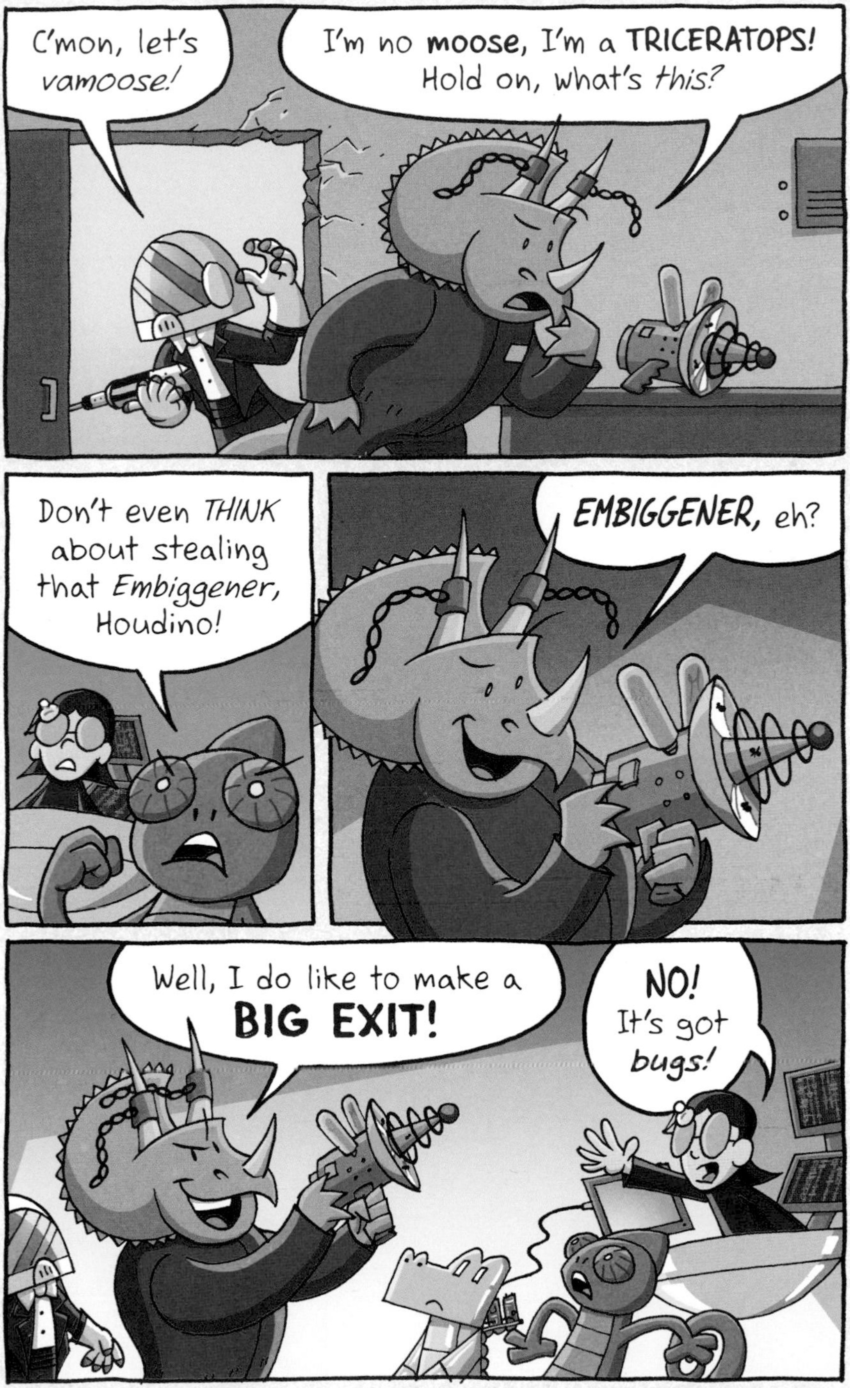
C'mon, let's *vamoose!*
I'm no **moose**, I'm a **TRICERATOPS!** Hold on, what's *this?*
Don't even *THINK* about stealing that *Embiggener,* Houdino!
**EMBIGGENER,** eh?
Well, I do like to make a **BIG EXIT!**
**NO!** It's got **bugs!**

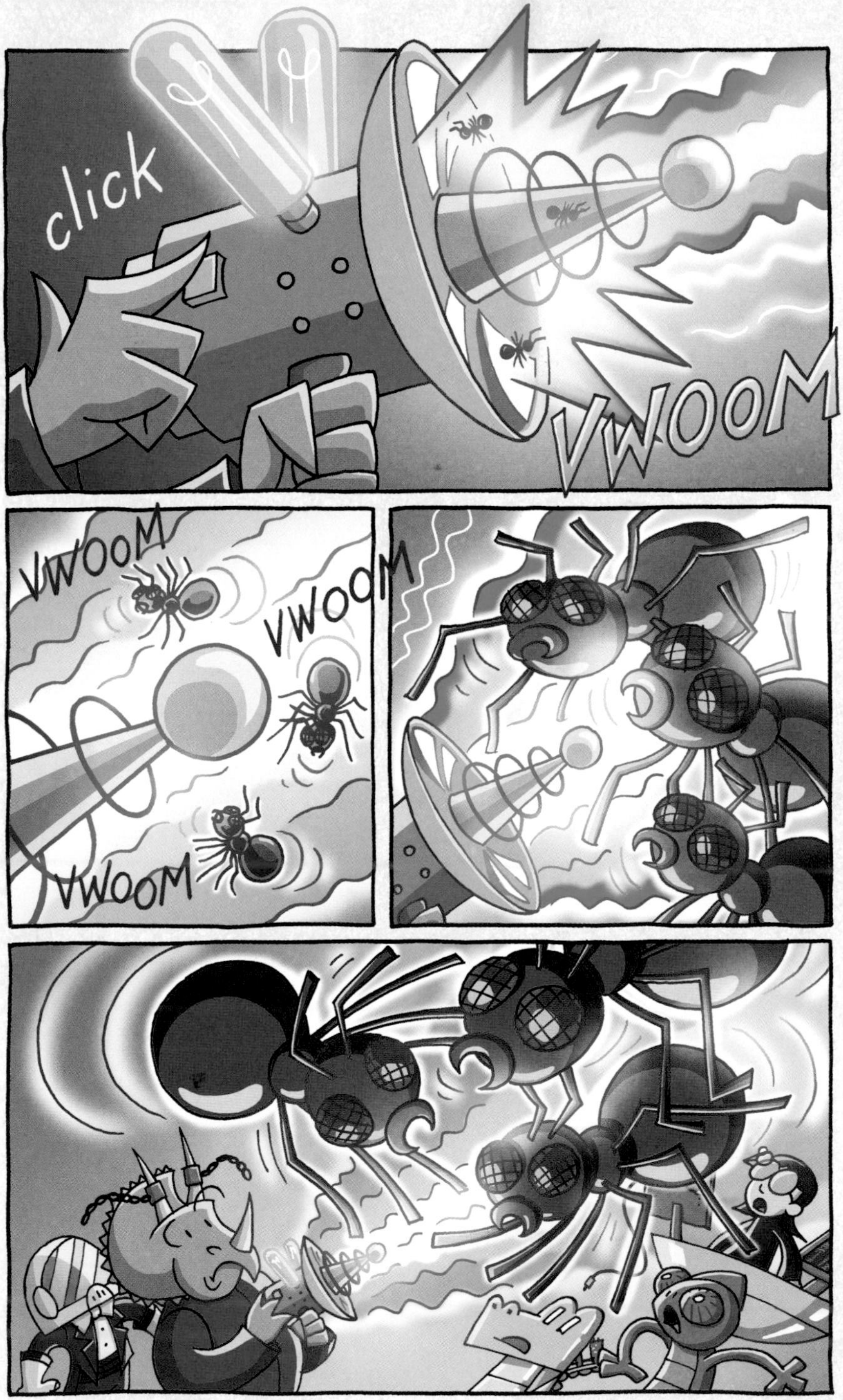
click
VWOOM
VWOOM
VWOOM
VWOOM

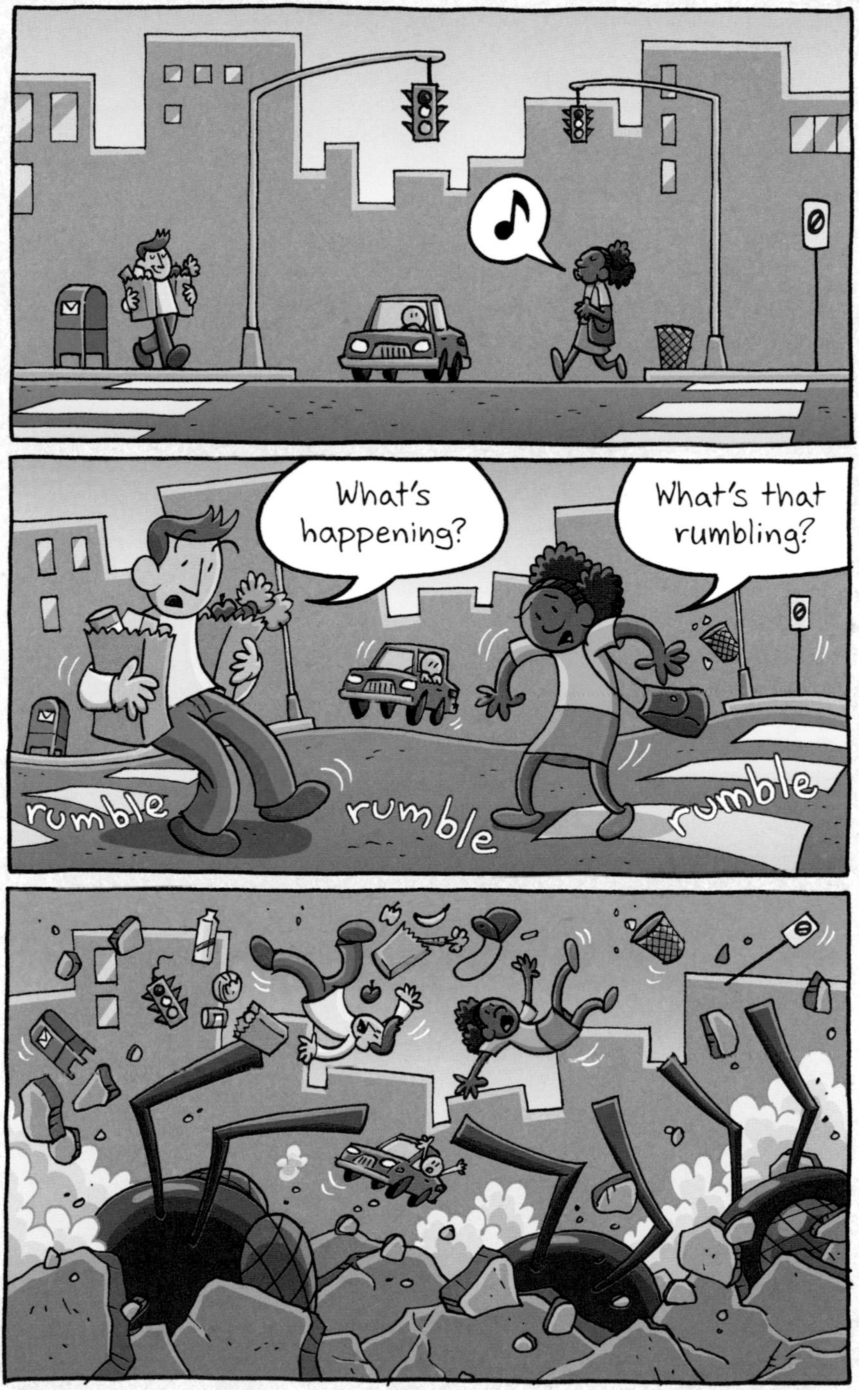
♪
What's happening?
What's that rumbling?
rumble
rumble
rumble

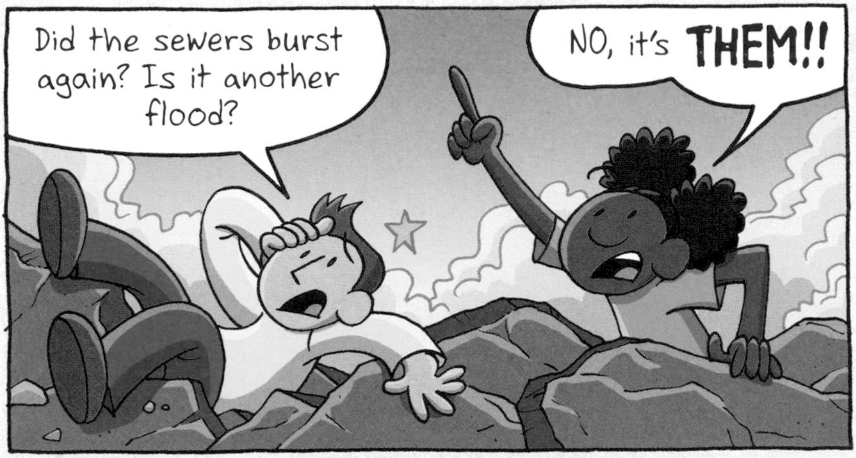
Did the sewers burst again? Is it another flood?
NO, it's THEM!!

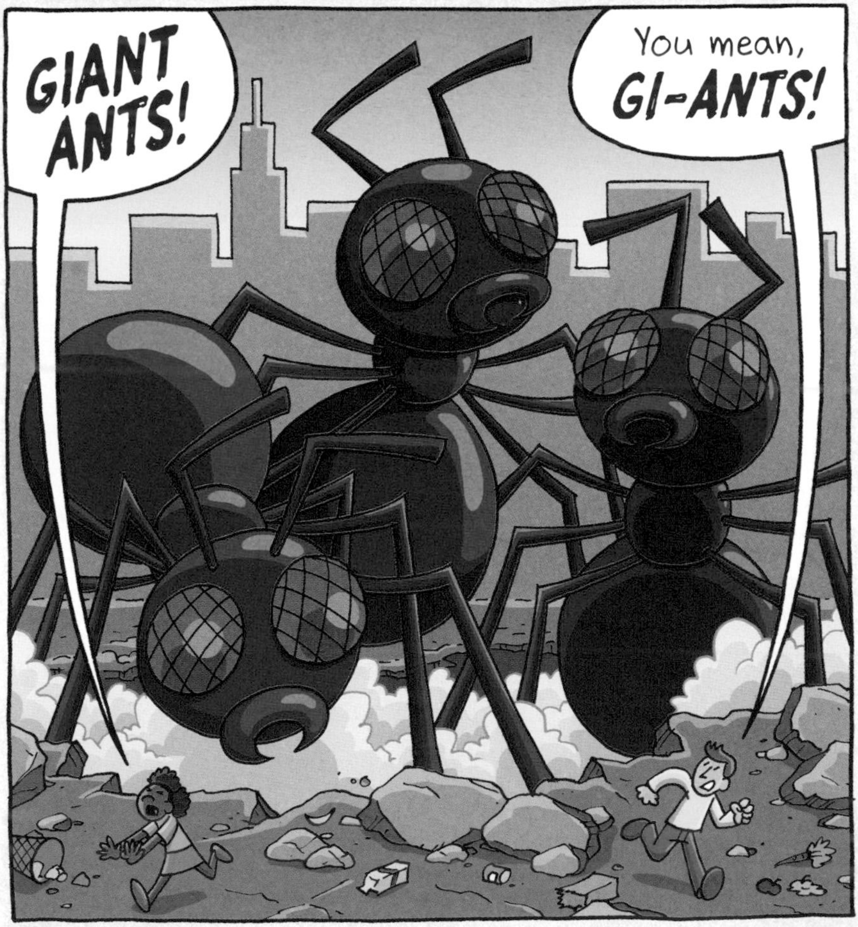
GIANT ANTS!
You mean, GI-ANTS!

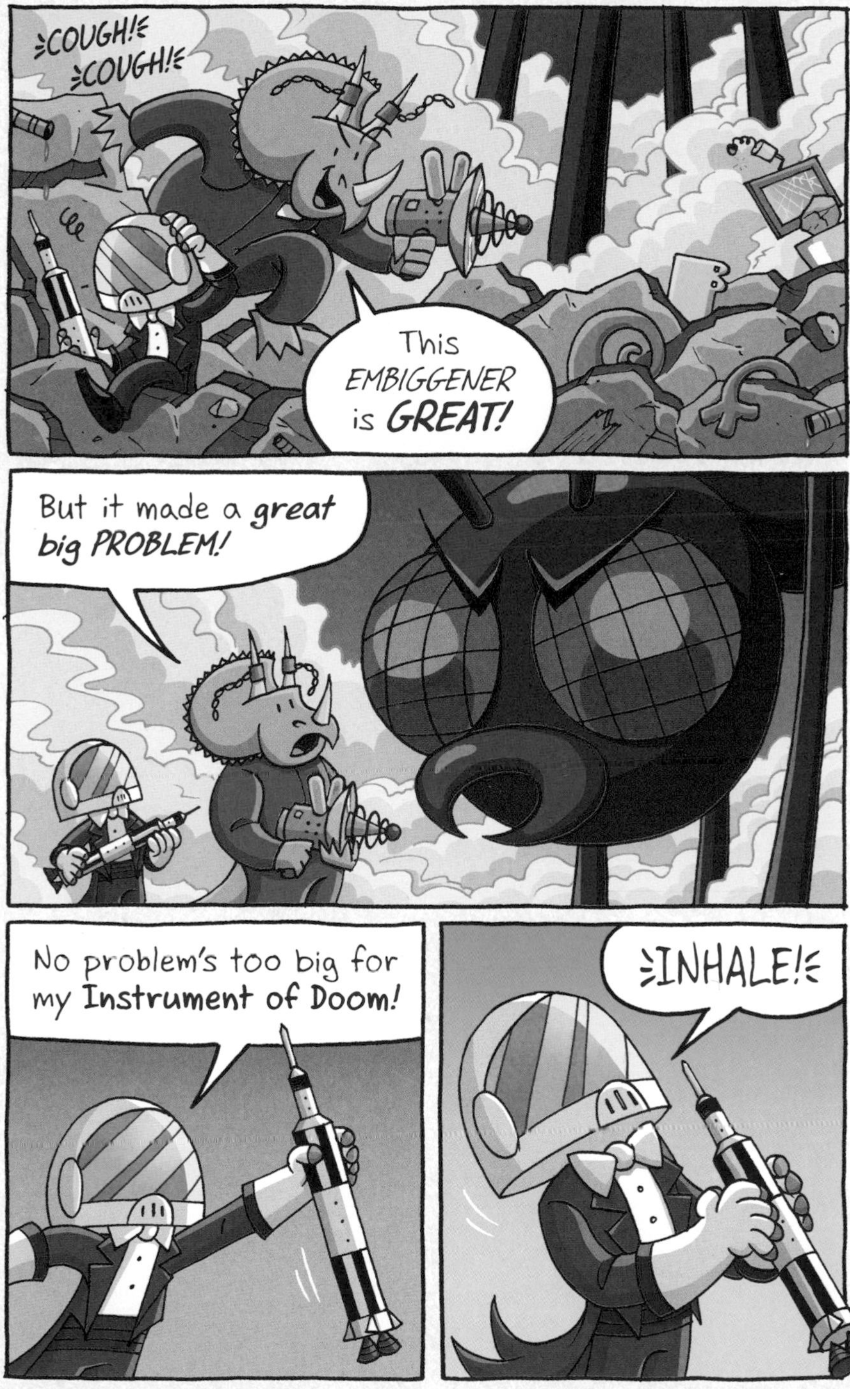

COUGH! COUGH!
This EMBIGGENER is GREAT!
But it made a great big PROBLEM!
No problem's too big for my Instrument of Doom!
INHALE!

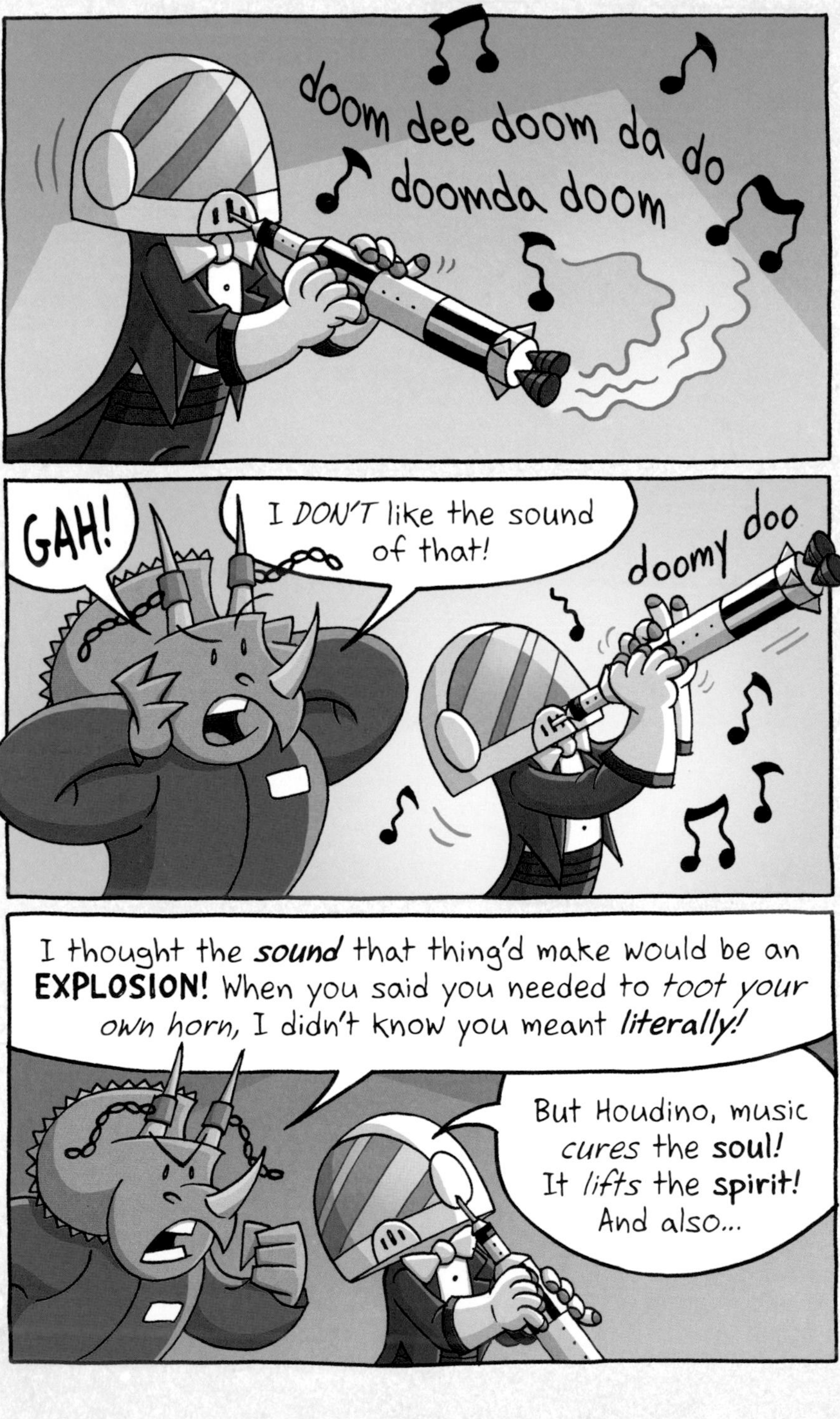
doom dee doom da do
doomda doom
GAH!
I *DON'T* like the sound of that!
doomy doo
I thought the ***sound*** that thing'd make would be an **EXPLOSION!** When you said you needed to *toot your own horn,* I didn't know you meant ***literally!***
But Houdino, music *cures* the **soul!** It *lifts* the **spirit!** And also...

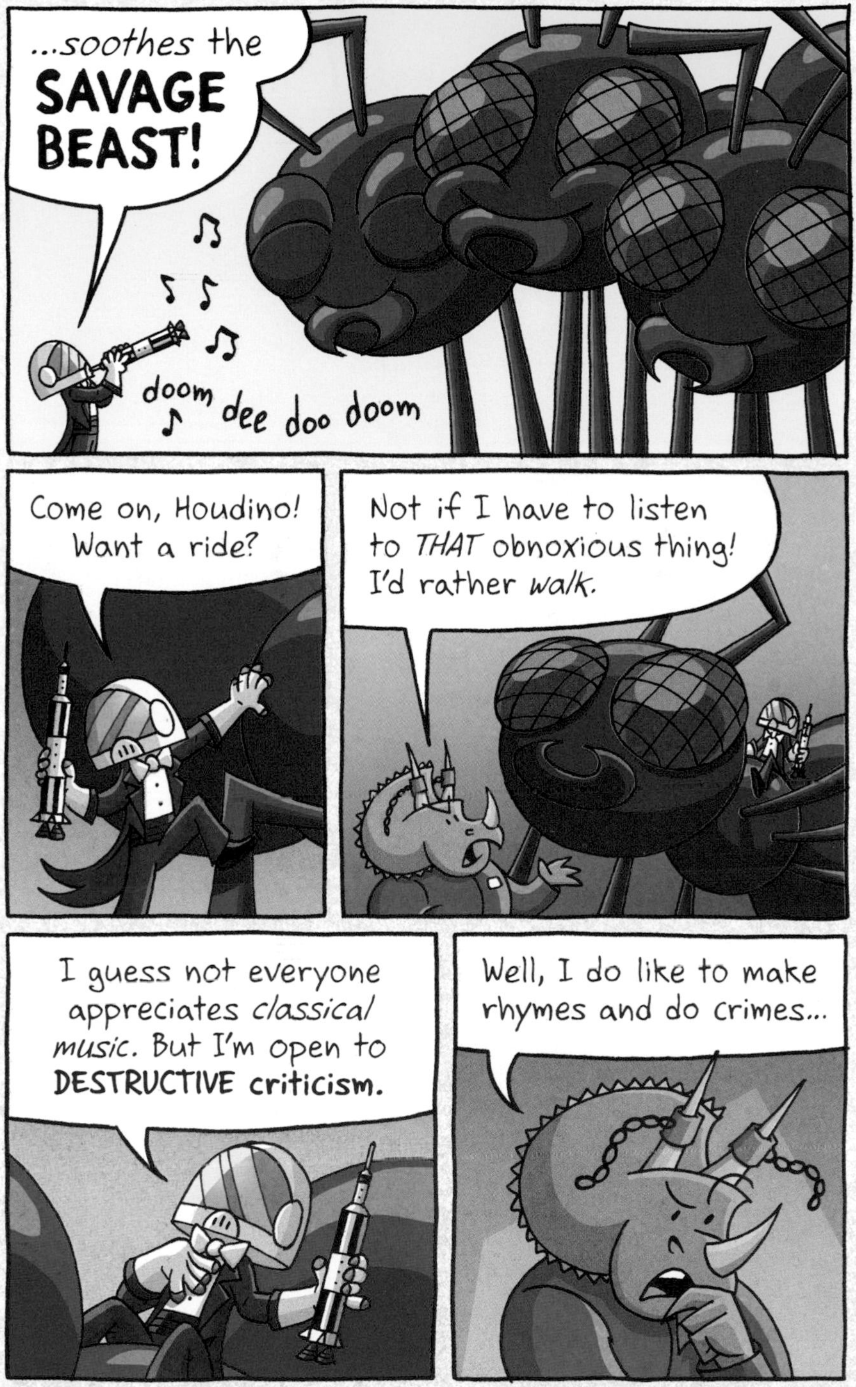
...soothes the SAVAGE BEAST!
doom dee doo doom
Come on, Houdino! Want a ride?
Not if I have to listen to *THAT* obnoxious thing! I'd rather *walk*.
I guess not everyone appreciates *classical music*. But I'm open to **DESTRUCTIVE** criticism.
Well, I do like to make rhymes and do crimes...

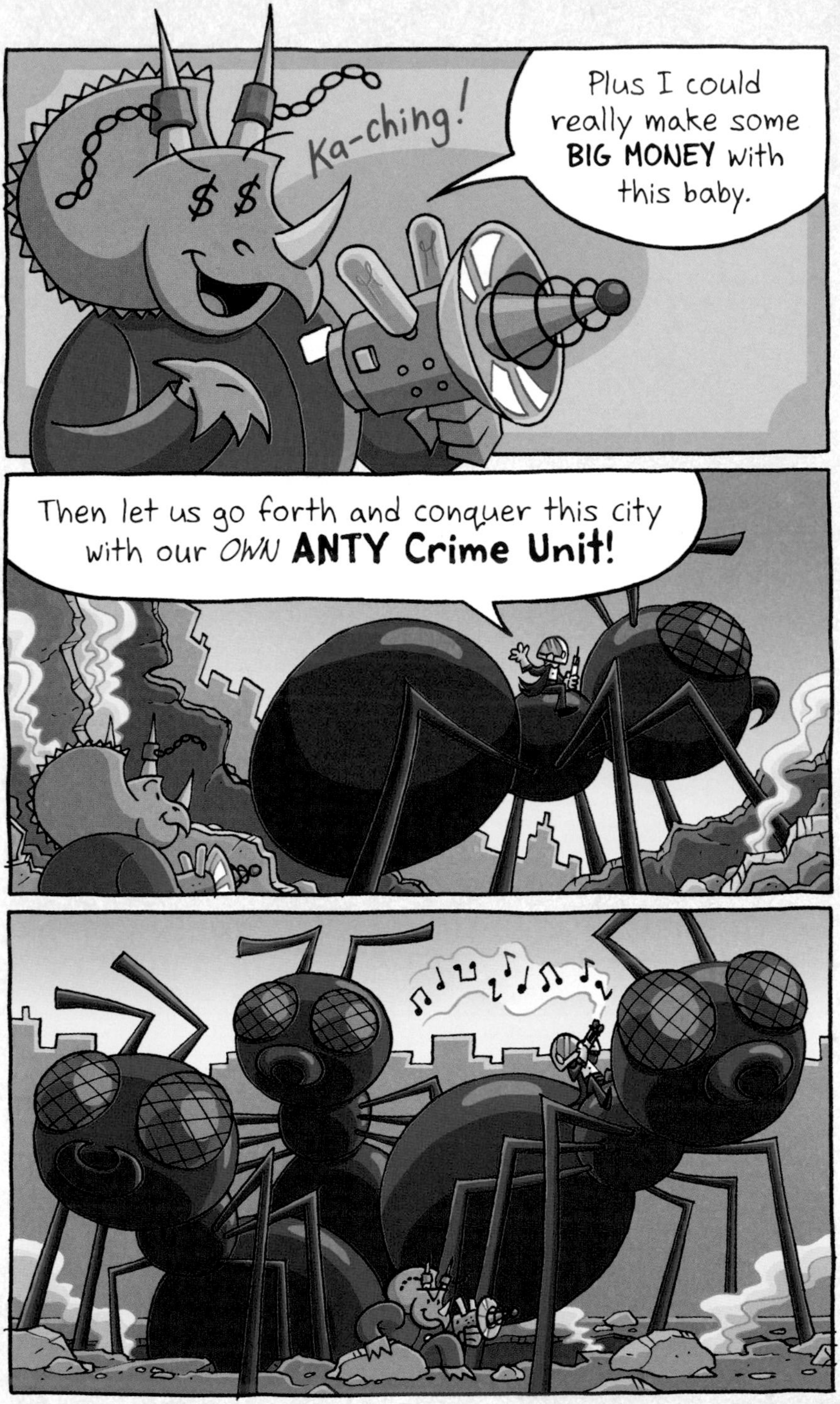
Ka-ching!
Plus I could really make some **BIG MONEY** with this baby.
Then let us go forth and conquer this city with our *OWN* **ANTY Crime Unit!**

# Chapter 11

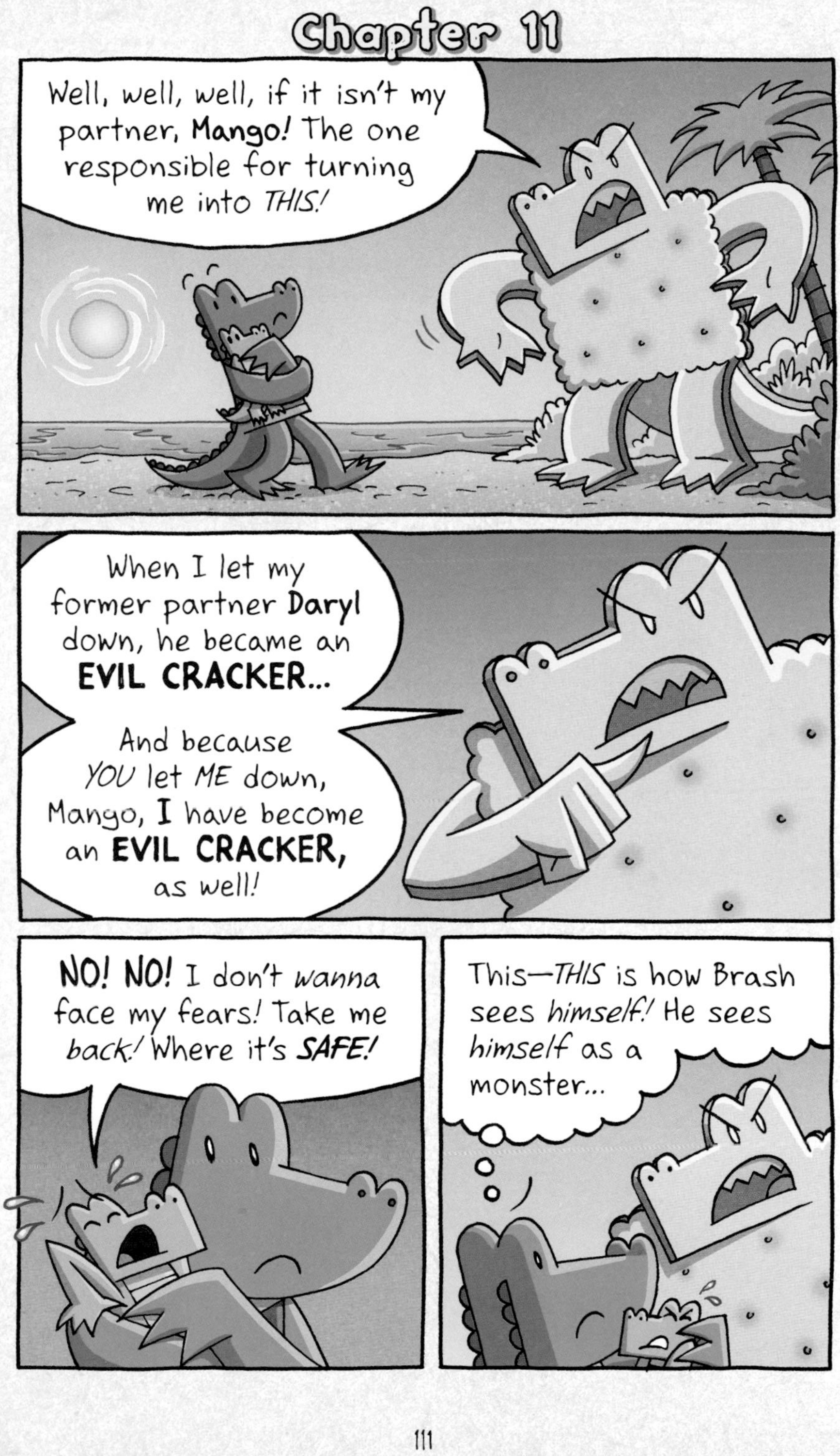
Well, well, well, if it isn't my partner, **Mango!** The one responsible for turning me into *THIS!*
When I let my former partner **Daryl** down, he became an **EVIL CRACKER...**
And because *YOU* let *ME* down, Mango, **I** have become an **EVIL CRACKER,** as well!
**NO! NO!** I don't *wanna* face my fears! Take me *back!* Where it's ***SAFE!***
This—*THIS* is how Brash sees *himself!* He sees *himself* as a monster...

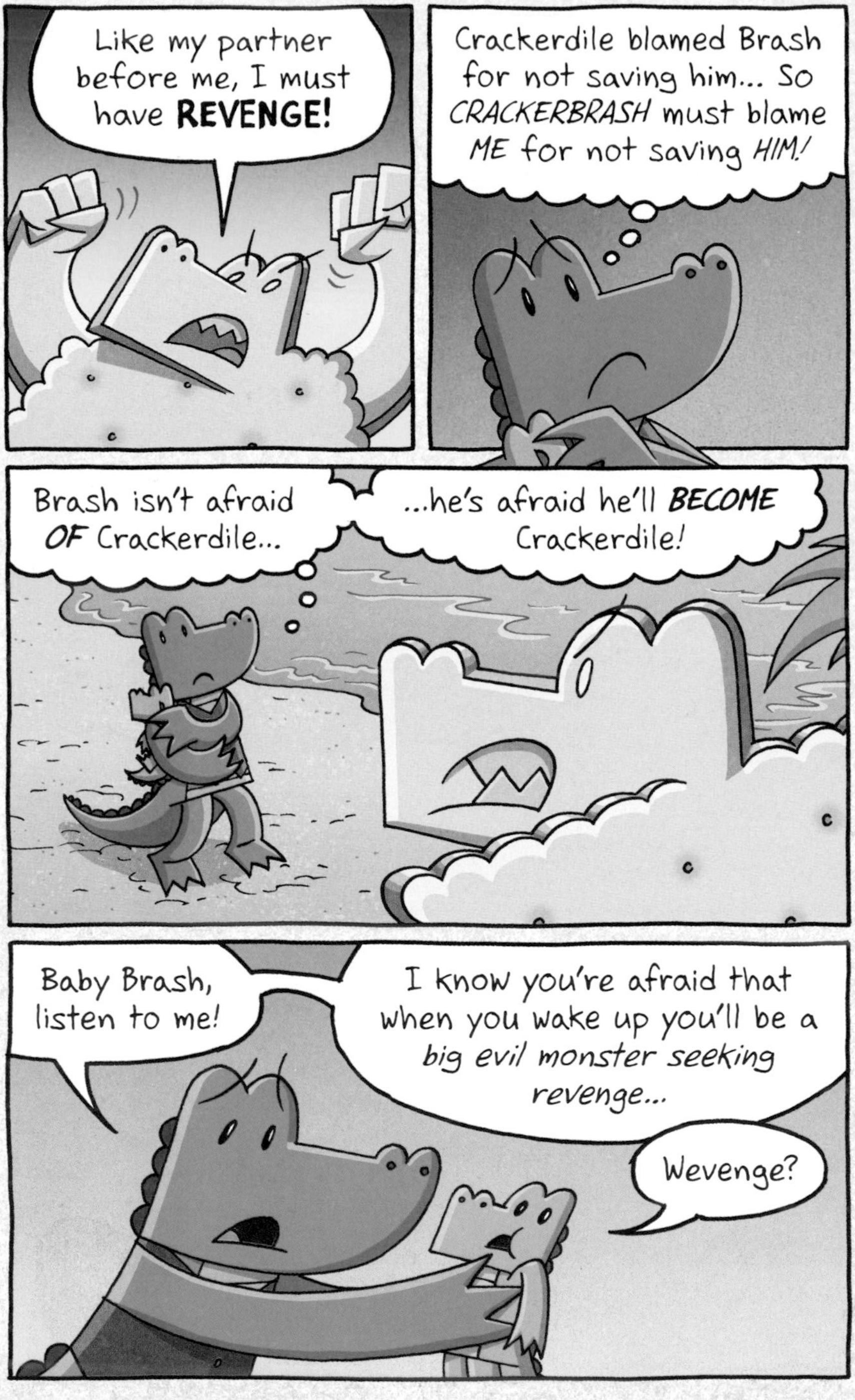

Like my partner before me, I must have **REVENGE!**
Crackerdile blamed Brash for not saving him... So *CRACKERBRASH* must blame *ME* for not saving *HIM!*
Brash isn't afraid *OF* Crackerdile...
...he's afraid he'll ***BECOME*** Crackerdile!
Baby Brash, listen to me!
I know you're afraid that when you wake up you'll be a *big evil monster seeking revenge...*
Wevenge?

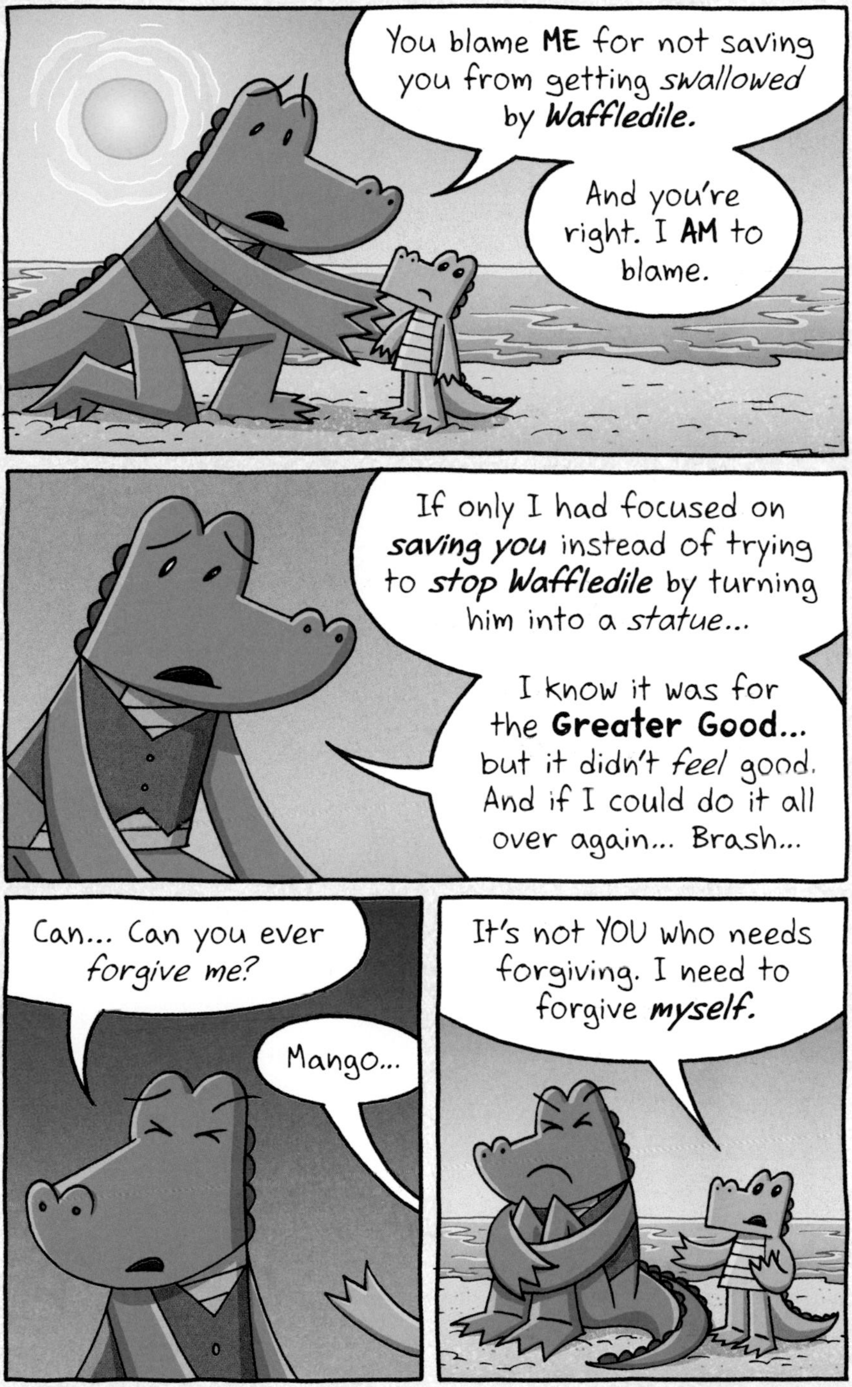
You blame **ME** for not saving you from getting *swallowed* by ***Waffledile.***
And you're right. I **AM** to blame.
If only I had focused on ***saving you*** instead of trying to ***stop Waffledile*** by turning him into a *statue*...
I know it was for the **Greater Good...** but it didn't *feel* good. And if I could do it all over again... Brash...
Can... Can you ever *forgive me?*
Mango...
It's not YOU who needs forgiving. I need to forgive ***myself.***

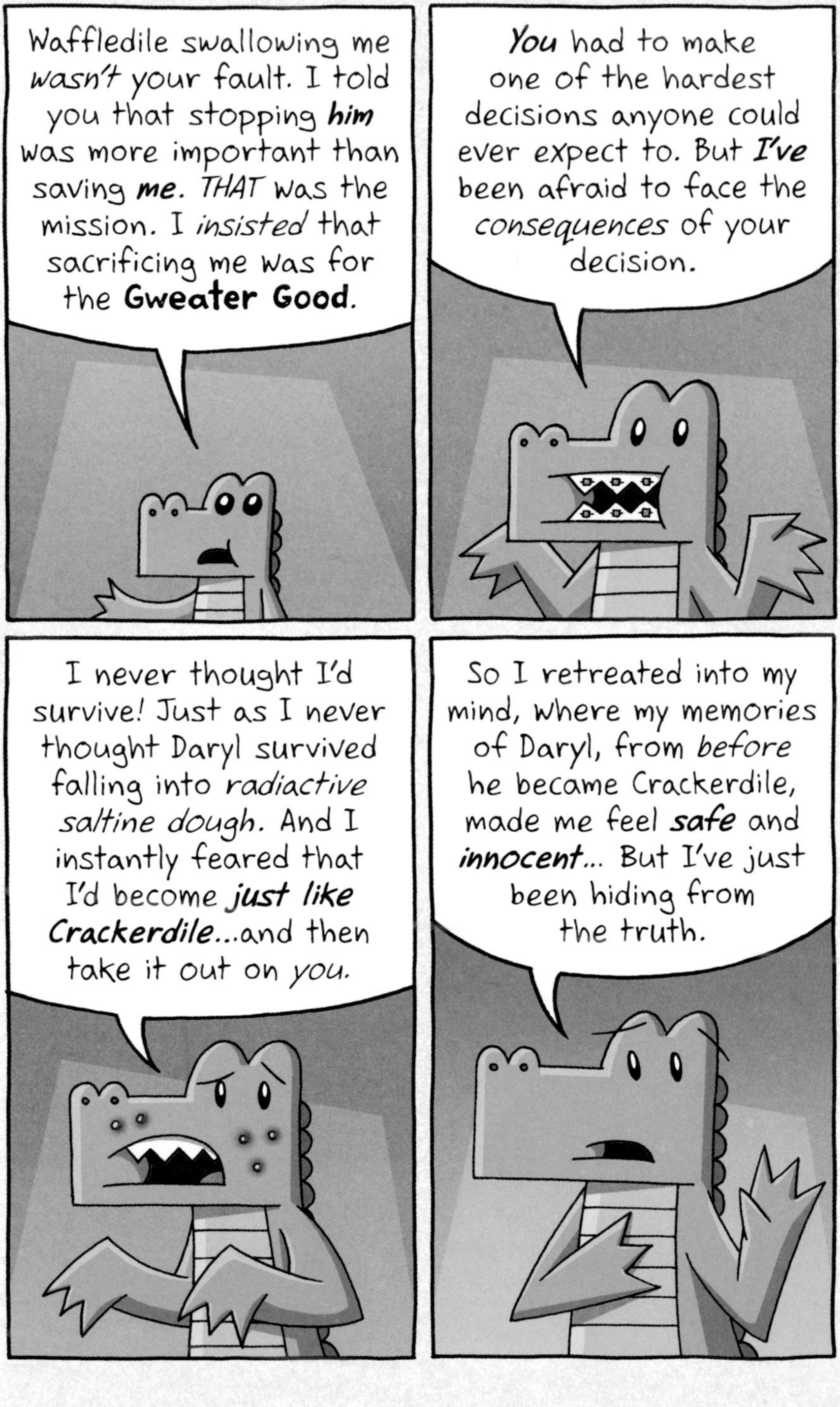
Waffledile swallowing me wasn't your fault. I told you that stopping him was more important than saving me. THAT was the mission. I insisted that sacrificing me was for the Gweater Good.
You had to make one of the hardest decisions anyone could ever expect to. But I've been afraid to face the consequences of your decision.
I never thought I'd survive! Just as I never thought Daryl survived falling into radiactive saltine dough. And I instantly feared that I'd become just like Crackerdile...and then take it out on you.
So I retreated into my mind, where my memories of Daryl, from before he became Crackerdile, made me feel safe and innocent... But I've just been hiding from the truth.

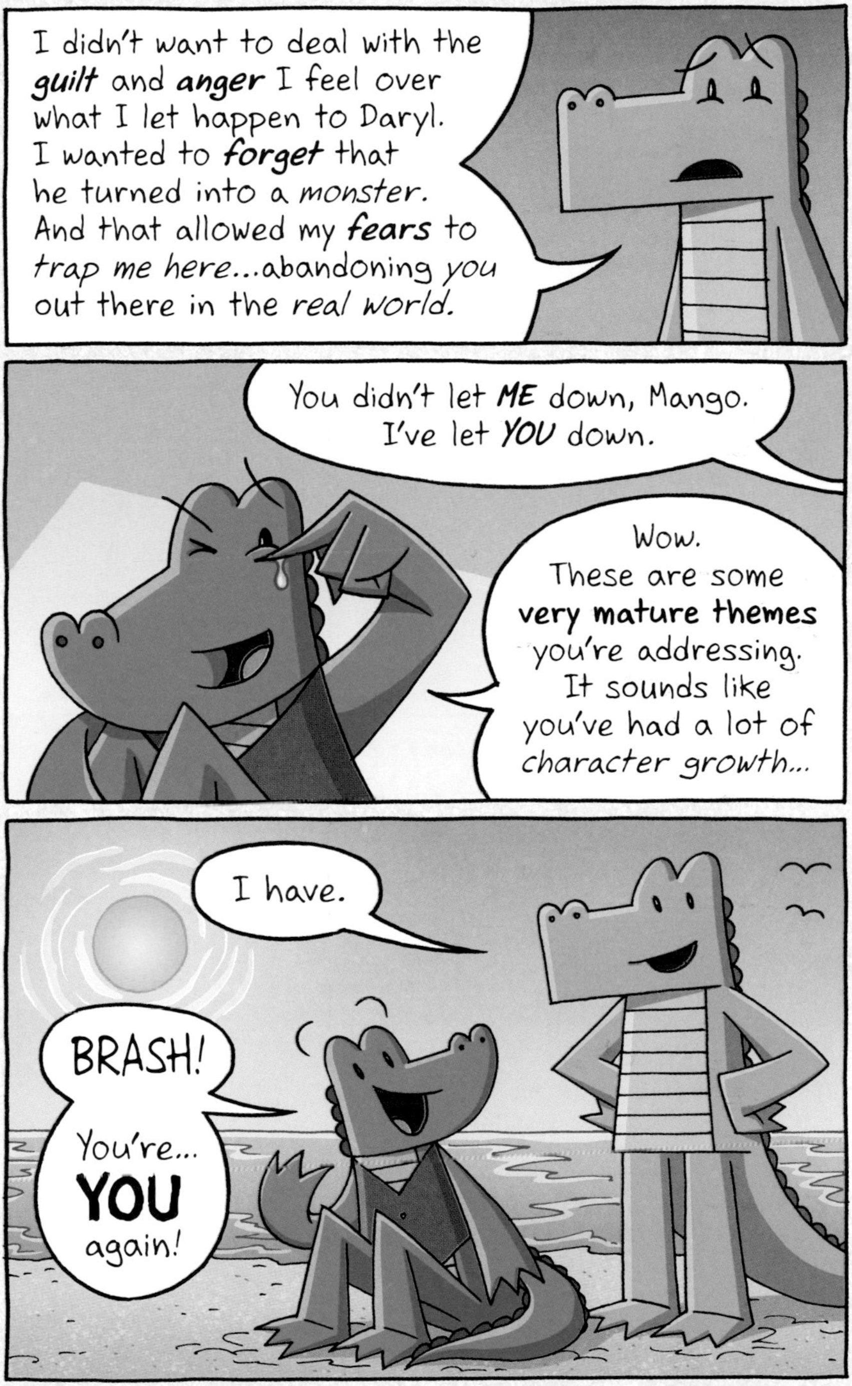
I didn't want to deal with the guilt and anger I feel over what I let happen to Daryl. I wanted to forget that he turned into a monster. And that allowed my fears to trap me here...abandoning you out there in the real world.
You didn't let ME down, Mango. I've let YOU down.
Wow. These are some very mature themes you're addressing. It sounds like you've had a lot of character growth...
I have.
BRASH!
You're... YOU again!

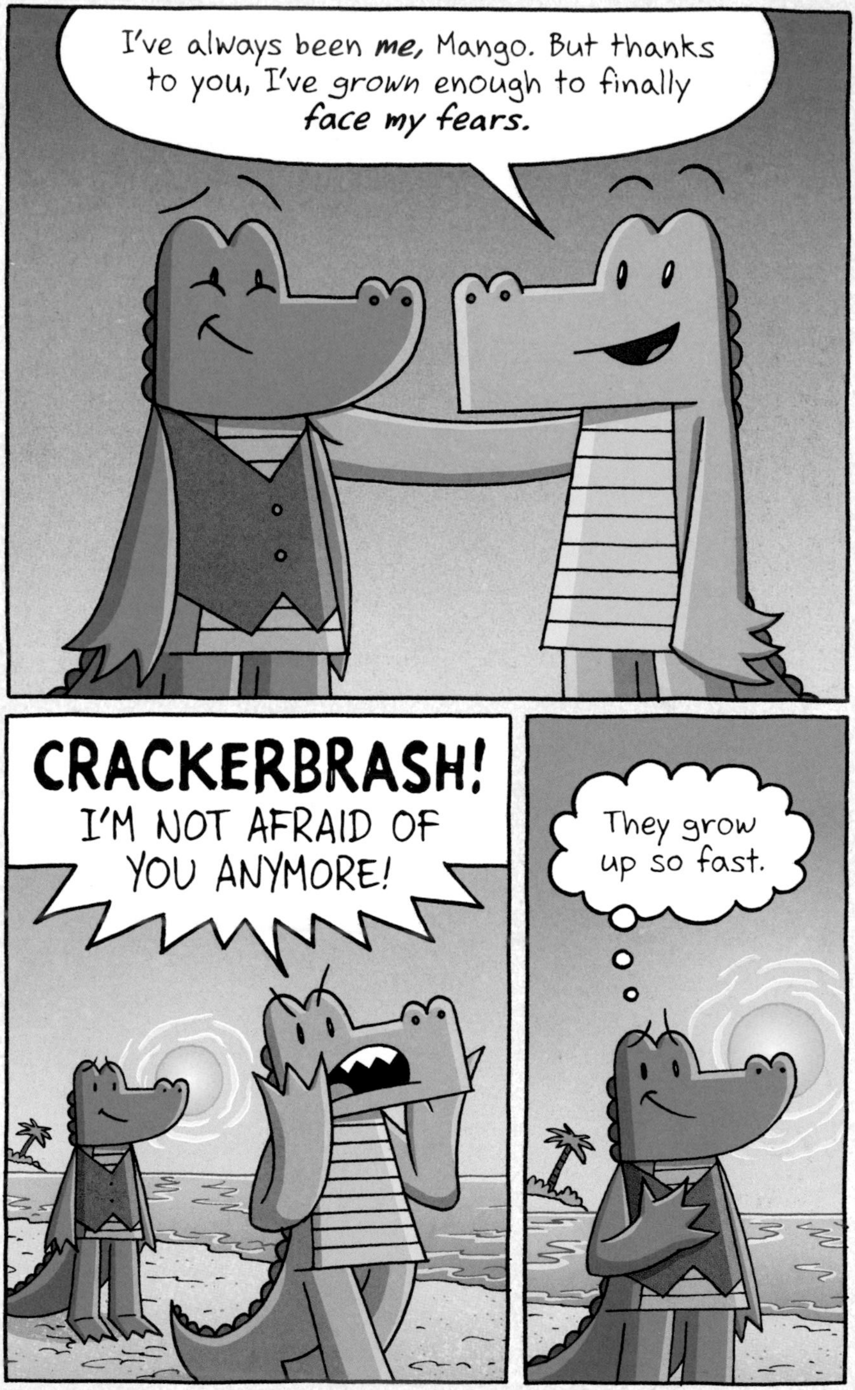
I've always been **me,** Mango. But thanks to you, I've grown enough to finally **face my fears.**
CRACKERBRASH! I'M NOT AFRAID OF YOU ANYMORE!
They grow up so fast.

# Chapter 12

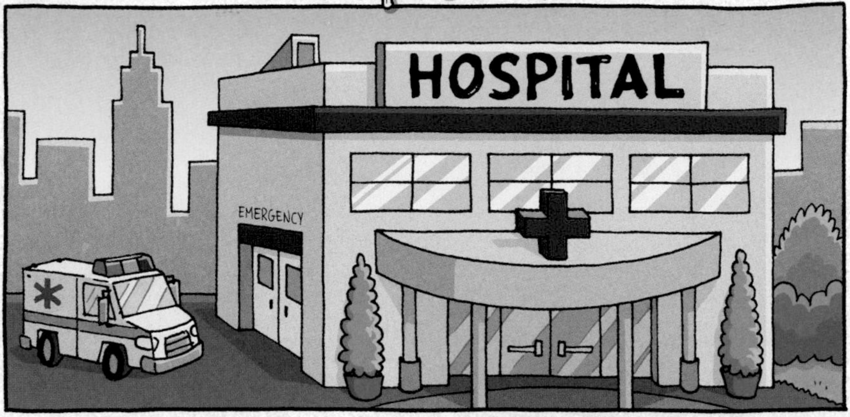
HOSPITAL
EMERGENCY

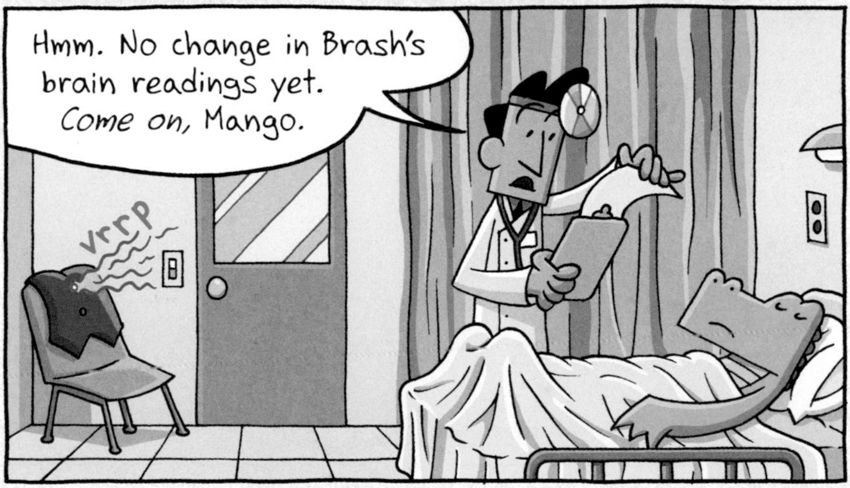
Hmm. No change in Brash's brain readings yet. Come on, Mango.
vrrp

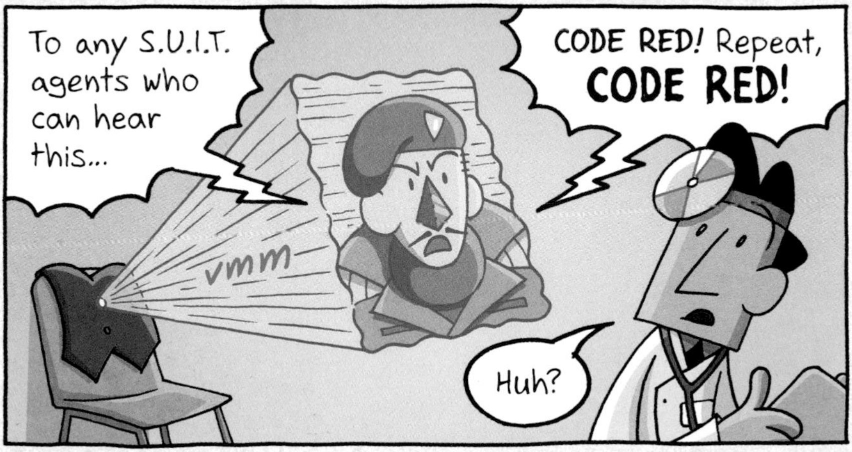
To any S.U.I.T. agents who can hear this...
CODE RED! Repeat, CODE RED!
vmm
Huh?

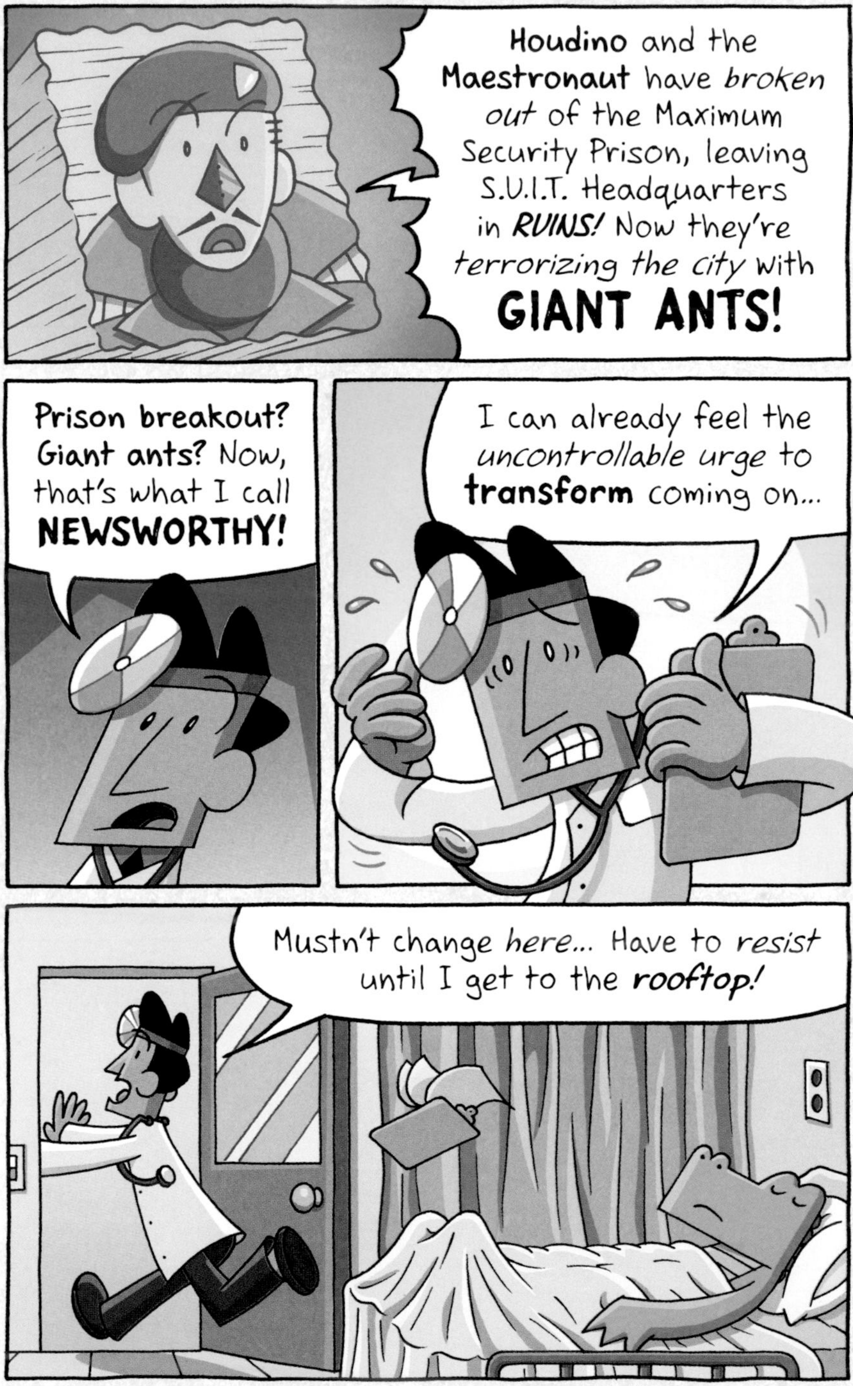
Houdino and the Maestronaut have broken out of the Maximum Security Prison, leaving S.U.I.T. Headquarters in RUINS! Now they're terrorizing the city with GIANT ANTS!
Prison breakout? Giant ants? Now, that's what I call NEWSWORTHY!
I can already feel the uncontrollable urge to transform coming on...
Mustn't change here... Have to resist until I get to the rooftop!

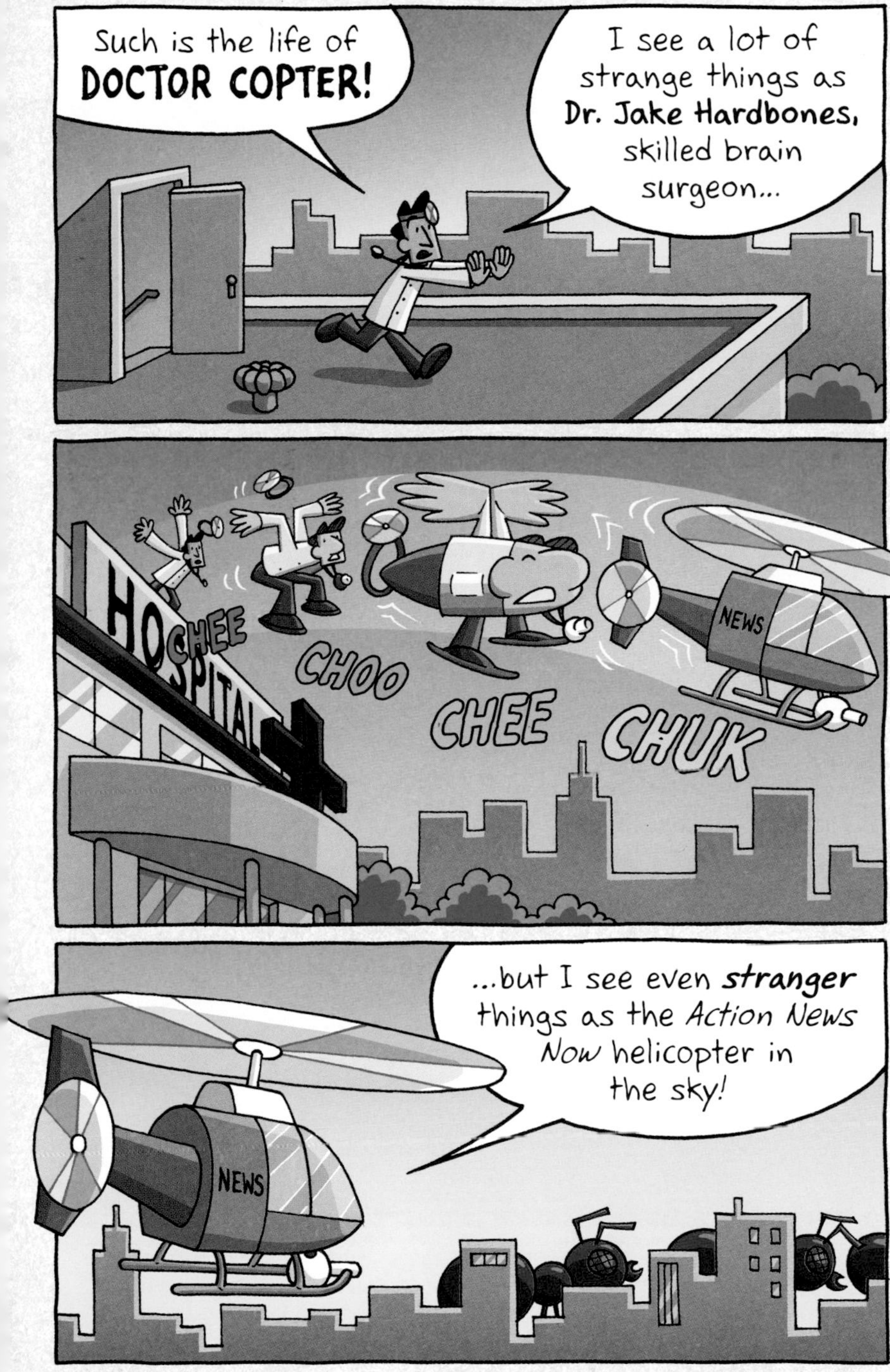
Such is the life of **DOCTOR COPTER!**
I see a lot of strange things as **Dr. Jake Hardbones,** skilled brain surgeon...
HOSPITAL
CHEE
CHOO
CHEE
CHUK
NEWS
...but I see even ***stranger*** things as the *Action News Now* helicopter in the sky!
NEWS

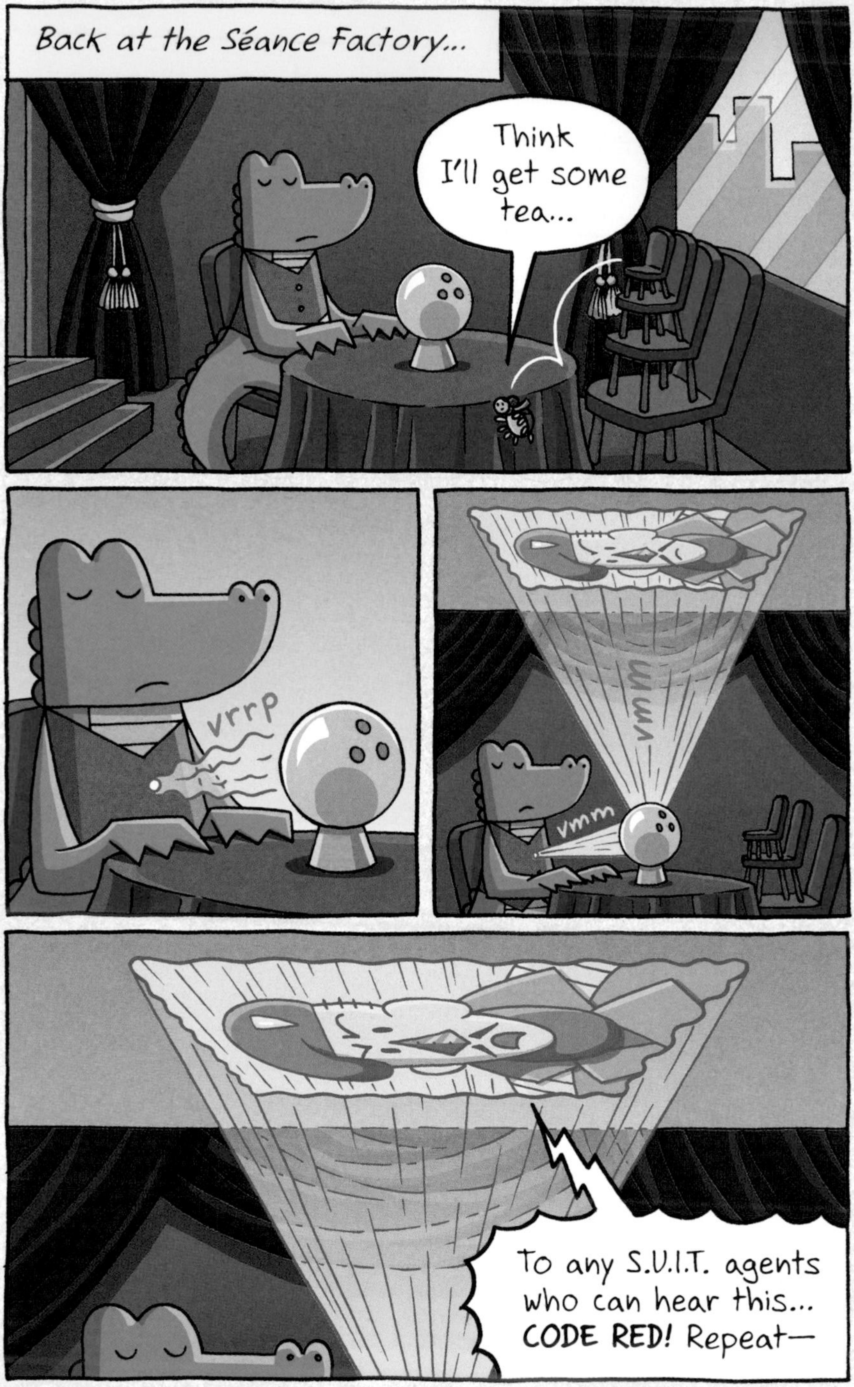
Back at the Séance Factory...
Think I'll get some tea...
vrrp
vmm
vmm
To any S.U.I.T. agents who can hear this... CODE RED! Repeat—

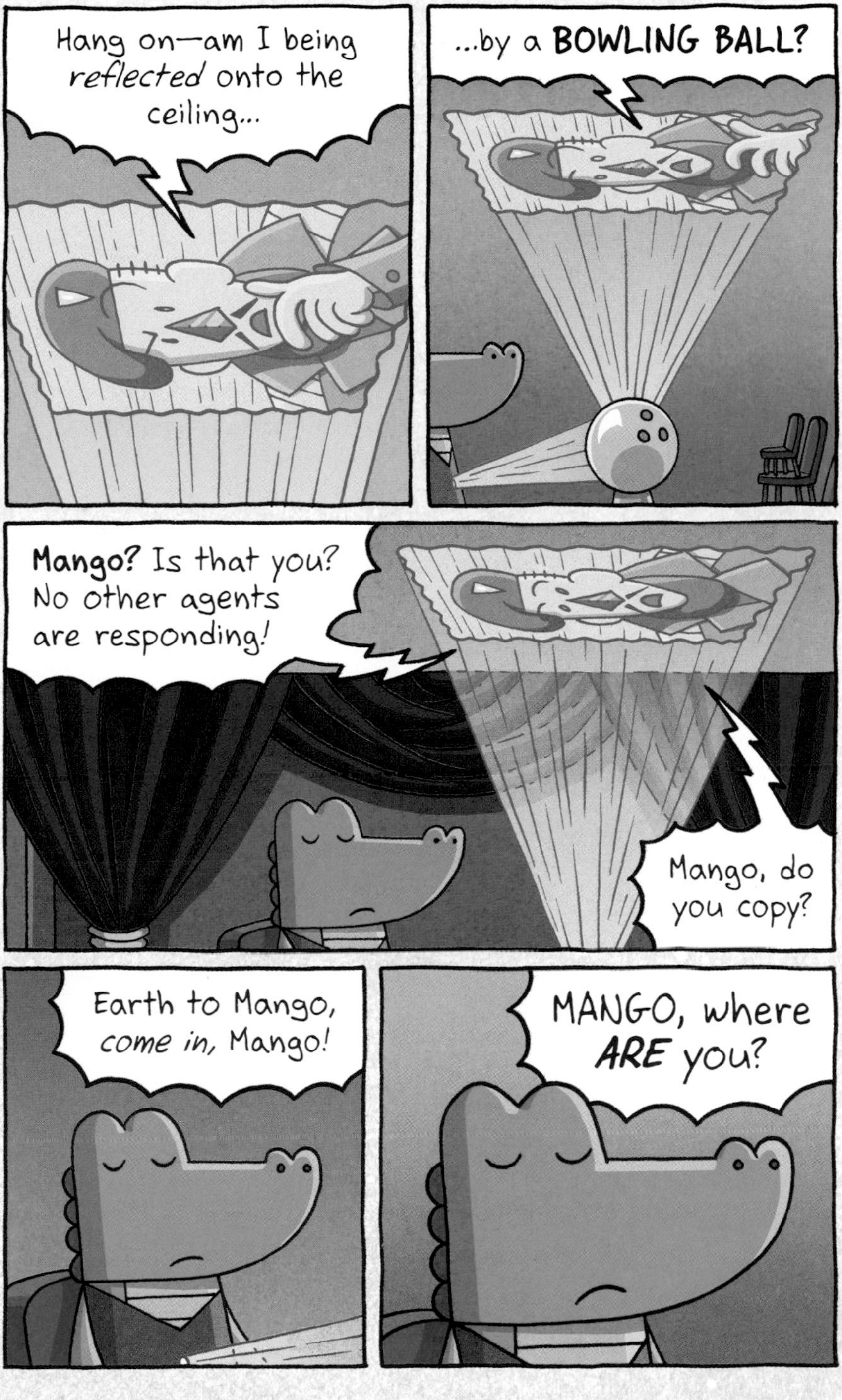
Hang on—am I being *reflected* onto the ceiling...
...by a **BOWLING BALL?**
**Mango?** Is that you? No other agents are responding!
Mango, do you copy?
Earth to Mango, *come in*, Mango!
MANGO, where ***ARE*** you?

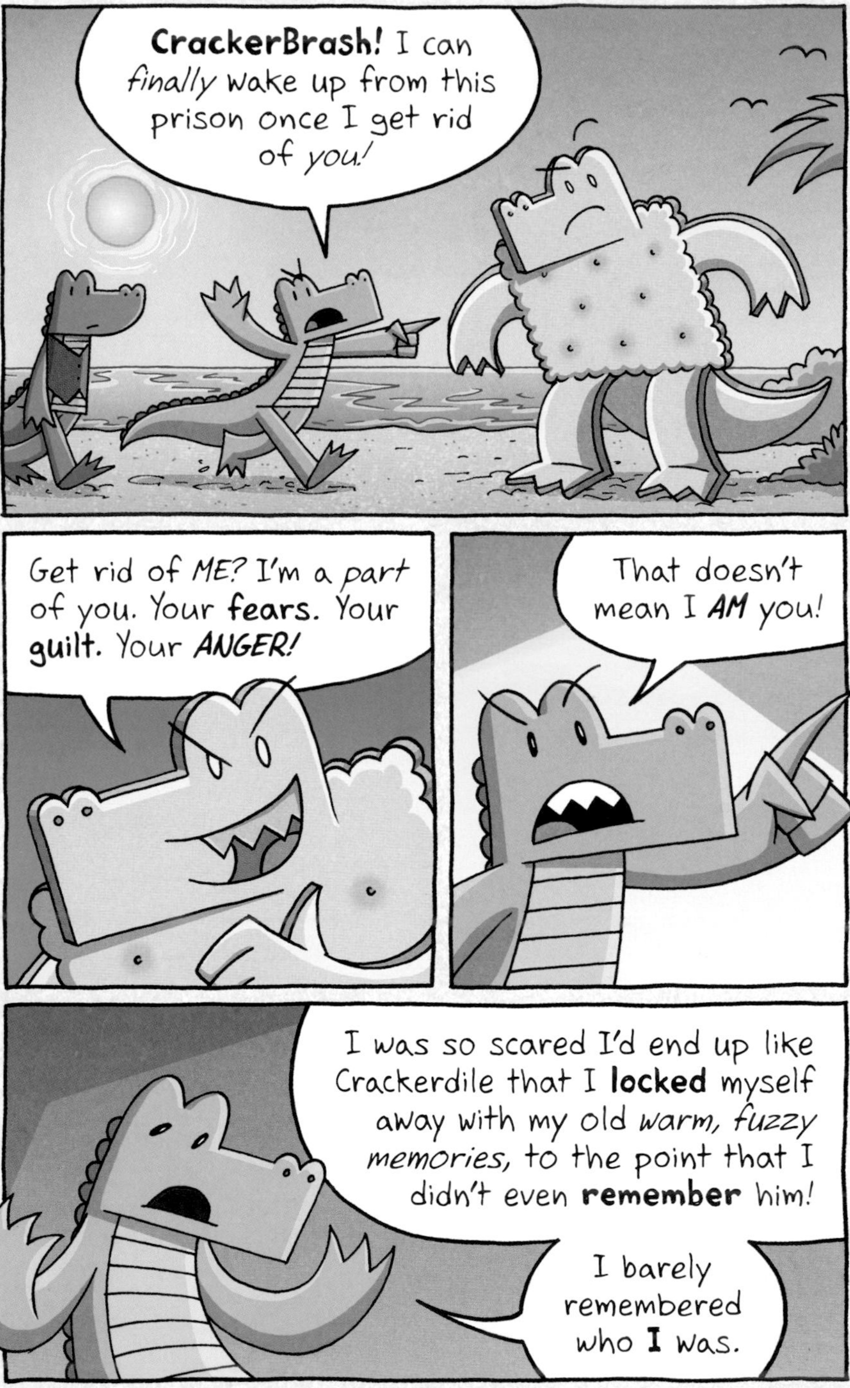
**CrackerBrash!** I can *finally* wake up from this prison once I get rid of *you!*
Get rid of *ME?* I'm a *part* of you. Your **fears**. Your **guilt**. Your ***ANGER!***
That doesn't mean I ***AM*** you!
I was so scared I'd end up like Crackerdile that I **locked** myself away with my old *warm, fuzzy memories,* to the point that I didn't even **remember** him!
I barely remembered who **I** was.

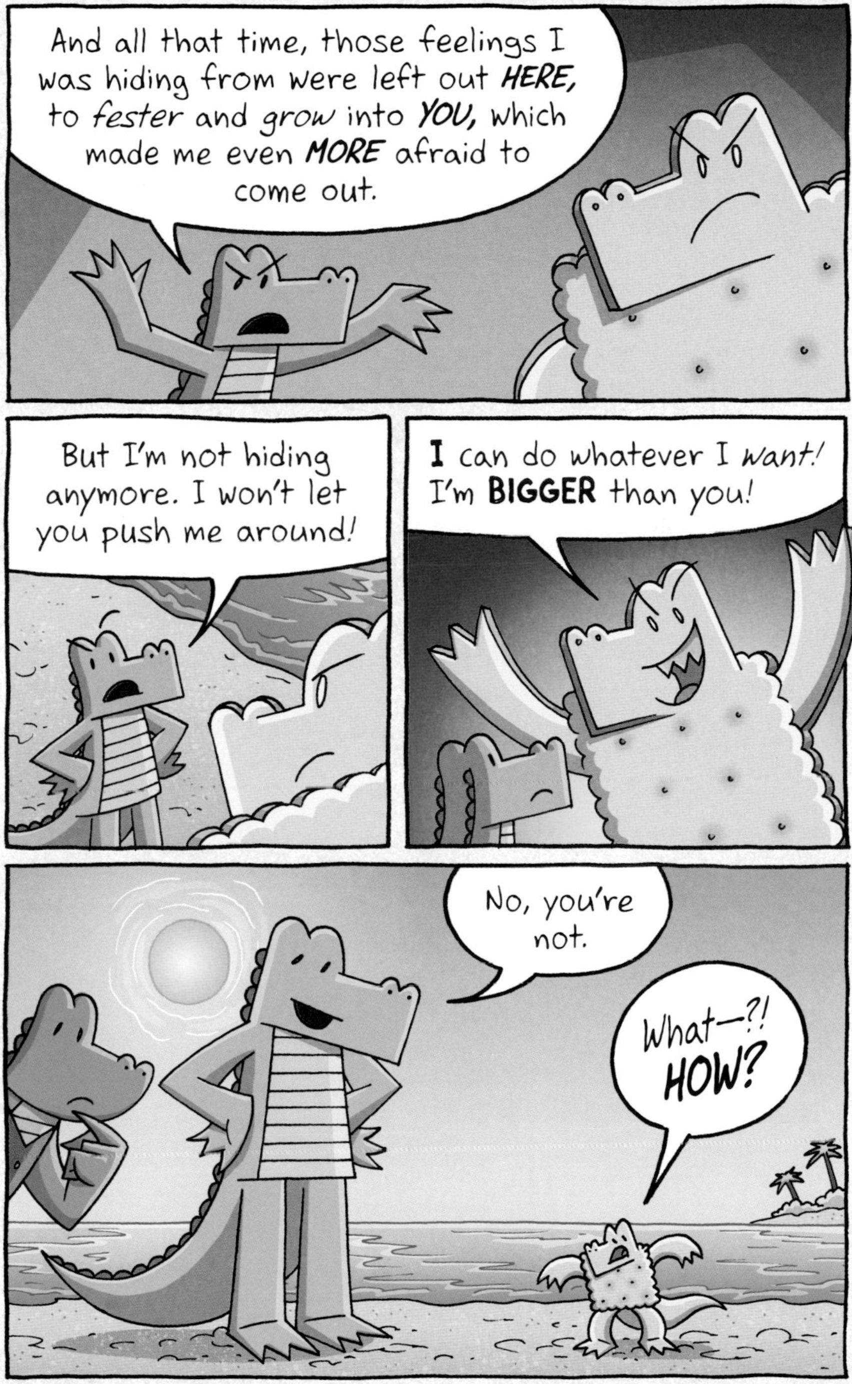

And all that time, those feelings I was hiding from were left out HERE, to fester and grow into YOU, which made me even MORE afraid to come out.
But I'm not hiding anymore. I won't let you push me around!
I can do whatever I want! I'm BIGGER than you!
No, you're not.
What—?! HOW?

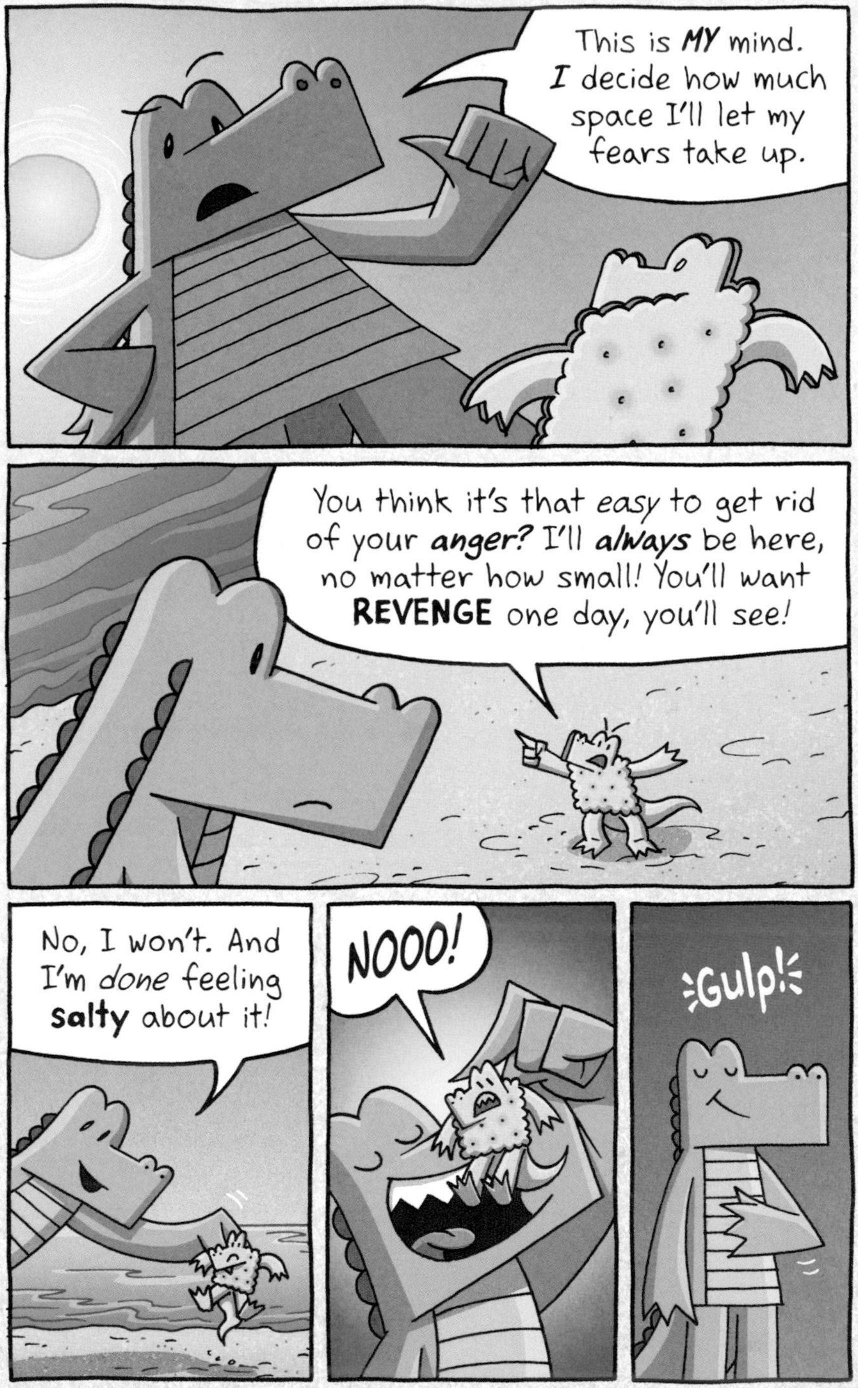
This is MY mind. I decide how much space I'll let my fears take up.
You think it's that easy to get rid of your anger? I'll always be here, no matter how small! You'll want REVENGE one day, you'll see!
No, I won't. And I'm done feeling salty about it!
NOOO!
Gulp!

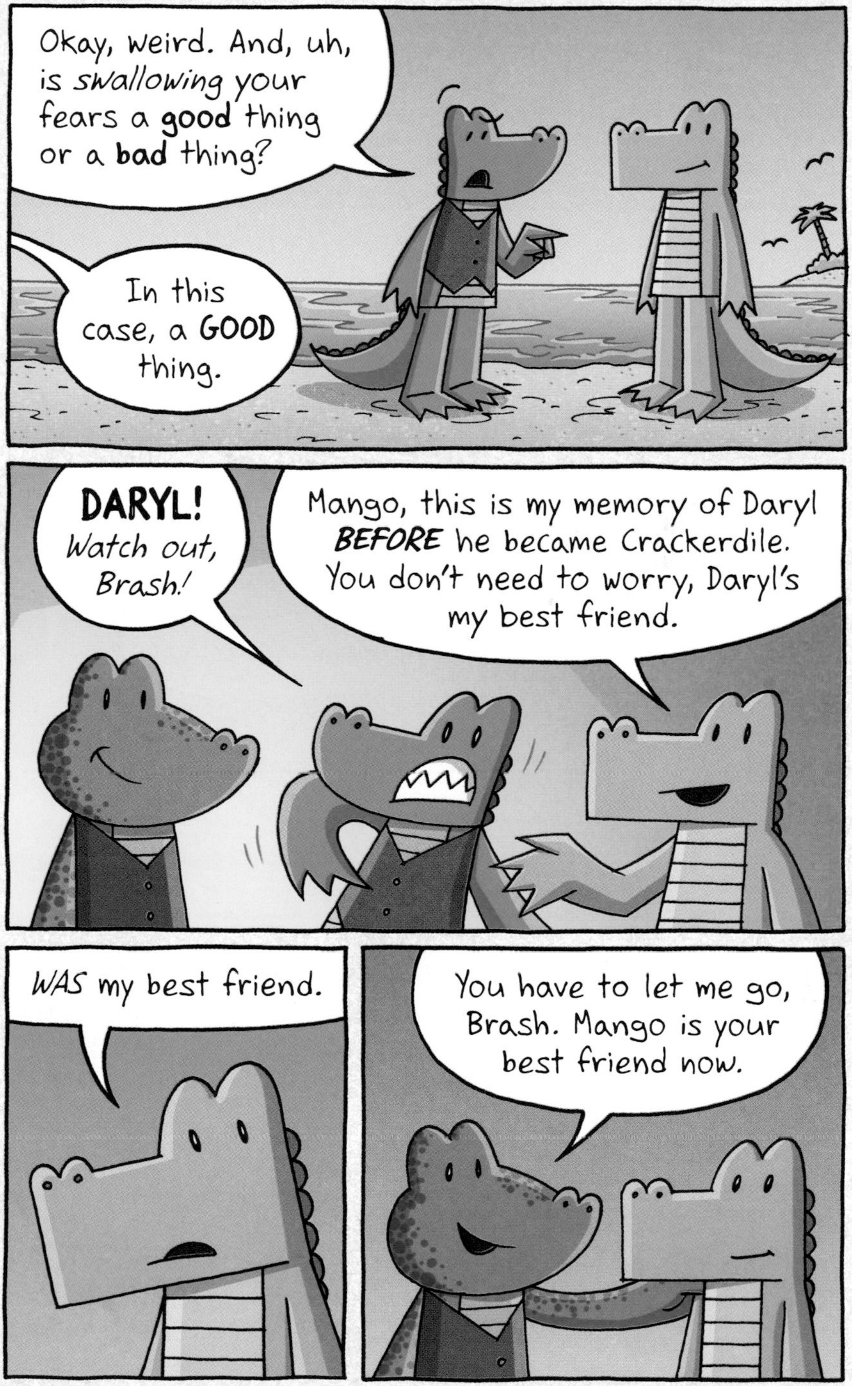

Okay, weird. And, uh, is *swallowing* your fears a **good** thing or a **bad** thing?
In this case, a **GOOD** thing.
**DARYL!** *Watch out, Brash!*
Mango, this is my memory of Daryl ***BEFORE*** he became Crackerdile. You don't need to worry, Daryl's my best friend.
*WAS* my best friend.
You have to let me go, Brash. Mango is your best friend now.

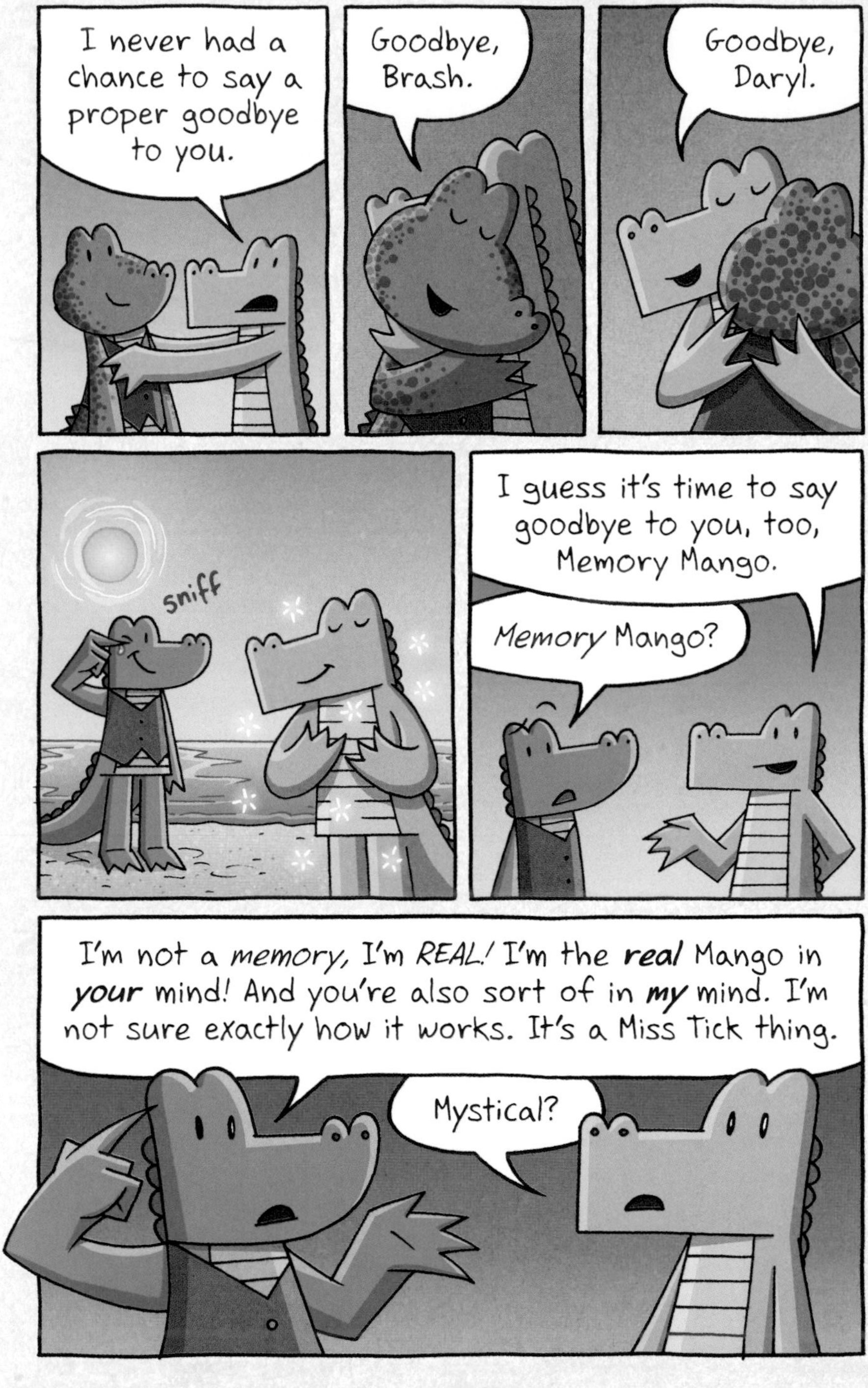
I never had a chance to say a proper goodbye to you.
Goodbye, Brash.
Goodbye, Daryl.
sniff
I guess it's time to say goodbye to you, too, Memory Mango.
*Memory* Mango?
I'm not a *memory*, I'm *REAL!* I'm the ***real*** Mango in ***your*** mind! And you're also sort of in ***my*** mind. I'm not sure exactly how it works. It's a Miss Tick thing.
Mystical?

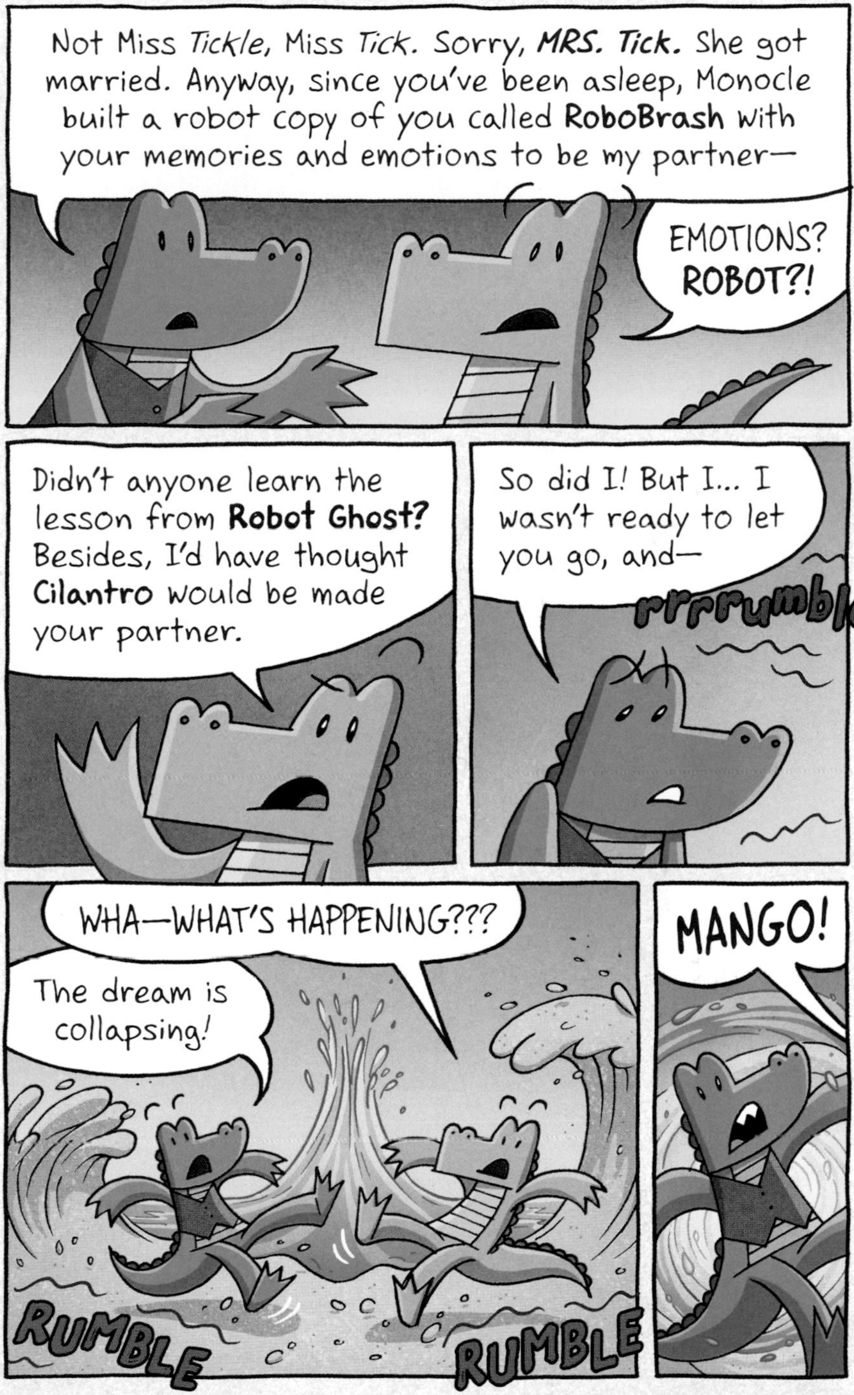
Not Miss *Tickle*, Miss *Tick*. Sorry, ***MRS. Tick.*** She got married. Anyway, since you've been asleep, Monocle built a robot copy of you called **RoboBrash** with your memories and emotions to be my partner—
EMOTIONS? **ROBOT?!**
Didn't anyone learn the lesson from **Robot Ghost?** Besides, I'd have thought **Cilantro** would be made your partner.
So did I! But I... I wasn't ready to let you go, and—
rrrrumble
WHA—WHAT'S HAPPENING???
The dream is collapsing!
RUMBLE
RUMBLE
MANGO!

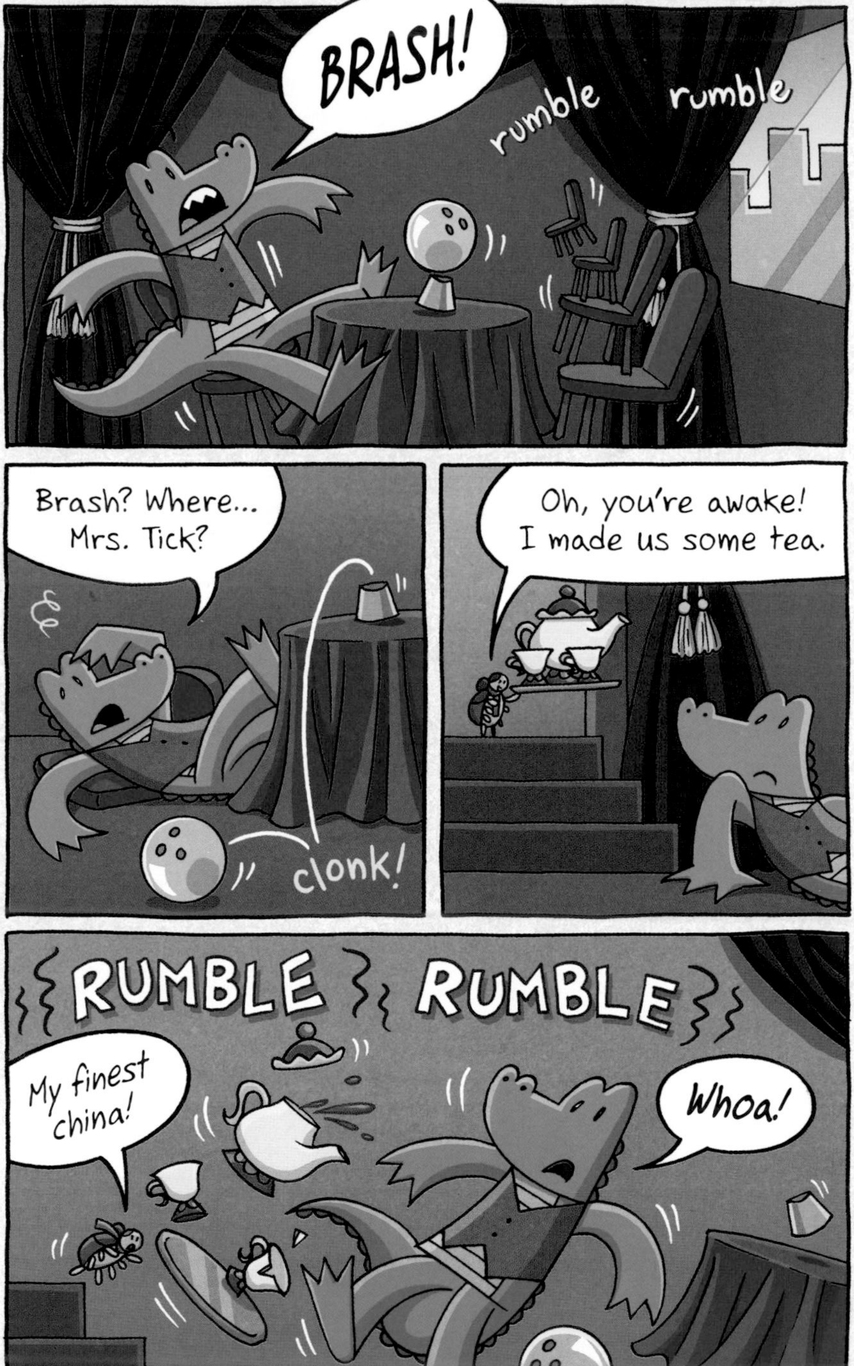
BRASH!
rumble rumble
Brash? Where...
Mrs. Tick?
clonk!
Oh, you're awake!
I made us some tea.
RUMBLE RUMBLE
My finest china!
Whoa!

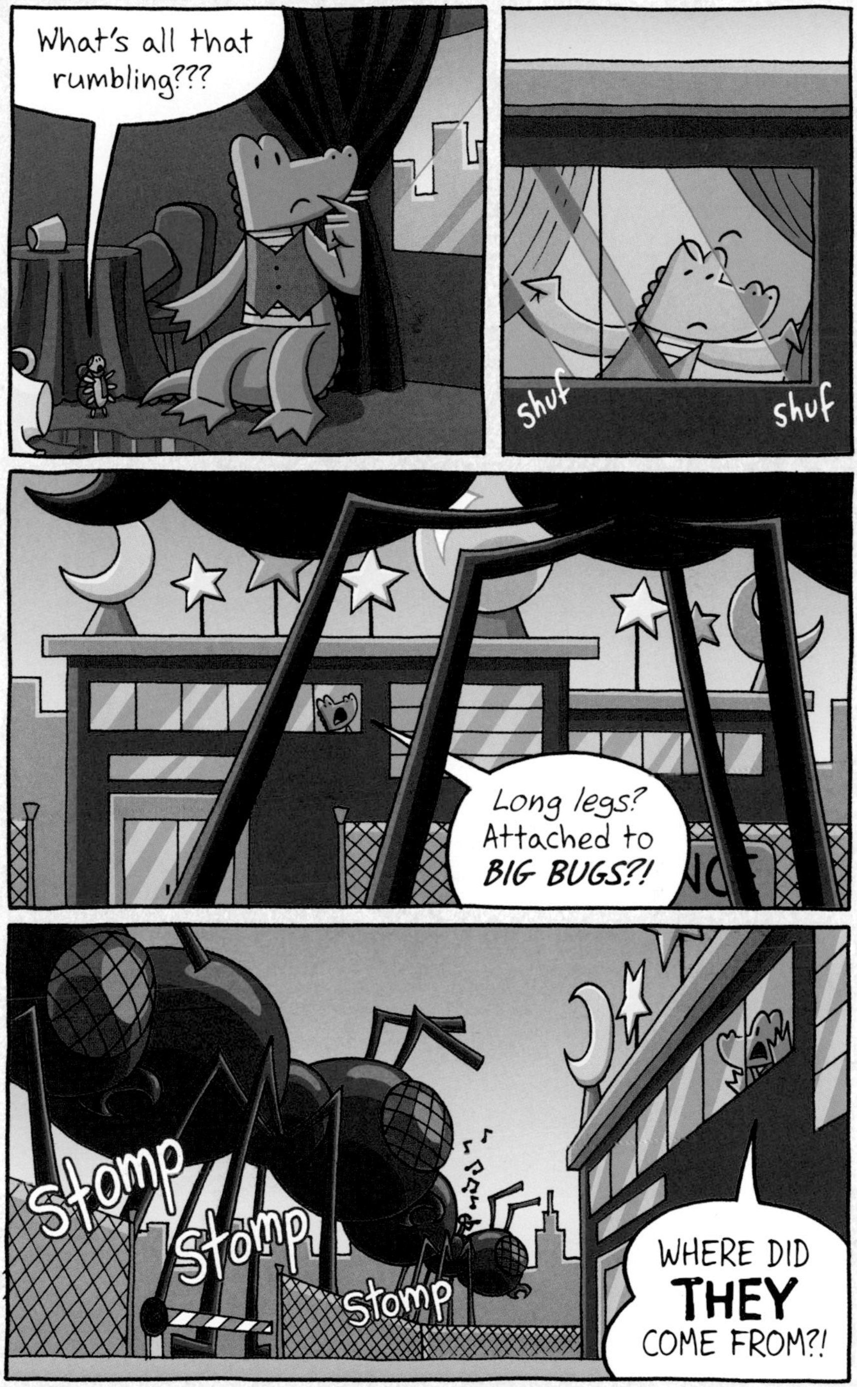
What's all that rumbling???
shuf
shuf
Long legs? Attached to BIG BUGS?!
Stomp
Stomp
Stomp
WHERE DID THEY COME FROM?!

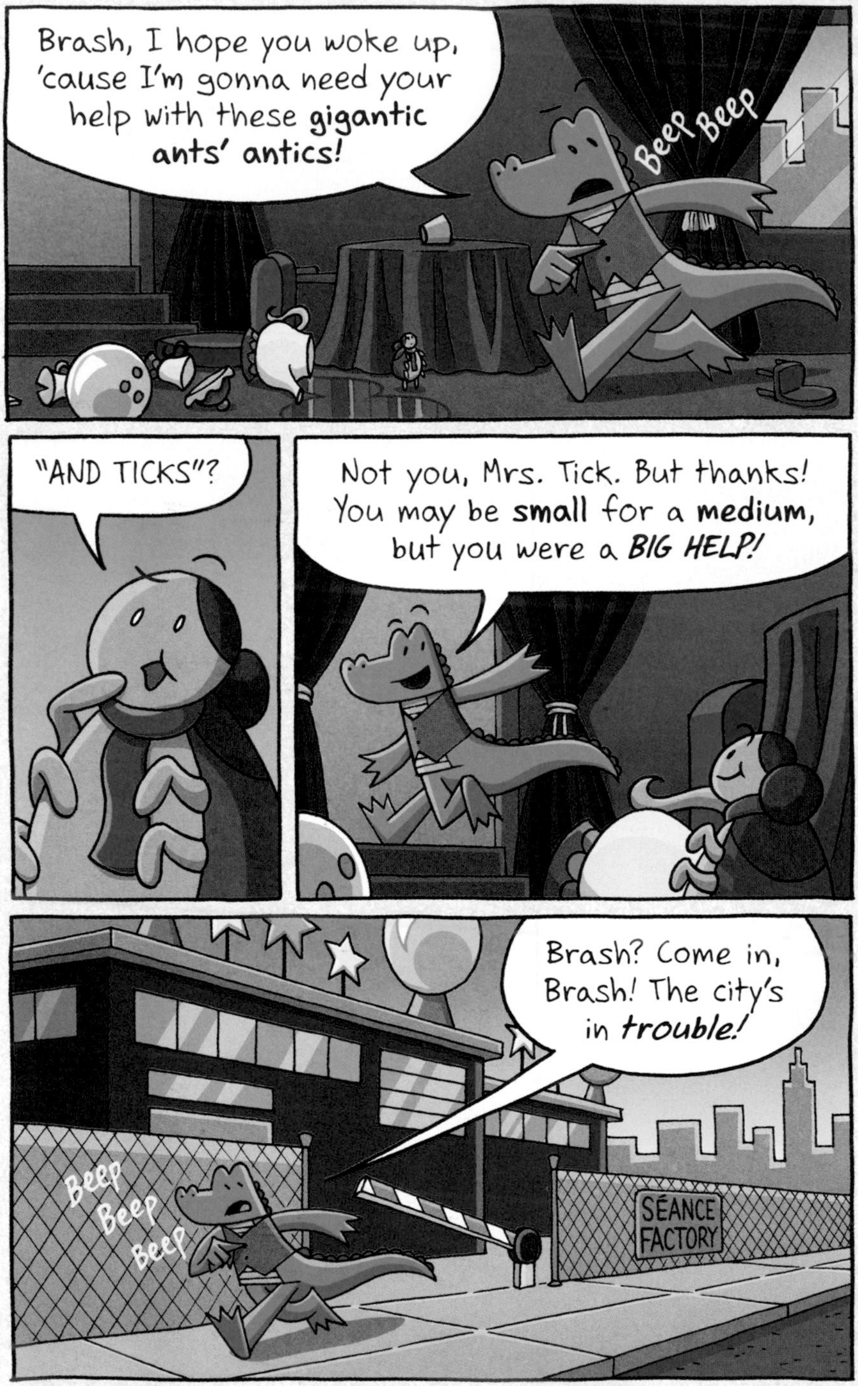
Brash, I hope you woke up, 'cause I'm gonna need your help with these **gigantic ants' antics!**
BEEP BEEP
"AND TICKS"?
Not you, Mrs. Tick. But thanks! You may be **small** for a **medium,** but you were a ***BIG HELP!***
Brash? Come in, Brash! The city's in ***trouble!***
Beep Beep Beep
SÉANCE FACTORY

# Chapter 13

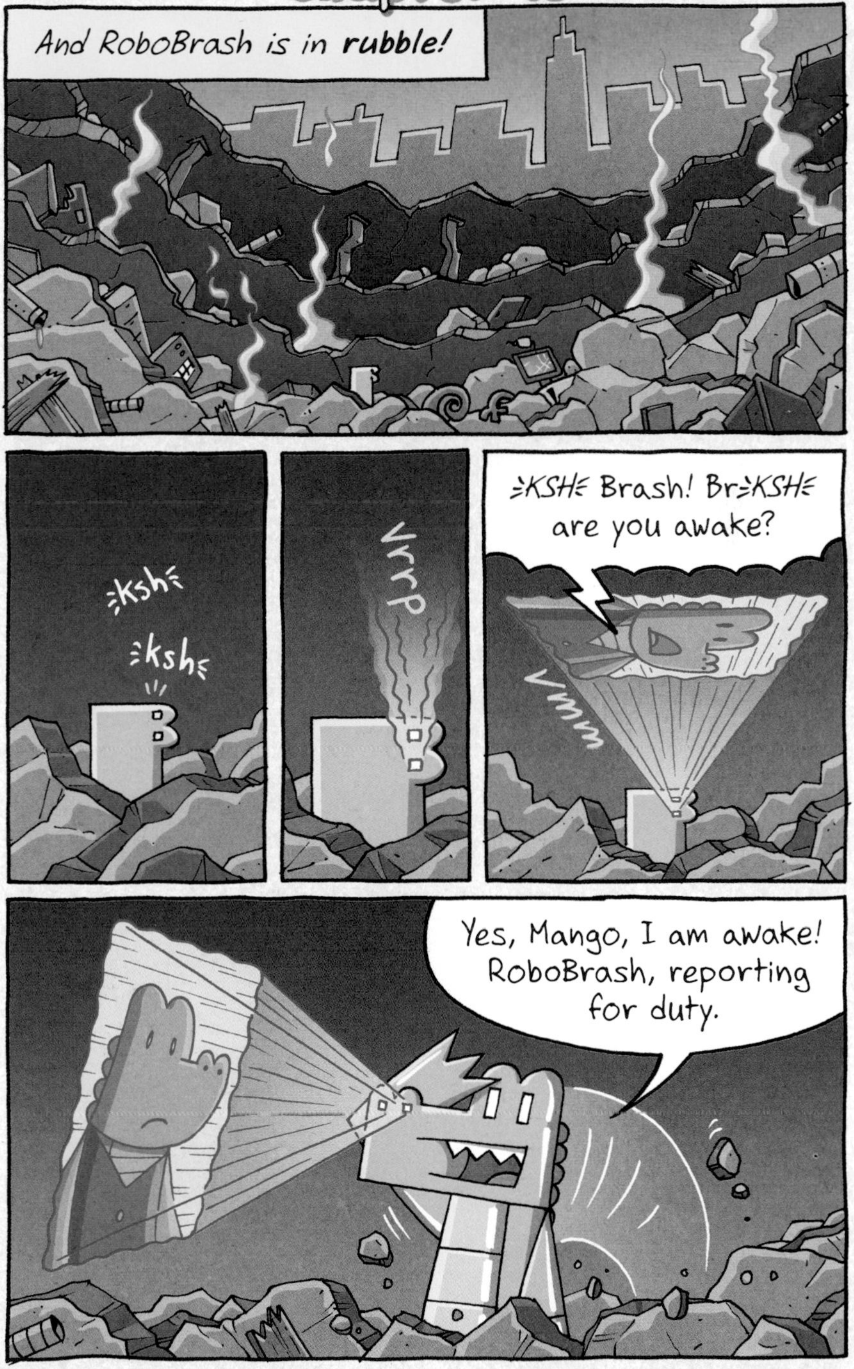
And RoboBrash is in **rubble!**
ksh
ksh
Vrrp
KSH Brash! Br KSH are you awake?
Vmm
Yes, Mango, I am awake! RoboBrash, reporting for duty.

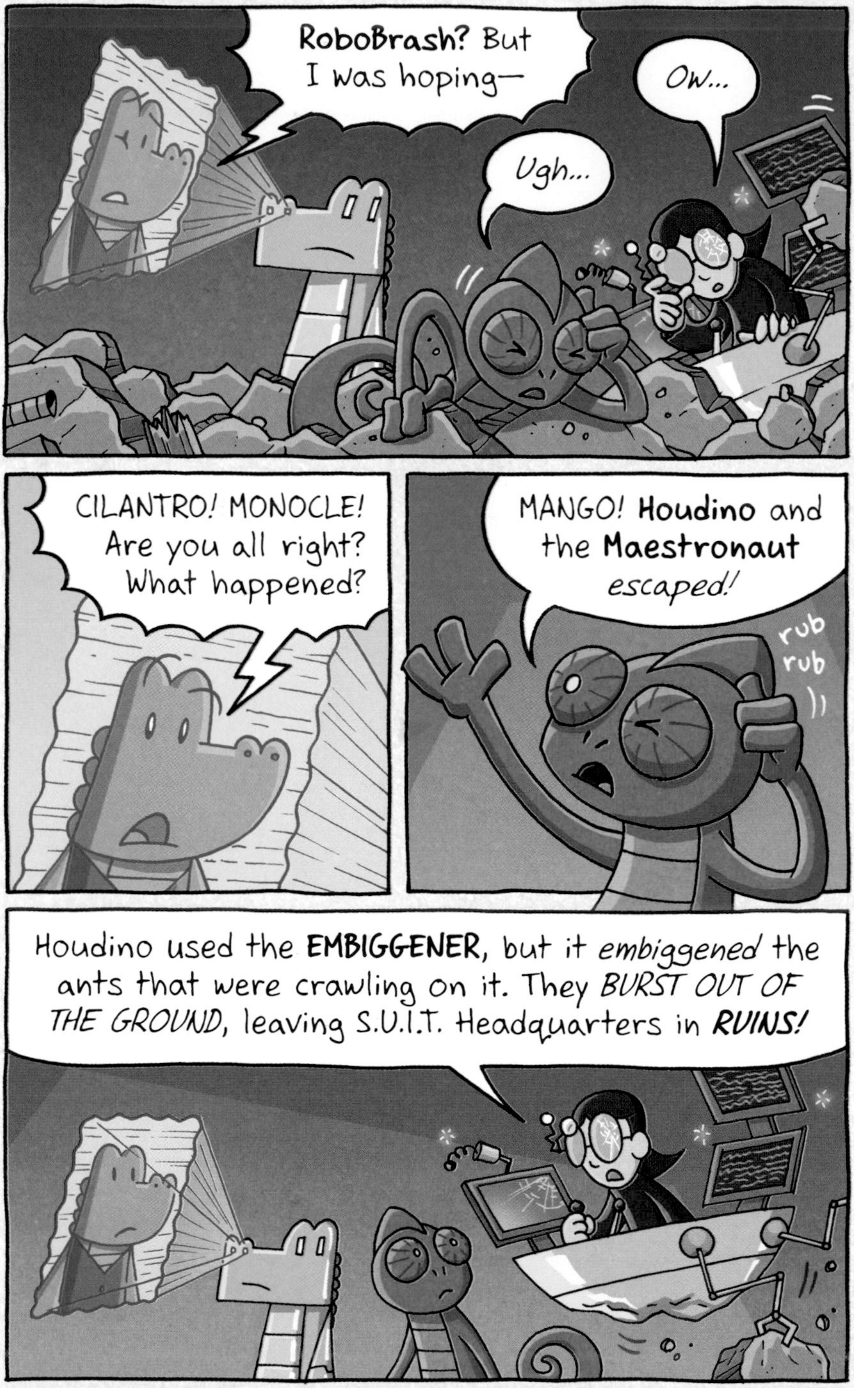
**RoboBrash?** But I was hoping—
Ow...
Ugh...
CILANTRO! MONOCLE! Are you all right? What happened?
MANGO! **Houdino** and the **Maestronaut** *escaped!*
rub rub
Houdino used the **EMBIGGENER**, but it *embiggened* the ants that were crawling on it. They *BURST OUT OF THE GROUND*, leaving S.U.I.T. Headquarters in ***RUINS!***

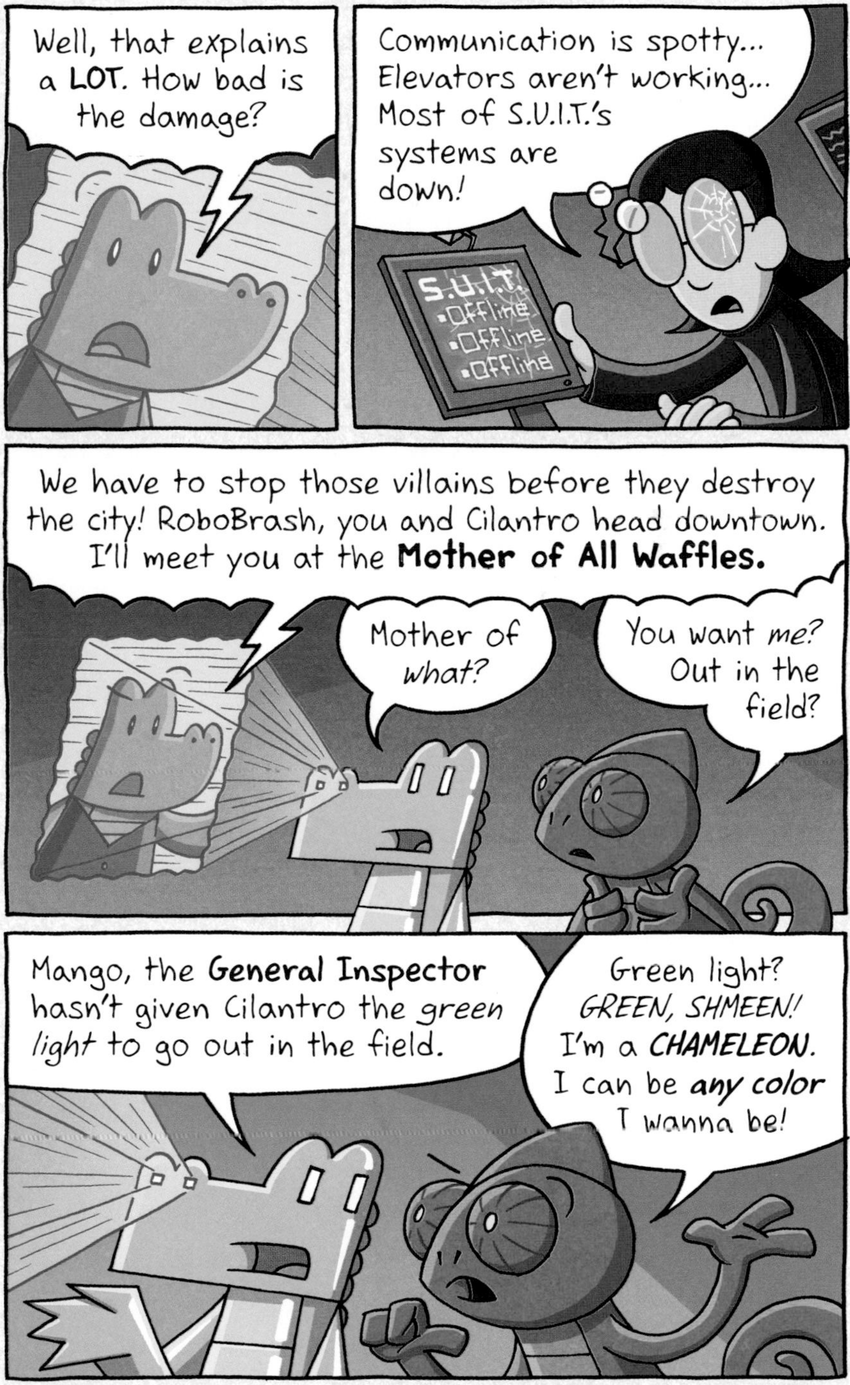
Well, that explains a LOT. How bad is the damage?
Communication is spotty... Elevators aren't working... Most of S.U.I.T.'s systems are down!
S.U.I.T.
Offline
Offline
Offline
We have to stop those villains before they destroy the city! RoboBrash, you and Cilantro head downtown. I'll meet you at the Mother of All Waffles.
Mother of what?
You want me? Out in the field?
Mango, the General Inspector hasn't given Cilantro the green light to go out in the field.
Green light? GREEN, SHMEEN! I'm a CHAMELEON. I can be any color I wanna be!

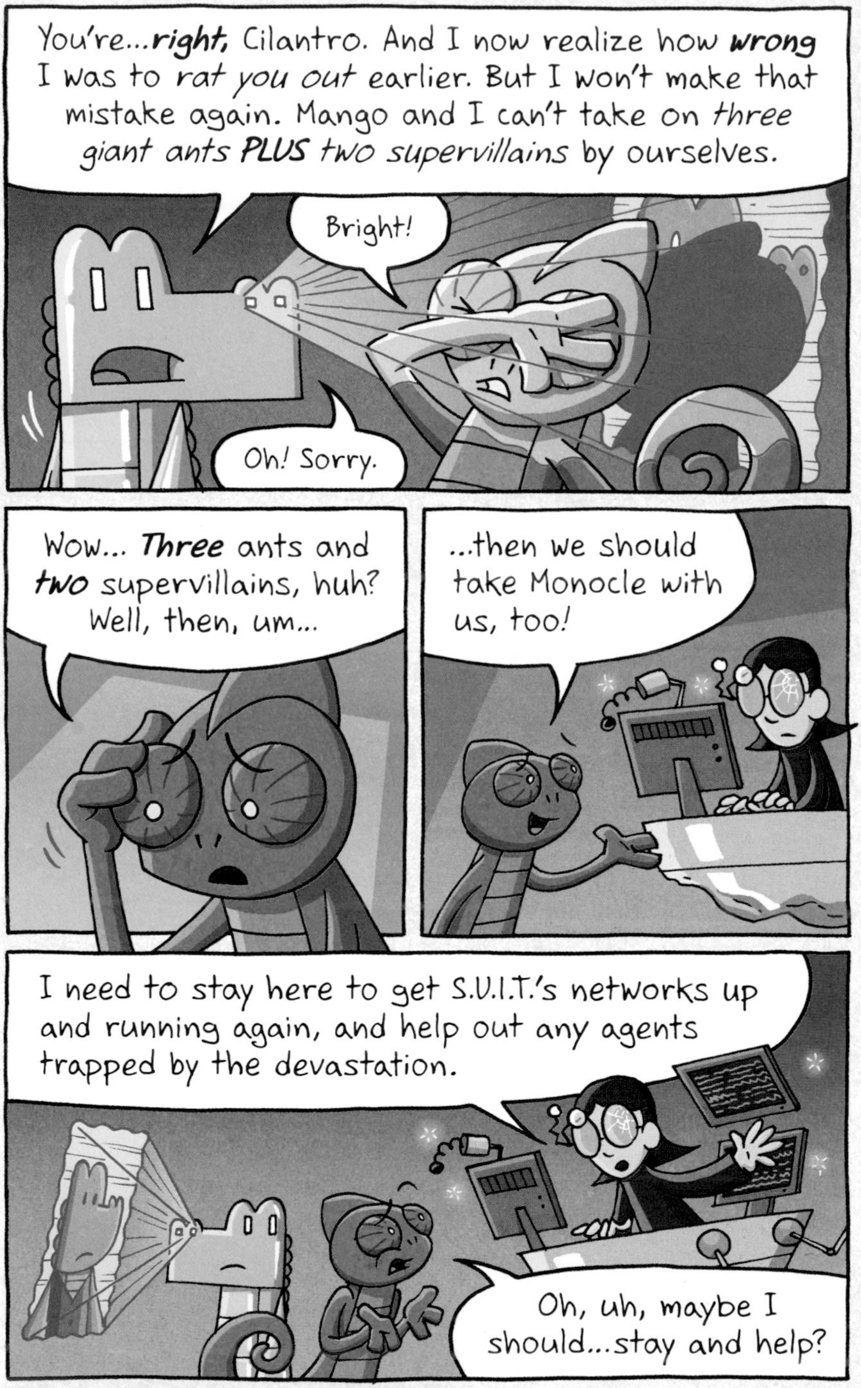
You're...**right,** Cilantro. And I now realize how **wrong** I was to *rat you out* earlier. But I won't make that mistake again. Mango and I can't take on *three giant ants* **PLUS** *two supervillains* by ourselves.
Bright!
Oh! Sorry.
Wow... **Three** ants and **two** supervillains, huh? Well, then, um...
...then we should take Monocle with us, too!
I need to stay here to get S.U.I.T.'s networks up and running again, and help out any agents trapped by the devastation.
Oh, uh, maybe I should...stay and help?

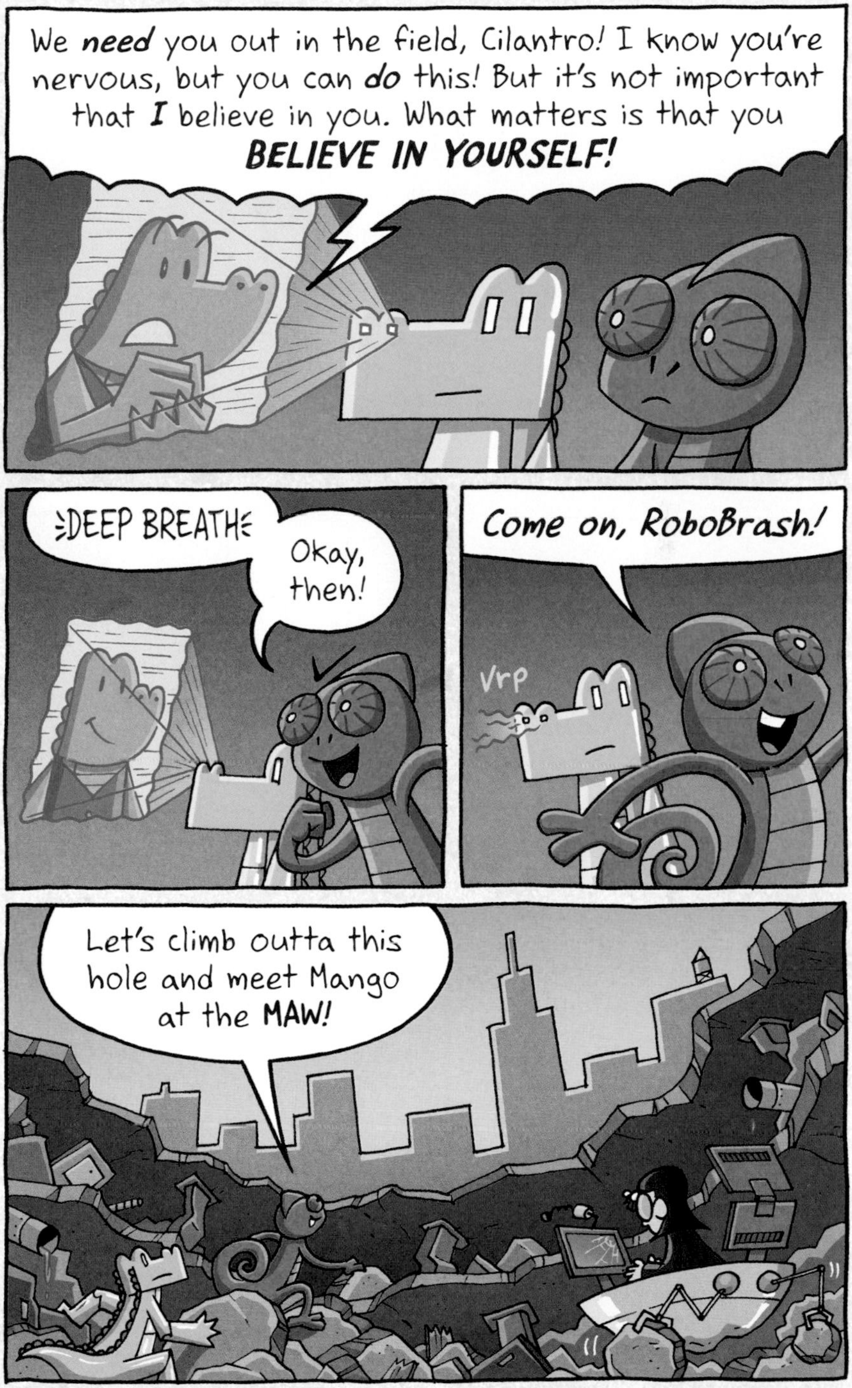
We *need* you out in the field, Cilantro! I know you're nervous, but you can *do* this! But it's not important that *I* believe in you. What matters is that you **BELIEVE IN YOURSELF!**
DEEP BREATH
Okay, then!
Come on, RoboBrash!
Vrp
Let's climb outta this hole and meet Mango at the **MAW!**

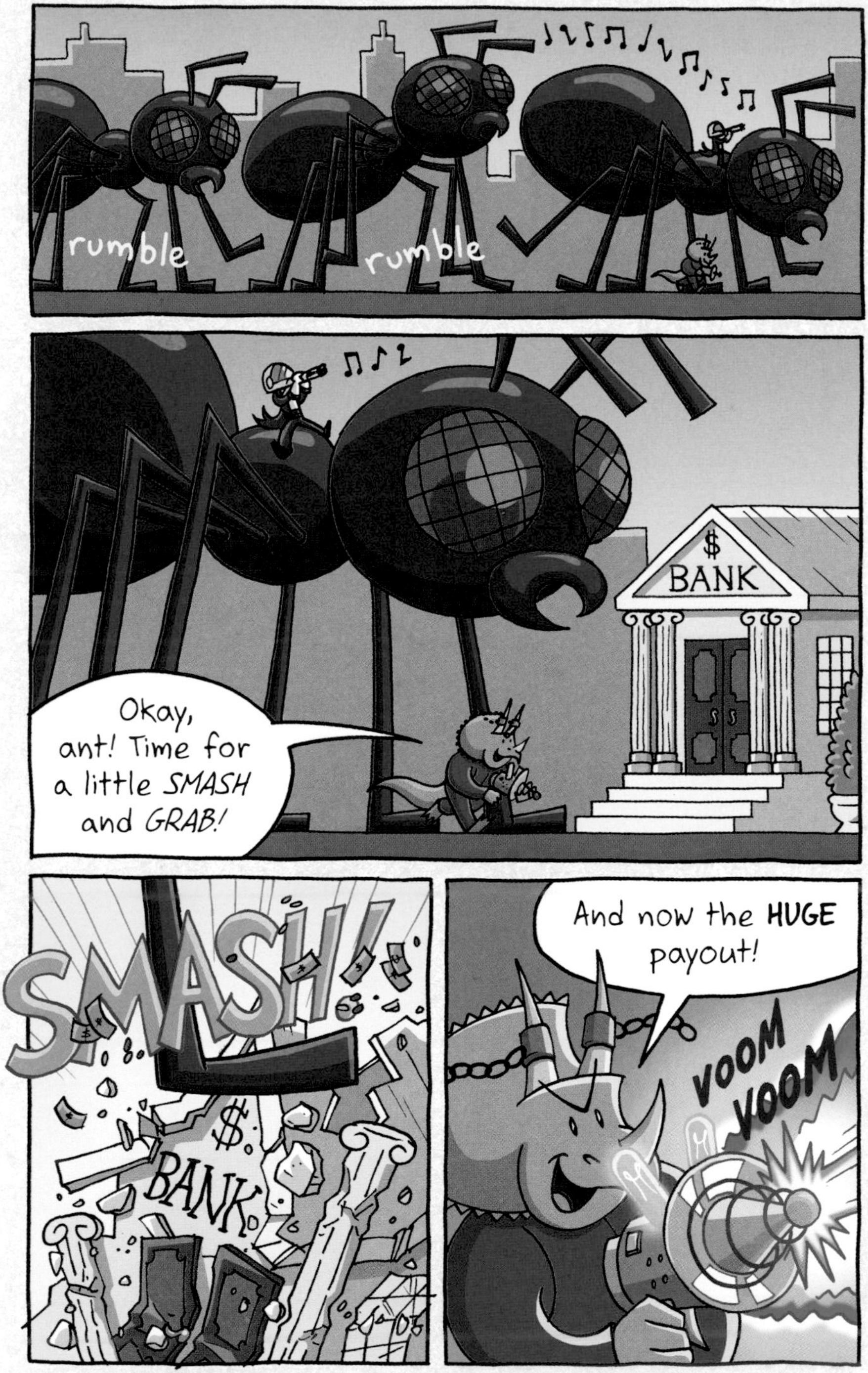
rumble
rumble
Okay, ant! Time for a little SMASH and GRAB!
BANK
SMASH!
BANK
And now the **HUGE** payout!
VOOM
VOOM

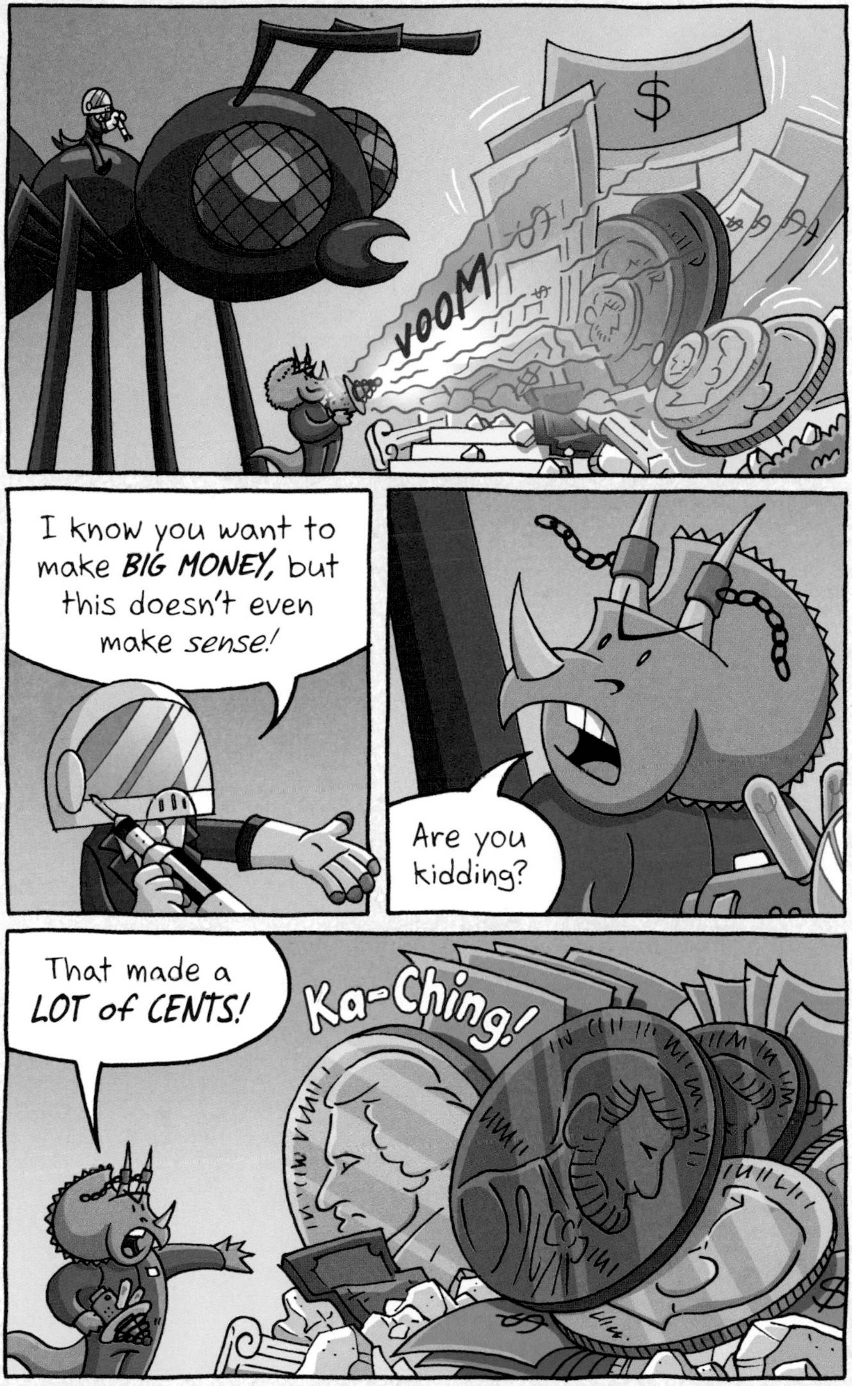
VOOM
I know you want to make BIG MONEY, but this doesn't even make sense!
Are you kidding?
That made a LOT of CENTS!
Ka-Ching!

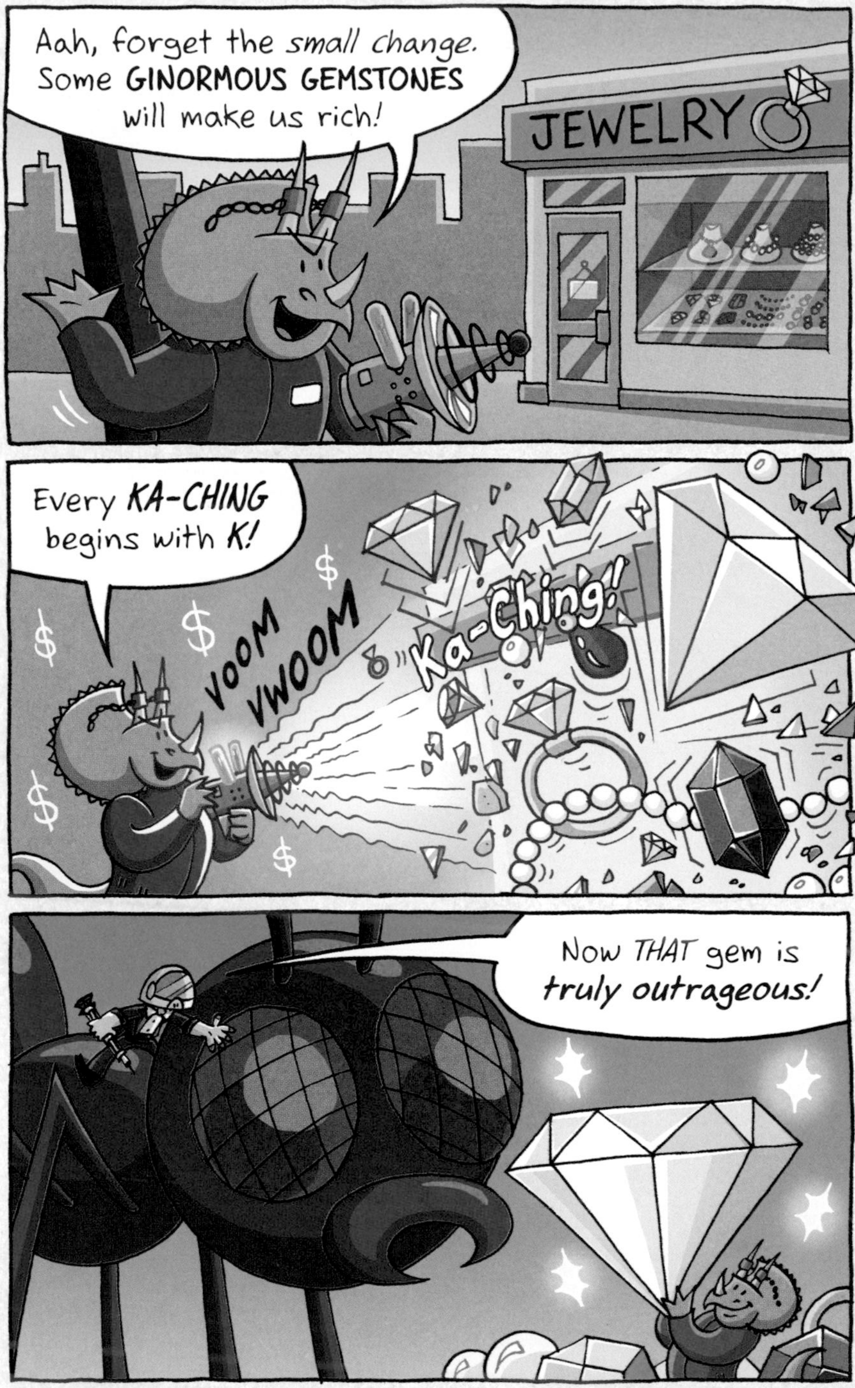

Aah, forget the *small change.* Some **GINORMOUS GEMSTONES** will make us rich!
JEWELRY
Every ***KA-CHING*** begins with ***K!***
VOOM
VWOOM
Ka-Ching!
Now *THAT* gem is ***truly outrageous!***

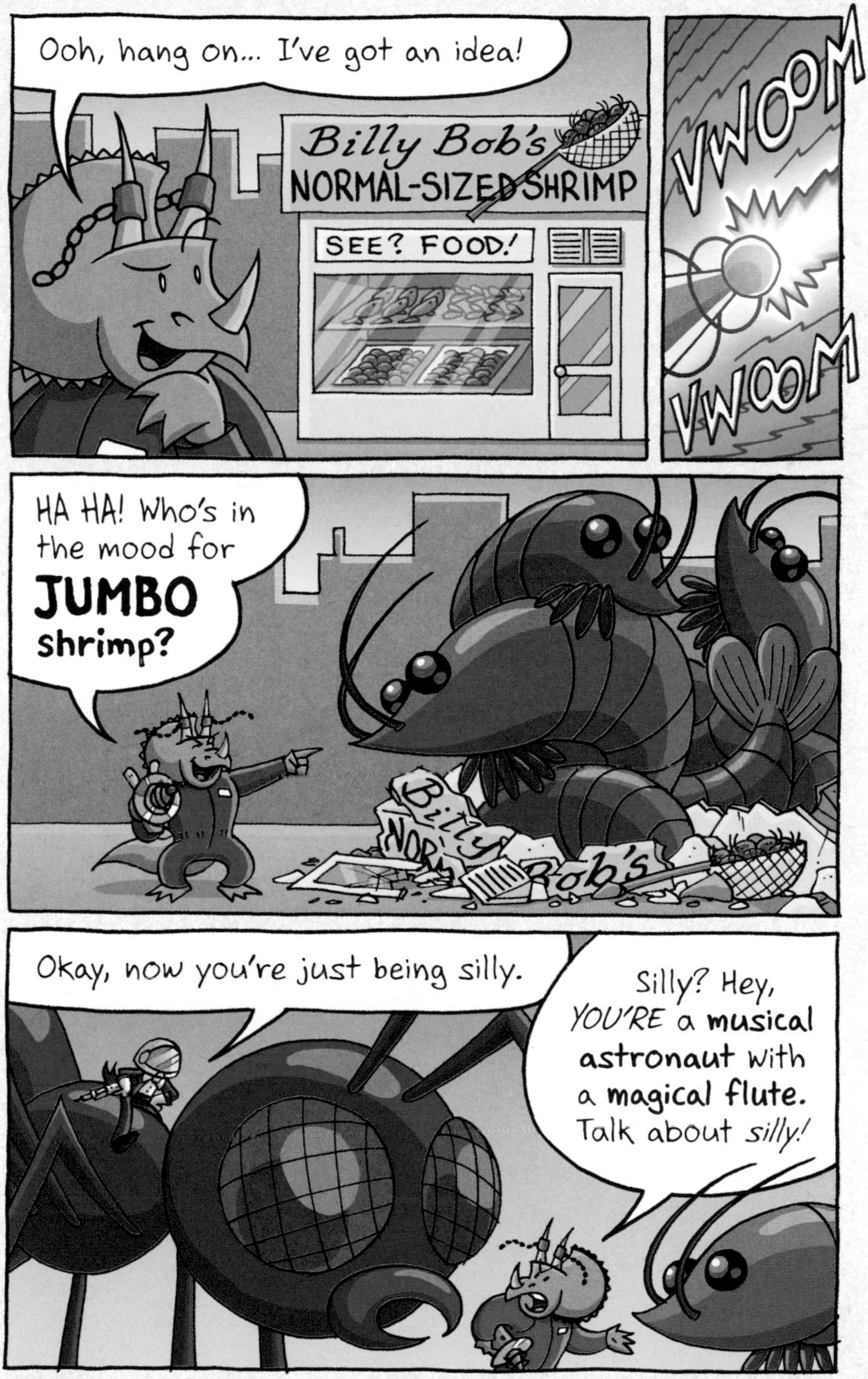
Ooh, hang on... I've got an idea!
Billy Bob's NORMAL-SIZED SHRIMP
SEE? FOOD!
VWOOM
VWOOM
HA HA! Who's in the mood for JUMBO shrimp?
Okay, now you're just being silly.
Silly? Hey, YOU'RE a musical astronaut with a magical flute. Talk about silly!

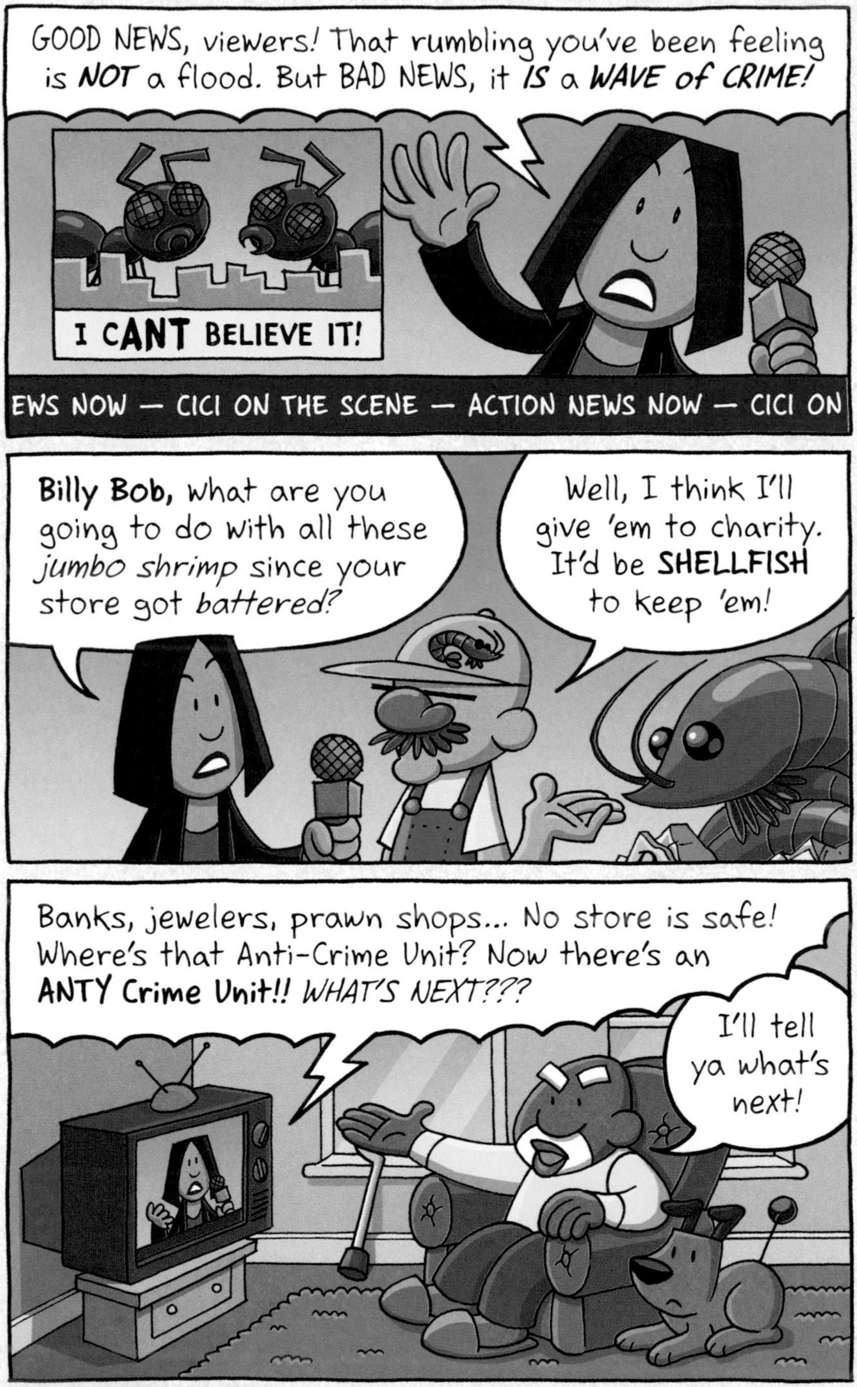

GOOD NEWS, viewers! That rumbling you've been feeling is NOT a flood. But BAD NEWS, it IS a WAVE of CRIME!
I CANT BELIEVE IT!
EWS NOW — CICI ON THE SCENE — ACTION NEWS NOW — CICI ON
Billy Bob, what are you going to do with all these jumbo shrimp since your store got battered?
Well, I think I'll give 'em to charity. It'd be SHELLFISH to keep 'em!
Banks, jewelers, prawn shops... No store is safe! Where's that Anti-Crime Unit? Now there's an ANTY Crime Unit!! WHAT'S NEXT???
I'll tell ya what's next!

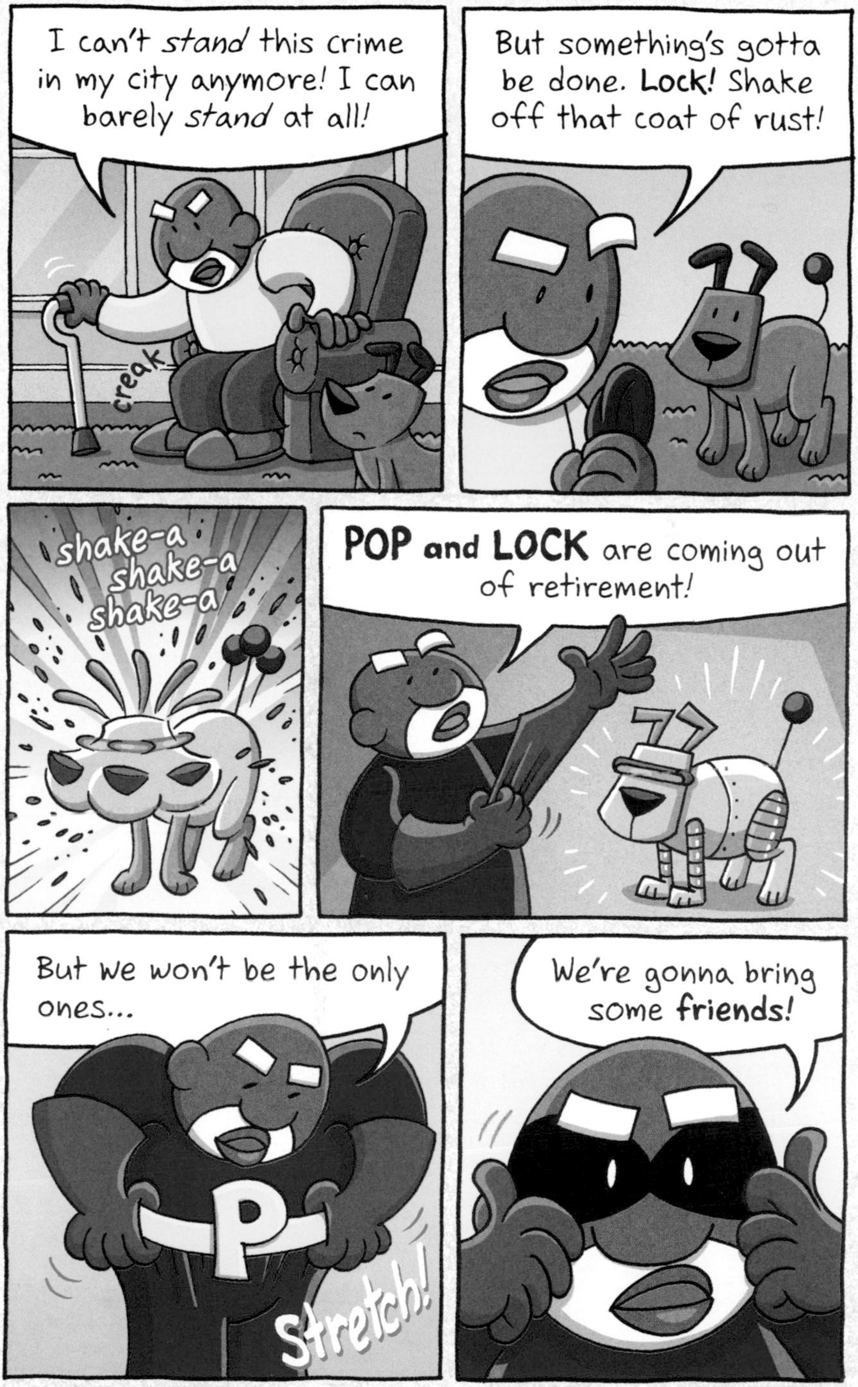
I can't *stand* this crime in my city anymore! I can barely *stand* at all!
creak
But something's gotta be done. **Lock!** Shake off that coat of rust!
shake-a shake-a shake-a
**POP and LOCK** are coming out of retirement!
But we won't be the only ones...
P
Stretch!
We're gonna bring some **friends!**

# Chapter 14

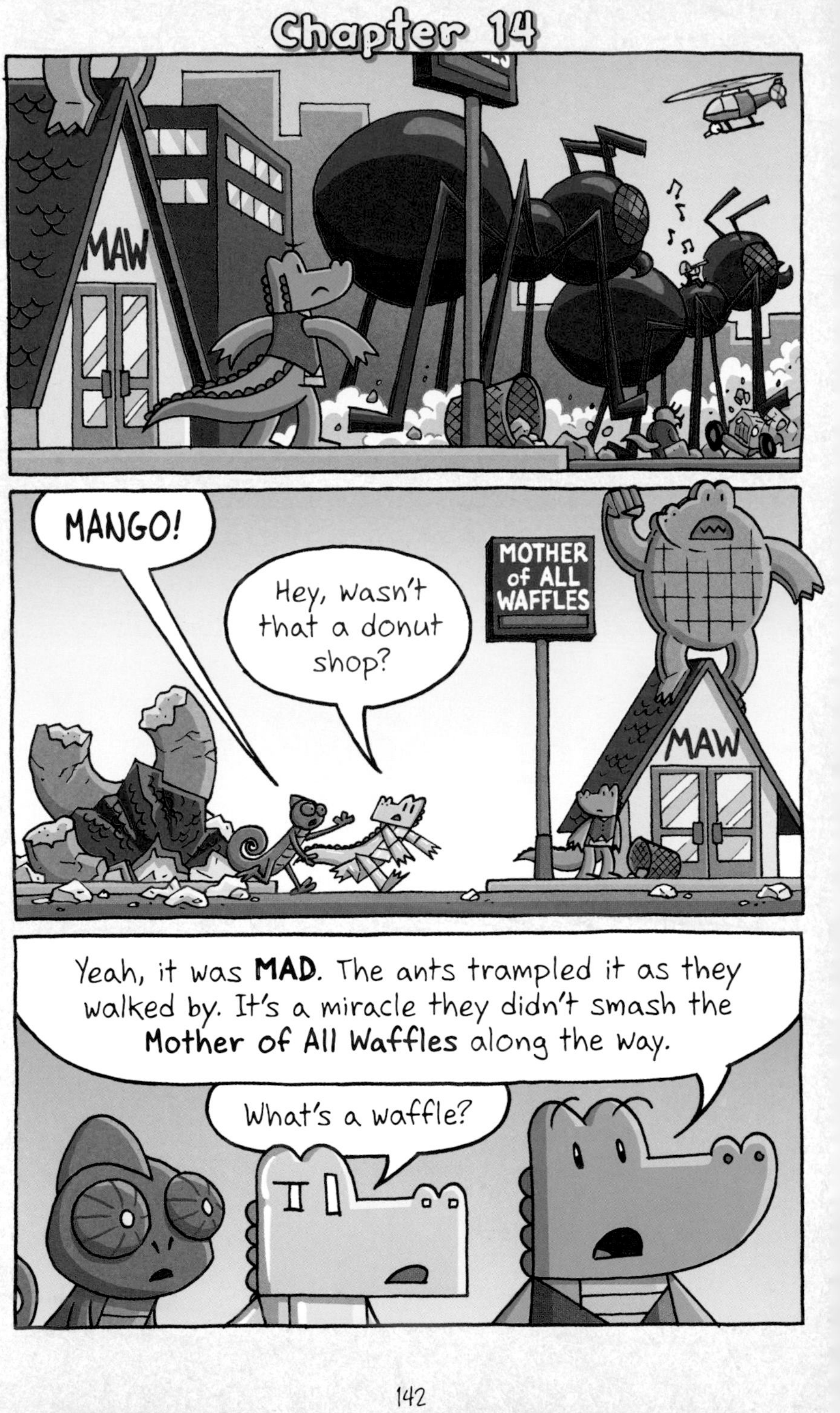
MAW
MANGO!
Hey, wasn't that a donut shop?
MOTHER of ALL WAFFLES
MAW
Yeah, it was **MAD**. The ants trampled it as they walked by. It's a miracle they didn't smash the **Mother of All Waffles** along the way.
What's a waffle?

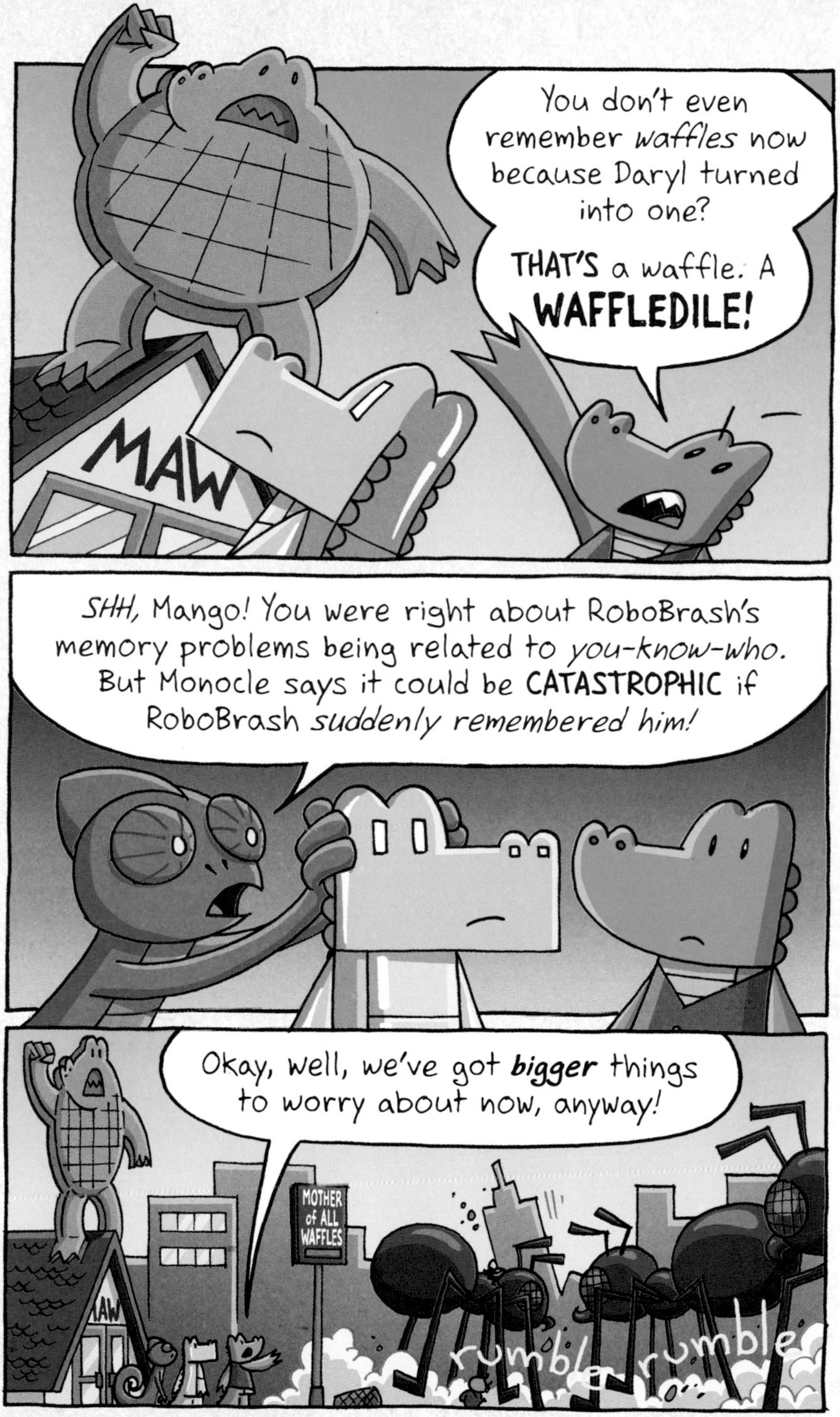
You don't even remember *waffles* now because Daryl turned into one?
**THAT'S** a waffle. A **WAFFLEDILE!**
MAW
*SHH,* Mango! You were right about RoboBrash's memory problems being related to *you-know-who.* But Monocle says it could be **CATASTROPHIC** if RoboBrash *suddenly remembered him!*
Okay, well, we've got ***bigger*** things to worry about now, anyway!
MOTHER of ALL WAFFLES
rumble rumble

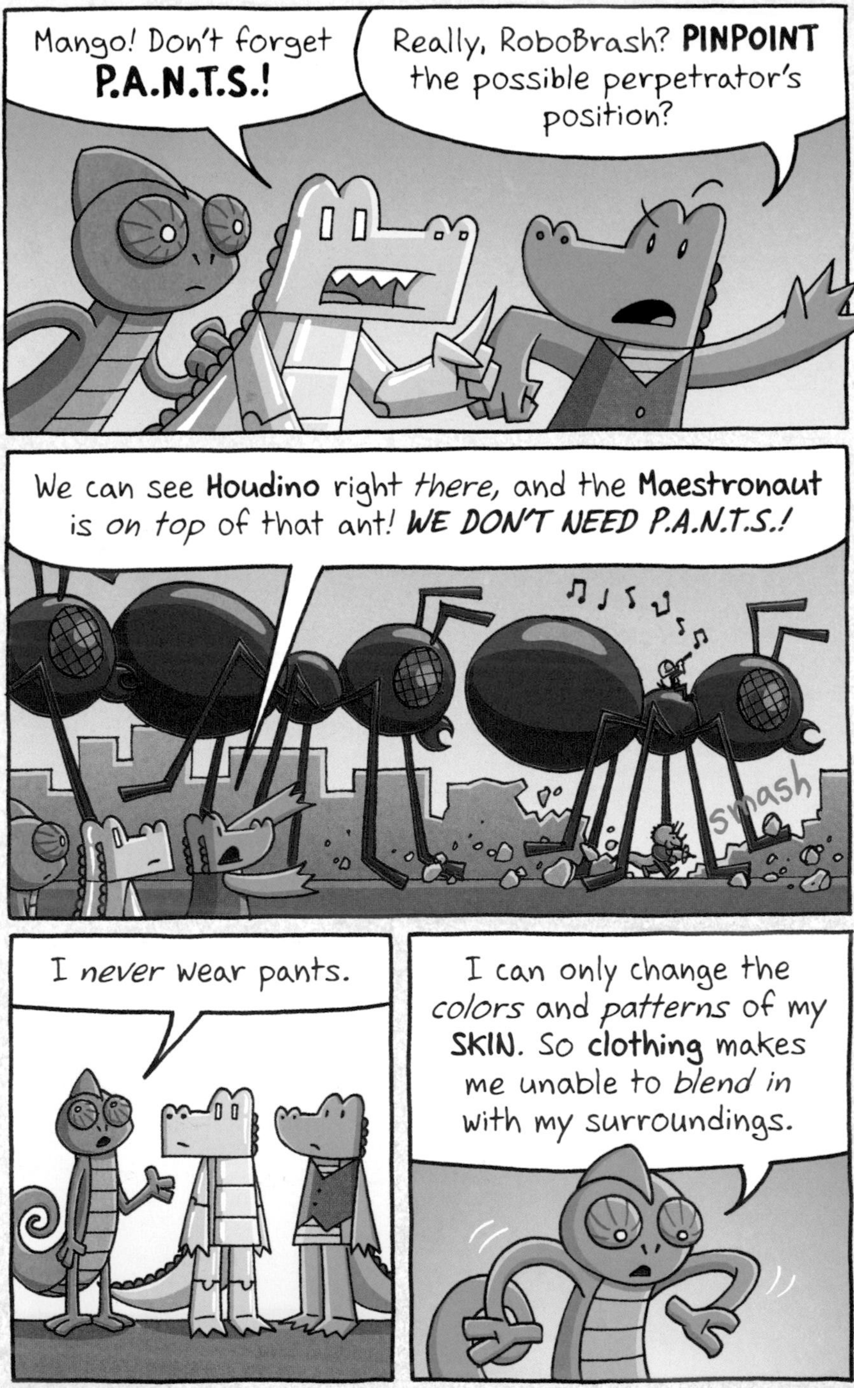
Mango! Don't forget **P.A.N.T.S.!**
Really, RoboBrash? **PINPOINT** the possible perpetrator's position?
We can see **Houdino** right *there*, and the **Maestronaut** is *on top* of that ant! ***WE DON'T NEED P.A.N.T.S.!***
smash
I *never* wear pants.
I can only change the *colors* and *patterns* of my **SKIN**. So **clothing** makes me unable to *blend* in with my surroundings.

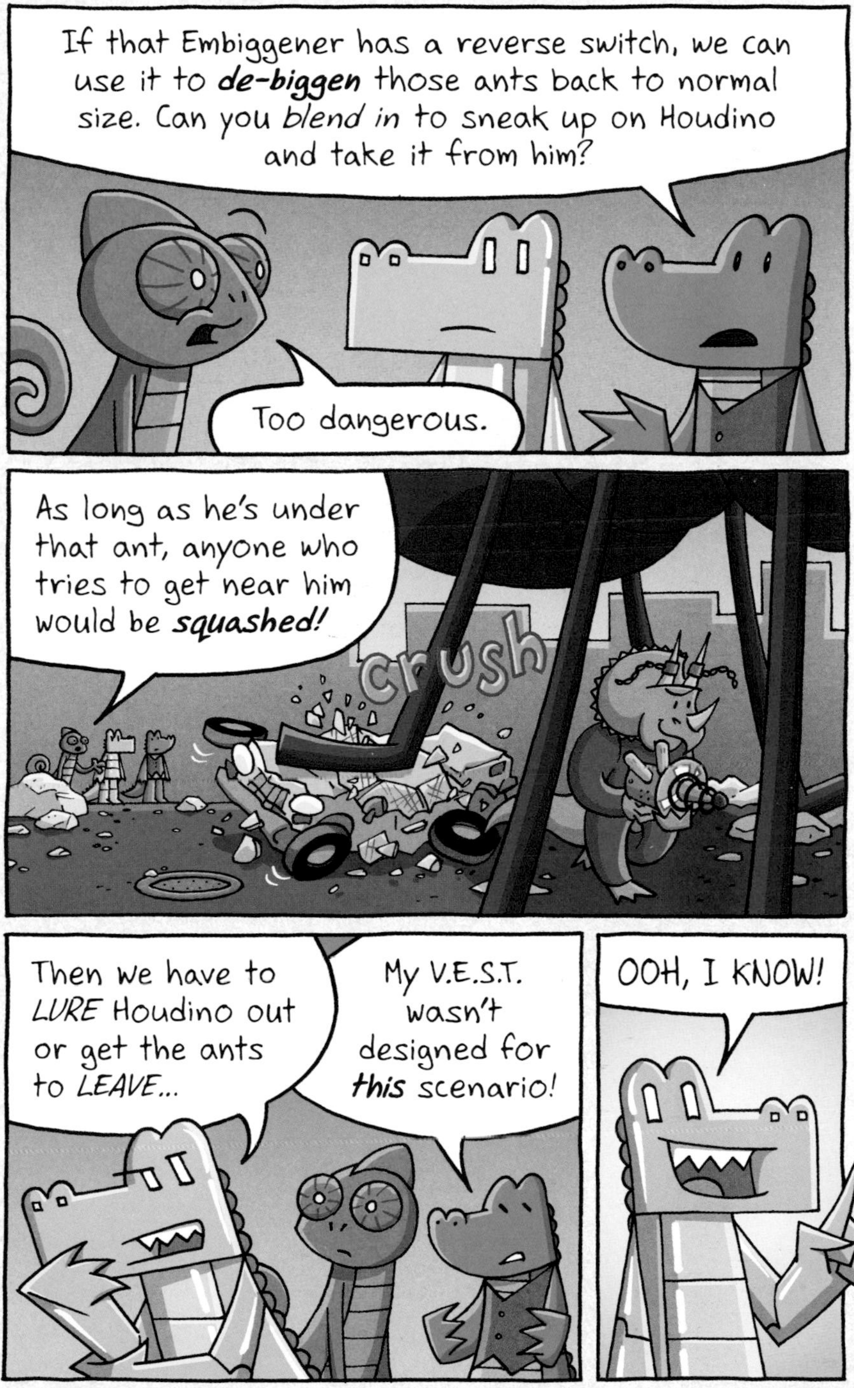
If that Embiggener has a reverse switch, we can use it to ***de-biggen*** those ants back to normal size. Can you *blend in* to sneak up on Houdino and take it from him?
Too dangerous.
As long as he's under that ant, anyone who tries to get near him would be ***squashed!***
CRUSH
Then we have to *LURE* Houdino out or get the ants to *LEAVE*...
My V.E.S.T. wasn't designed for ***this*** scenario!
OOH, I KNOW!

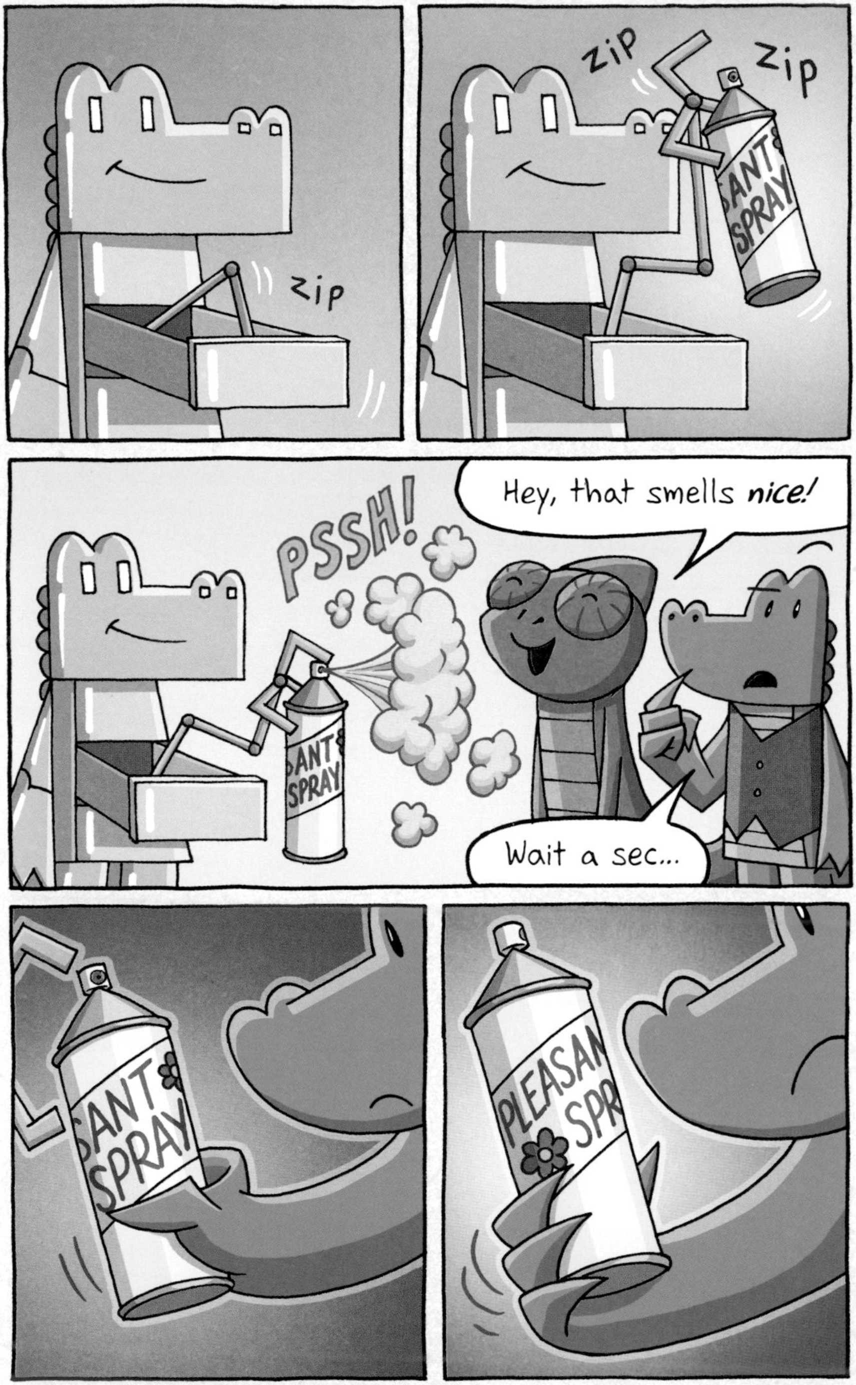
zip
zip
zip
PSSH!
Hey, that smells nice!
Wait a sec...
ANT SPRAY
PLEASAN SPR

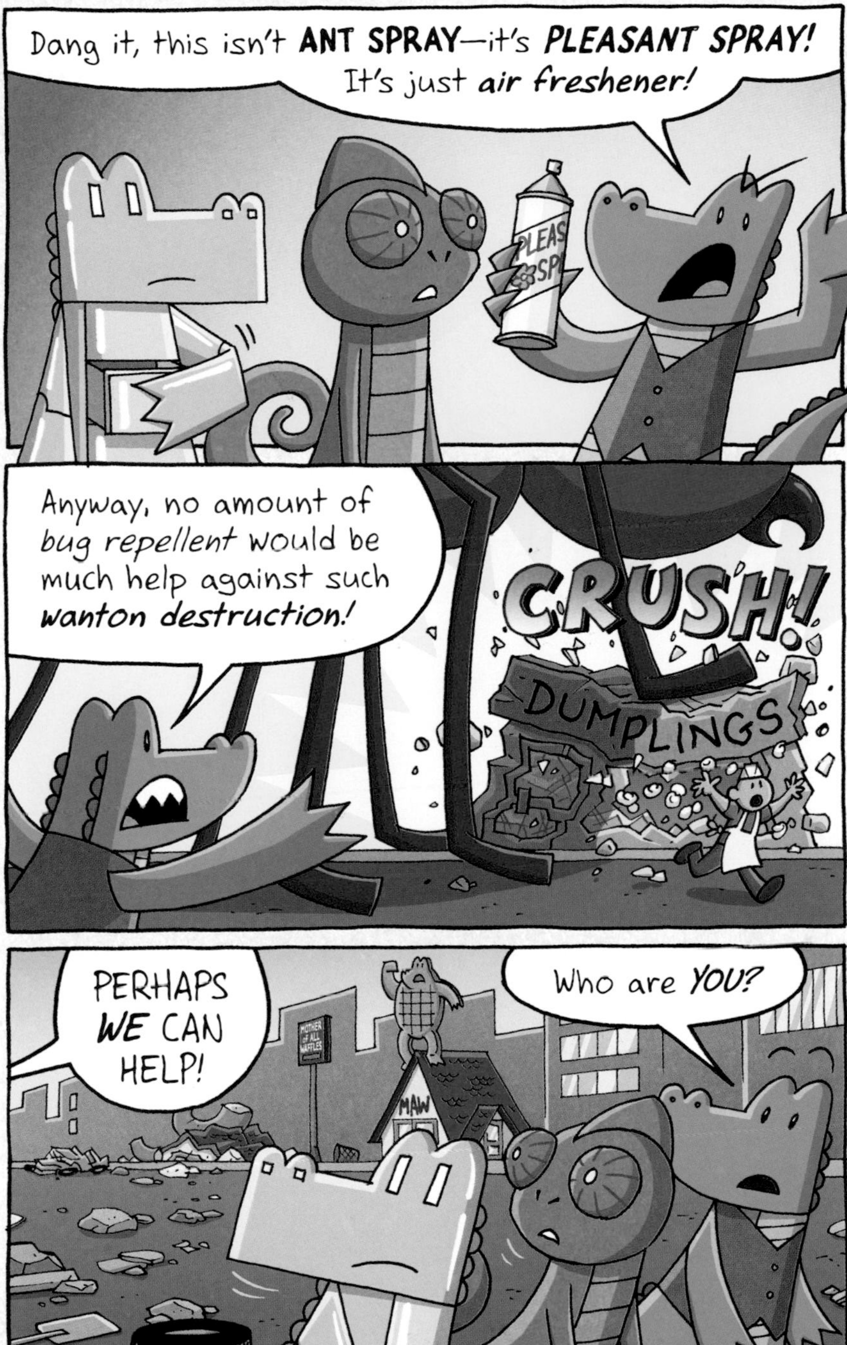
Dang it, this isn't ANT SPRAY—it's PLEASANT SPRAY! It's just air freshener!
Anyway, no amount of bug repellent would be much help against such wanton destruction!
CRUSH!
DUMPLINGS
PERHAPS WE CAN HELP!
Who are YOU?
MOTHER OF ALL WAFFLES
MAW

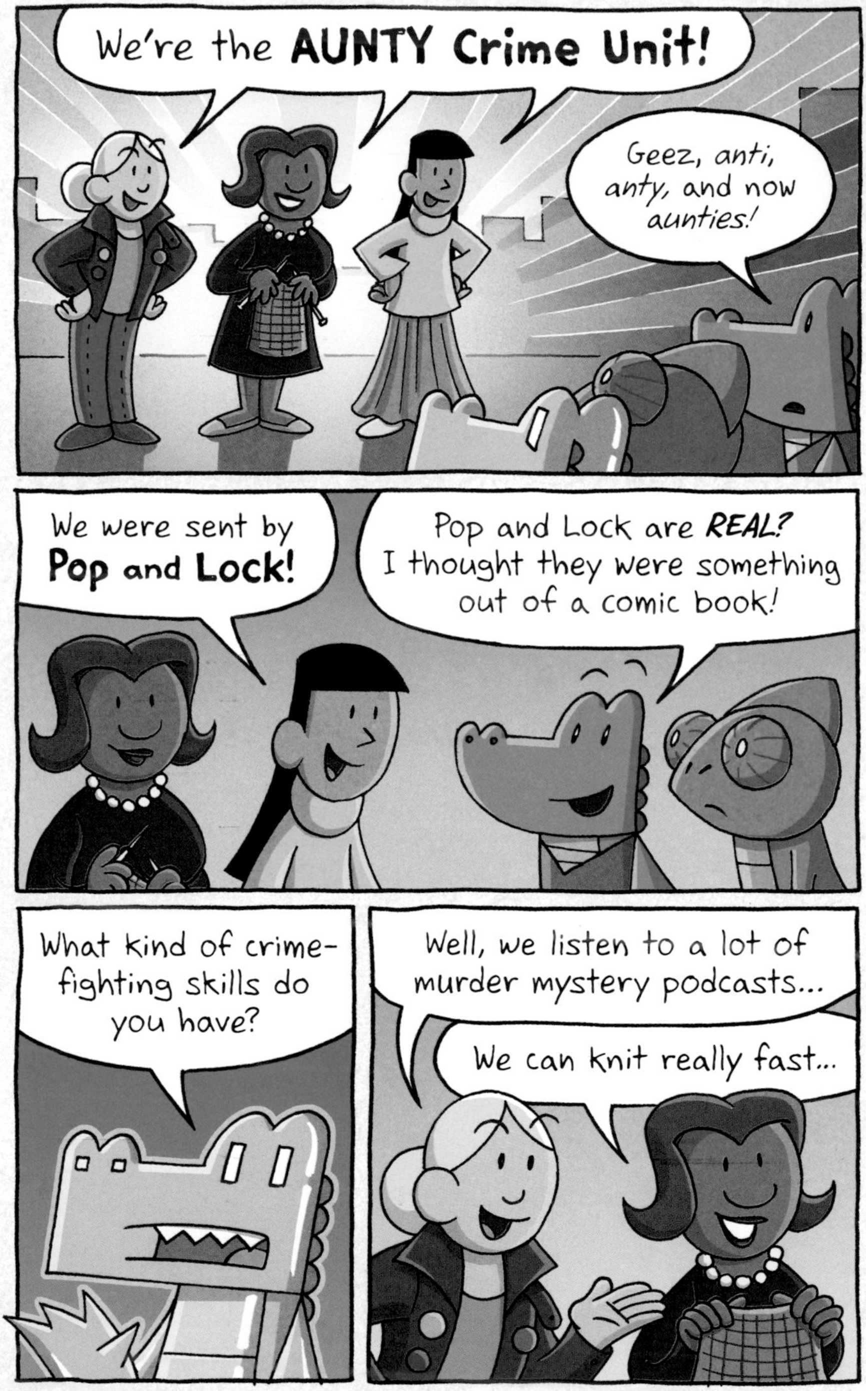
We're the **AUNTY Crime Unit!**
Geez, anti, anty, and now aunties!
We were sent by **Pop and Lock!**
Pop and Lock are ***REAL?*** I thought they were something out of a comic book!
What kind of crime-fighting skills do you have?
Well, we listen to a lot of murder mystery podcasts...
We can knit really fast...

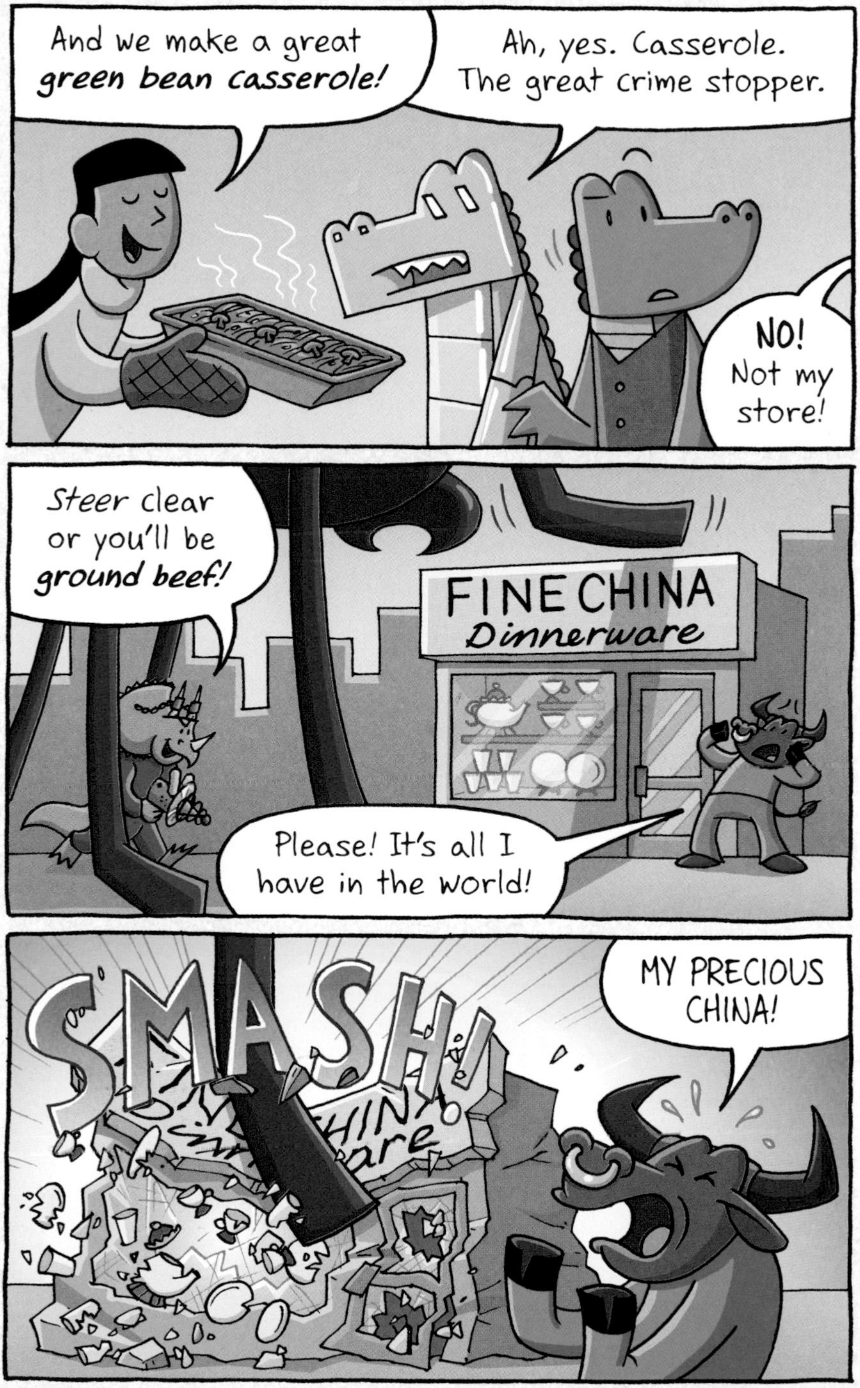
And we make a great **green bean casserole!**
Ah, yes. Casserole. The great crime stopper.
**NO!** Not my store!
*Steer* clear or you'll be **ground beef!**
FINE CHINA Dinnerware
Please! It's all I have in the world!
SMASH!
MY PRECIOUS CHINA!

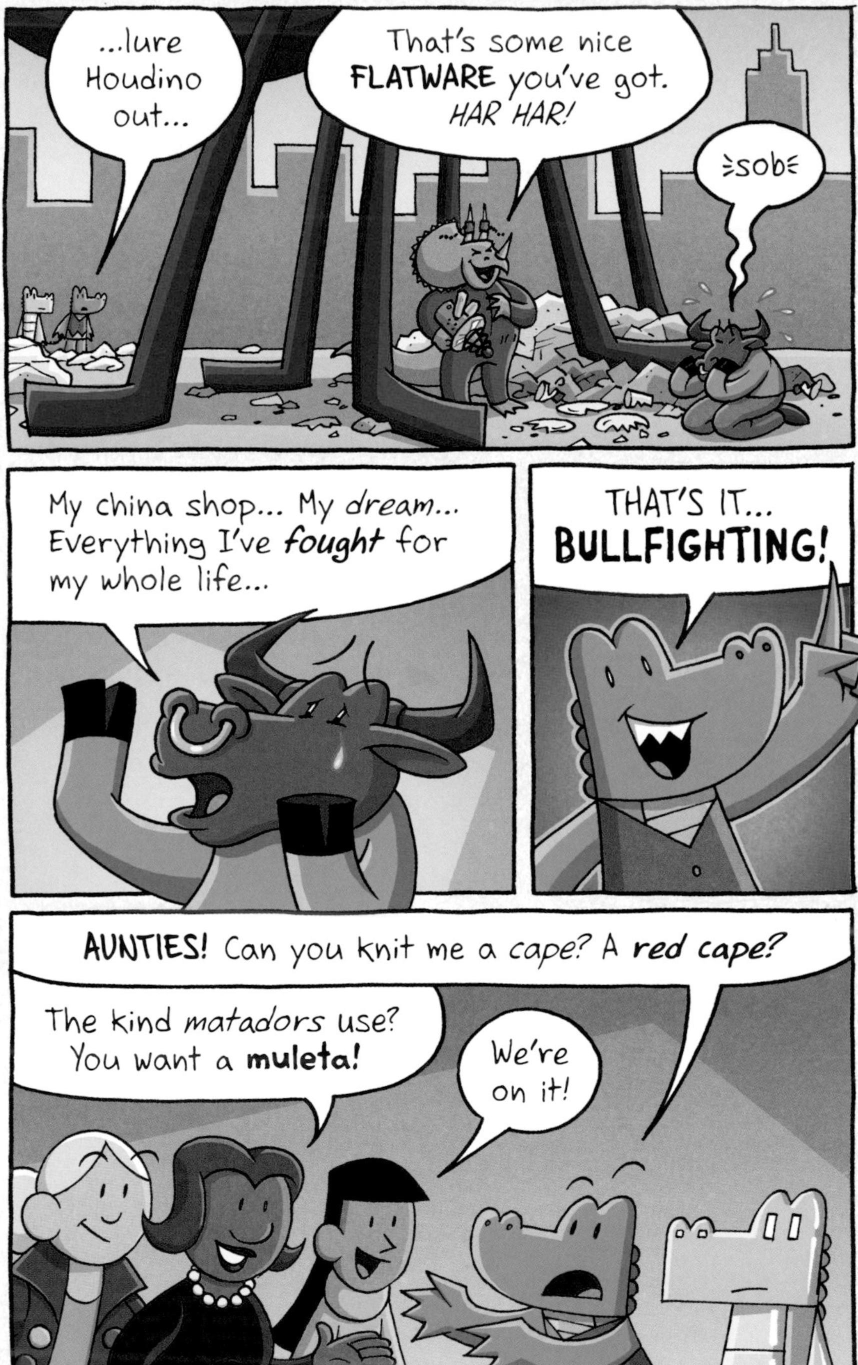

...lure Houdino out...
That's some nice **FLATWARE** you've got. *HAR HAR!*
sob
My china shop... My *dream*... Everything I've ***fought*** for my whole life...
THAT'S IT... **BULLFIGHTING!**
**AUNTIES!** Can you knit me a *cape?* A ***red cape?***
The kind *matadors* use? You want a **muleta!**
We're on it!

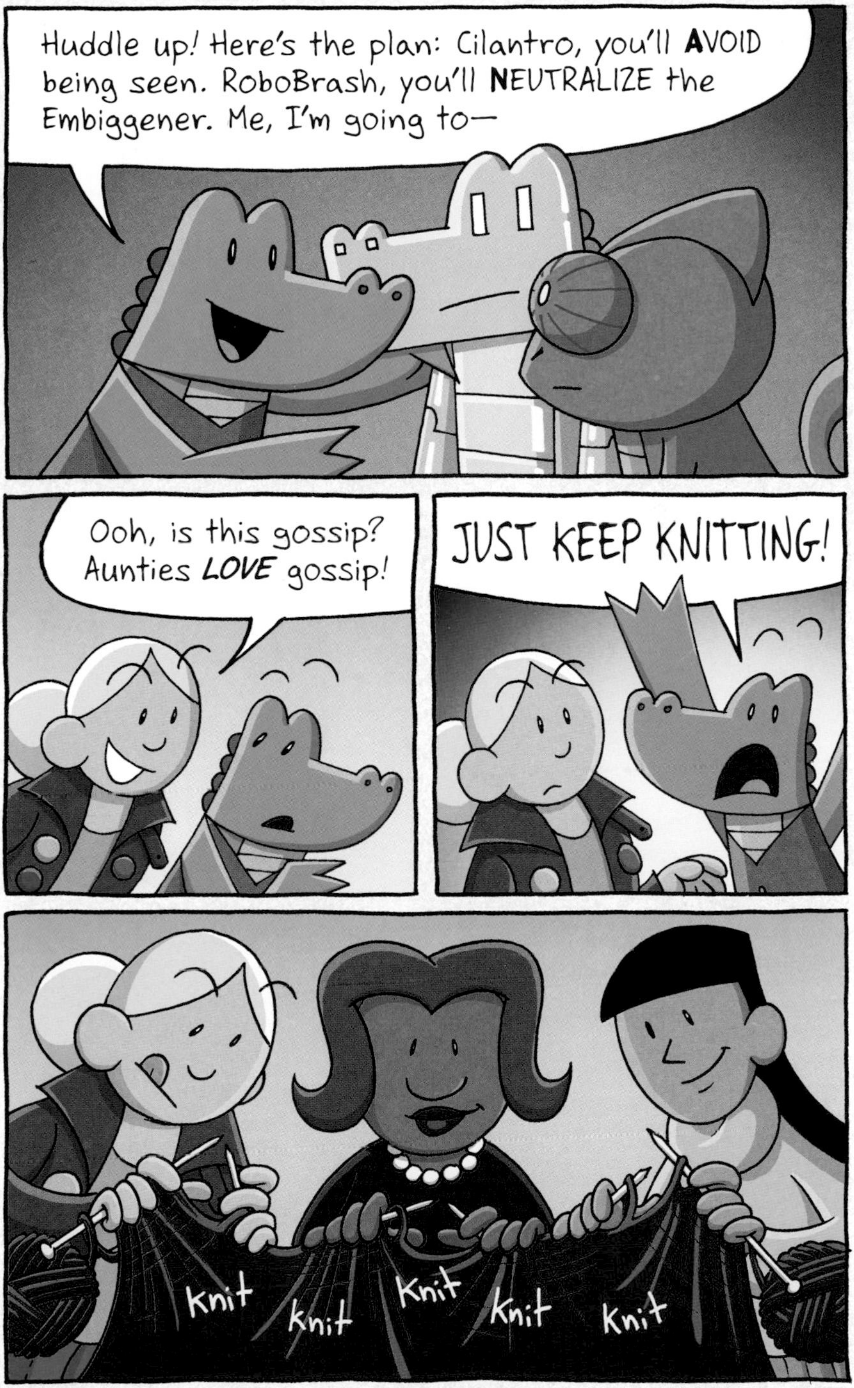
Huddle up! Here's the plan: Cilantro, you'll AVOID being seen. RoboBrash, you'll NEUTRALIZE the Embiggener. Me, I'm going to—
Ooh, is this gossip? Aunties LOVE gossip!
JUST KEEP KNITTING!
knit
knit
knit
knit
knit

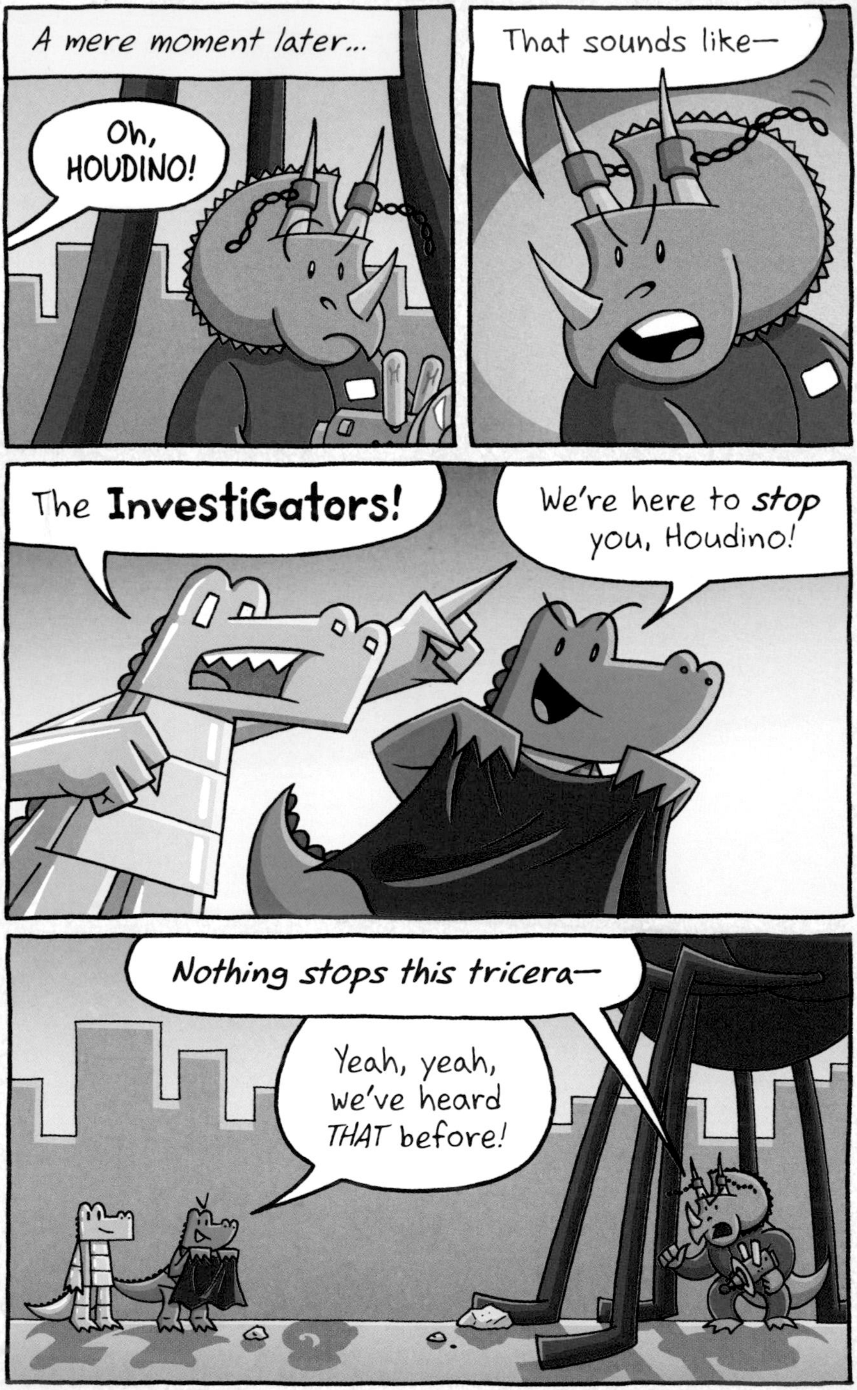
A mere moment later...
Oh, HOUDINO!
That sounds like—
The **InvestiGators!**
We're here to *stop* you, Houdino!
*Nothing stops this tricera—*
Yeah, yeah, we've heard *THAT* before!

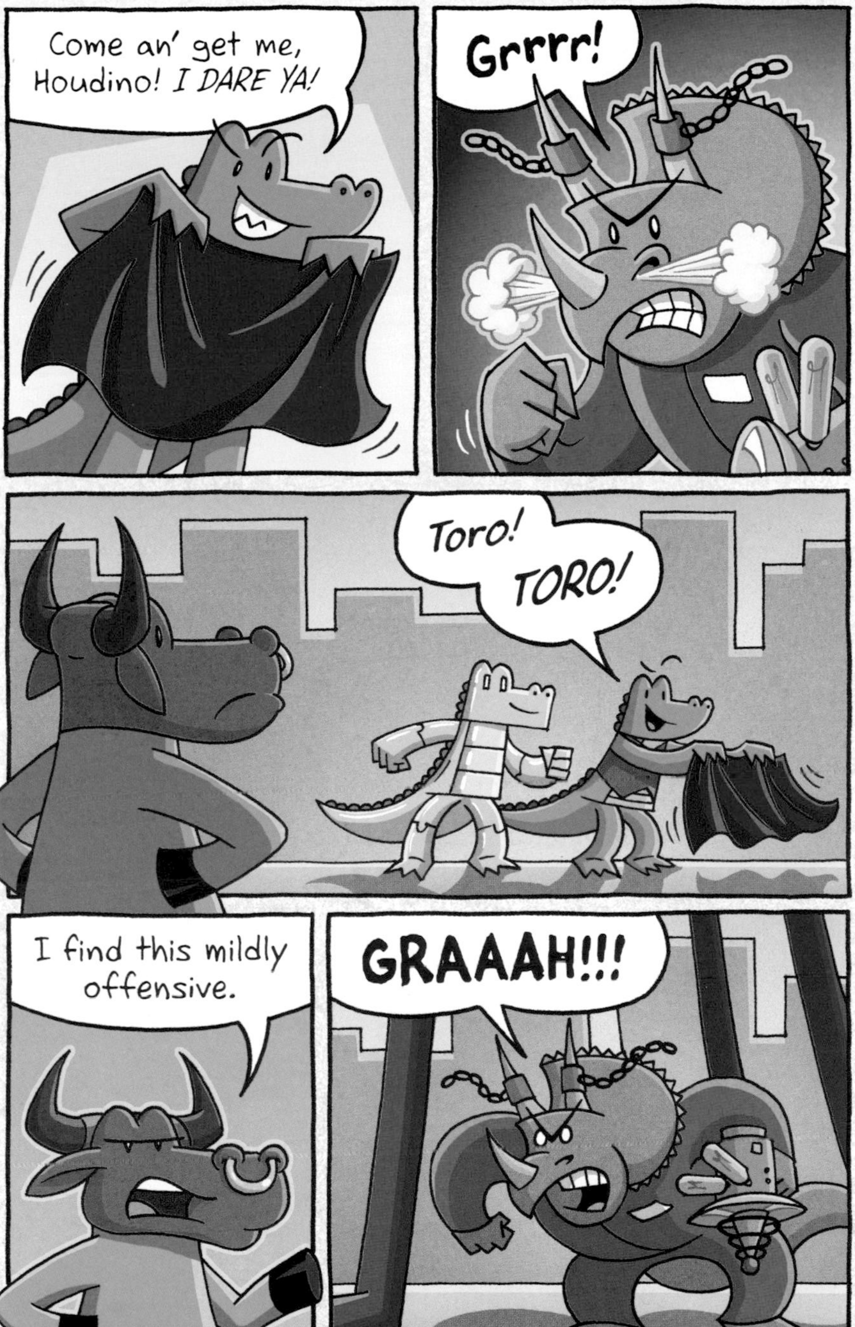
Come an' get me, Houdino! *I DARE YA!*
Grrrr!
*Toro!*
*TORO!*
I find this mildly offensive.
GRAAAH!!!

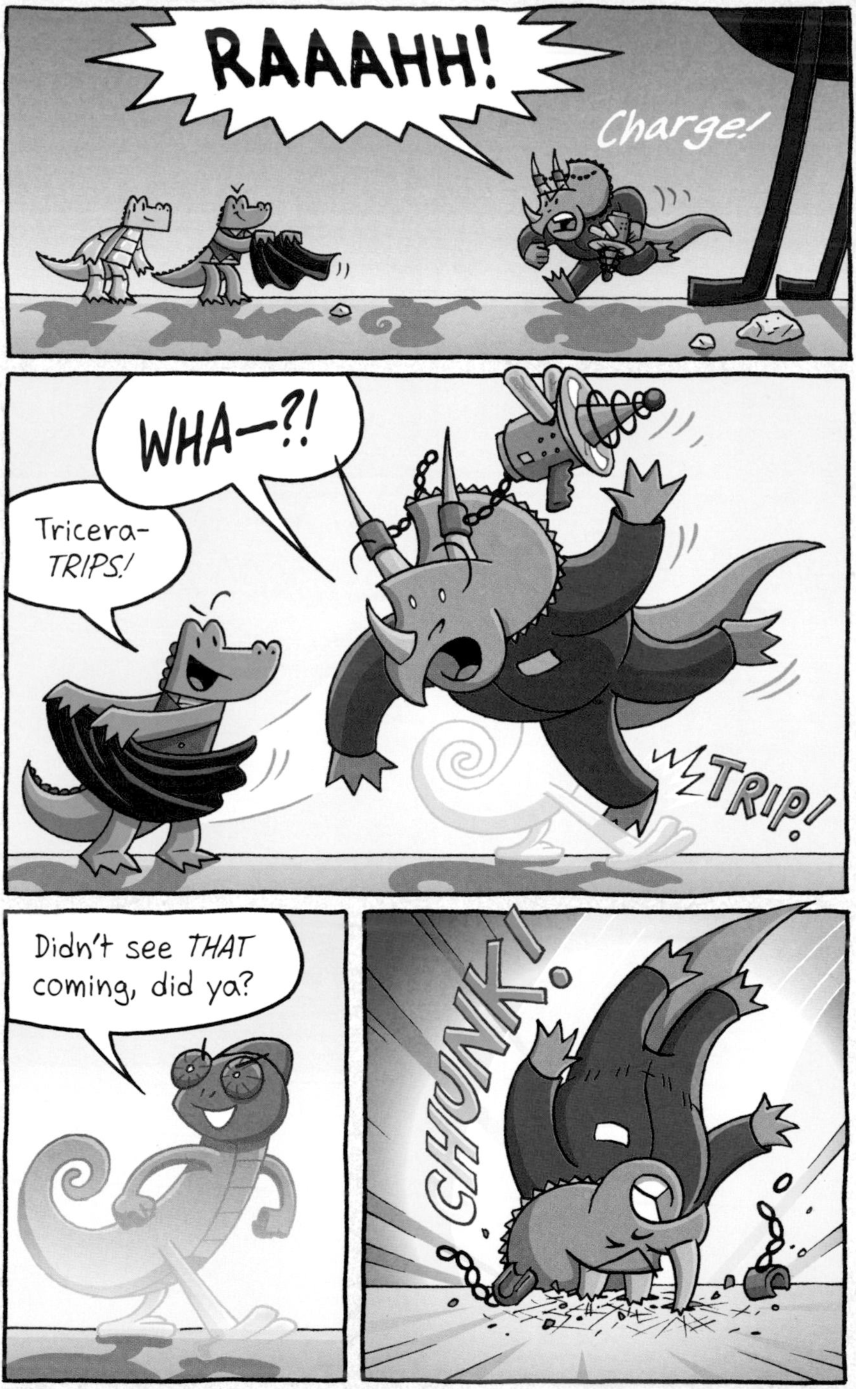

RAAAHH!
Charge!
WHA—?!
Tricera-
TRIPS!
TRIP!
Didn't see THAT
coming, did ya?
CHUNK!

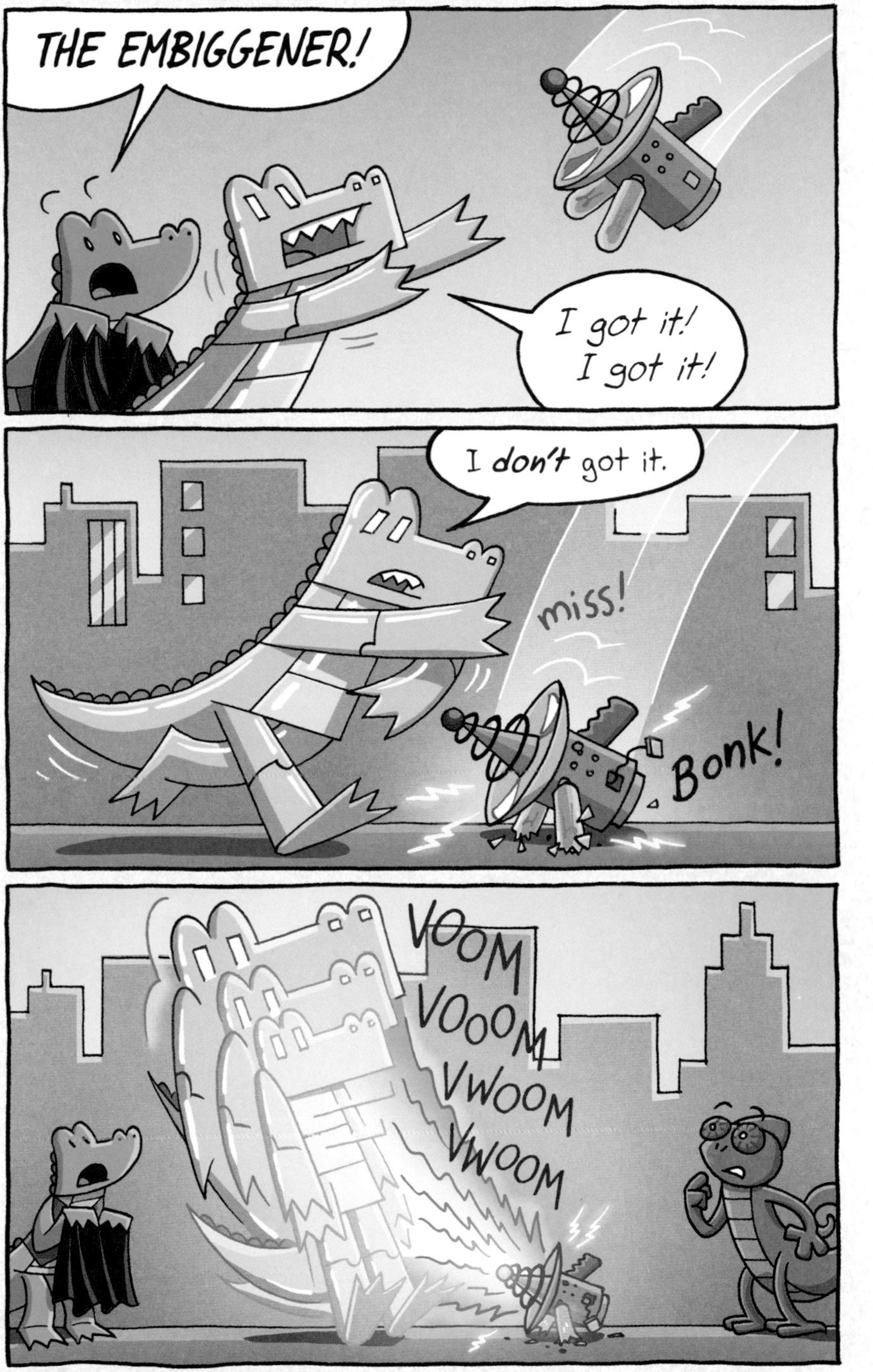
THE EMBIGGENER!
I got it! I got it!
I don't got it.
miss!
Bonk!
VOOM
VOOOM
VWOOM
VWOOM

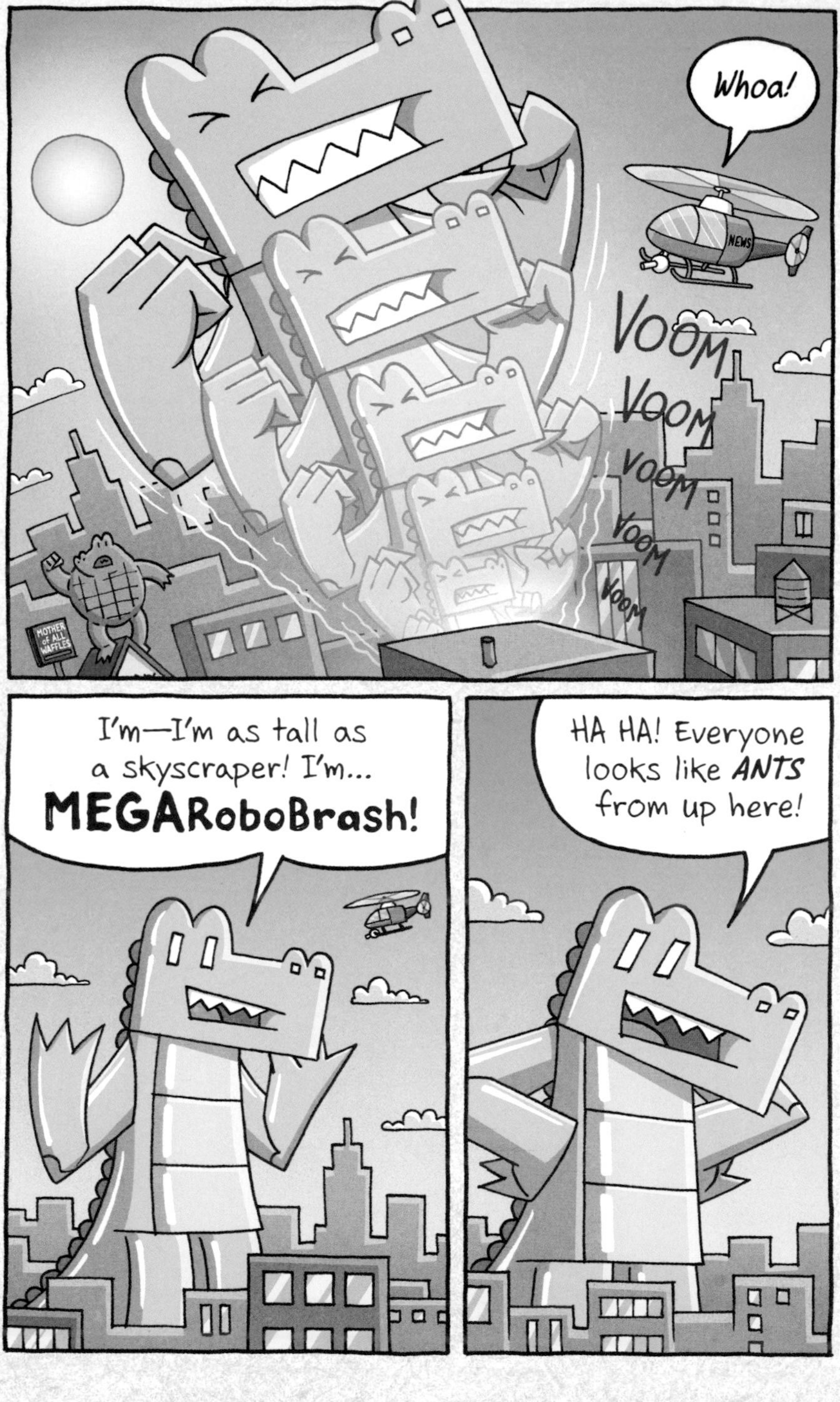
Whoa!
NEWS
VOOM VOOM VOOM VOOM VOOM
MOTHER of ALL WAFFLES
I'm—I'm as tall as a skyscraper! I'm... **MEGARoboBrash!**
HA HA! Everyone looks like ***ANTS*** from up here!

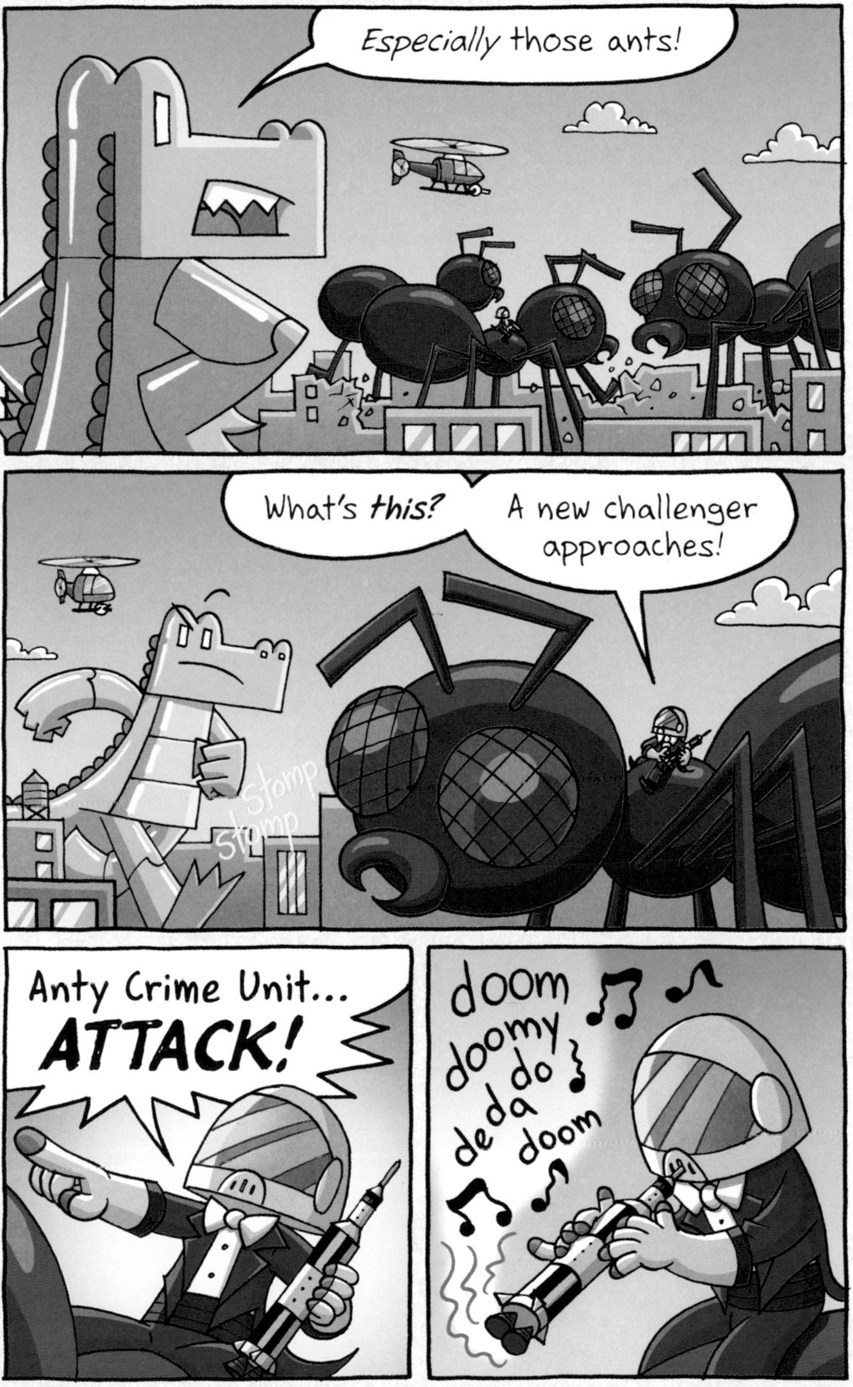
Especially those ants!
What's this?
A new challenger approaches!
Stomp
stomp
Anty Crime Unit... ATTACK!
doom doomy do de da doom

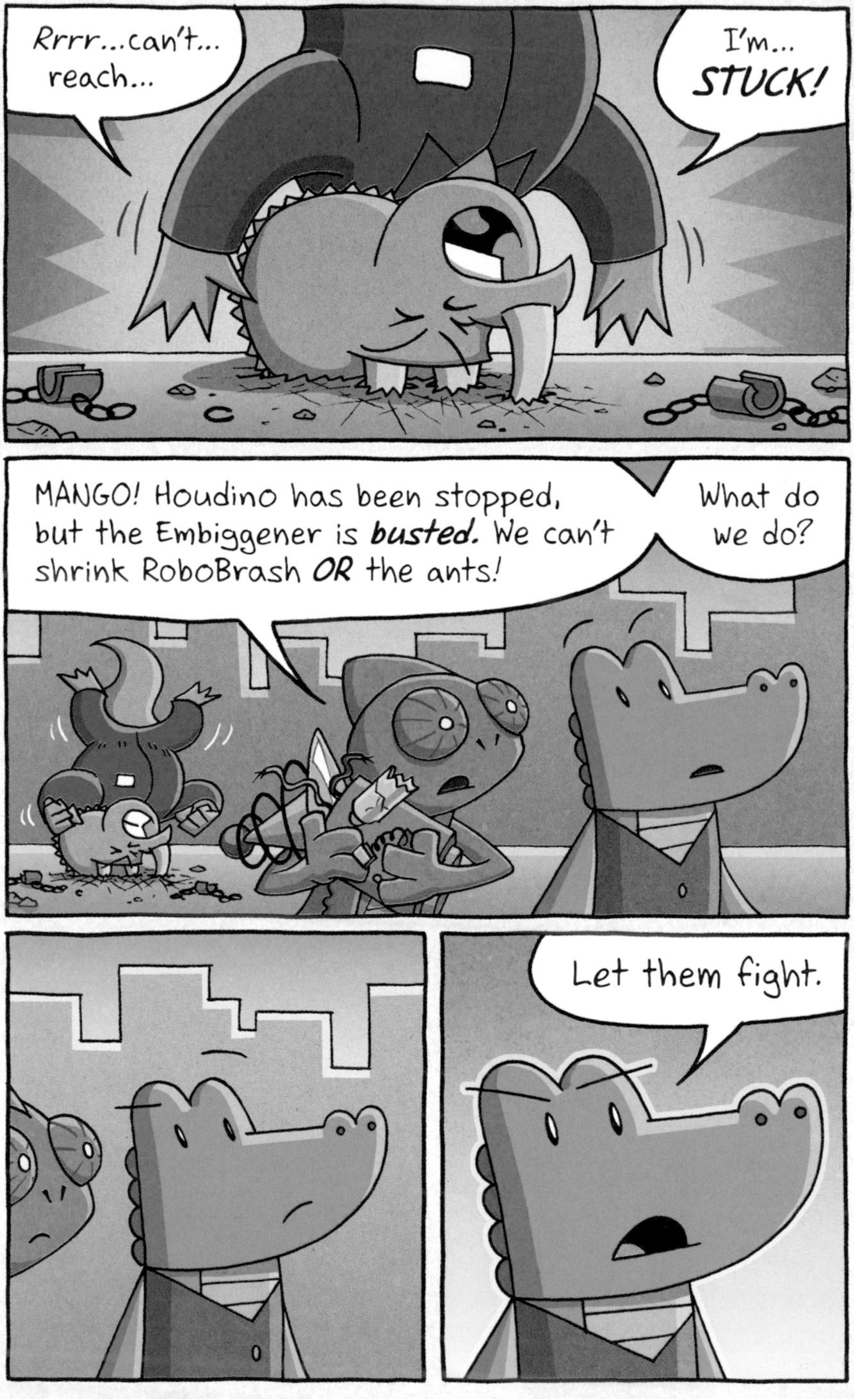
Rrrr...can't... reach...
I'm... STUCK!
MANGO! Houdino has been stopped, but the Embiggener is busted. We can't shrink RoboBrash OR the ants!
What do we do?
Let them fight.

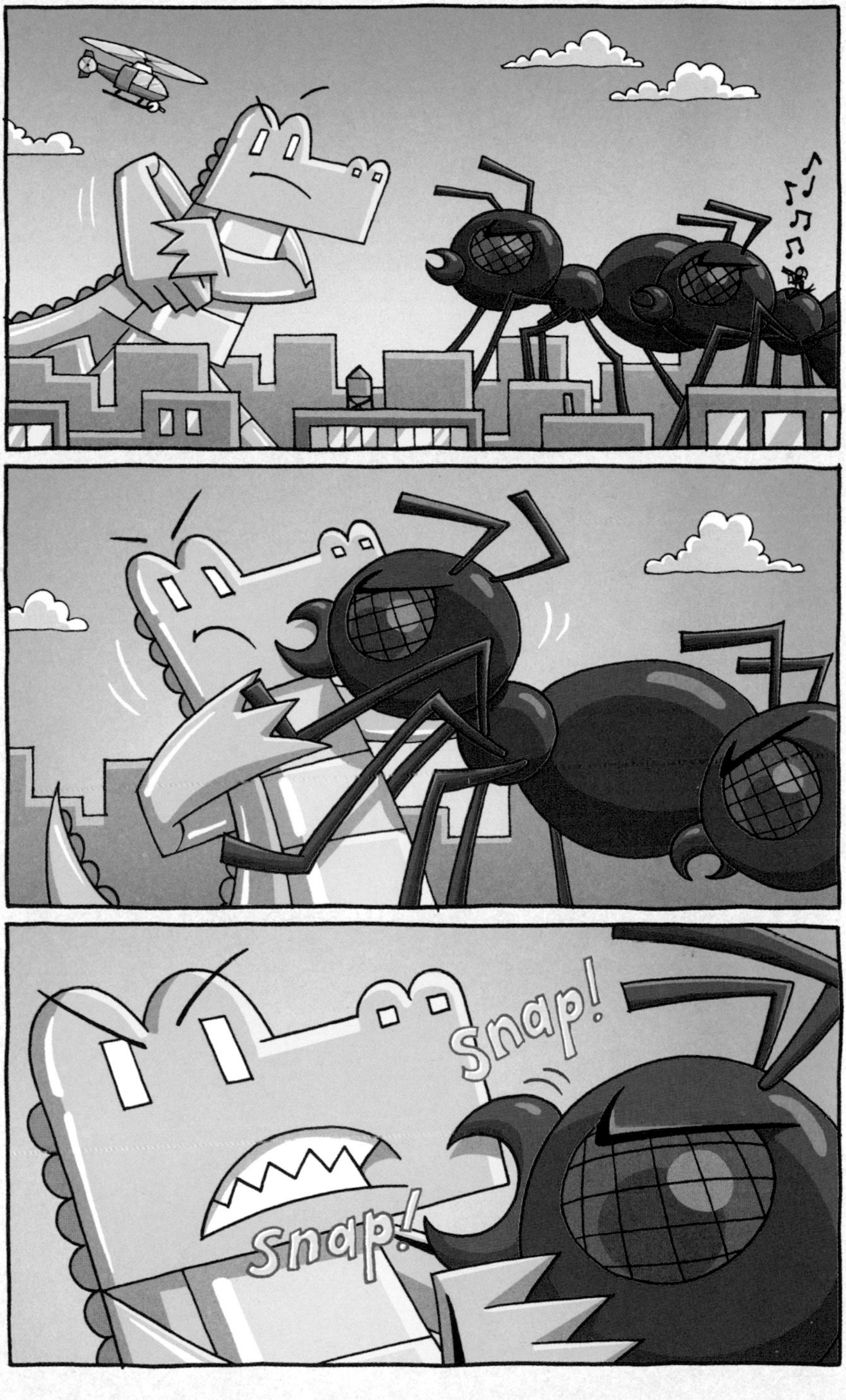
Snap!
Snap!

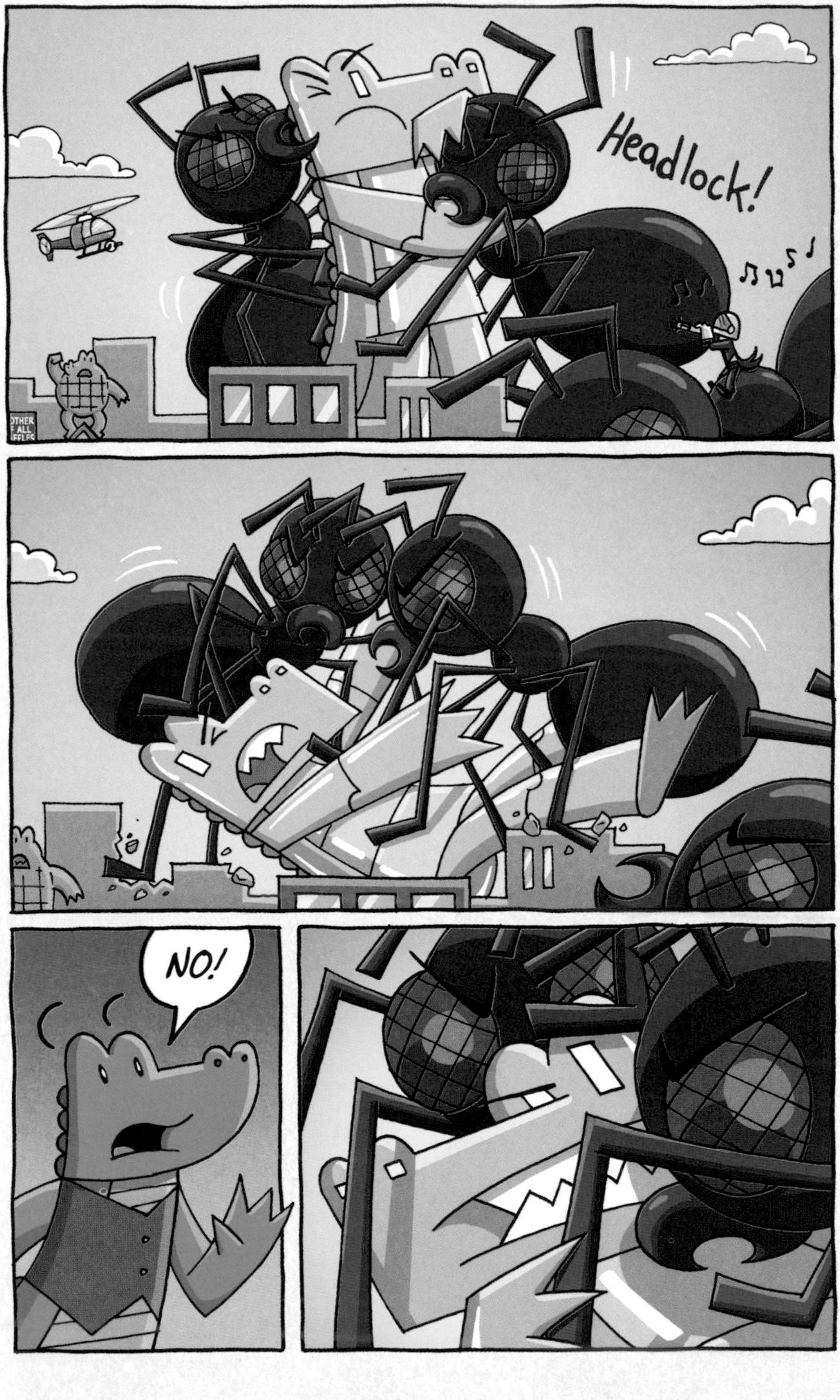
Headlock!
NO!

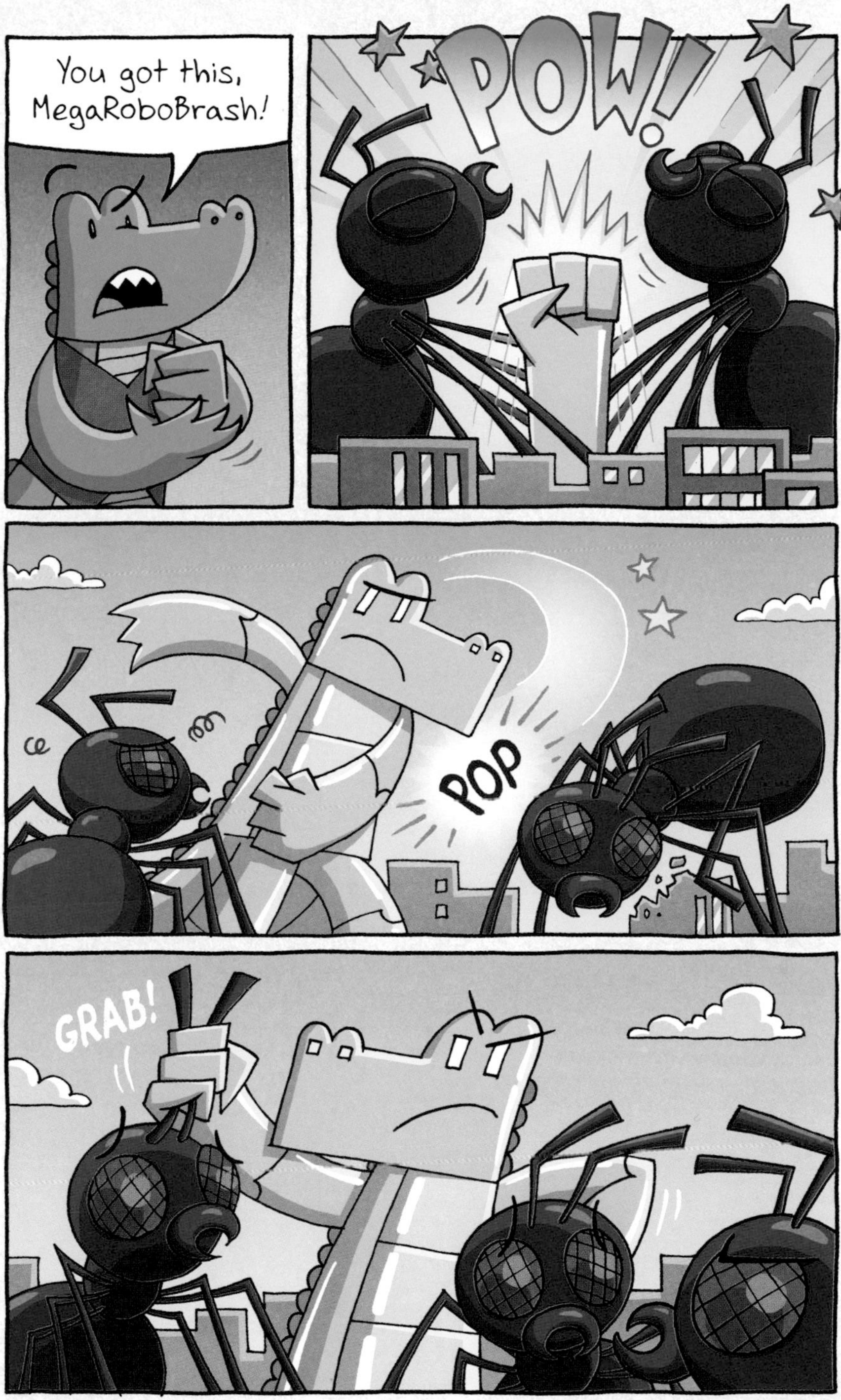
You got this, MegaRoboBrash!
POW!
POP
GRAB!

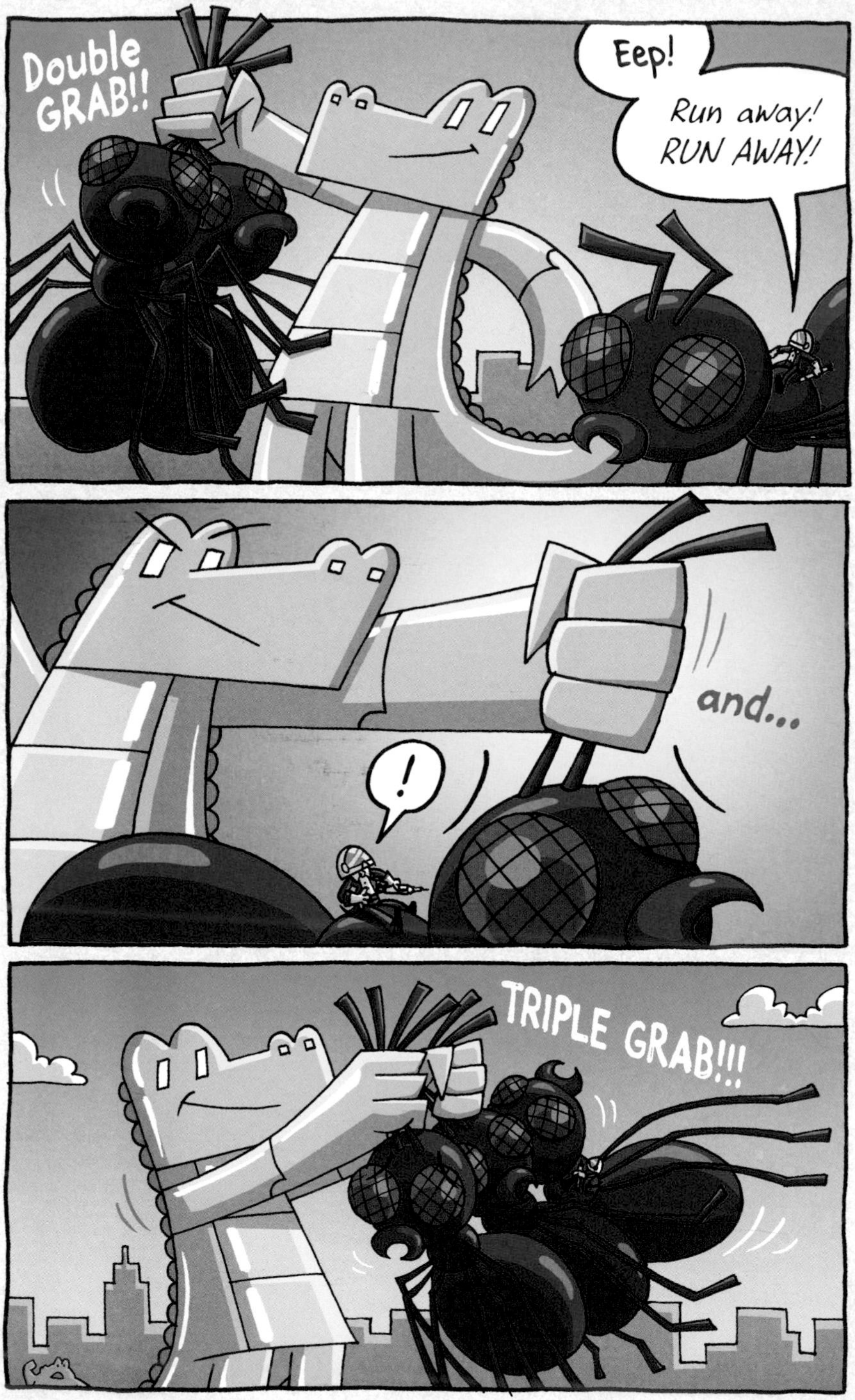
Double GRAB!!
Eep!
Run away! RUN AWAY!
and...
!
TRIPLE GRAB!!!

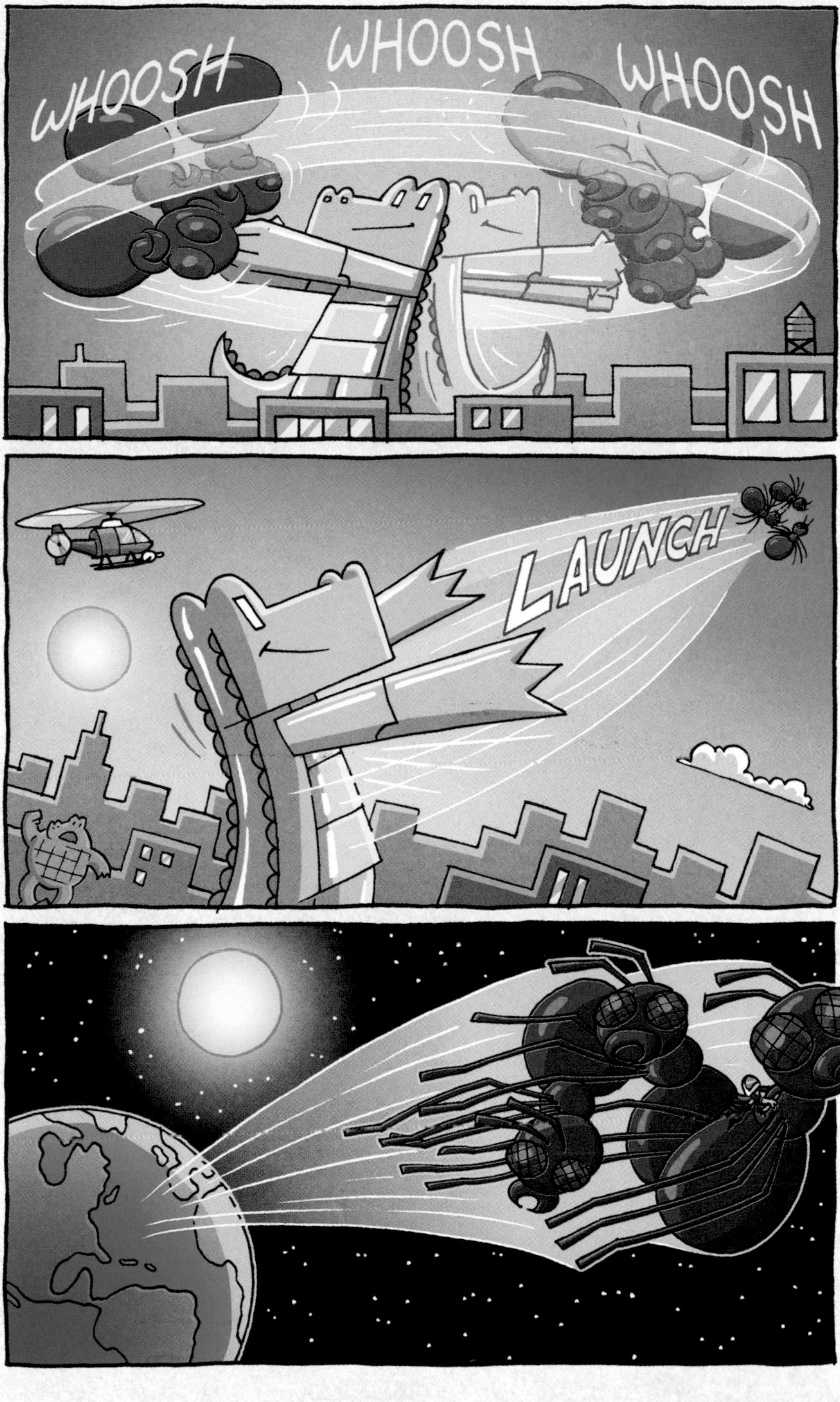
WHOOSH
WHOOSH
WHOOSH
LAUNCH

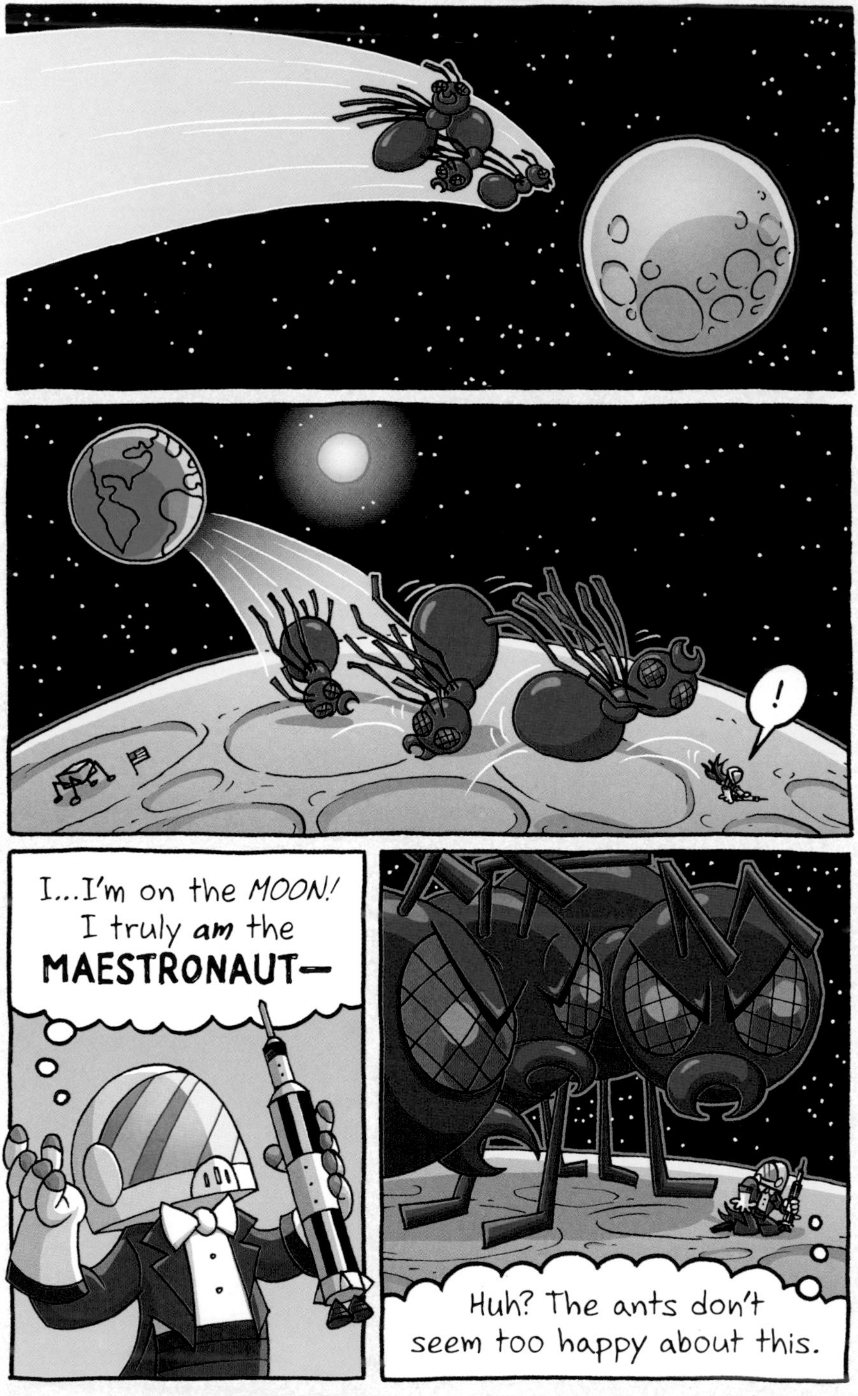
!
I...I'm on the *MOON!* I truly **am** the **MAESTRONAUT—**
Huh? The ants don't seem too happy about this.

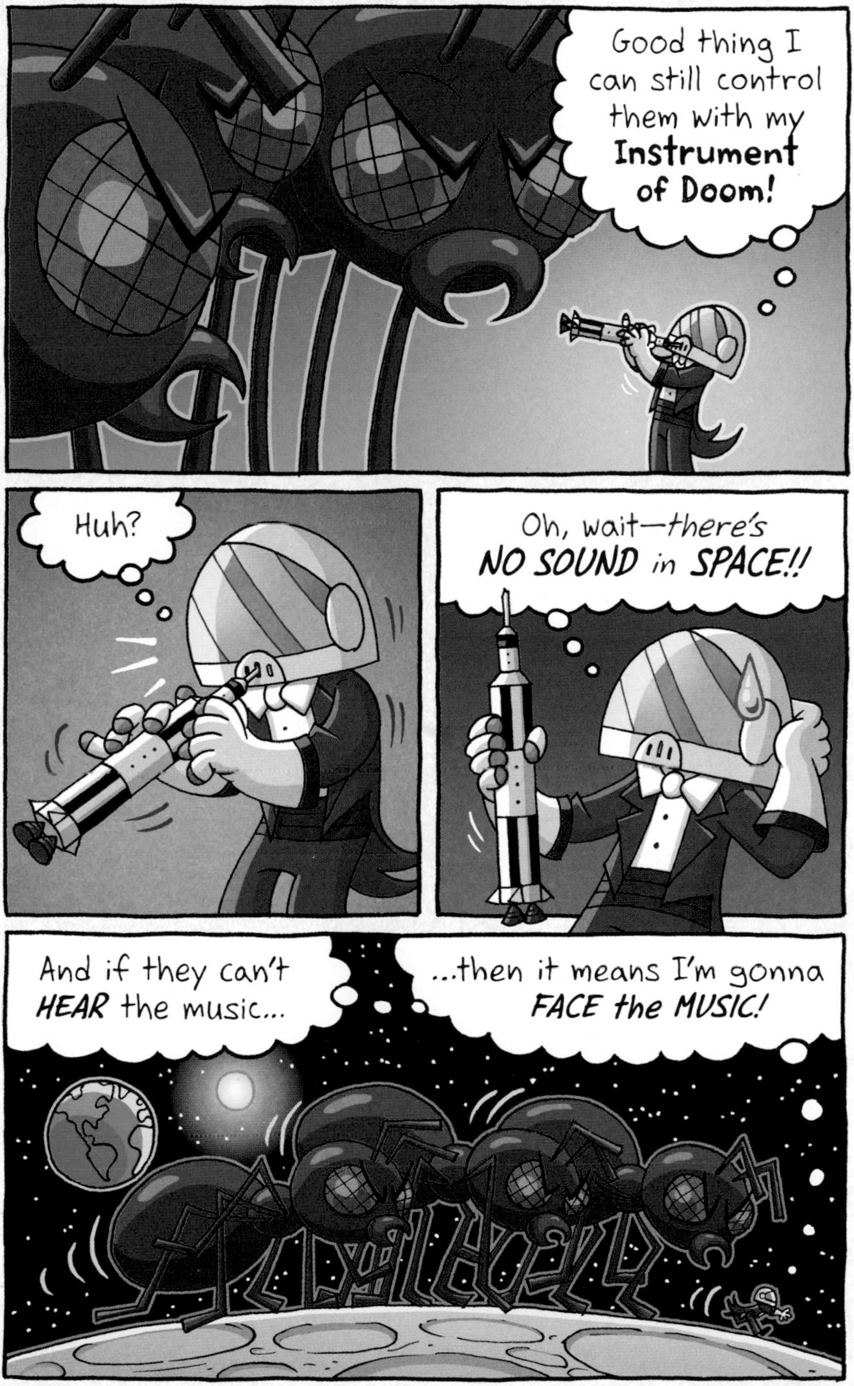
Good thing I can still control them with my **Instrument of Doom!**
Huh?
Oh, wait—*there's* ***NO SOUND*** *in* ***SPACE!!***
And if they can't ***HEAR*** the music...
...then it means I'm gonna ***FACE the MUSIC!***

# Chapter 15

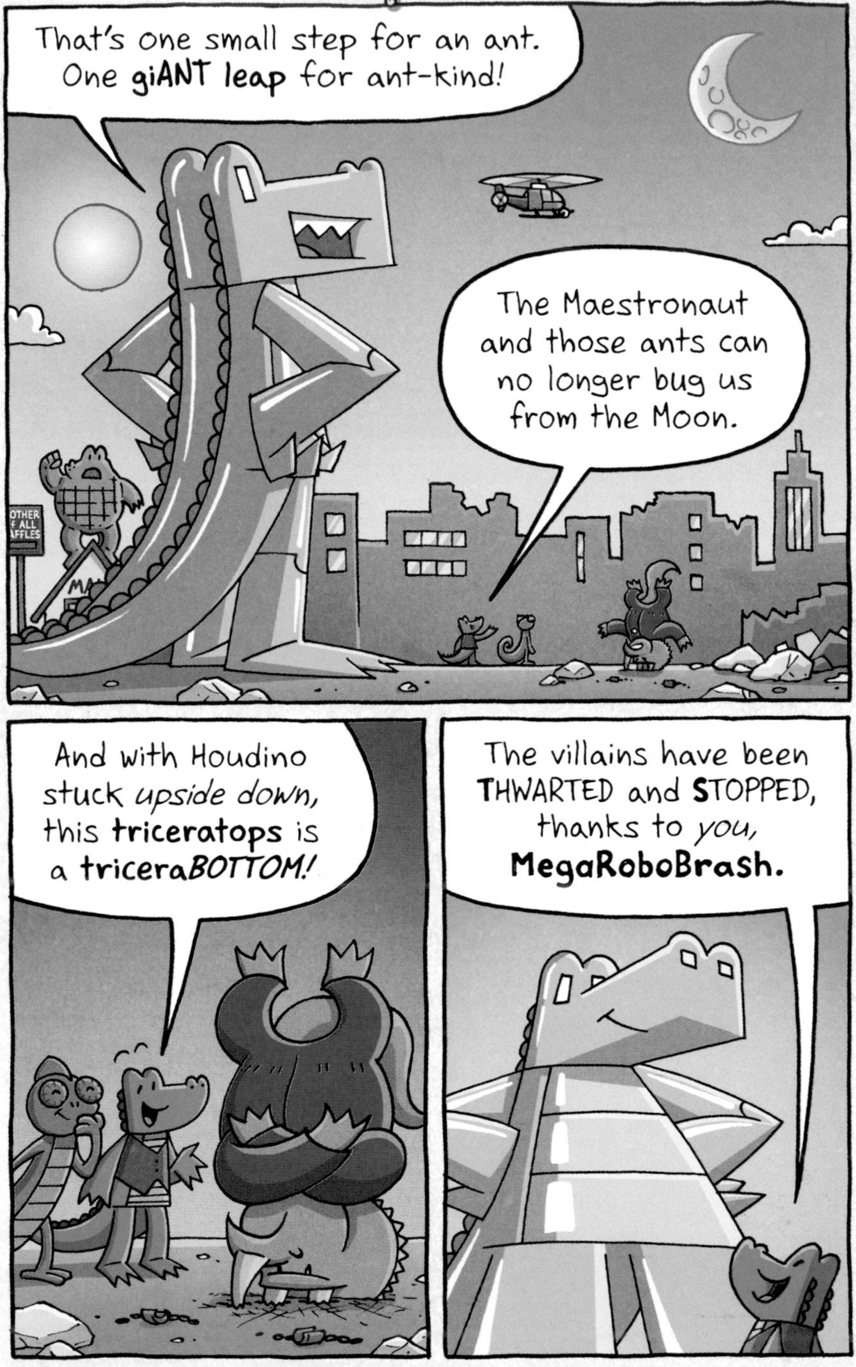
That's one small step for an ant. One **giANT leap** for ant-kind!
The Maestronaut and those ants can no longer bug us from the Moon.
And with Houdino stuck *upside down*, this **triceratops** is a **tricera*BOTTOM!***
The villains have been **T**HWARTED and **S**TOPPED, thanks to *you*, **MegaRoboBrash.**

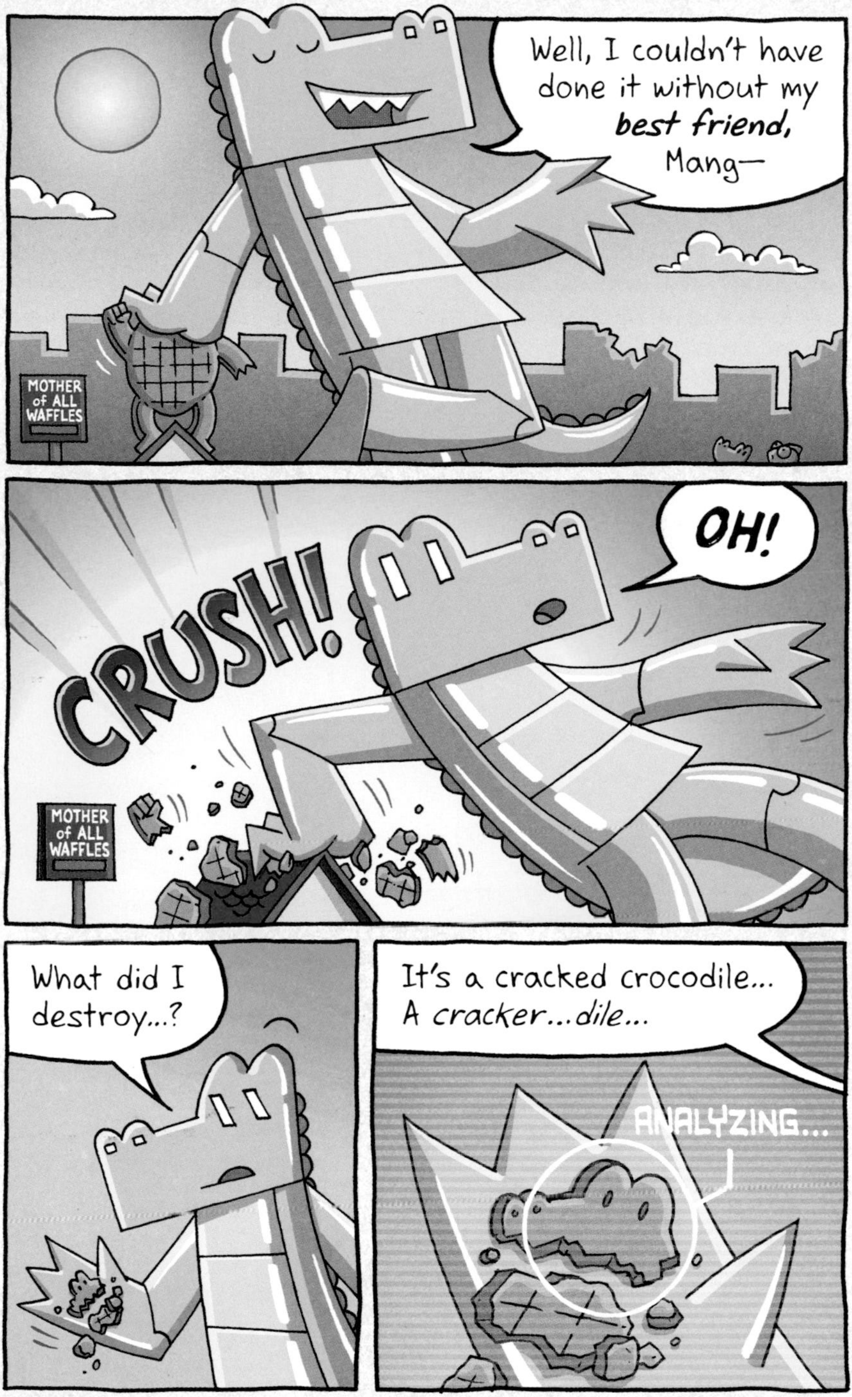
Well, I couldn't have done it without my **best friend,** Mang—
MOTHER of ALL WAFFLES
CRUSH!
OH!
MOTHER of ALL WAFFLES
What did I destroy...?
It's a cracked crocodile... A *cracker...dile...*
ANALYZING...

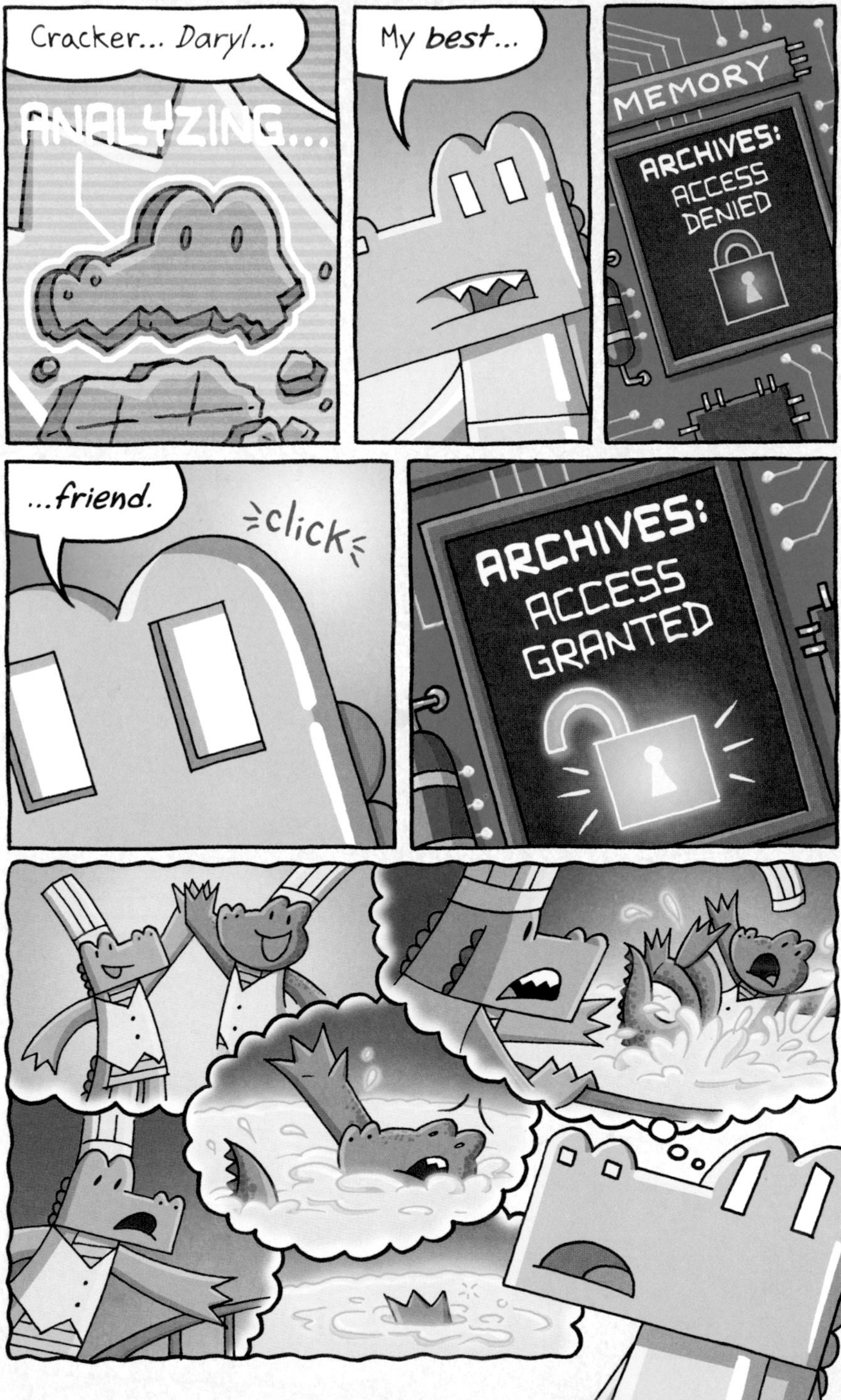
Cracker... Daryl...
ANALYZING...
My best...
MEMORY
ARCHIVES: ACCESS DENIED
...friend.
click
ARCHIVES: ACCESS GRANTED

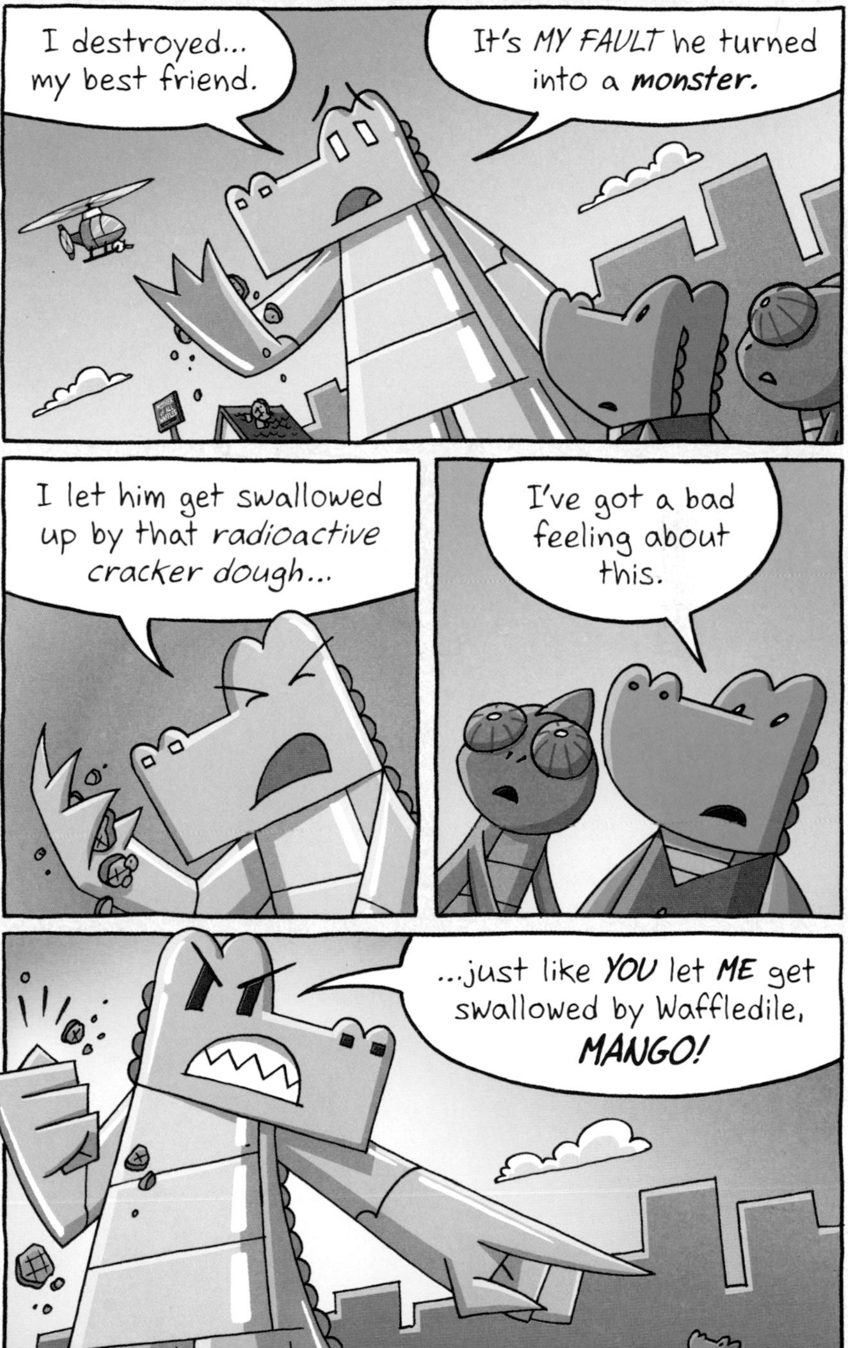
I destroyed... my best friend.
It's *MY FAULT* he turned into a **monster.**
I let him get swallowed up by that *radioactive* cracker dough...
I've got a bad feeling about this.
...just like **YOU** let **ME** get swallowed by Waffledile, **MANGO!**

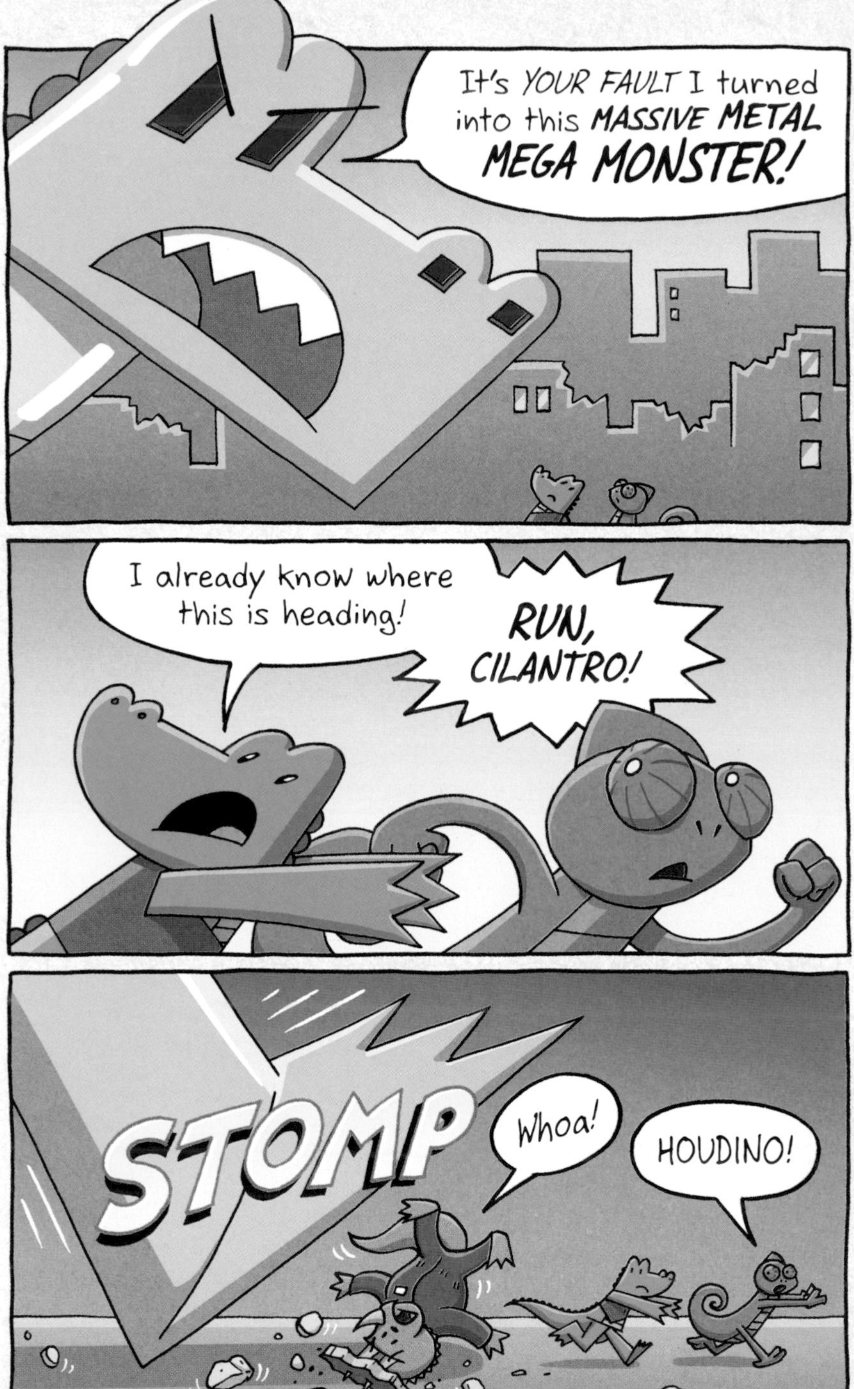
It's YOUR FAULT I turned into this MASSIVE METAL MEGA MONSTER!
I already know where this is heading!
RUN, CILANTRO!
STOMP
Whoa!
HOUDINO!

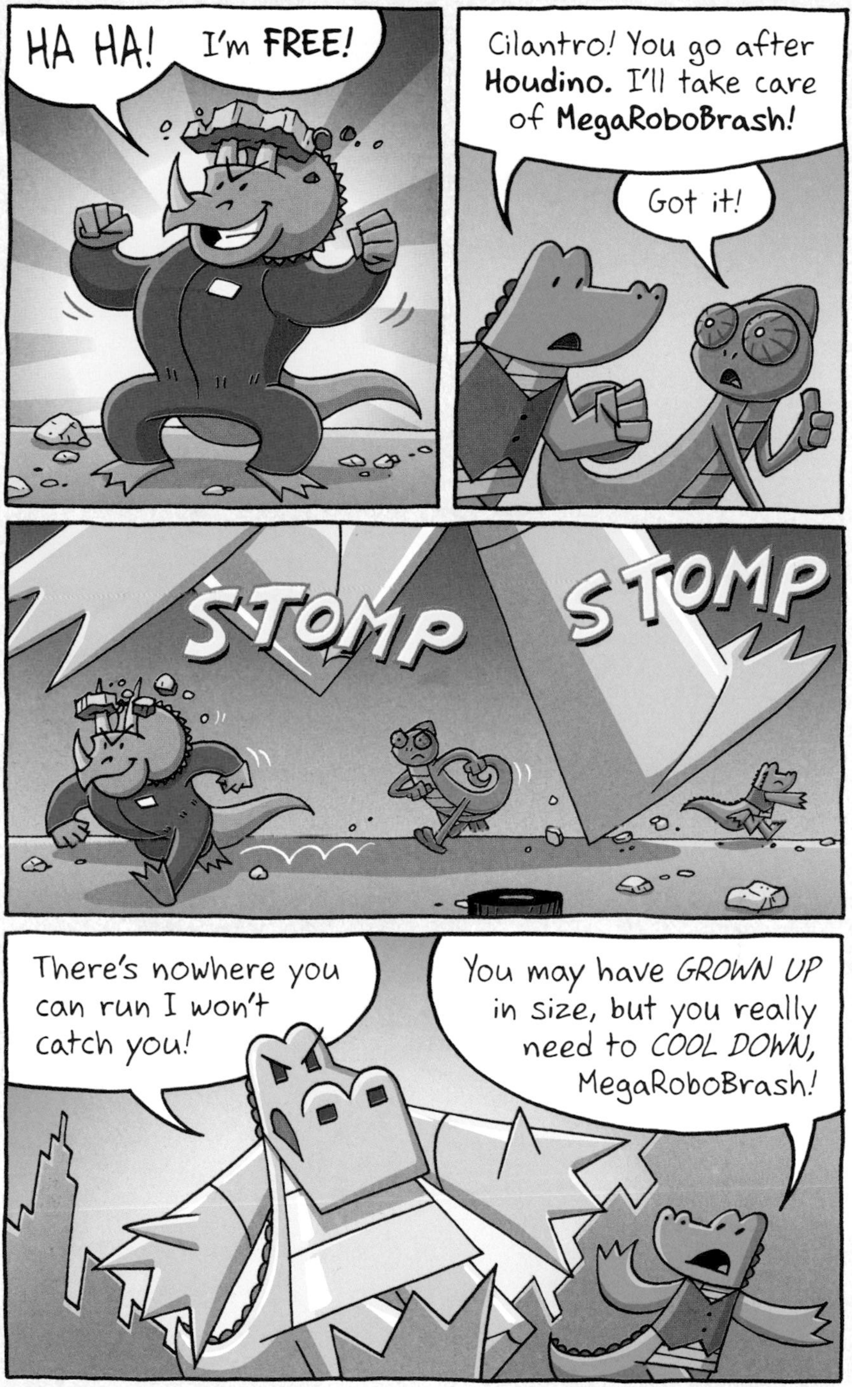
HA HA! I'm FREE!
Cilantro! You go after Houdino. I'll take care of MegaRoboBrash!
Got it!
STOMP
STOMP
There's nowhere you can run I won't catch you!
You may have GROWN UP in size, but you really need to COOL DOWN, MegaRoboBrash!

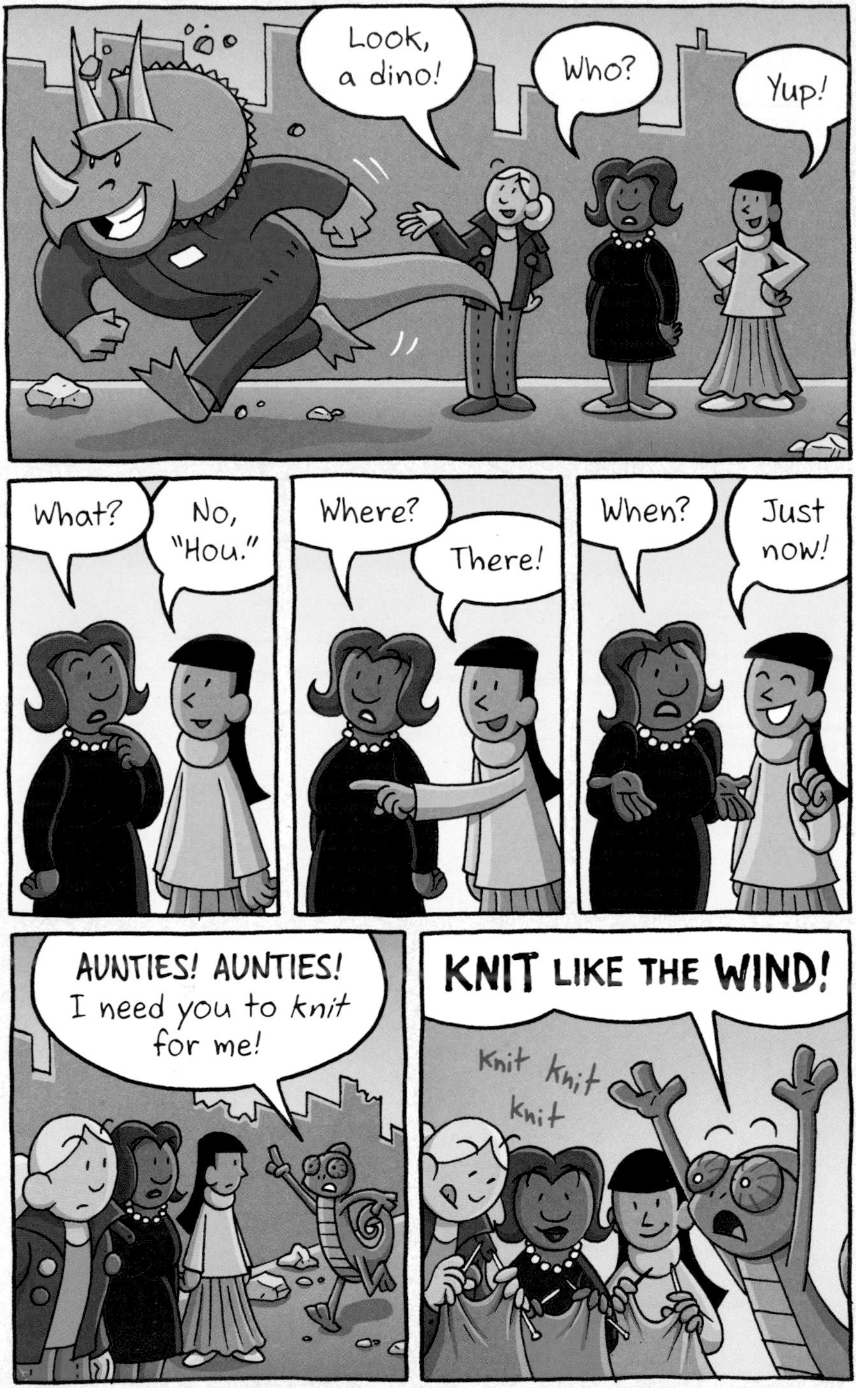

Look, a dino!
Who?
Yup!
What?
No, "Hou."
Where?
There!
When?
Just now!
AUNTIES! AUNTIES! I need you to knit for me!
KNIT LIKE THE WIND!
Knit knit knit

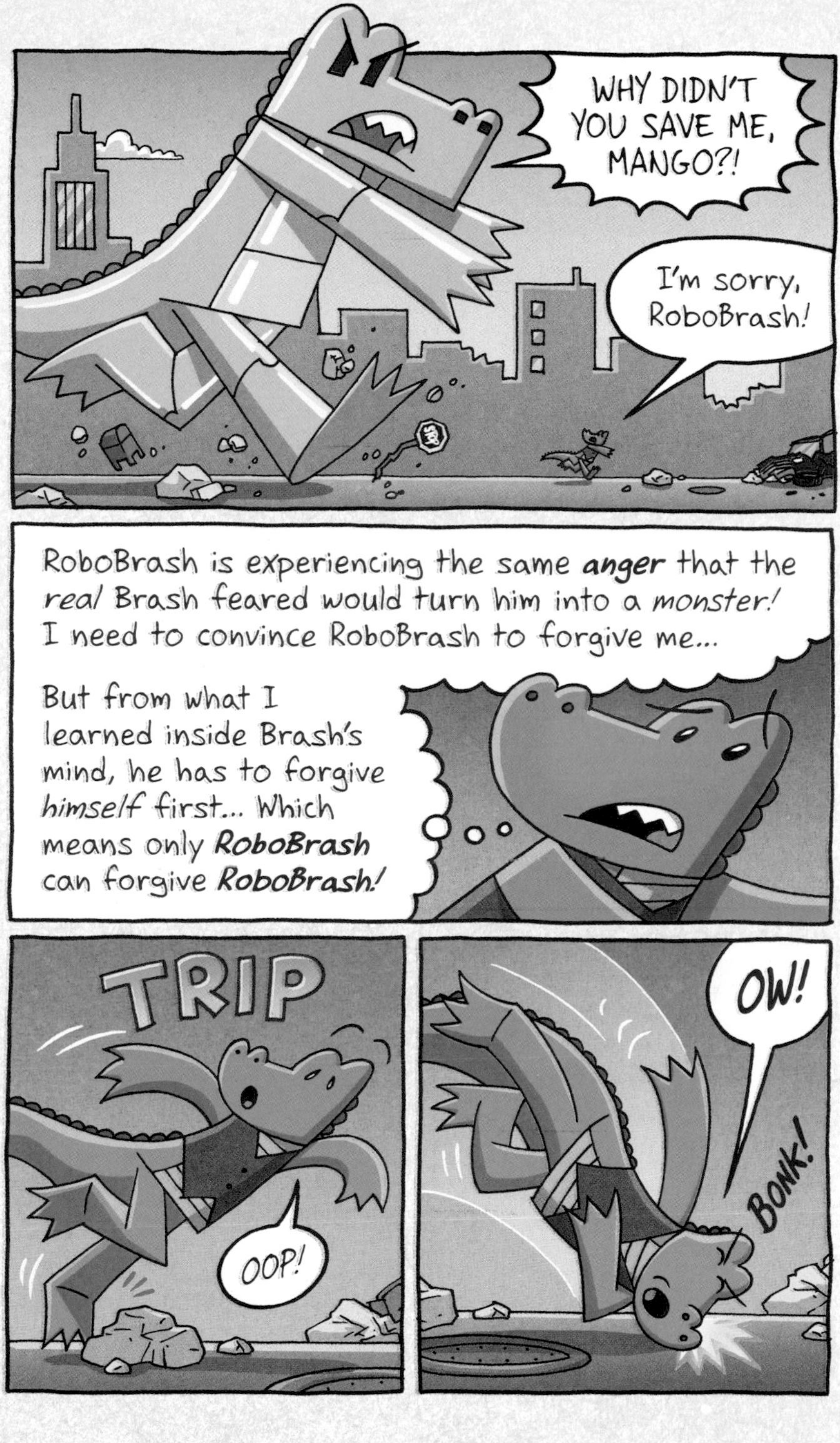
WHY DIDN'T YOU SAVE ME, MANGO?!
I'm sorry, RoboBrash!
STOP
RoboBrash is experiencing the same **anger** that the *real* Brash feared would turn him into a *monster!* I need to convince RoboBrash to forgive me...
But from what I learned inside Brash's mind, he has to forgive *himself* first... Which means only **RoboBrash** can forgive **RoboBrash!**
TRIP
OOP!
OW!
BONK!

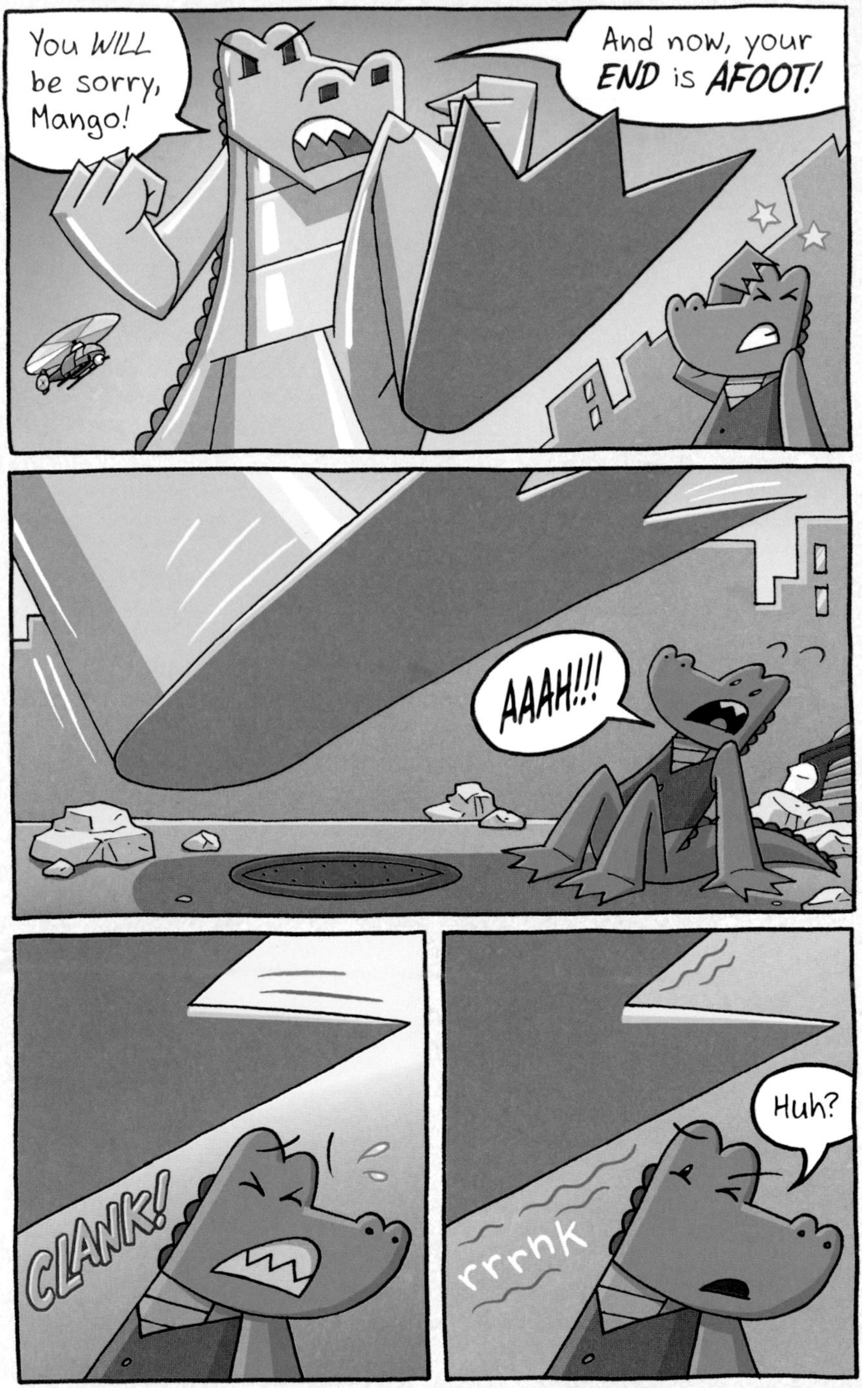
You WILL be sorry, Mango!
And now, your END is AFOOT!
AAAH!!!
CLANK!
rrrnk
Huh?

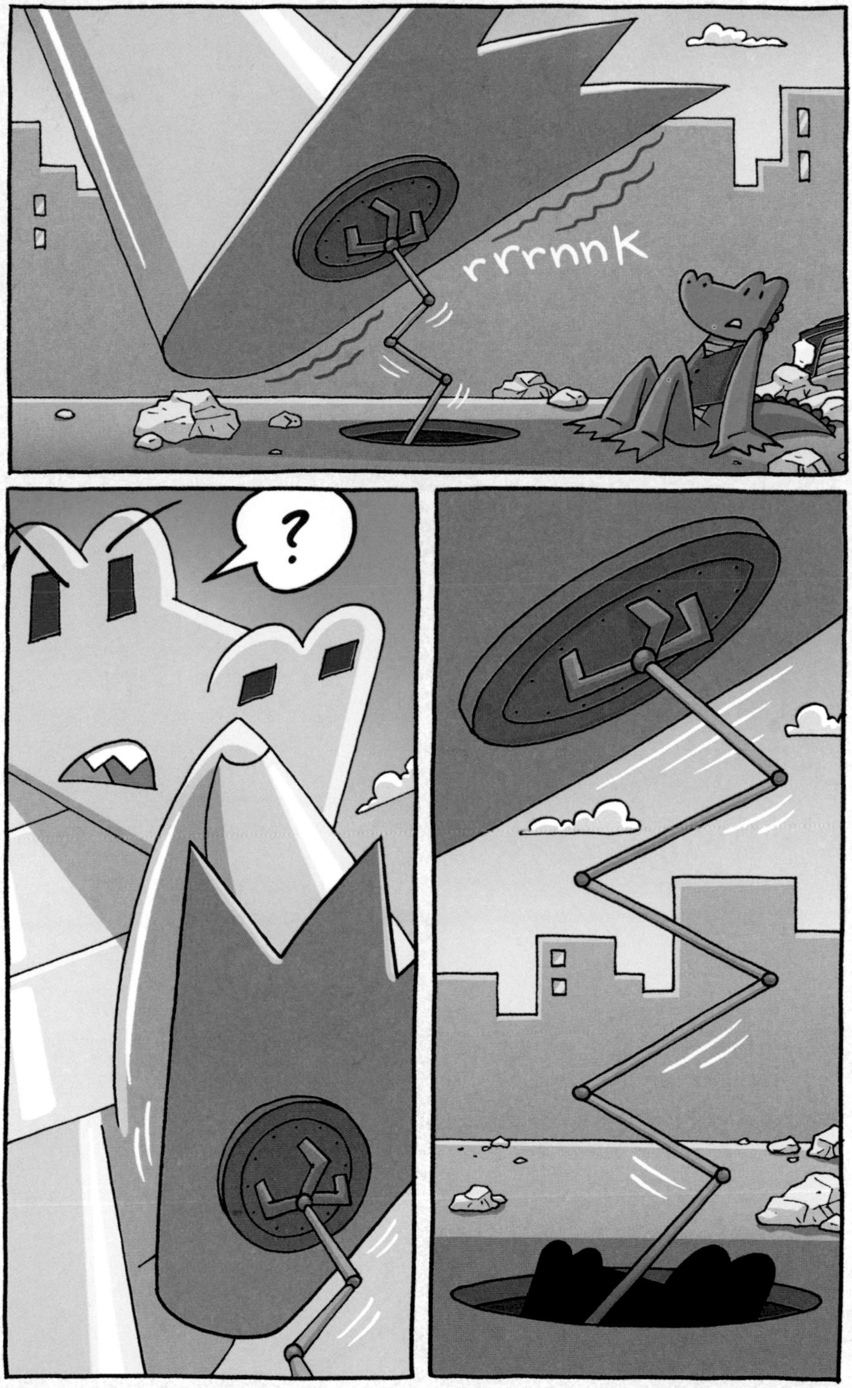
rrrnnk
?

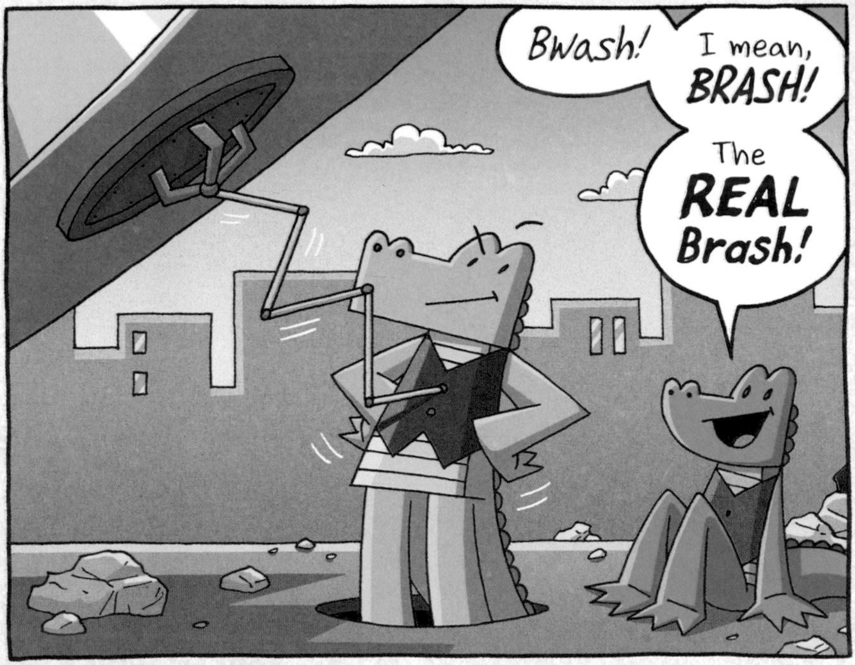
Bwash!
I mean, BRASH!
The REAL Brash!

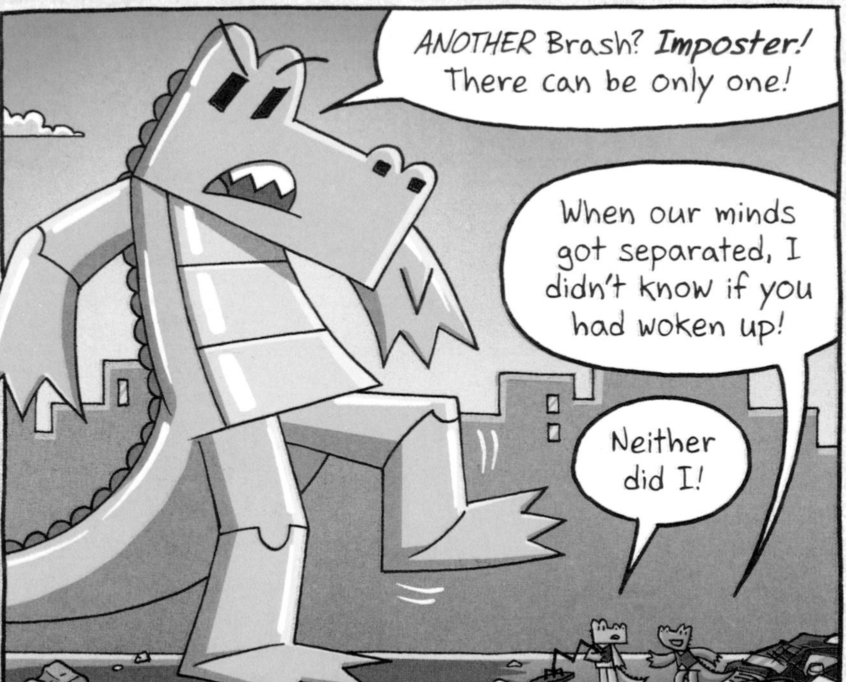
ANOTHER Brash? Imposter! There can be only one!
When our minds got separated, I didn't know if you had woken up!
Neither did I!

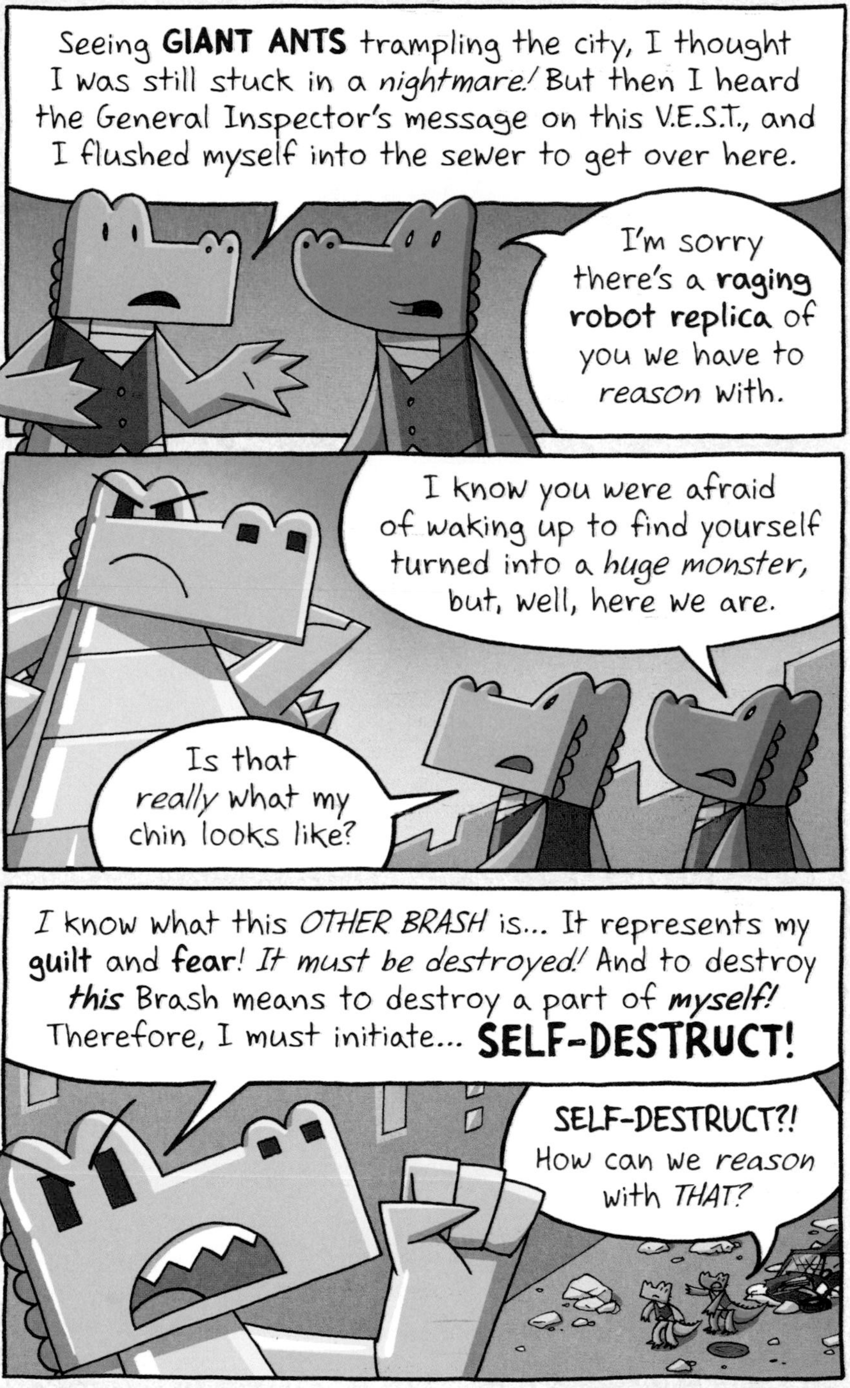
Seeing GIANT ANTS trampling the city, I thought I was still stuck in a nightmare! But then I heard the General Inspector's message on this V.E.S.T., and I flushed myself into the sewer to get over here.
I'm sorry there's a raging robot replica of you we have to reason with.
I know you were afraid of waking up to find yourself turned into a huge monster, but, well, here we are.
Is that really what my chin looks like?
I know what this OTHER BRASH is... It represents my guilt and fear! It must be destroyed! And to destroy this Brash means to destroy a part of myself! Therefore, I must initiate... SELF-DESTRUCT!
SELF-DESTRUCT?! How can we reason with THAT?

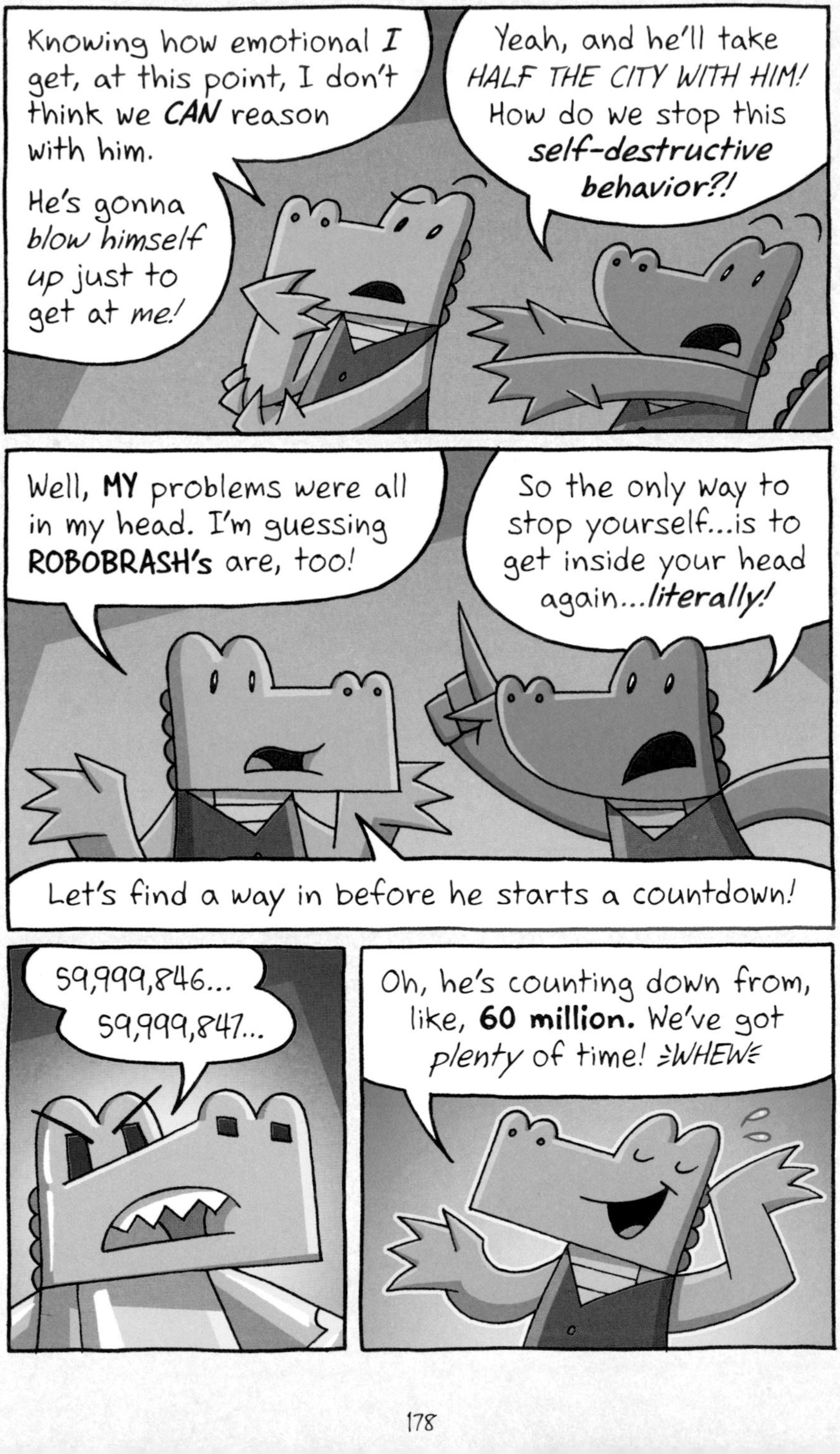
Knowing how emotional *I* get, at this point, I don't think we **CAN** reason with him.
He's gonna *blow himself up* just to get at *me!*
Yeah, and he'll take *HALF THE CITY WITH HIM!* How do we stop this ***self-destructive behavior?!***
Well, **MY** problems were all in my head. I'm guessing **ROBOBRASH's** are, too!
So the only way to stop yourself...is to get inside your head again...***literally!***
Let's find a way in before he starts a countdown!
59,999,846... 59,999,847...
Oh, he's counting down from, like, **60 million.** We've got *plenty* of time! *WHEW*

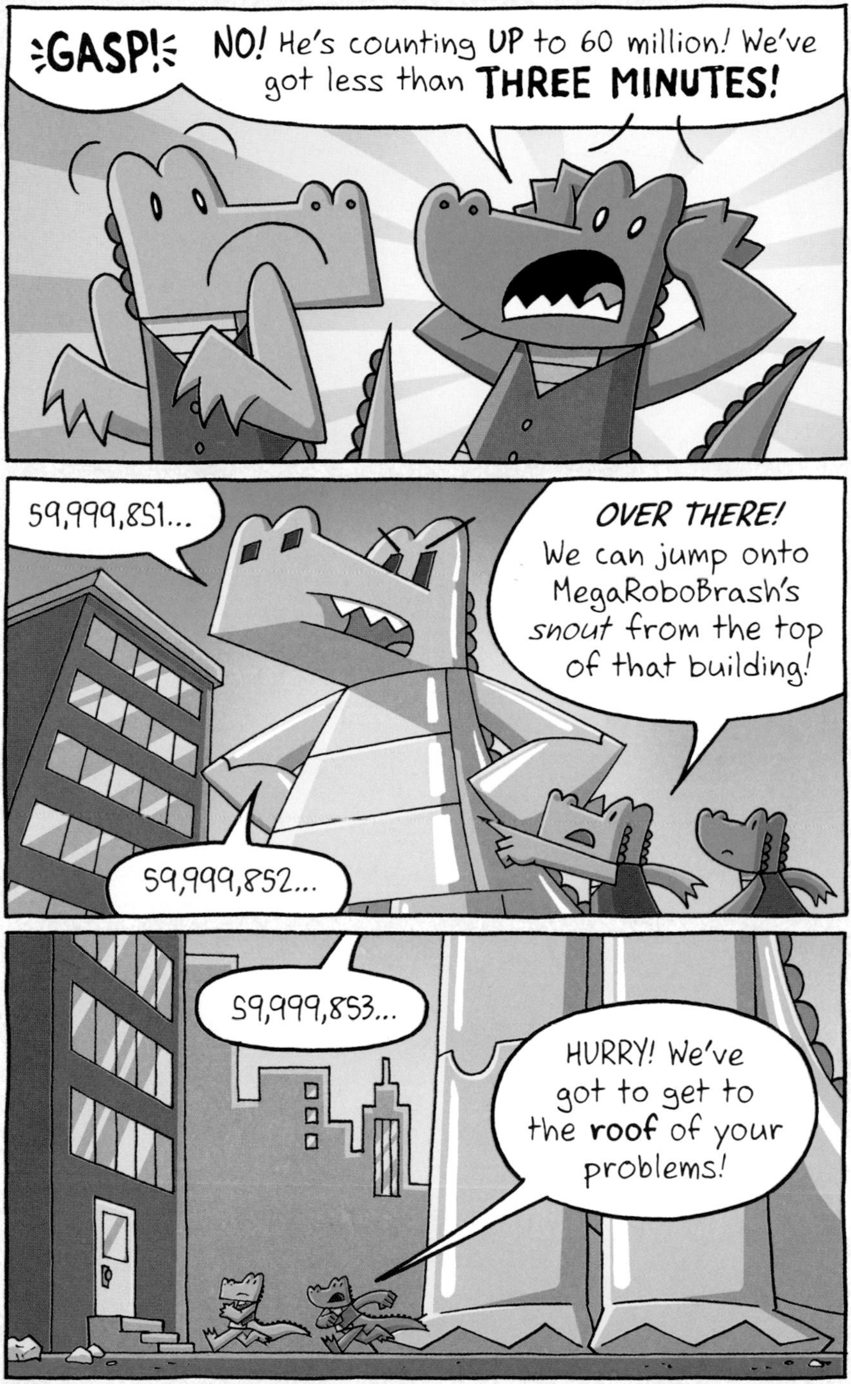
GASP!
NO! He's counting UP to 60 million! We've got less than THREE MINUTES!
59,999,851...
OVER THERE! We can jump onto MegaRoboBrash's snout from the top of that building!
59,999,852...
59,999,853...
HURRY! We've got to get to the roof of your problems!

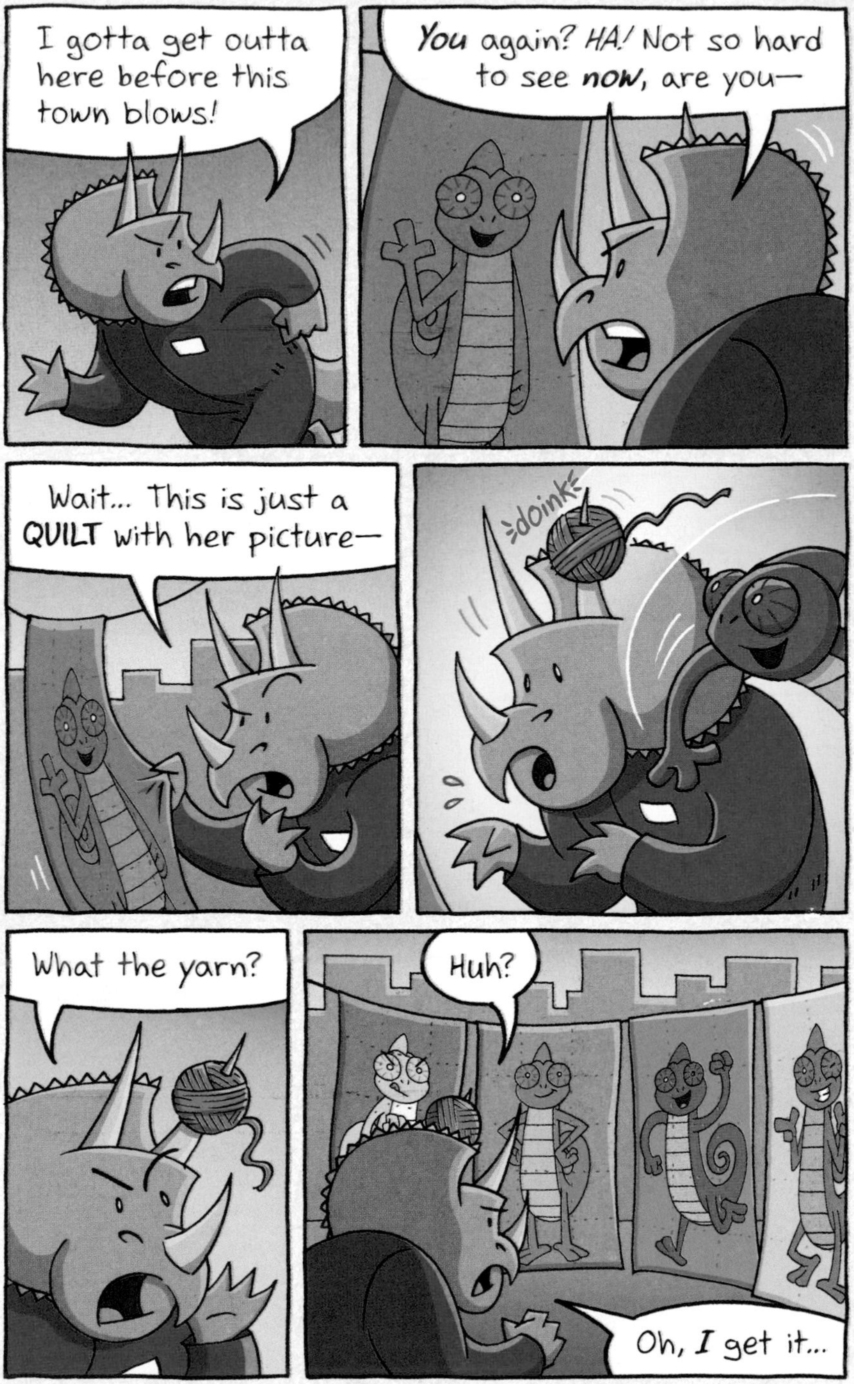
I gotta get outta here before this town blows!
*You* again? *HA!* Not so hard to see **now**, are you—
Wait... This is just a **QUILT** with her picture—
doink
What the yarn?
Huh?
Oh, *I* get it...

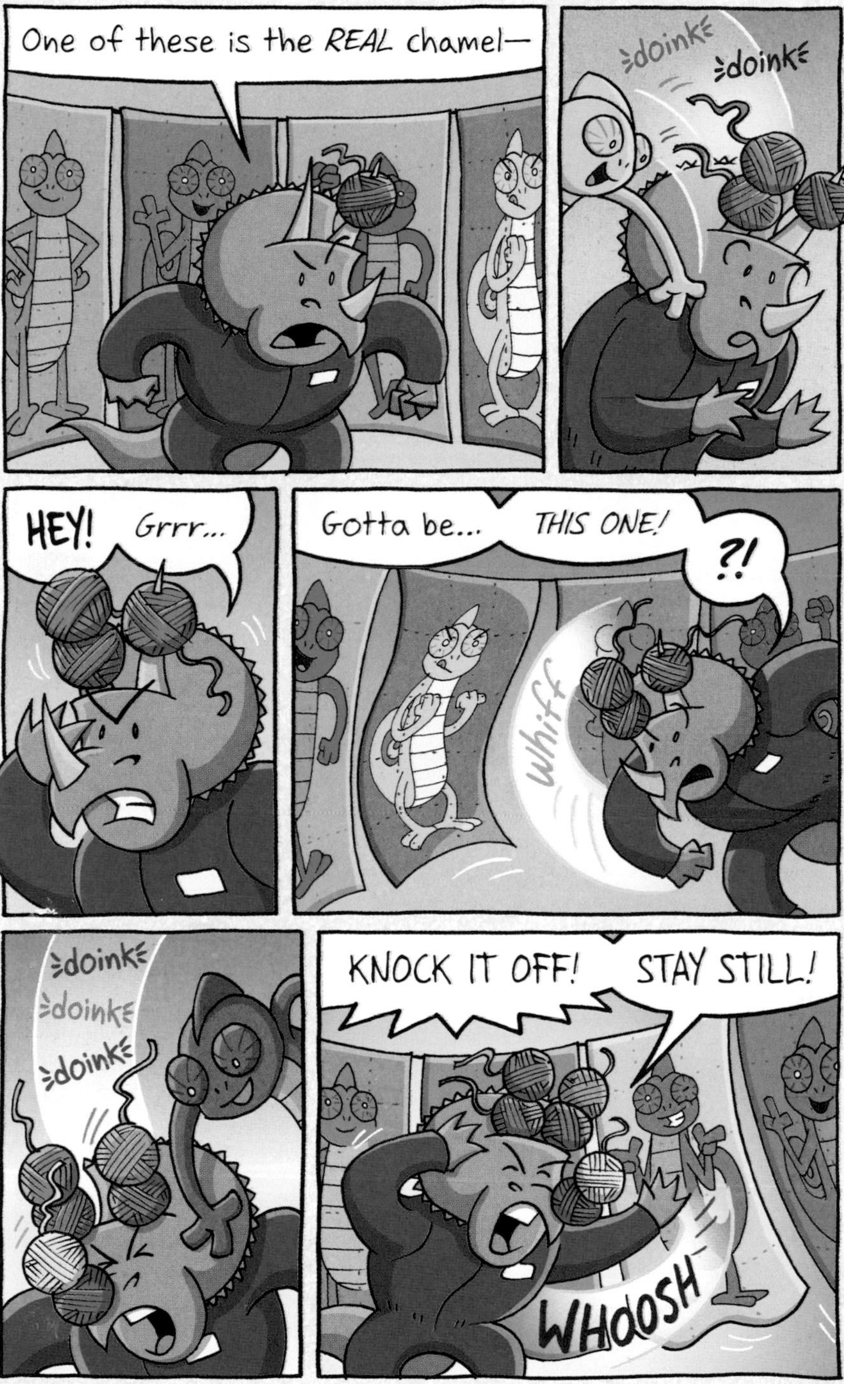
One of these is the REAL chamel—
doink
doink
HEY! Grrr...
Gotta be... THIS ONE!
?!
whiff
doink
doink
doink
KNOCK IT OFF! STAY STILL!
WHOOSH

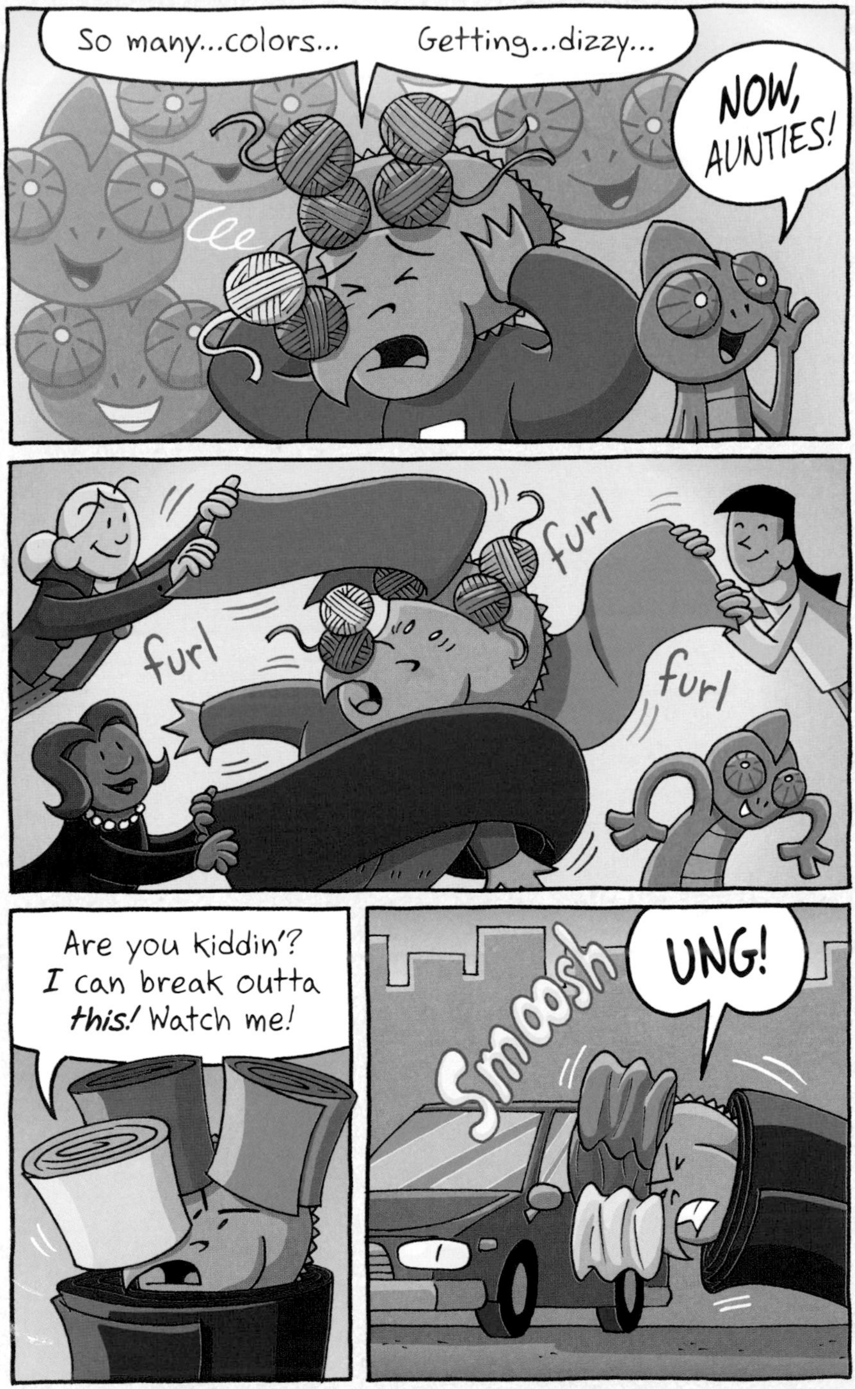
So many...colors... Getting...dizzy...
NOW, AUNTIES!
furl
furl
furl
Are you kiddin'? I can break outta *this!* Watch me!
Smoosh
UNG!

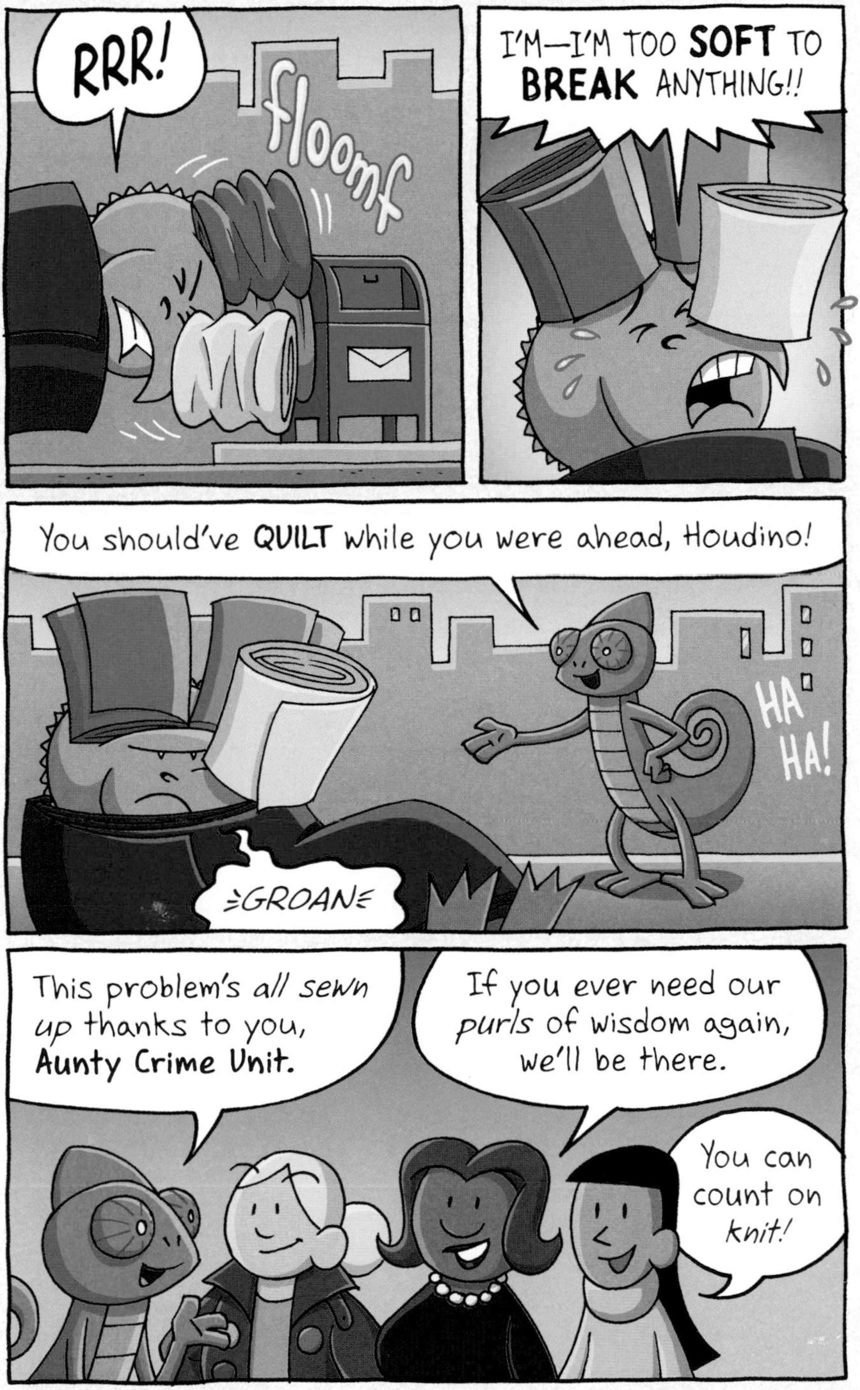
RRR!
floomf
I'M—I'M TOO SOFT TO BREAK ANYTHING!!
You should've QUILT while you were ahead, Houdino!
HA HA!
GROAN
This problem's all sewn up thanks to you, Aunty Crime Unit.
If you ever need our purls of wisdom again, we'll be there.
You can count on knit!

# Chapter 16

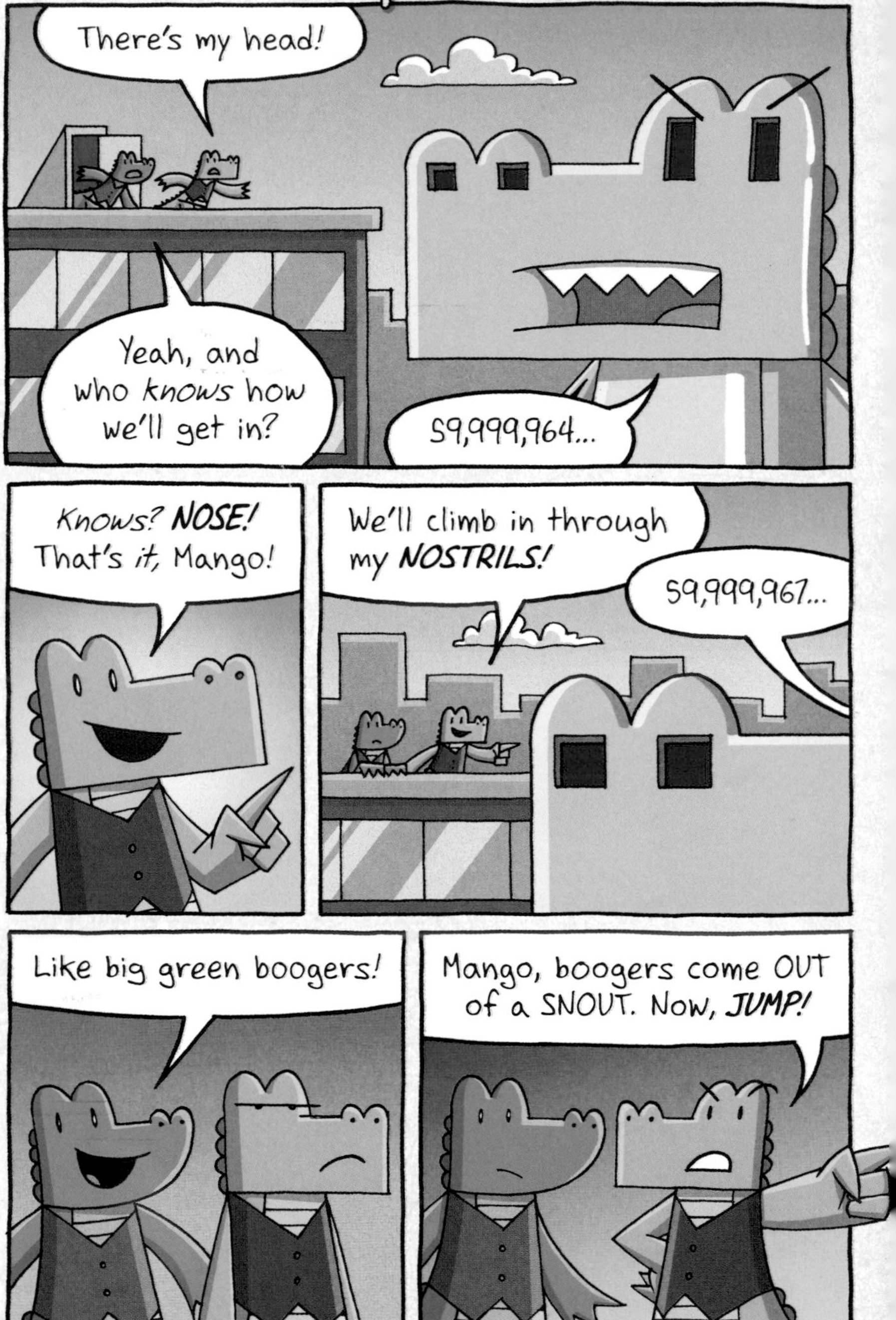

There's my head!
Yeah, and who *knows* how we'll get in?
59,999,964...
*Knows?* **NOSE!** That's *it*, Mango!
We'll climb in through my **NOSTRILS!**
59,999,967...
Like big green boogers!
Mango, boogers come OUT of a SNOUT. Now, ***JUMP!***

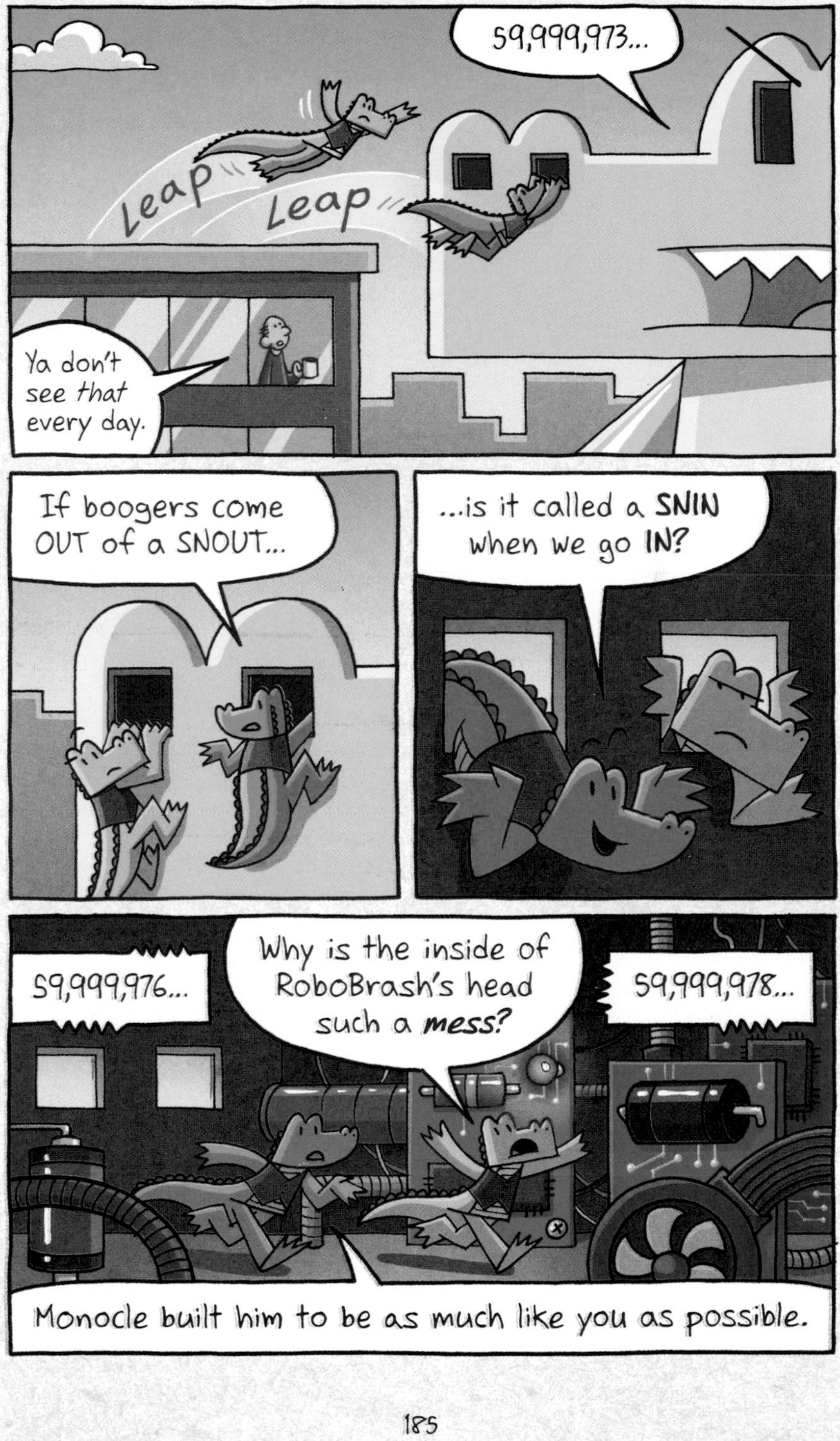
59,999,973...
Leap
Leap
Ya don't see *that* every day.
If boogers come OUT of a SNOUT...
...is it called a **SNIN** when we go **IN**?
59,999,976...
Why is the inside of RoboBrash's head such a ***mess?***
59,999,978...
Monocle built him to be as much like you as possible.

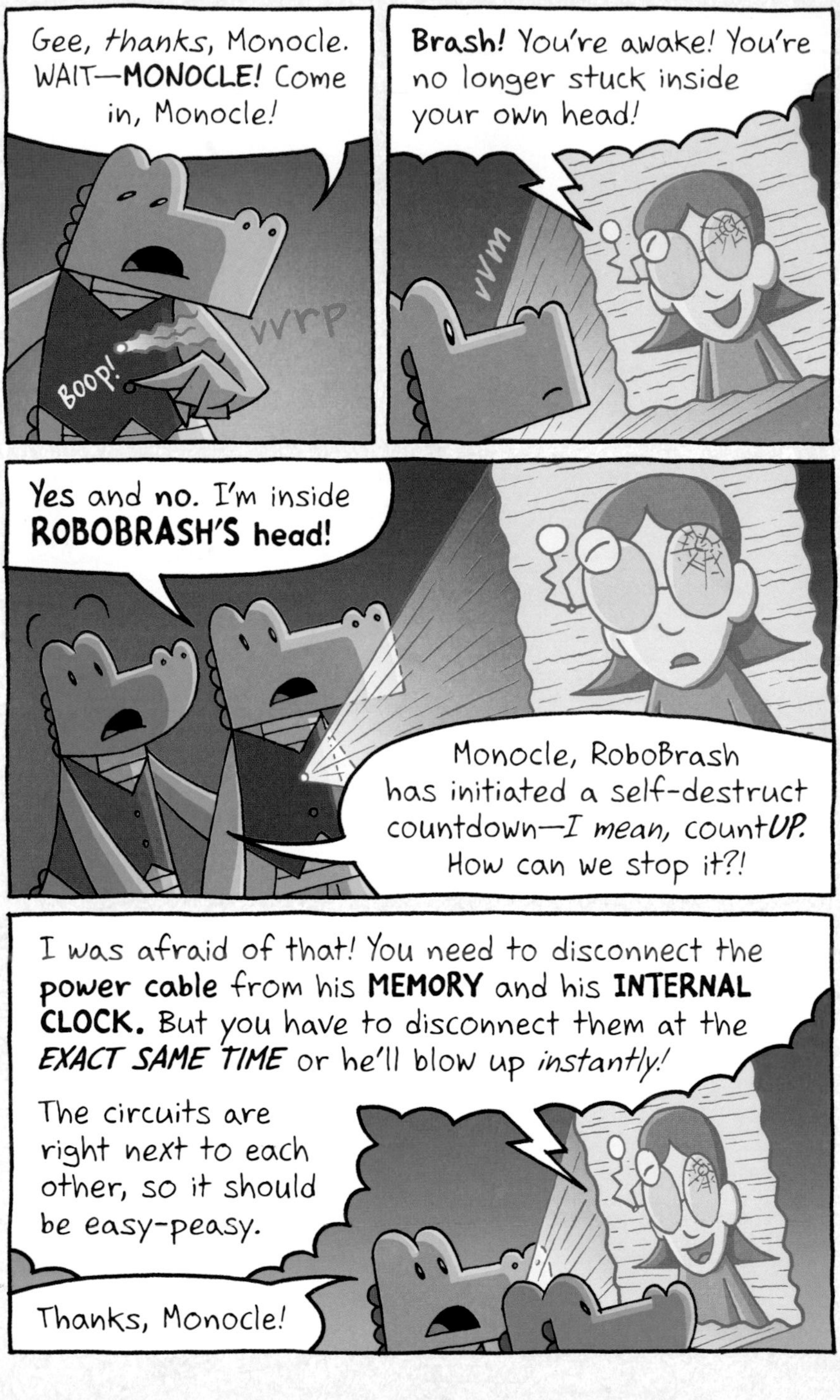
Gee, *thanks*, Monocle. WAIT—**MONOCLE!** Come in, Monocle!
BOOP!
VVRP
**Brash!** You're awake! You're no longer stuck inside your own head!
VVM
**Yes** and **no.** I'm inside **ROBOBRASH'S head!**
Monocle, RoboBrash has initiated a self-destruct countdown—*I mean,* count*UP.* How can we stop it?!
I was afraid of that! You need to disconnect the **power cable** from his **MEMORY** and his **INTERNAL CLOCK.** But you have to disconnect them at the ***EXACT SAME TIME*** or he'll blow up *instantly!*
The circuits are right next to each other, so it should be easy-peasy.
Thanks, Monocle!

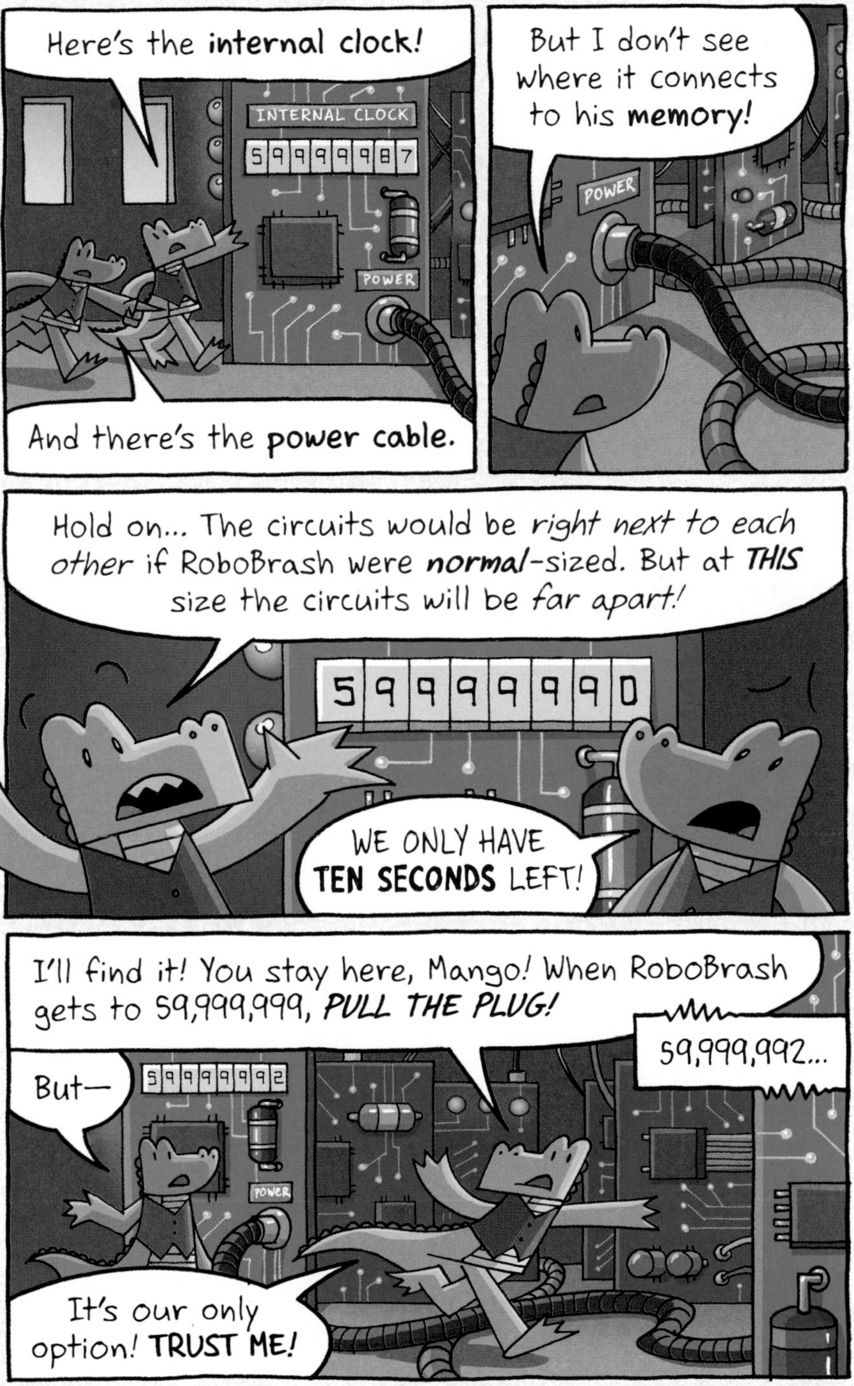
Here's the **internal clock!**
INTERNAL CLOCK
59999987
POWER
And there's the **power cable.**
But I don't see where it connects to his **memory!**
POWER
Hold on... The circuits would be *right next to each other* if RoboBrash were ***normal***-sized. But at ***THIS*** size the circuits will be *far apart!*
59999990
WE ONLY HAVE **TEN SECONDS** LEFT!
I'll find it! You stay here, Mango! When RoboBrash gets to 59,999,999, ***PULL THE PLUG!***
59,999,992...
But—
59999992
POWER
It's our only option! **TRUST ME!**

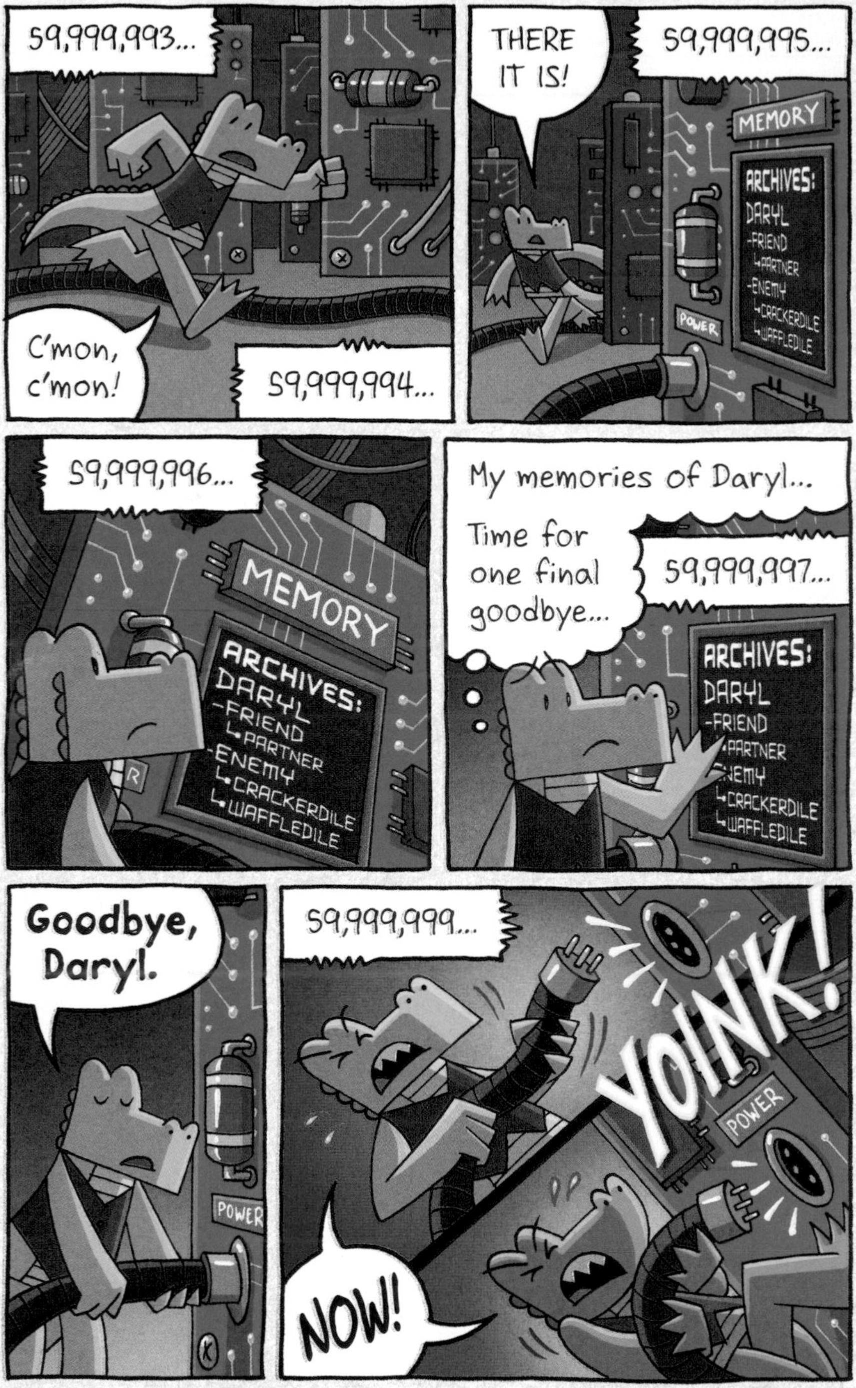
59,999,993...
C'mon, c'mon!
59,999,994...
THERE IT IS!
59,999,995...
MEMORY
ARCHIVES:
DARYL
-FRIEND
↳PARTNER
-ENEMY
↳CRACKERDILE
↳WAFFLEDILE
POWER
59,999,996...
MEMORY
ARCHIVES:
DARYL
-FRIEND
↳PARTNER
-ENEMY
↳CRACKERDILE
↳WAFFLEDILE
My memories of Daryl...
Time for one final goodbye...
59,999,997...
ARCHIVES:
DARYL
-FRIEND
↳PARTNER
ENEMY
↳CRACKERDILE
↳WAFFLEDILE
Goodbye, Daryl.
POWER
59,999,999...
YOINK!
POWER
NOW!

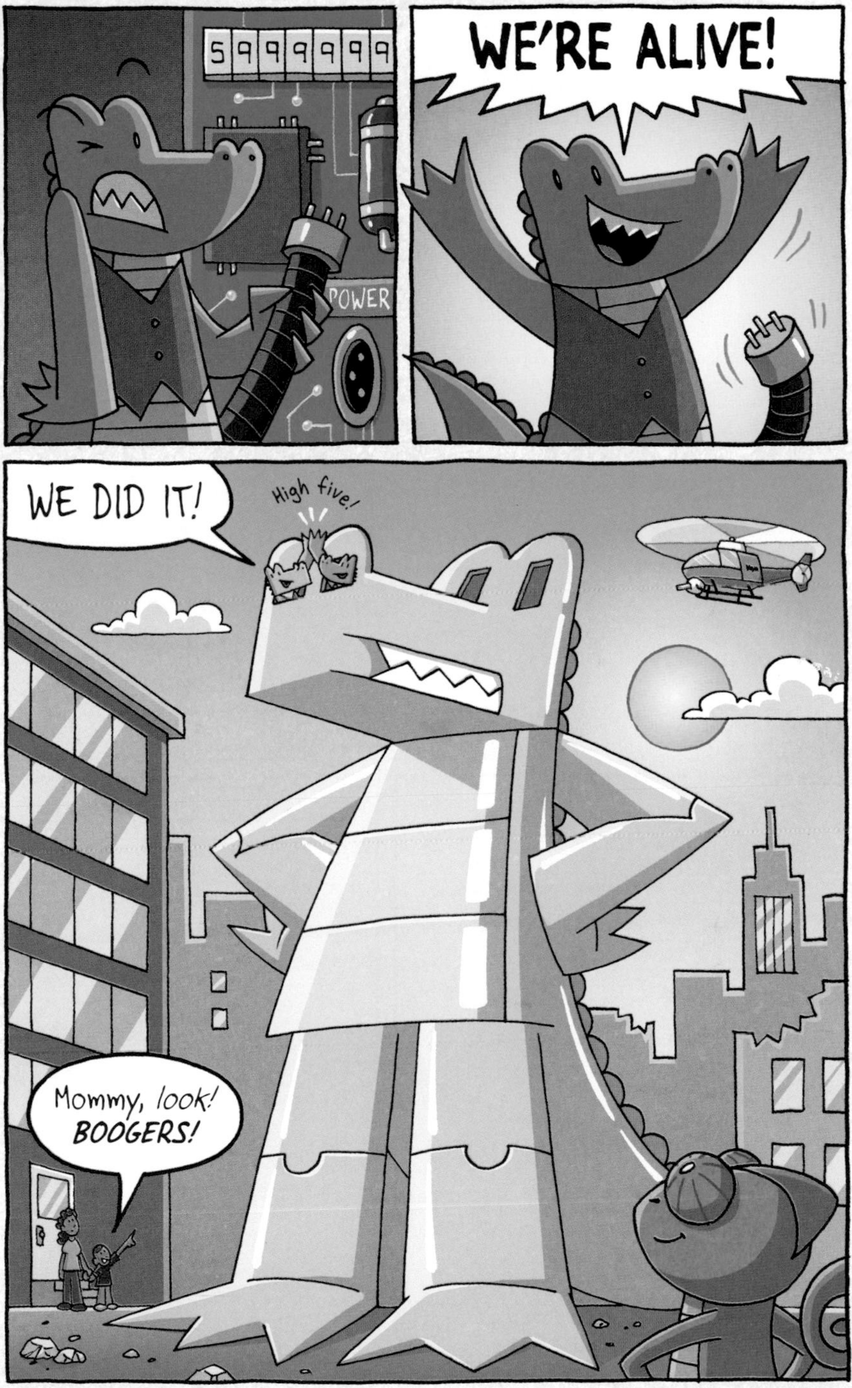
5999999
POWER
WE'RE ALIVE!
WE DID IT!
High five!
Mommy, *look!*
***BOOGERS!***

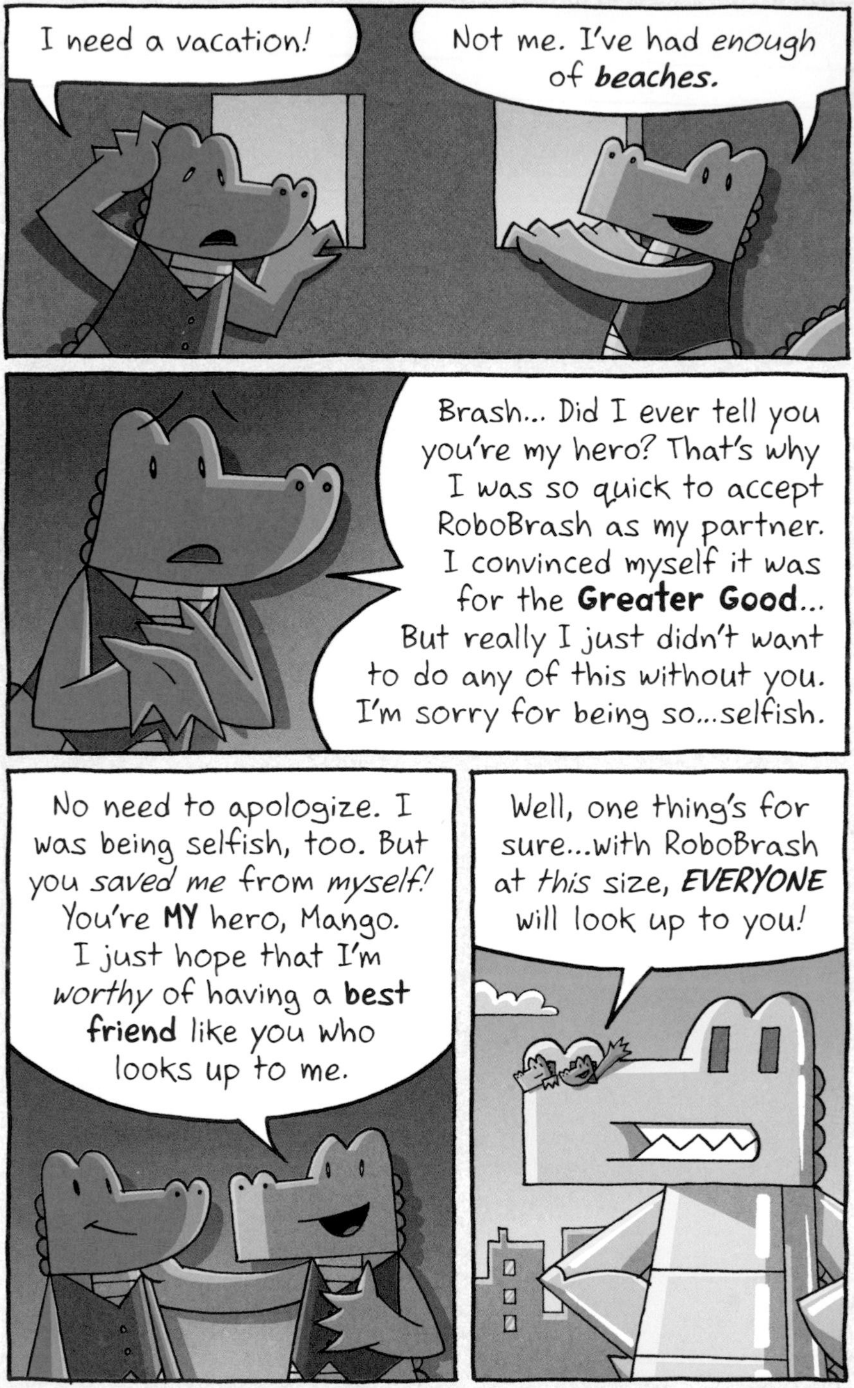
I need a vacation!
Not me. I've had *enough* of **beaches.**
Brash... Did I ever tell you you're my hero? That's why I was so quick to accept RoboBrash as my partner. I convinced myself it was for the **Greater Good**... But really I just didn't want to do any of this without you. I'm sorry for being so...selfish.
No need to apologize. I was being selfish, too. But you *saved me* from *myself!* You're **MY** hero, Mango. I just hope that I'm *worthy* of having a **best friend** like you who looks up to me.
Well, one thing's for sure...with RoboBrash at *this* size, ***EVERYONE*** will look up to you!

# Chapter 17

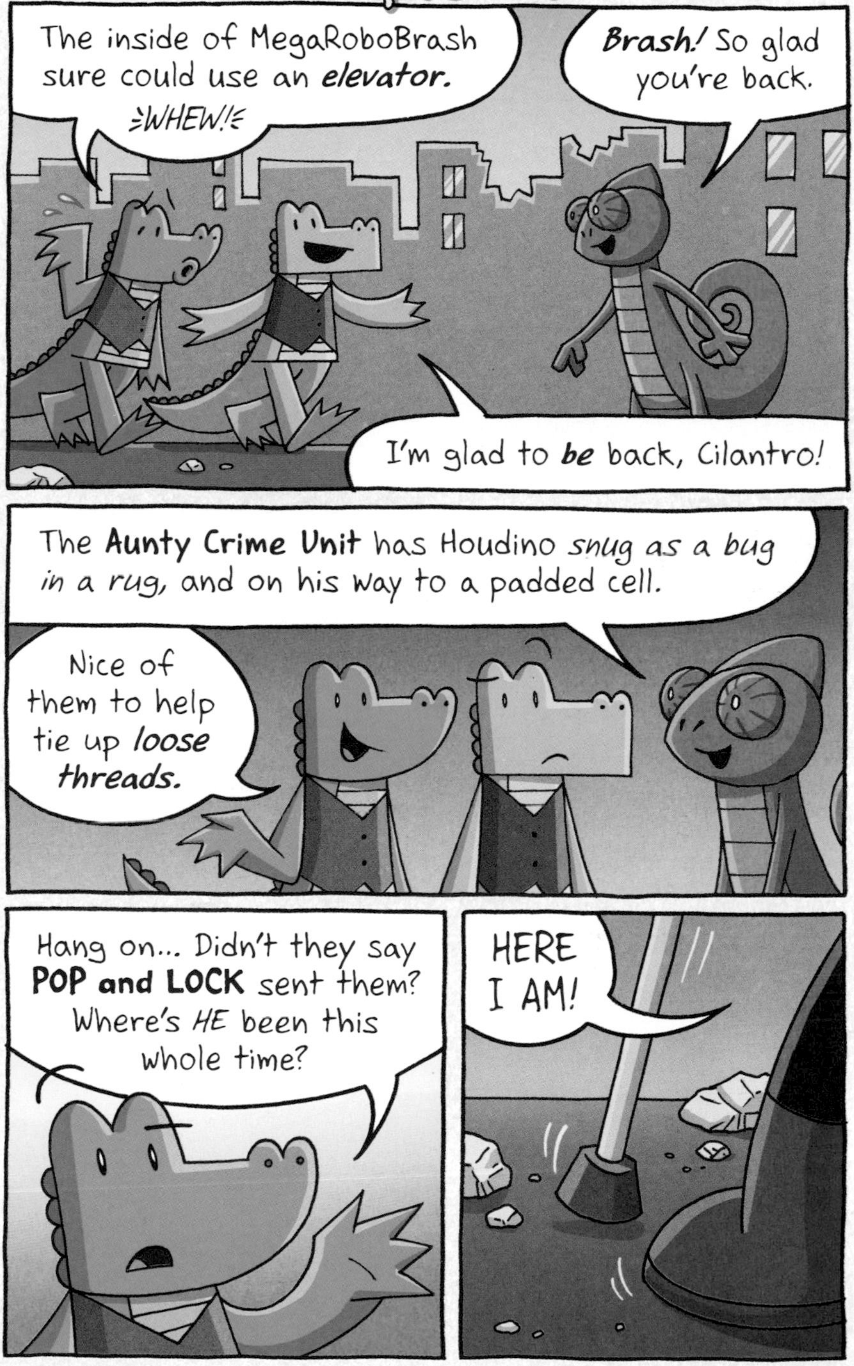
The inside of MegaRoboBrash sure could use an *elevator.*
WHEW!
*Brash!* So glad you're back.
I'm glad to *be* back, Cilantro!
The **Aunty Crime Unit** has Houdino *snug as a bug in a rug,* and on his way to a padded cell.
Nice of them to help tie up *loose threads.*
Hang on... Didn't they say **POP and LOCK** sent them? Where's *HE* been this whole time?
HERE I AM!

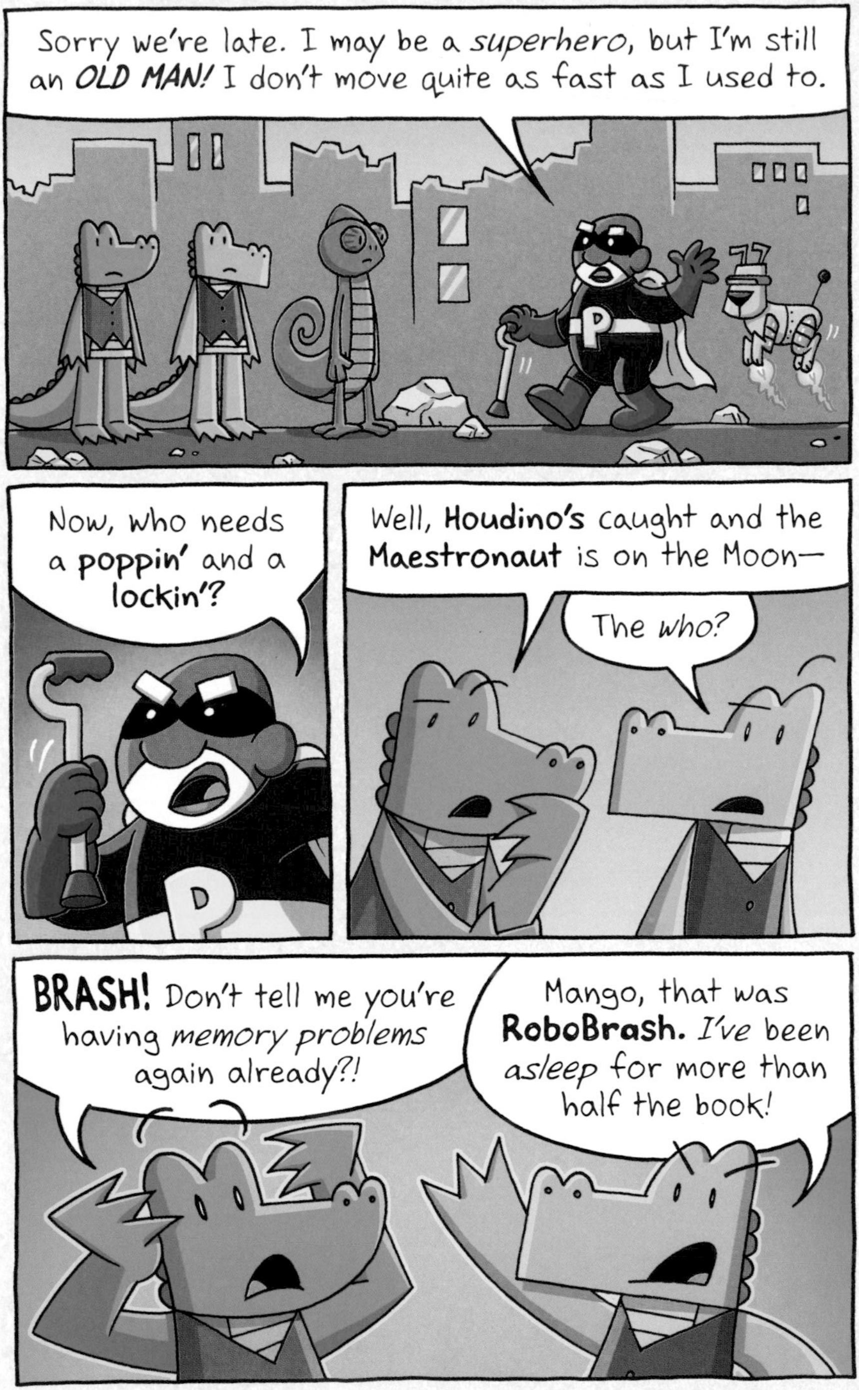
Sorry we're late. I may be a *superhero*, but I'm still an **OLD MAN!** I don't move quite as fast as I used to.
Now, who needs a **poppin'** and a **lockin'**?
Well, **Houdino's** caught and the **Maestronaut** is on the Moon—
The *who?*
**BRASH!** Don't tell me you're having *memory problems* again already?!
Mango, that was **RoboBrash.** *I've* been *asleep* for more than half the book!

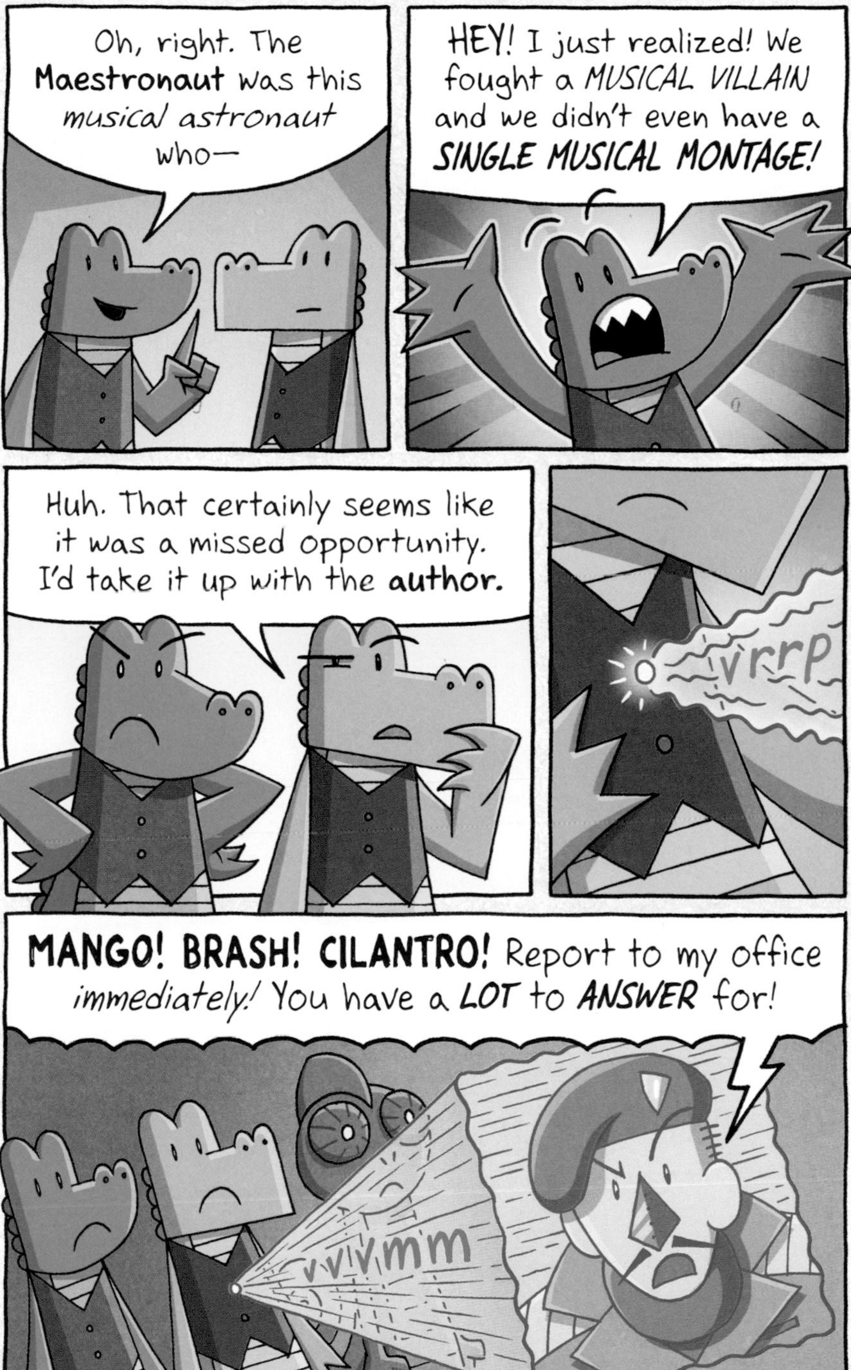

Oh, right. The **Maestronaut** was this *musical astronaut* who—
HEY! I just realized! We fought a *MUSICAL VILLAIN* and we didn't even have a ***SINGLE MUSICAL MONTAGE!***
Huh. That certainly seems like it was a missed opportunity. I'd take it up with the **author.**
vrrp
**MANGO! BRASH! CILANTRO!** Report to my office *immediately!* You have a ***LOT*** to ***ANSWER*** for!
vvvmm

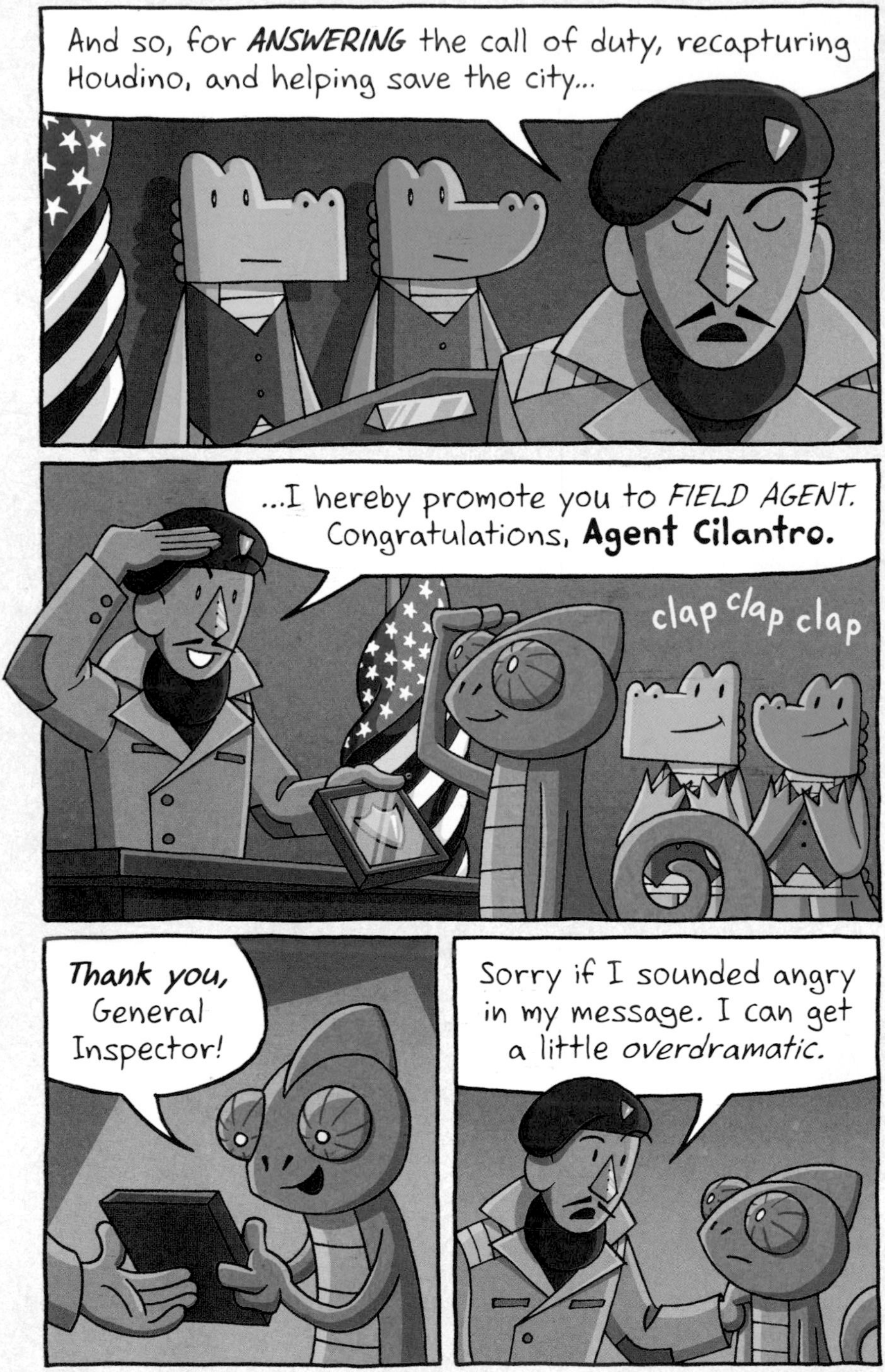

And so, for **ANSWERING** the call of duty, recapturing Houdino, and helping save the city...
...I hereby promote you to *FIELD AGENT.* Congratulations, **Agent Cilantro.**
clap clap clap
***Thank you,*** General Inspector!
Sorry if I sounded angry in my message. I can get a little *overdramatic.*

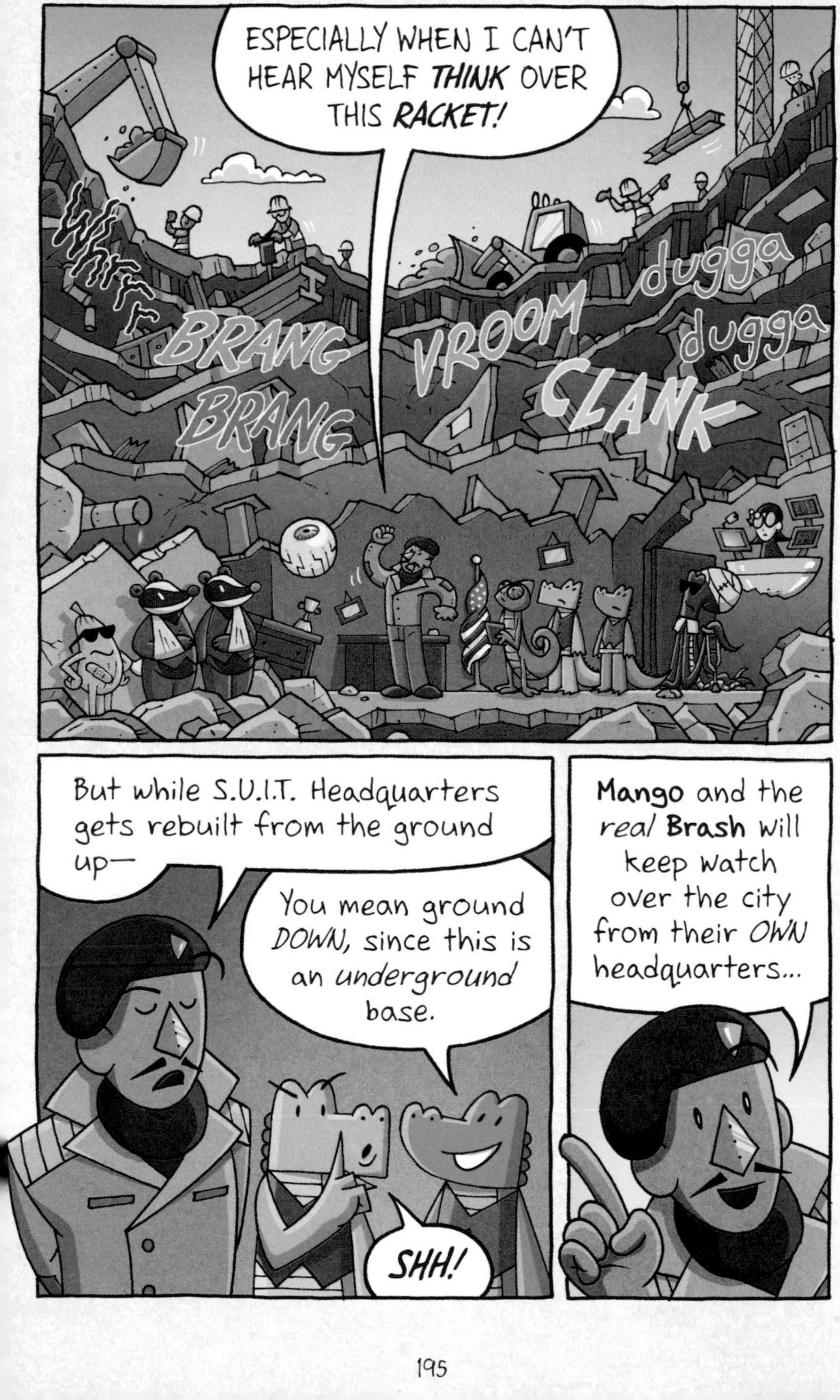

ESPECIALLY WHEN I CAN'T HEAR MYSELF THINK OVER THIS RACKET!
Whrrr
BRANG
BRANG
VROOM
dugga
dugga
CLANK
But while S.U.I.T. Headquarters gets rebuilt from the ground up—
You mean ground DOWN, since this is an underground base.
SHH!
Mango and the real Brash will keep watch over the city from their OWN headquarters...

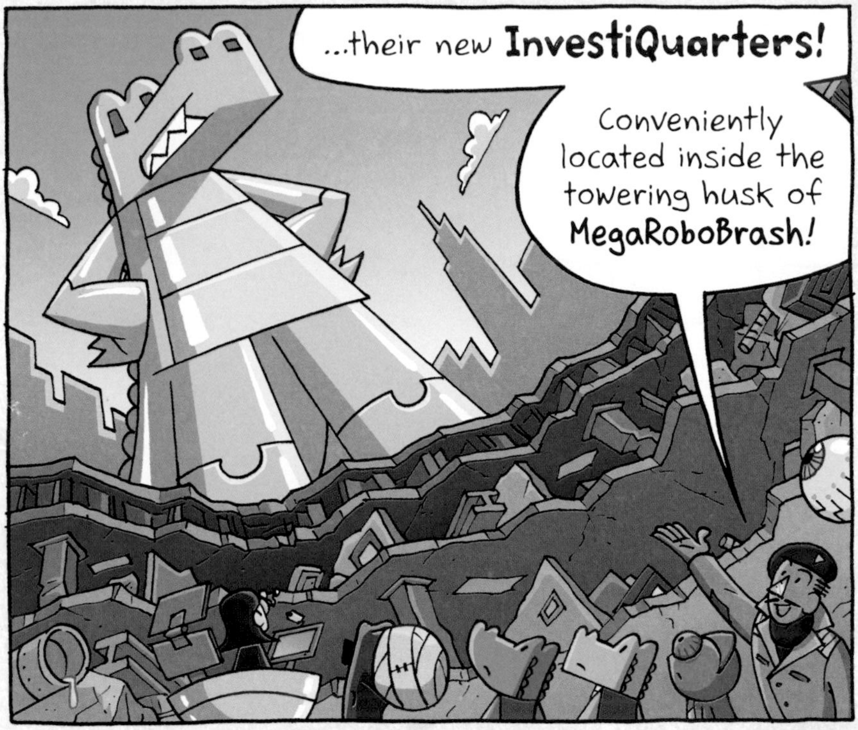
...their new **InvestiQuarters!**
Conveniently located inside the towering husk of **MegaRoboBrash!**

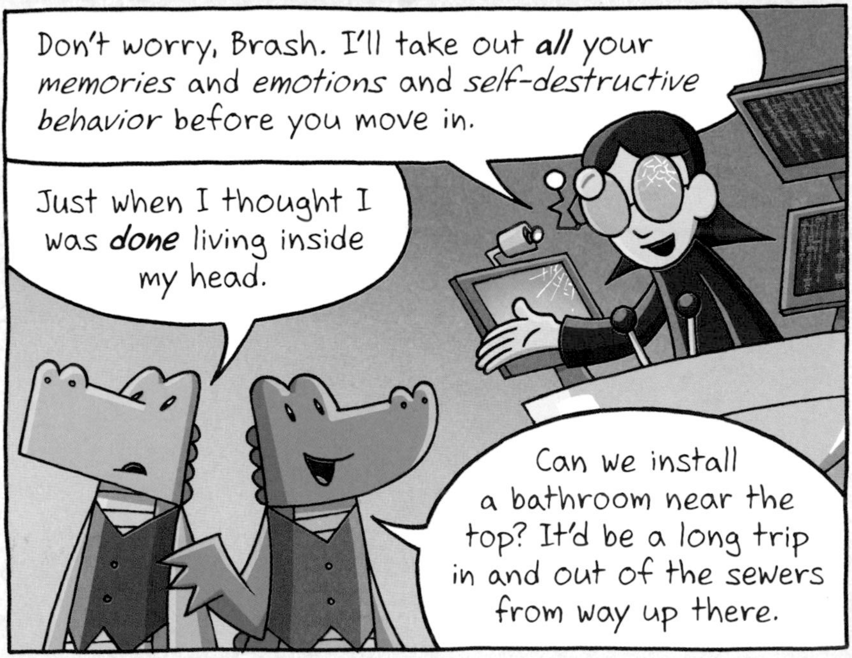
Don't worry, Brash. I'll take out *all* your *memories* and *emotions* and *self-destructive behavior* before you move in.
Just when I thought I was *done* living inside my head.
Can we install a bathroom near the top? It'd be a long trip in and out of the sewers from way up there.

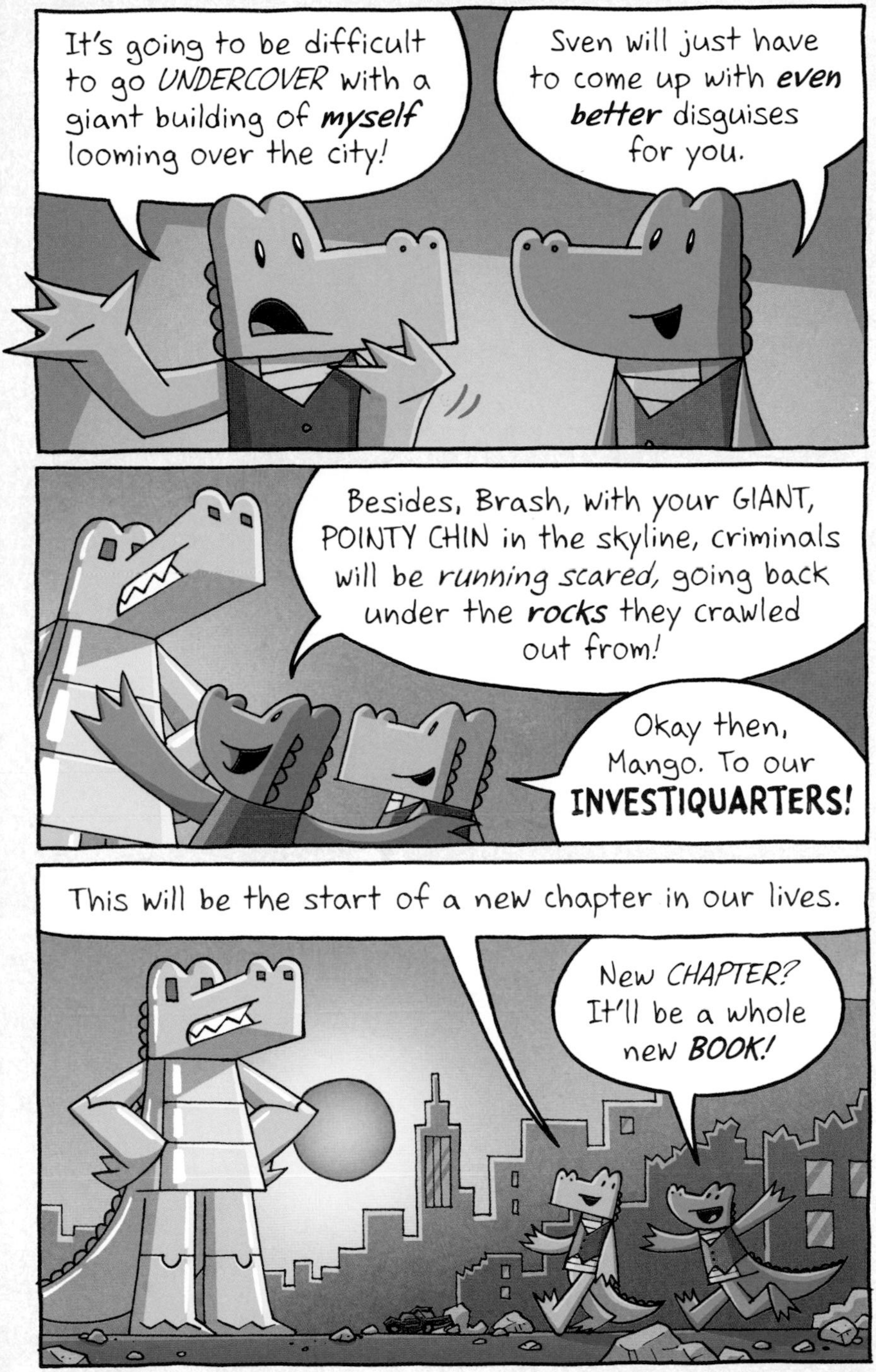
It's going to be difficult to go *UNDERCOVER* with a giant building of ***myself*** looming over the city!
Sven will just have to come up with ***even better*** disguises for you.
Besides, Brash, with your GIANT, POINTY CHIN in the skyline, criminals will be *running scared,* going back under the ***rocks*** they crawled out from!
Okay then, Mango. To our **INVESTIQUARTERS!**
This will be the start of a new chapter in our lives.
New *CHAPTER?* It'll be a whole new ***BOOK!***

# Epilogue

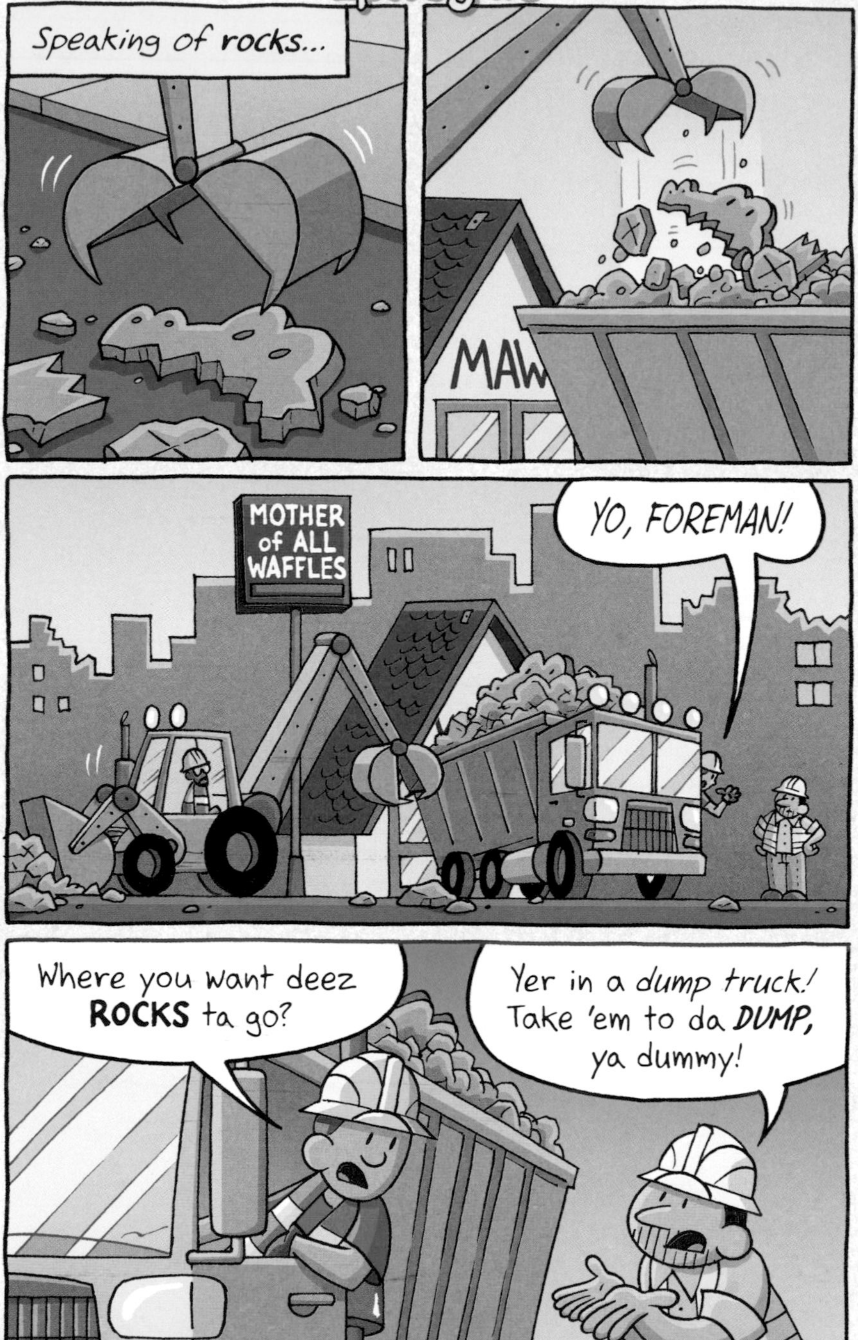

Speaking of rocks...
MAW
MOTHER of ALL WAFFLES
YO, FOREMAN!
Where you want deez ROCKS ta go?
Yer in a dump truck! Take 'em to da DUMP, ya dummy!

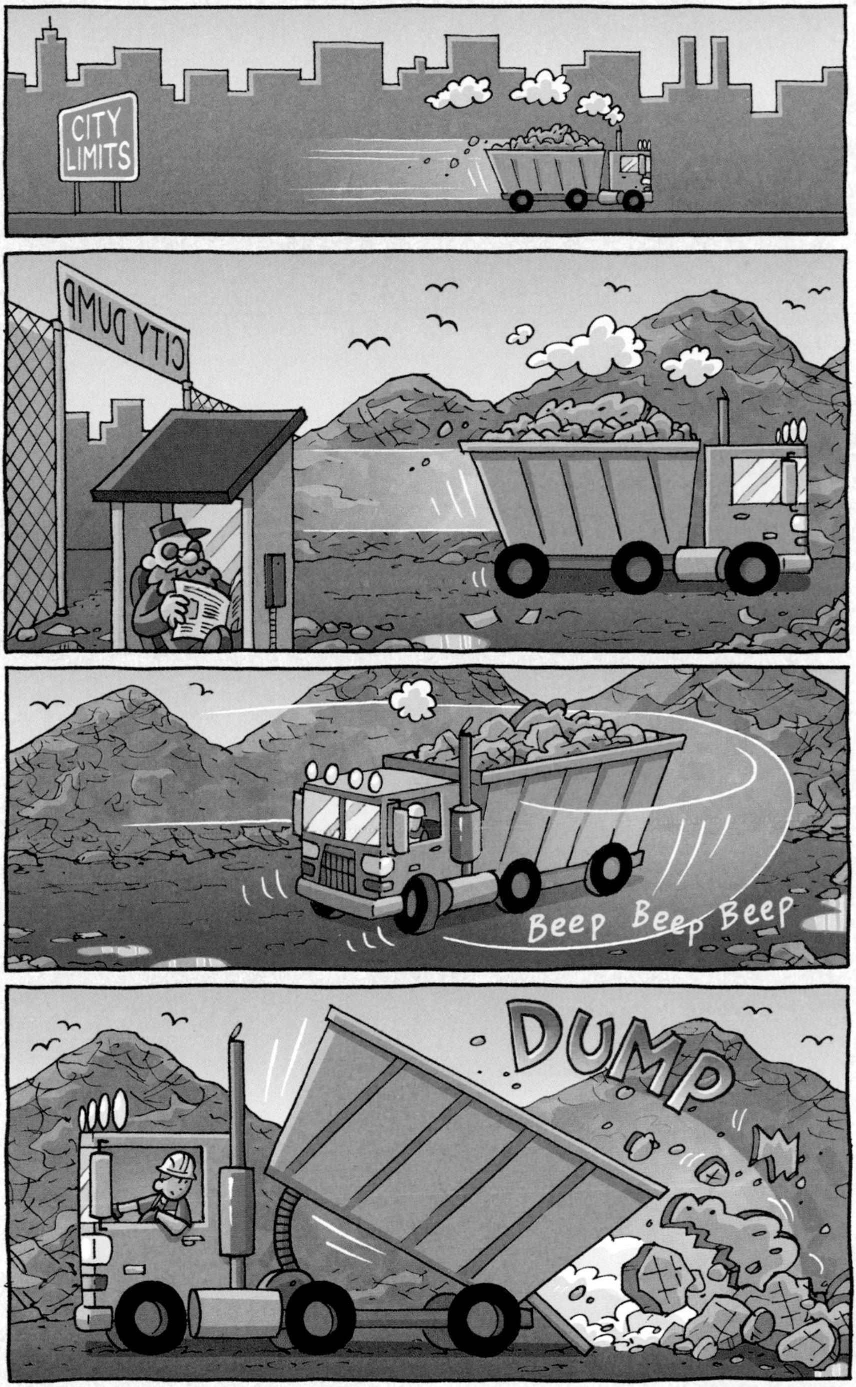
CITY LIMITS
CITY DUMP
Beep Beep Beep
DUMP

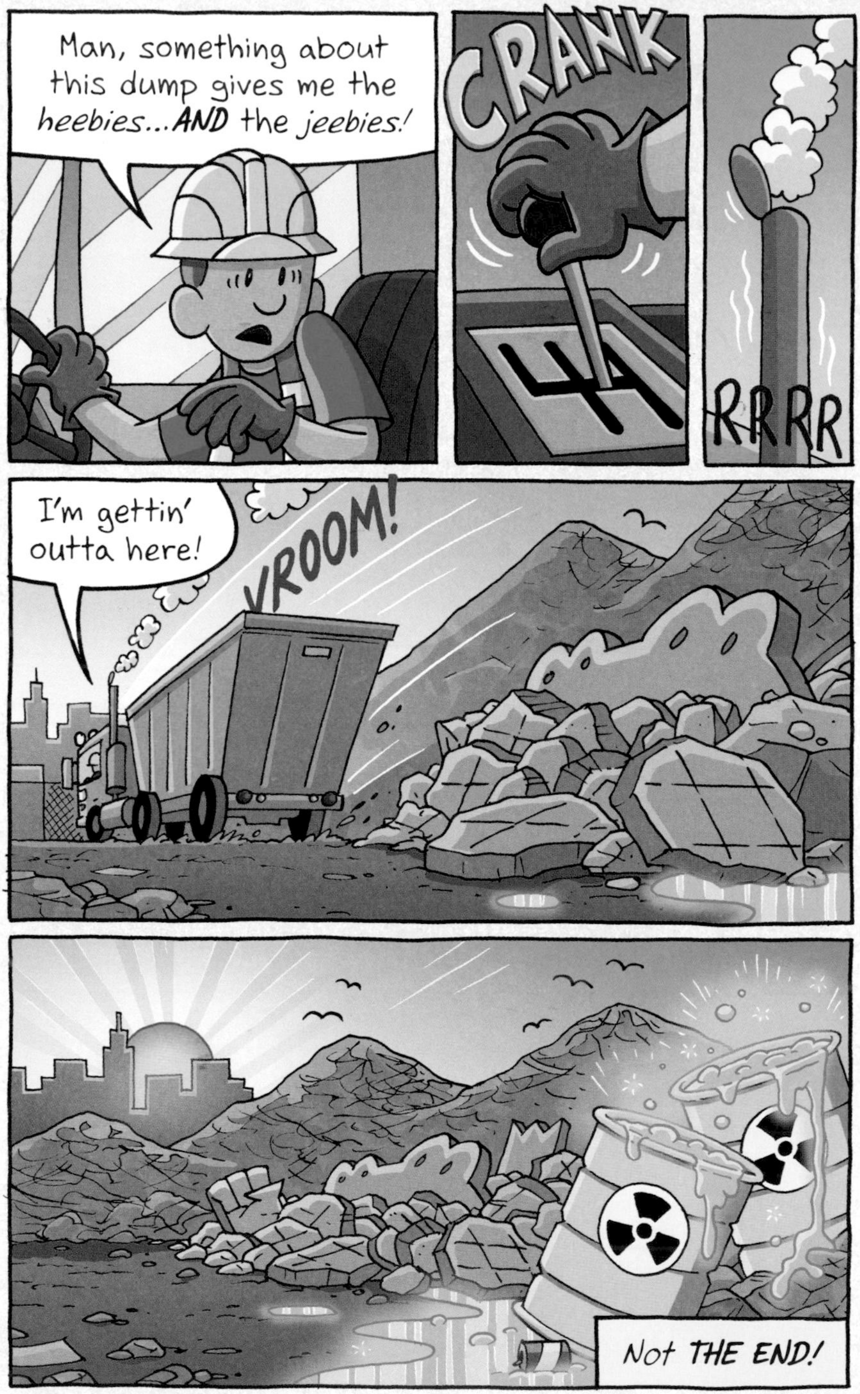
Man, something about this dump gives me the *heebies*...***AND*** the *jeebies!*
CRANK
RRRR
I'm gettin' outta here!
VROOM!
*Not* ***THE END!***

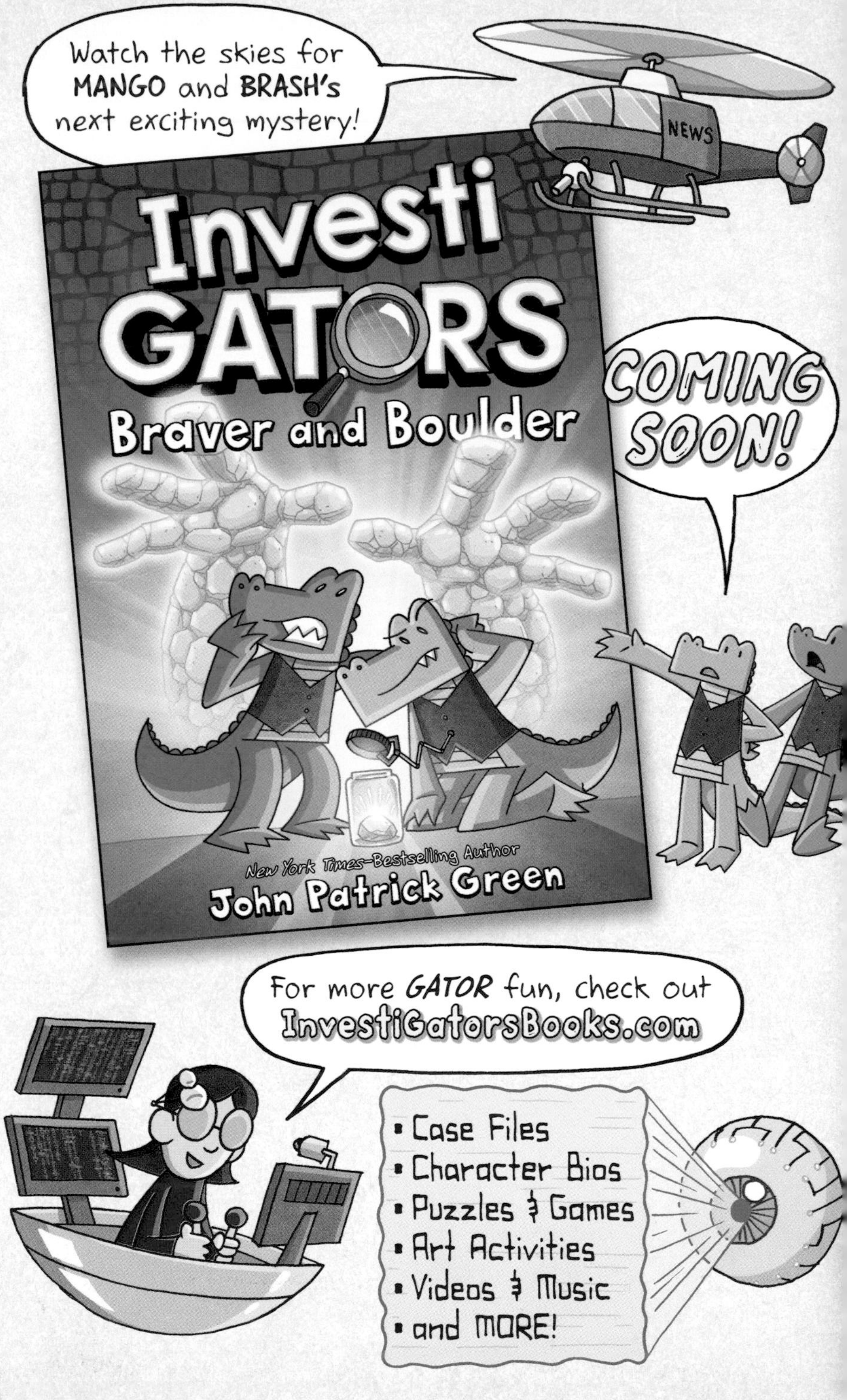
Watch the skies for MANGO and BRASH's next exciting mystery!
NEWS
InvestiGATORS
Braver and Boulder
New York Times–Bestselling Author
John Patrick Green
COMING SOON!
For more GATOR fun, check out InvestiGatorsBooks.com
• Case Files
• Character Bios
• Puzzles & Games
• Art Activities
• Videos & Music
• and MORE!

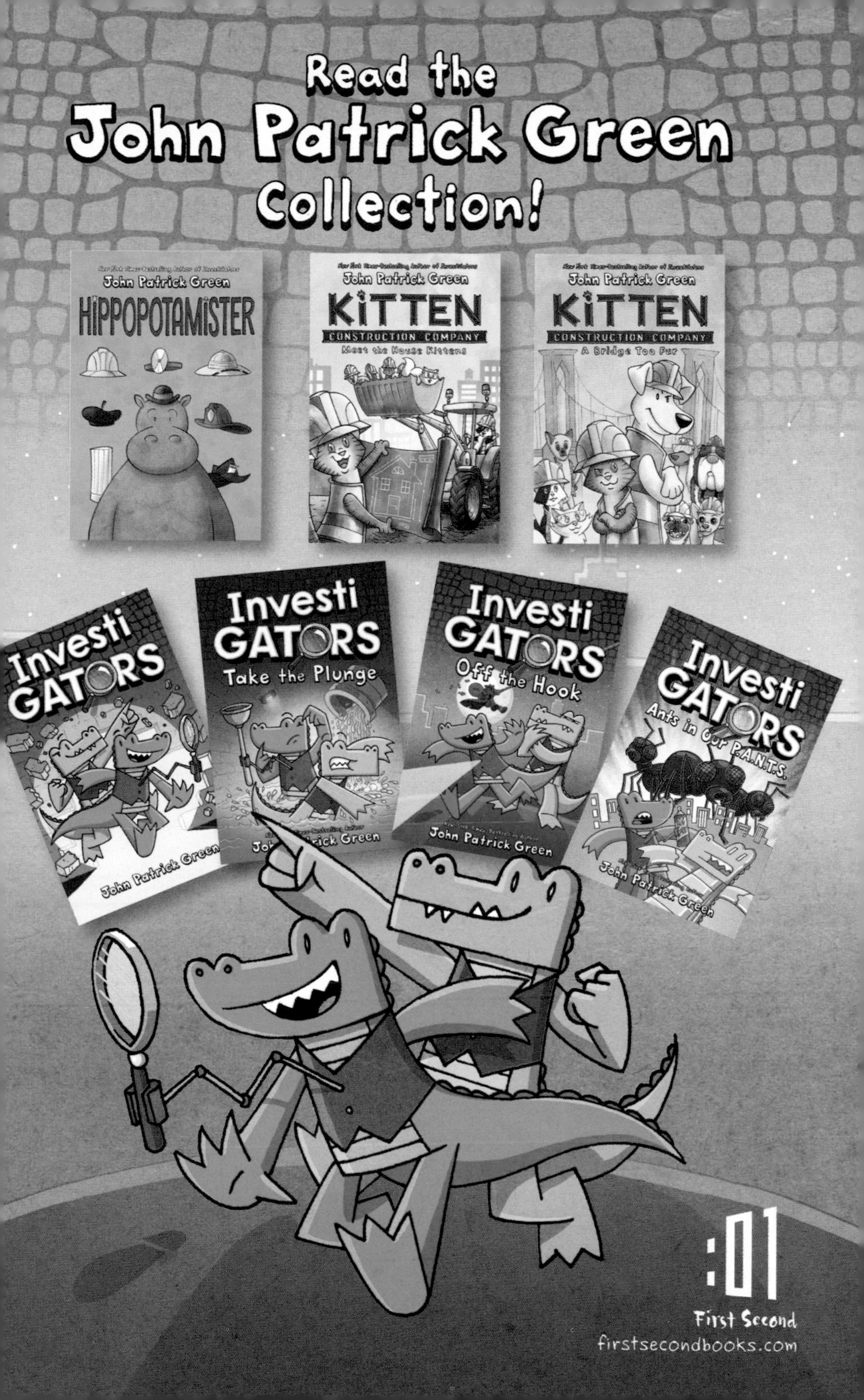

Read the
John Patrick Green
Collection!
New York Times-Bestselling Author of InvestiGators
John Patrick Green
HIPPOPOTAMISTER
New York Times-Bestselling Author of InvestiGators
John Patrick Green
KITTEN
CONSTRUCTION COMPANY
Meet the House Kittens
New York Times-Bestselling Author of InvestiGators
John Patrick Green
KITTEN
CONSTRUCTION COMPANY
A Bridge Too Fur
InvestiGATORS
John Patrick Green
InvestiGATORS
Take the Plunge
InvestiGATORS
Off the Hook
New York Times-Bestselling Author
John Patrick Green
InvestiGATORS
Ants in Our P.A.N.T.S.
John Patrick Green
:01
First Second
firstsecondbooks.com

## *Special thanks to...*

Wes Dzioba for his wonderful colors.
Everyone at Macmillan and First Second,
notably my editors, Calista Brill and Dave Roman.
My amazing agent, Jen Linnan, for navigating this maze.
Lizzy Itzkowitz and Abe Erskine, for all the assistance.
Rachel Stark, for helping get the series to where it is now.
Aaron Polk, for establishing so much of the palette.
My brother, Bill, for being the first
person who I wanted to draw like.
And my parents, for all that feeding and
clothing and keeping me alive stuff.

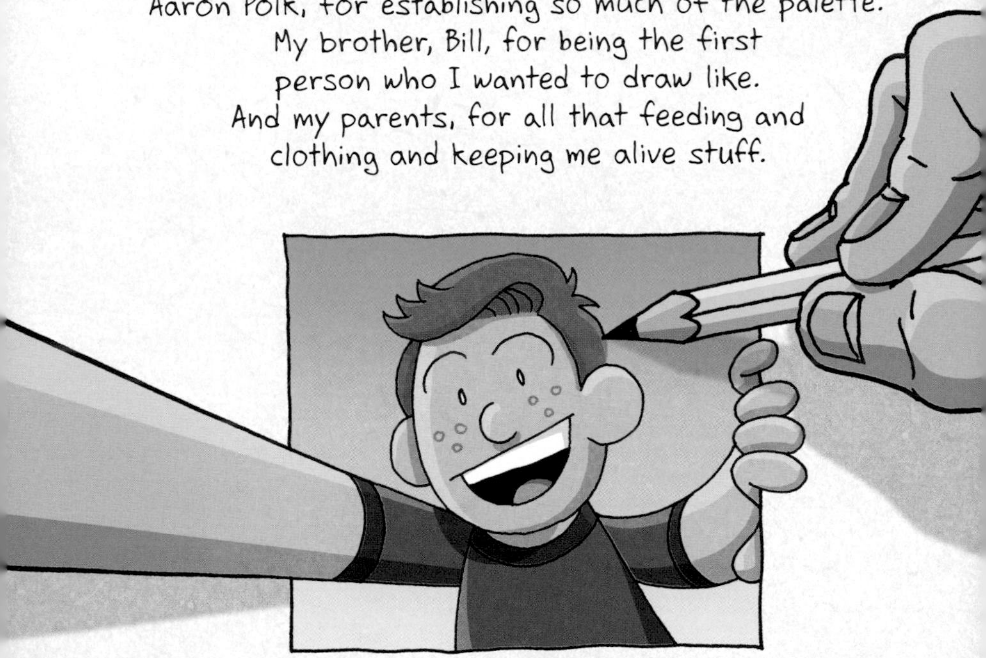

**John Patrick Green** is a *New York Times*-bestselling author who makes books about animals with human jobs, such as *Hippopotamister*, the Kitten Construction Company series, and the InvestiGators series. John is definitely not just a bunch of animals wearing a human suit pretending to have a human job. He is also the artist and co-creator of the graphic novel series Teen Boat!, with writer Dave Roman. John lives in Brooklyn in an apartment that doesn't allow animals other than the ones living in his head.